BEYOND THE SURFACE

Trisha Ridinger McKee

Happy Reading!

Trisha Ridinger McKee

ISBN-13: 9781234567890
ISBN-10: 1477123456

Cover design by: Jennifer Gordon
Library of Congress Control Number: 2018675309
Printed in the United States of America

Thanks goes out to so many in the writing community. Abigail, thank you for answering my questions without impatience. Allison, thank you for your encouragement. And major thanks to Jennifer Anne Gordon for listening to me gush about my characters and designing a book cover that portrays them better than I could have imagined.

Many thanks to my beautiful family. Thank you to my amazing husband, Matthew, who never doubted me in all the years I hemmed and hawed about getting my writing out there. Who sometimes took over the mopping of floors and scrubbing of counters so I could work on creating other worlds. Thank you to my son, Eric, for the many visits and the pure joy over my success even as his own life is gaining momentum. And thanks to my daughter, Lexie, for making me laugh on many nights I was about to cry and give up.

Thanks to my friends. E, for always being there, willing to straighten me up when my body sagged in defeat, reminding me that pretty never gives up. And to my group: Dana, Emily, Melanie, Amy, and Nicole for enduring many late night messages, for attending the dinner parties so I could have a chance to wear my frilly skirt, and for reminding me why laughing so much my ribs hurt is good for the soul.

This book is dedicated to my Critter, my baby girl, Lexie. My best friend. Dream as hard as you can, and work even harder. It's worth it.

CHAPTER 1

Dennis never thought of himself as a hero, as someone looking to save anyone. That day at the lake, he was trying to unwind, to clear his head and simply fish. And… sure, he was looking for that woman, hungry for another glance, curious about her story, perhaps even lulled by her mere presence, as silent and impersonal as it was. But he had not the slightest inkling that she was in danger. He had not suspected that she would need someone there to intervene… to, in summary, save her.

Not that he resented it. Of course, he was relieved he had been there to stop… to help… to save…. It just was not what he had planned for his lazy Saturday of fishing. Meeting her was not what he had planned for his quiet, routine life.

The first time he had seen her, Dennis had done a double take. Perhaps it was the first day of warm weather, the sunlight finally kissing the Earth after a long slumber… perhaps it was the euphoric feel of a fishing rod in his hand. Whatever it was, the sight of that woman less than twenty feet away left him breathless. He was a fifty-year-old man and suddenly he felt like he was an awkward teenager with little experience. How could that be? What was it about this woman? He studied her openly, noticing that she was completely oblivious to anything but the water in front of her. Beautiful. Probably late twenties, early thirties. Long auburn hair with gold highlights and large green eyes. He noticed her lips were curved down and her face was clouded in a sadness that tugged at him. Something about her drew his attention - no, demanded it.

It was that first day of ever seeing her that he got caught

staring. She turned and jumped, as if she had expected to be alone. As if she had never noticed she was out in public with people all around her. Or maybe she was startled to find a stranger staring.

"Hi," she called out. She motioned to the space between them. "Am I too close? It's been awhile since I've fished here, and ... should I move?"

For a moment, he could only grin. That voice... soft and delicious, like warm apple crisp in the fall or daisy petals in the summer. Finally, he shook his head. "No. You're fine... good. You're good there. I just... have we met before?" It was a horrendously obvious pick up line, but he needed an excuse for ogling her. Especially since she appeared to need her space.

And to prove that point, she solemnly shook her head. "I don't think so."

He started to say something more, ask her name and comment on the weather, but she had turned back to fishing, her face never changing from that expression of deep misery, of loss. And he knew it would not be right to interrupt that. To impede on whatever reflection she was deep in or answers she was seeking. This was her time and his suddenly alert hormones would have to just suffer in silence.

Two weeks later, she was there again. Her face was scrubbed clean of makeup and still, she looked young and fresh, stunning. She was dressed in an oversized flannel and sweats, her hair tied up in an impossibly high ponytail. She flashed a smile at his greeting, sincere and warm, but then turned her focus back to the water.

Within a half hour, she started tugging at her line. He put his rod down and stepped closer to her. "Line get stuck?" When she nodded, her face contorted into such helplessness, his heart jumped, and he walked over to her. "Can I try?"

She stood and handed over the rod. "This is the first time in years I've gone fishing. I've missed it but..." she flung her hand toward the water in a helpless motion, "I don't remember how to not get stuck."

"Oh, there's no sure solution for that. And the water's so low…" He tugged at the line and felt it break. "Shit. I'm sorry. I can tie your line back on, get the hook on there…."

She sighed and bent down to grab her book. "No, thanks. I don't want to bother you. I'll just go and -"

"No, ma'am, it's really no trouble."

She straightened and met his gaze, studying him as he tried to catch his breath. "Okay. And it's Ella. I feel old enough without being called ma'am." She put her hand on his arm, peeking over as he stooped to tie the line. "Can you show me? In case you're not around the next time this happens."

He felt his face bursting with a grin, his arm on fire from her touch. Did she not feel that? Did she not realize her effect on him? "Okay. I'll explain step by step. And I'm Dennis. Nice to meet you, Ella."

She had this way of paying attention, of seeming so enthralled by his actions that she absently chewed her lip and furrowed her brow. As if he were showing her the secret of life. Not wanting to lose that attention, that intensity once he handed the rod back to her, he asked, "Not fishing in a while? What made you start up again?"

She lifted a delicate shoulder as she juggled the rod and tried to catch the swinging hook. "I don't know." Then she laughed. "That's a lie. I'm trying to be more independent. Trying to do things I've always loved but …. didn't have time for before."

He studied her as she avoided his gaze and he slowly nodded. "Good for you." And he suspected a deep pain, a heartbreak that rang in tune with a long-ago memory.

That slight sliver of encouragement seemed to give her a nudge. "Yes. I … I'm trying. I need to get out there and do things on my own. My daughter is fifteen and spending more time with her friends, as she should."

"Fifteen?" He spoke out of pure surprise. "I'm sorry. Pardon my bluntness, but you must have been a child when you had her."

Her lips curved up and she rolled her eyes. "Not quite. I was 24."

Doing the math in his head, he gave a low whistle. "No. You can't be... I thought you were maybe 30."

She laughed. "You are great for my ego. Unfortunately, I feel every second of my 39 years." She held up her rod. "Thanks again." And then she returned to her spot, the smile fading, her eyes glazing. That sadness returned as if it had just been waiting at the sidelines to wash over once again.

There were short greetings for the next few weeks, a comment here or there about the weather, and a few smiles. But no true conversation. Dennis sensed she was sorting through some heavy life situations, and he respected that need for privacy.

But one Saturday morning, she stared over at him and called out, "I took a big step."

"Oh yeah?" He set down the fishing rod and turned toward her. "What did you do?"

"I went out on a date. After twenty-three years... I went on a first date again."

The simple manner in which she relayed the information, the earnest expression and the light in her eyes, he found himself cheering her on, despite the stab of unreasonable jealousy. "You did? Ella, that's fantastic. Good for you. How was it?"

"Terrible." They laughed, and then she shrugged. "I honestly think I'm not cut out for it. I was so nervous. I'm clumsy anyway, but I spilled my drink. He cursed. He complained about the prices of everything. He tried to kiss me. Ugh. It was the worst."

"Blind date?" he guessed.

"Yes. Set up from my friend who insists I need to get back out there."

He nodded and then softly asked, "How long has it been? Since it ended?"

She paused, swallowing as she stared out toward the

lake. Finally, she answered, "Six months. He left six months ago."

And his heart broke for her. "That's really recent. If you're not ready, there's nothing wrong with stepping back from dating, Ella."

She faced him and attempted a smile, but the corners of her lips quivered. "He's engaged to her. He left six months ago and is now engaged."

"I'm so sorry."

"No, I'm sorry. You don't need to hear about that. I'm just… tired and stressed and talking to strangers about things they don't want to hear." She stood and gathered up her belongings.

"Hey, Ella, don't go. Stay and fish. If you want to talk, we'll talk. If you don't want to talk, then we won't."

She stared at the ground and then slowly, she nodded, and he saw the wetness leak out of the corner of her eye. Carefully, she set her items down and sat on the chair. "Does it get easier?"

"Heartbreak or dating? Either way… it does. I think the hardest thing is the break in routine. People are such comfort creatures. We crave that familiarity, the safeness of what we know. But you'll eventually set your own routine and get used to not being with him daily. It will get easier. You'll be able to breathe better. To come across a random piece of clothing left behind and not cry. You'll meet some guy and the differences between him and your ex won't make you shudder in disgust."

He stopped and glanced over at her. She was staring back, her eyes wide and watery and beautiful and her mouth open. Finally, she replied, "You've been there."

"I have. I survived. You will too."

She smiled briefly, as if she was not sure she could believe that. Then she cast out and leaned back in the folding chair, her eyes shutting, the tears still falling.

It was the following week. Dennis tried not to remember. He still had nightmares. He still found himself chasing fragments of thoughts away before they could fully form into the memories of that day. That deceivingly beautiful late spring morning. Seemingly tranquil, hauntingly still and fragrant. He remembered being pleased there were no other people. He liked talking to her when no one was around because she was less self-conscious, more talkative.

The silence was one of the reasons he heard the rustling a distance away. He heard people talking and then a sharp cry of surprise. Then a louder scream of terror, of pain. And he was on his feet and running toward the sound without any hesitation or doubt. He ran on instinct.

It was hard to make out at first- the image that stayed with him. Terrorized him. Made him believe that there truly was evil in this world. There was a man behind some bushes, and he appeared to be clearing out the brush with his foot. Then he realized with a sickening start that the man was kicking someone. Someone who was on the ground trying to scream. Trying to make a sound but only gurgling came out.

"Hey!" He shot forward, and the man's head jerked up in surprise before he turned and ran. Dennis started to run after him, screaming, but then he remembered there was a person lying on the ground hurt. He pulled out his phone, calling for an ambulance. He didn't remember his words or the response. He was on automatic and he hung up, anxious to help the person...

Stomping through the bushes, he stared down and had to bite back a cry.

"Ella," he crouched down, afraid to touch her swollen, bloody face. "Ella, it's me. Dennis. I called for help. Okay? Hang in there. You're okay. You're going to be fine."

She groaned, her arm at an unnatural angle, her shirt torn, and her face almost unrecognizable.

She gasped for air, and then managed, "My daughter - other side of the lake. She's waiting-"

"Okay. Try not to talk too much. We'll make sure -"

And then her eyes focused on him, and her voice was

stronger. "He might find her. Her dad dropped her off. I don't think he stayed. She's alone-"

By then there were a few other people gathered around, and he wondered where they had come from. He nodded and stood, addressing the small crowd. "There's help on the way. Please keep her still. Don't let her get up."

"Gumdrop!" she called out after him, and he wondered if she were delirious from pain.

But he knew she was right. The man that attacked her could very well be on the other side of the lake, and there was a teenage girl waiting for her mother. He sprinted over, his chest burning and mind numb, and then he saw her. A tiny version of Ella sitting on the bench and glancing around.

"Ma'am." He approached her and she sat upright, startled. "I'm sorry. I … your mom is being taken to the hospital. She's okay. She's going to be okay but there was an incident."

Her eyes widened, and she grabbed her phone. "I'll call my dad. What happened? Where is she?" She stood and stepped away from him, craning her neck to try to see to the other side. Before he could answer, she was on her phone, cursing. "He's not answering." She narrowed her eyes. "I just talked to her. How do you know mom?"

"I fish here every Saturday. I-"

"What happened to her?" She was on her phone again, cursing. "She's not answering. No. Wait. I don't know you." She had a wild look in her eyes, and she stepped back. "You're trying to kidnap me. Oh my God!"

She turned to flee and suddenly, he realized what Ella had been trying to tell him. "Gumdrop!" he called out and immediately, she stopped, slowly turning toward him. He stepped forward just as the sound of sirens grew louder. He considered taking her to her mother, but he didn't want her to see her mother lying on the ground beaten. No. "I can take you to the hospital. Or I can wait here with you while you wait for your father. I can't, however, in good faith leave you here alone. Not safe."

And he saw her eyes clear with an understanding. "What happened? Is she okay? Did someone hurt her? Is that why you won't leave me alone?" Then she shook her head as if to chase away the questions. "Please take me to the hospital."

The morning was a blur of asking questions, explaining things to the daughter, Lila, answering questions from police. He hated hospitals, but didn't everyone? So, he felt uncomfortable, miserable, and fidgety.

Lila blurted out after a half hour of sitting there, "There was that guy. My mom went out on a date set up by her friend. It was a disaster. He kept calling. He even showed up at her job. That's really creepy after one date. Isn't it?"

"It is," he agreed, trying to hide his rage. Trying to disguise the guilt because Ella had mentioned the date to him. But there was a scared little girl beside him. So, he had to put his emotions aside. "Your mom is going to talk to the police. I'm telling the police everything I know. The guy is going to pay for this. And your mom is okay. You heard the doctor. They just want to keep her overnight to monitor the concussion."

"Broken arm. Broken nose. Fractured jaw. Concussion - she's not okay!" She curled up and started sobbing and he drew her to him.

"She is. Your momma's strong."

"She's been through hell this year. It's not fair this is happening. She's the best person in the world and doesn't deserve this."

Before he had a chance to agree, a man charged up to them with a woman following not far behind. He addressed Lila in a frantic, almost screeching manner. "What happened? How is she?"

"Dad! You brought her? Really?" She slammed back against her seat in true teenage fashion, and Dennis took the chance to study the man that had broken Ella's heart. He was tall and thin, his eyes blue and droopy as if he had not gotten enough sleep, permanently tired. Dennis supposed women fell for that puppy dog look. He was not a fan. He noticed with inappropriate joy that the man's hairline was receding at an awkward angle so that it looked like he had an ill-fitted toupee on his head. But he looked young and had a smooth face, compared to Dennis's pot-marked skin. And the man's beard was full and even, not like Dennis's own patches of thick black facial hair.

He almost laughed out loud. Fifty years old and comparing himself to another man.

"Lila, Connie was with me when I got your message. Stop. Now."

Dennis took in the woman by his side, the one he was now engaged to while still married. She was thin and tall, her face long and hair short. She had no expression on her face, as if this was an everyday stop. Just at the hospital to look around and leave - no need for a facial reaction.

He stood and held out his hand. "Sir, I'm Dennis. I ... I was there."

"Alex. You were there?"

"I stopped... the attack."

And Alex's eyes watered just as Dennis's throat constricted, and his chest felt heavy. "Thank you."

"I'm going to go. Let you visit with her. Please... give her my best." He started to walk away when suddenly he felt arms fly around him. He stopped and hugged Lila back.

"Thank you, Dennis. Thank you so much for saving my mom."

"Hey," he nudged her away and stooped so they were at eye level. "Your mom is going to be fine. I promise."

And then he walked away. He could say he walked away from the chaos and trouble, but he actually walked away from the woman that stirred up things he had thought were dead. Emotions and cravings and... it was too much and yet, not enough.

The following morning, he was there with flowers and chocolate and a gift card to a bookstore. He found her sitting up, her face bandaged and arm in a cast.

"You!" she tried to smile and then grimaced in pain. Setting down the items, he made his way to the side of her bed.

"El, are you okay? Should I get a nurse?"

"No. I'm okay. But I'm glad you came back today. I wanted to see you yesterday, and Lila said you'd left. I have to thank you. Dennis, thank you. I don't even want to think about what might have happened if -"

"No, don't even let yourself go there." He gave her a breath of a smile and gently brushed her hair away from her face. "I heard you're leaving today. Going home. That's great."

"Yes. Off work for a week because of the damn head injury but... I'll manage. But listen, you ... my daughter is everything to me. Thank you for getting to her."

He nodded. "I talked to the police. They have him in custody. So...it was that guy... the date?" It was her time to nod and he added, "Your friend set you up with him? Did your friend not know?"

She sighed. "It was a coworker that wanted to have more time with her new boyfriend, so she figured giving his weird, lurking friend something to distract him..." She glanced over at the table. "You brought me gifts? You saved my life. I should be showering you with presents."

"No. Stop. I got you a gift card to a bookstore. I notice you always have a book with you."

"Yeah. I'm a nerd."

"Me too. The book you had with you the other week. The one about time dimensions and the family hiking in the mountains with the landslide... what did you think about it?"

She sat up straighter, wincing slightly. "You read it too?"

"Last year. I don't remember details but know it gave me the creeps for weeks afterward. If you liked it, I can give you a list of other authors that write similar stories."

They talked for the next half hour about books and movies. And then he patted the side of her bed. "I'm going to let you rest, El. You'll have to reserve your strength to go home later."

There was not much more to say. She looked exhausted, her eyes heavy and body sinking back into the pillows. He paused at the door to wish her the best, but she was already asleep.

CHAPTER 2

Ella was going through the worst time of her adult life. That was not being dramatic or thinking the worst of everything…. She honestly was not sure how she could continue. Finding out her husband of twenty-one years was having an affair with a co-worker… that still puzzled her because he was home every night. Were they screwing in the lunchroom? Perhaps behind the forklift? Or in it?

She had to steer her thoughts away from that, from any images that might form in her mind and torture her all over again. Ella could not even claim to be terribly surprised. He had obviously lost interest in her long ago. It was just that when she would bring it up, when she pleaded for them to attend therapy or talk about it… when she asked how to fix it, he acted as if she were crazy.

"You worry too much," he always retorted, a look of exasperation twisting his features.

The real kick in the ass was that she had made him leave. Alex had been willing to stick around, to be her husband and live out the happily ever after. But who wanted that? What woman wanted to be the obligation? The result of vows whispered long ago when they were both just naive kids?

Alex had always been a homebody. She tried to get him to take trips with her, to go fishing and kayaking, all the things she loved. But he would go once or twice and then insist it was not his thing.

And once Ella had kicked him out of their marriage… he had scurried to Connie's, insisting he had chosen her. And Ella was not about to be the one to shatter that illusion. Not her business. But since he had moved in with Connie, he had bought a fishing boat. He went hiking every week. The one time she had tortured herself by going to his social media page, she had cried for hours. And she had cursed the grinning, tanned couple who were arm in arm at the top of a mountain trail. She had practically spit at the lovebirds as they ziplined through the very park she had begged Alex to take her to. Boats and kayaks and fishing gear. He was a whole new person. The one Ella had tried for years to bring out. But had not been good enough to succeed.

It was when she felt faint, suffocated from the necessary niceties to him and his soulmate, that she realized she was becoming bitter. The very thing she wanted to resist. So, she had gone out and spent money she did not necessarily have on a fishing rod and fishing line, bobbers and bait. This could be a positive thing. She could do all the things she had been wanting to. And she did not have to explain her time or money. She did not have to answer the phone and assure some impatient, suspicious man that she was on her way home, and she was sorry, it just took longer to shop for Christmas gifts than she had planned. Or longer to drive out to the lake and take pictures. Or have lunch with friends.

Now she was independent. Her daughter, her precious, amazing lifeline, was now old enough to fend for herself for a few hours. Or to tag along. Lila was mature for her age, and although this divorce was affecting her greatly, she loved both parents and remained neutral. And Ella treaded carefully, trying to talk in positive words and insist she was okay with her daughter going to stay with her father at Connie's. Of course, it was okay! That was her father. She left out the torturously lonely nights, the sobbing and anguish... the darkness that was dangerously close.

So, she went to the lake early on a Saturday morning. And for the first time in months, she saw a break in the darkness. There was a possibility of good moments ahead.

She had even agreed to go out with a man her co-worker knew. This was part of her new, bold self. Of course, she would date. Despite her ridiculous age and her plain looks, the extra pounds and bland personality.... She deserved to have fun.

But that night was a disaster. She had to excuse herself to the bathroom where she could weep and wish her husband back. No man would ever measure up. He might have been mad when she spilled her drink, but then he would apologize and laugh at her clumsiness, his hazel eyes taking her in.

Instead, she was stuck with this rude, shaggy-haired, red-eyed man, Blaine, who bore no resemblance to anyone she would associate with. A man who cursed at her when she spilled some water and rolled his eyes at the price of what she had ordered.

At the end of the night in the parking lot beneath the fluorescent streetlights, he had leaned in for a kiss and she had responded by ducking into her car.

She was initially surprised when he called the next day. Then she was irritated when he kept calling after her gentle turn-down. The unease settled in when he showed up at her job, leaning over the counter and hollering her name.

"This has to stop," she had hissed when she walked over. "I said no. I don't want to see you again. Stop calling, stop following. Just stop."

Perhaps it was the drastic jump from nice to downright rude that had triggered him. Maybe she should have been rude from the start. But when he stepped back from the counter, she actually shuddered at the look in his eyes, the curl of his lips.

"You don't have to be such a bitch about it!"

She worked at keeping her expression blank, watching him as he glared back at her. He muttered some crude comment about the size of her ass and then he was gone, and she found herself finally letting out a breath.

She thought nothing more of it, and four days later, she arrived at the lake early, excited because her ex was dropping their daughter off. Lila wanted to go fishing with her mom, to experience the calm and beauty of a spring morning. This was now Ella's meditation, her happy place.

Ella decided to walk around in the twenty minutes before Lila would get there. She did not see Dennis in his usual spot, but with a slight, unfamiliar shiver, she realized he would be there within minutes. And she laughed at herself for the silly crush. He was a gorgeous man, rugged and striking with a gentleness that belied all appearances. She enjoyed their talks, his comfort with her random confessions. He seemed to take it all in stride, and reflecting back, she felt silly. Vapid. Bland. Someone he tolerated because she was sitting beside him at a lake.

She was deep in thought and did not notice Blaine until she bumped into him. "Oh, sorry, I - Blaine!" She glanced over her shoulder, not wanting her daughter to see this man, to be seen by him, as he was obviously not a safe person to have around. He was too aggressive and unpredictable. He had been on the same date, right? Then why try to torture himself with a second chance. They both had been miserable.

"I wanted to apologize. I heard you say you come here-"

"I never told you that I came here. I just said I go fishing."

He shrugged, trying to appear nonchalant despite being caught in a lie. "I just assumed it was here... but I'm pretty sure I heard you say Lake Batlan. Can we talk? I want to explain-"

"It's fine. Forget it. No explanation needed."

"Please." His face crumbled, and she felt a tug at her heart. He was just as clueless as she was about dating. Who was she to destroy any self-worth he had? She nodded and followed him to the edge of the woods. She would listen, she would nod in understanding even if what he said might not jive with how she perceived the situation, then she would bid him farewell and good luck. Despite the oddities, she was positive he would find his match. Everyone had a match, right?

She tipped her head up at him, ready to forgive and move on graciously. Her first lesson in dating as an older woman. She had this.

His expression seemed to darken, to distort in a flash as

his voice came out strangled. "Why did you feel the need to embarrass me when I came to talk to you the other night?"

"What? Blaine, I … you showed up at my work."

"I deserved an explanation. You blew me off every time I tried to see you again-"

Warning bells burst through her head as he got closer and with a snort, she tried to move around him. "I am not doing this."

The rest is hazy at best. She remembered being hit… shoved…falling back… pain in her head, her jaw…. Landing on her arm and feeling a snap… and her whole body screaming out in unbearable pain that kept coming and coming until she blissfully blacked out. Then a familiar, safe voice spilling into her ear and coating her with relief.

Something refused to let her fall back into the darkness and trying to sit up, she found she could not move. Ella had to focus and say the words she was trying to grab from her spinning mind. What was so urgent… what kept her from escaping into unconsciousness? And suddenly she found herself gasping and scratching out words through a sore throat and broken lips. Her daughter. Lila. She could not be out there alone while some maniac was running loose. She managed to see through blood and tears Dennis running at full speed, and that was when she allowed herself to pass out.

They had her on pain medication in the hospital, so she was in and out of consciousness. She remembered seeing Dennis, talking to him and noticing the shock in his eyes. It had affected him. She heard it in his voice, the tremble and the shake of his hands as he patted the covers. She wanted to reassure him and explain that she should not have trusted that guy. That she learned her lesson in following instincts. But her thoughts were like petals dancing in the wind, light and forgettable. And then she remembered- Lila! She found the words to sufficiently say her thanks, to at least start to express her gratitude. And just as she was saying the words, taking in the sight of him, the next moment, she opened her eyes, and he was gone. The only evidence was the gifts he had left for her. And over the next several weeks, she wondered if she had ever really met Dennis, or if she had dreamed him up to get her through the worst of the storm.

**

Ella shot Alex a sidelong glare before returning to the task of chopping vegetables. "Quite a rock on her hand. Must be nice to get a ring somewhere other than Walmart."

"Ellie..." Alex drew out her name, his lips turned up in that cocky smile. "I didn't pay for it. She bought it herself."

She angled herself around him and reached for an onion. "You're such a lying ass, Alex. Seriously."

"Dad, that means leave." Lila bounced into the room and gave her father a kiss on the cheek. "I'll see you tonight. I'll have Brad drop me off." She watched him walk out the door, waiting until she heard the screen shut after him, and then she faced her mom. "That was a bit hostile."

"Sorry," Ella murmured, not pausing in the chopping.

Lila walked up to her mom and gently pushed her shoulder. "Stop. Save this for another day. Let's go out to eat. Come on. I know you got overtime on your check. I have time before the movies. Food and shopping. Get you out of this funk."

There was nothing to do but agree. Ever since the attack two months ago, she had gone to work and then home, not many other places. She was spending the start of summer inside staring out at the sunshine and flowers... sometimes venturing out to sit on the porch. But she knew she was worrying Lila, and that was no good.

During their meal at their favorite restaurant, Lila confirmed her fears. "Mom, you're not yourself, and I get it. But maybe if you get out there. Go fishing again. Hiking. You can't be afraid all your life. You just can't. And you can't be miserable either. I miss my happy mom. You don't laugh anymore. You snap a lot. Look, I'll cancel plans with dad, and we'll go somewhere tomorrow. Enjoy the nice weather."

"No. Don't cancel. He always has something fun planned for you." And it was true. As shitty a husband as he was, he was a fantastic father. She felt fortunate to have a daughter that cherished both parents. Ella did not want to destroy that. "You go, and I promise I'll take a walk outside. Maybe go to some yard sales."

Lila shot her mother a doubting glare. "Well... all right but more than just a walk around the block. Do something!"

They visited a few stores, laughing at some odd items and marveling at the sales. It felt good. Ella felt lighter and each laugh seemed to shake off the darkness weighing her down. She almost felt delirious from the sensation. Old times. Good times. She had Lila, and while her job was stressful and low paying, it was enough to allow her to slide by. She would have a home once the divorce was final, and she could sell the current one, the one she could not afford. Things would work out, and she would have good days again. Like this one.

"Moooom," Lila sang out, tugging at her sleeve and re-minding her of when she had been a little girl wanting her attention. "Look at that sale!"

She absently followed the direction of her daughter's stare and then gave a surprised jump. There was a kayak with a price tag that seemed too good to be true.

As she stared, Lila voiced the very words she had been thinking, "Meant to be."

**

There could not have been a better morning to reclaim her independence. To familiarize herself once again with kay-aking. There was a warm breeze, gentle sunlight glinting off the water, and birds announcing the start of the day. That is not to say she wasn't petrified to be at the place... to stare down the memories and residual terror. She was glancing over her shoulder every second, although no one was there while the night sky was just beginning to break into a spectacular canvas of color. By the time she untied the kayak from the roof of her car and lugged it over to the water's edge, the sun was overtaking any leftover night. She was paddling to the center of the lake by the time the colors were thrown up against the sky, and she took it all in, feeling calmer than she had in months. Content. For the next hour, she paddled and relaxed, adjusting to this sport once again, to the freedom allotted to her through less than happy circumstances. This was her time. She had been a teenager when she'd met her ex. Barely an adult when they had married. And for some reason, somehow... she had become the female that turned over control.

Now here she was paddling on a Saturday morning in full control. Not having to worry about someone else's comfort or level of fun. She did not have to hear complaints about sitting in the tight space of the kayak for too long or making it home in time for whatever sports game was playing on the television. She did not have to worry about starting or messing up dinner or cooking what he liked. No fear, no worry.

Still unsure and unsteady, she had decided not to attempt fishing in a kayak. Wielding a rod while balancing in the kayak was not yet on her comfort list, and after accomplishing so much just this one day, she was willing to give herself a break.

Ella focused on steering the kayak to the spot she had started from, her arms suddenly tired and mind racing. Being on the water seemed safer than land. Maybe she would just head home. She could try fishing another time.

But just as she reached the shore, she glanced up and involuntarily grinned. There stood Dennis, staring at her with his own wide smile. She realized her memory had been weak... had not lived up to his actual good looks. Those almond shaped cocoa-colored eyes and full lips. He had on shorts and sandals and a tank top that displayed biceps Ella could not help but notice. She felt exhilarated and vulnerable all at once, and just as she stopped paddling, he stepped forward, feet in the water and grabbed the rope to pull her in.

"Wait!" she cried out, laughing despite her embarrassment.

He stopped, raising his eyebrows.

"You can pull me over there, but then you have to turn around. It's so awkward getting out of these. I can't let you watch that."

Not showing any sign of hearing her, he pulled the kayak up to land. Then he bent down so that his mouth was near her ear. "I can help you with that. Getting out." He motioned toward her. "May I?" He waited, and when she gave an uncertain nod, he moved closer and before she had a chance to protest, before she even realized what was happening, he had his hands under her armpits and hoisted her up and out, onto land with quick, gentle movements. He kept his hands in place until she had her footing. "See? Easy Peasy."

Ella marveled at how he had moved her as if she were a feather and not a middle-aged pile of extra pounds. And she tried to keep the warmth of his body in memory.

"I'm glad to see you. I've been... been looking for you. I didn't have your information to get in touch..."

There was not much to say to that. She felt the sun on her face, and she felt protected. Like the warmth was a cocoon around her, a shell. She smiled up at him, and he simply grinned back, as if not expecting a response. And after some more words, she found herself sitting beside him, using an extra fishing rod he had brought and enjoying the day.

"You look great, El."

"So do you."

He laughed. "Thank you. But I meant... I know it hasn't been easy." She lifted her shoulder, and he gave a nod of understanding. "Okay. Fishing. Nice and simple, right?"

"You're very wise."

The morning slipped away in the manner that all good things seemed to do. Time could be so delicate and fickle. For the most part, the chatter between them was vague... weather and former beach trips, favorite restaurants and unique locations. Light. Airy. Almost fake.

Because there was something brewing beyond the surface. Ella realized it was one-sided, but she longed to dig deeper, to betray her own words to him and find out what terrified him, what elated him, what made him get up in the morning, every morning over and over again. What did he work toward? What drove him? Because she wanted to tell him, to confess that the act of waking up each day was becoming more of a chore than a delight. She craved that piece of passion that fueled a person. That made the mornings more than a necessity. She wanted to feel something other than a longing to simply go back to sleep, to slip into that escape.

Instead, Ella asked, "What is it you do, Dennis?"

He widened his eyes as he reeled in his line. "I'm a professor. I teach at the university in Clawston."

"Oh." Ella let that sink in for a moment. "What do you teach?"

"Economics." He laughed when he caught the look on her face. "Not a fan?"

"Seems dry."

Still grinning, he nodded. "To some. I find it fascinating. It's how money works, how our resources work."

"I graduated from that university. Long ago. Longer than I care to admit."

"Major?"

"English."

He nodded. "Great English department there."

"Sure. Didn't do me much good. I'm working a job that I hate that pays practically nothing."

"Have you tried applying for a job elsewhere?"

"Well… sure, but there isn't much out there."

"You're kidding. Ella, there are so many jobs out there. I know we are always hiring at the university. They always pay at national level and benefits… the benefits alone are amazing."

She took her time casting out, trying to not feel his stare, not flush with embarrassment. Finally, she turned toward him and confessed, "Dennis, I am 39 years old. I got my degree when I was 26. I had a few jobs in editing but not many and not for several years. I am not qualified for anything except customer service and maybe cashier."

Dennis listened carefully, his gaze heavy and attention all-encompassing. Once she was done, he leaned back. "Were you any good at editing?"

She laughed. "I was damn good. Unfortunately, the companies folded under the economic crash."

"You're smart." It was a statement, not a question. She simply stared back, her eyes narrowed in question. Then he said, "Can I have your number? Because there is an opening in my department-"

"Economics?"

"Yes," he chuckled. "Dry, boring economics. But we still need website content and online courses and articles... we need someone that can write and edit and save those of us that are unfortunately talented in anything except English."

There were a few minutes of silence as she felt the gentle morning sun give way to the blazing midday shine and heat. She shifted in her seat. "I appreciate it, but... I don't want to put you out."

"Hey. Ella. Look at me." He waited until she swung her gaze toward him. "This is a job opening we need filled. I have a great feeling you have the skills needed. I can't guarantee you'll get it, but at least you can try. Or do you like customer service with low pay and high stress?"

"I don't like it!" she exclaimed with a giggle. There was not much more to argue, so they exchanged numbers.

As she got ready to leave, he insisted on helping tie the kayak to the roof of her car. As they lifted it up, he burst out laughing. "How the hell did you get this on the car yourself? Your height... I am just picturing an entire ordeal!"

"Wasn't easy," she admitted. "There was some trial and error, some falling and cursing...."

He laughed. "Well, I have to tell you, I was very happy to see you this morning, Ella. It makes Saturdays a little more colorful when you're around."

"Thank you." She blushed, fumbling with the straps holding the kayak in place. "It's nice to be back outside. I feel like I've lived in a cave away from everyone the past couple of weeks. I missed this."

The rest of the day seemed both flat and vibrant. Whenever she remembered his smile, the conversation, the sunshine... she felt alive, as if every nerve was plugged into some electric source... and then she remembered it would be a week until she would see him, and the color drained from the day. The most exciting part of her week had already happened.

She felt ridiculous. He could be married or in a relationship. She was assuming a man she had talked to a handful of times was available. She was even assuming he would look twice at her in a romantic way. Someone like Dennis.... Someone like Dennis noticed the stunning women. He appreciated all women, respected them, indulged in conversation with them. Sometimes he even saved them. But for a relationship, he probably romanced women with perfect, toned stomachs and perky boobs. Women with smooth skin around their eyes and the perfect shade of blond or even red in their thick, shiny hair. Women who matched designer purses with heels and ironed their jackets that would go over shimmery tops. And Ella was willing to bet that those kinds of women never found cat hair on their slacks or pizza grease on their shirts.

Ella was also certain they did not spend Saturday nights curled up on the couch watching a cheesy romance film while indulging in jalapeno poppers and sour cream. But she refused to feel bad about that. Perhaps she was never going to have a chance with a man as hot as Dennis... perhaps she was never going to have a chance with any guy ever again. But she had her evenings to unwind. To watch mindless television or read a book... to not have to pick up after a husband that barely muttered a greeting to her.

She had to admit, she still missed Alex. Sometimes it was all she could do to keep from falling to her knees and crying over the heartbreak. But on nights like this... she was now comfortable with her new routine.

It was early in her evening that the text came through. "Where are you from, El? Are you close to the university?"

She tucked her feet underneath her. "I live in Oaks. Thirty minutes from the university and the lake."

"May I call?"

Within seconds of her consent, she was on the phone with him. "Oaks, huh? Nice neighborhood. I live in Burkland... in between. So, I'm only fifteen minutes from you. Which means close enough to visit or have you visit me and work on getting your application and resume in."

A light laugh fell from her lips. "You're determined."

"Well, yeah. We need some capable people in our department. And you need a better job. It's just a win win. So... did I call at a bad time? Did I interrupt something like... a hot date or something?" There was a beat of silence, and then his voice came through lower, huskier. "I'm sorry, Ella. I wasn't thinking... I -"

"It's okay. I'm actually curled up on the couch watching movies. Exciting weekend plans. I'm afraid I'm extremely boring."

"Are you kidding?" His chuckle was deep and rich and seemed to seep into her skin, intoxicating her. "That sounds like my kind of night. Love watching movies."

"Oh, I think your taste in movies is much different from mine. Unfortunately, I am a true girly girl in this area. Chick flicks."

"Nothing wrong with that. I don't mind those movies once in a while. Are you strictly chick flick? No action or comedy?"

"No, I love action and comedy. I really love scary movies."

"You're kidding!"

"I do! But my daughter hates them, and I can't watch them alone because... well, for obvious reasons, so it's been awhile since I've seen any good ones. Or even bad ones because sometimes, the bad horror films are the best kind of movies!"

There was a gasp on his end of the line. "El, I so agree! Tell you what, if you let me work with you in getting your resume in for the university position, as a reward, we'll go to the dollar theater when they run the marathon of old time horror flicks. Deal?"

For a moment, she shut her eyes and imagined he was asking her out on a real date. Asking her because he was mesmerized by her eyes and enthralled by her voice. She pretended for just a second that she was a real woman to be desired and pursued. But after that space of an instant was gone, she remembered she was a frumpy middle-aged woman that was evoking pity in a man that would hang up the phone and probably go see one of his many beautiful options.

"Sure," she chirped in a desperate attempt to sound normal, to sound unfazed by such a suggestion.

CHAPTER 3

Just as she had suspected, she heard nothing from Dennis for the rest of the week. But it was just enough for her to focus on keeping her own situation together. Lila was fighting with the boy she was dating, and her attitude was horrendous. Ella's work was threatening to change hours so that she would be forced to work in the evenings and every other weekend. And Alex was fighting her on trivial matters and dragging the divorce out.

"Alex, seriously, I'm letting you off the hook for support and alimony. I'm just asking that you let me have the house, payments and all. Hear that? You don't have to worry about the mortgage for this house. Let me have my car. And you help pay for college when Lila attends."

"College? What kind of help are you talking about?"

She stopped herself from rolling her eyes. "Fifty fifty."

"See…. no. She should pay her own way. I can't afford that."

Leaning back against the counter in an attempt to move away from this man that had taken arrogance and selfishness to a level she had not known he was capable of, she sighed. "I'm not saying we are paying it all upfront. There will be financial aid and scholarships and loans. But help out."

Alex wandered over to the refrigerator and opened it, leaning in before pulling out a soda. Casually he took a sip, moving his gaze over her slowly. "You know…. It is so much easier now. Here, I had to worry about the bills and low-paying jobs… do you know she gets alimony? And he pays for the house. He's worth a lot. It's so much easier to relax and just enjoy things. She and I are taking a trip to Florida. Never had the money to do that before."

Ella almost slumped forward and begged him to stop, asked him why he was doing this. The torment and cruelty. But instead she straightened. "Then what are you waiting for? Let's get this divorce over with and move on. Please."

And suddenly his eyes narrowed and cheeks reddened. "Why are you in a rush for this? New guy in your life?"

The conversation was exhausting her. "I just want us both to move on."

To her surprise, Alex nodded, his expression suddenly somber. "I just got tired, Ellie. Tired of trying to get ahead. Of making the old new, the routine exciting. Aren't you tired?"

How does one answer such questions? Everyone got tired, right? Everyone longed for something different, but did that mean throwing everyone else away? Did it mean going out to find a better, skinnier, more successful version of a spouse? Fortunately, Ella was saved from answering by Lila returning to the house.

"Lila…last night…," she drew out, gathering what energy she had to muster up a stern expression.

"Mom! I know. I'll try to get home earlier. But my curfew is ridiculous."

And then began the art known as teenage bartering and convincing. Of course, her inability to get home at a decent hour was due to her boyfriend's flat tire or traffic. And it was summer, so why shouldn't she be allowed some freedom? All her other friends at the same age were able to stay out later.

To Alex's credit, he stepped in and agreed there would be a hold on extra social activities until Lila was able to follow the rules, including curfew. Then he left, taking Lila with him for the weekend. Such a flurry of noise and news and movement, and then there was silence. Sometimes Ella craved that quiet time. But sometimes it seemed to close in around her, slowly suffocating any life she might have left.

She mowed the lawn and weeded out the garden, basking in the late afternoon sun. She tried to make a deal with herself to leave behind the worries for the weekend. She would deal with the probable work schedule on Monday when she could discuss her concerns with her supervisor. And she would not care what her ex and his fiancé were doing with their lives. Eyes straight ahead on her own journey.

It was not until she went in the house to find something to eat that she saw her phone blinking. And despite it all, her heart jumped.

The text was from Dennis. "Traveling close to your neck of the woods - going to pick up a few fishing supplies. Care to come along?"

The text had been sent an hour ago. She responded. "Sorry, I was outside gardening. Am I too late?"

Her phone rang a minute later. "I hate trying to plan over text," he confessed, his tone low, as if confessing something intimate to her. "You're definitely not too late. I was just catching up on some end-of-the-week tasks. Can I pick you up?"

"Sure. But do I have time to get ready? I'm garden dirty."

His low chuckle came through the line. "Garden dirty? Sounds interesting. Yes. Say about an hour?"

She agreed and gave him her address. After she hung up, Ella wondered if she were being too trusting by giving out her information. It was not that long ago…. But she reasoned that her instincts had warned her about Blaine. She had sensed something was off.

And with Dennis… she felt comfortable and happy. Not to mention, he was the man that had saved her.

It was a little under an hour when the car pulled into her driveway, gravel alerting her to the arrival. She met him at the door, and with a self-conscious grin, she waved him into the house. "I am sorry, almost ready. Just have to brush my hair super quick."

Dennis stepped into the house, his tall, sturdy frame dwarfing the room. "You're fine. I'm early." He glanced around the living room, and she quickly peeked to see if she had cleaned up enough, if perhaps the carpet was too worn and the walls too dark. But he nodded and smiled as if he were being shown some spotless, impeccably decorated mansion he had always wanted to see. As if this were amazing. "You have a beautiful home."

Ella smiled politely. "Thanks. It works for us. So, do you want something to drink?"

"No. Actually I wanted to ask if you'd join me for dinner. There's this new Italian restaurant not far from here, and you'd be doing me a favor. I hate eating alone. My treat."

He drove to the hunting and fishing store first. Ella had never been in there, and she was overwhelmed by the size and beauty. She never thought she would be interested in such a store, but there were kayaks and tents, coolers and fishing rods. Dennis led her to the fish finder systems and explained how they worked.

"I have one," he informed her, pushing a button to show the heat vision feature. "I have a boat and use it, but this summer..." He shrugged before moving onto another topic. And she wondered what that trailing off meant. What about this summer? Was she to blame due to that incident... did it put a damper on things? Smudge the time and make it difficult for him to enjoy because the memory of some ridiculously naive woman getting beat was just too depressing?

Ella did her best to focus because Dennis was showing her a type of crankbait, explaining why it worked and sharing some stories of great catches he'd had. She nodded and then happened to look up, over his tilted shoulder and froze.

There staring right back at her was her husband's fiancé, Connie. Ella had little contact with the woman who had stolen her husband's heart. There was no reason to confront her, and even less reason to befriend her. Lila seemed to be okay with her, so there was not an issue of protecting her daughter.

But now the woman was staring at her, watching her with a disapproving glint in her eyes and an upward tilt of her jaw. When she caught Ella's eye, she shook her head and then glanced at Dennis, who was still oblivious. And it hit her. The woman's dark glare and chastising gestures were in regard to Ella being out with a man. Really! This woman was judging her?

Too late, she noticed Dennis had stopped talking and had turned to see what had her attention. Calmly, smoothly, he called out, "Can I help you, ma'am?"

Ella touched his arm and leaned in to inform him softly, "Dennis... that's... she's ..."

"I know who it is," he revealed in a low grunt. When she narrowed her eyes, he glanced back at her and explained, "She was at the hospital. Lila was upset he'd brought her along." He swung his gaze back to the spot where she had been standing only to see that she had left. "Why is she stalking you?"

"I think it was more of a coincidence. She's obsessed with the outdoors, so this is... probably her place."

"And the staring?" He paused to grab the package of bait he had been showing her. "That was just unnecessary. What you do, who you're with - how is that any of their business?"

So he had picked up on that also. She simply stared at the floor, embarrassed by the scene she had caused, the drama.

He continued, "She looks like she lives here. Should work here. Probably wrestles bears in her spare time."

And a surprised laugh burst from Ella's mouth. "Dennis!"

He grinned. "I'm sorry. I don't want to be disrespectful to any woman, but that grizzly girl ... damn! Your ex probably needed protection and sought that out."

"Stop!" She clasped his arm as she bent forward, unable to catch her breath. Even when she caught a glimpse of Connie peeking around the corner, she continued to laugh. Everything suddenly seemed okay, better... good, in fact. The colors of her world were more vibrant and alive, breathing out the fadedness. She did not feel so alone. Someone was on her side. *He* was on her side.

After paying for his purchases, Dennis led her out with a gentle hand on her elbow. He gave her a wink and a slight nod to indicate that they were still being watched. And Ella felt a rush of both irritation and bravery as she tugged him to her and rose up on her toes. Dennis immediately lowered his head as if he knew, he sensed what she wanted. Despite being the one to initiate it, the kiss threw Ella off guard. She felt his arms wrap around her to steady her, and then everything in her mind went blank. Because that kiss....

It was Dennis who pulled away first, and as she stared up at him, stunned, he flashed a grin at the greeter who was staring in shock. "We just really, really love your store."

"I'm sorry," Ella managed to sputter out in the parking lot. "I just... she wants to spy so..."

"If that is how you kiss just for show, I'd love to be there when you kiss just for a kiss sake." He opened the car door for her, his tone teasing, but his eyes taking her in carefully.

"Funny. I was thinking the same about you," she quipped, feeling brave and shy all at once.

On the way to the restaurant, her phone erupted with texts and calls from her ex. Excusing herself, she called her daughter. "Lila, is anything wrong? Are you okay?"

"Mom? I'm fine."

"That's all I needed to know. Love you." She hung up and explained, "If he isn't calling to discuss our child, I don't need to answer."

"He's calling because she saw us, El. Your ex has not let go."

"No. He's let go. He doesn't want me to let go."

For a few minutes, he drove in silence, but by the clenching of his jaw, she knew he was thinking, trying to broach the subject. And she wanted to speak up to tell him to say what he had to say, but she could not find her voice.

"Do you think.... Forgive me if I'm treading on sensitive ground... but do you think you're not assertive enough with him? The guy hasn't been the best to you. You don't owe him anything after he left you-"

"I kicked him out. I made him leave."

He took his eyes off the road to regard her with surprise.

"What?"

"I found out about Connie... about others. I kicked him out. So no, I'm not terribly assertive except when it counts."

"Wow. I'm sorry. I just assumed... but good for you. That could not have been easy."

"No. It wasn't. It was the hardest thing I've ever done. Because I considered that man my best friend. To realize that he was far from my friend... to figure out the lies and betrayals - or rather, to admit to it all. I knew all along. I just pretended to everyone, including myself."

"That's not uncommon. You give your everything to a person, and you don't want to face the facts that they just... trampled all over that. But that's on him, El. Nothing to do with you."

"Of course, it had something to do with me. I was his wife. I was with him for over twenty years. I supported him through bad times and celebrated with him during the good. And I'm left wondering... do those years count for anything or was it all just...a big fraud? Because looking back, I realize my heart wasn't fully in it either. I was willing to stay, to suffer... but I was never fully in love." She leaned her head back and exhaled. "Shit. I'm sorry. I talk too much."

"No. You don't. So, tell me... if you were never in love, why stay? Why torture yourself until he commits the ultimate betrayal?"

"Because we had made vows. And we had a daughter. I mean, is there such a thing as love described in movies? That explosive, can't get enough of each other love and does it last? No."

"No?" He gave a short shake of his head. "Wait - are you kidding me? Yes. There is such a thing. And you need to hold out for that."

"And you know because...?" she asked in a curious tone, not doubting, not amused... curious.

For a few moments, he focused on the road and said nothing. Then he answered, "I've felt it... had it. The kind of love that fills every corner of your life. It invades your thoughts and feelings, when you chew your food, when you open your eyes in the morning... Even when you get used to the person and the relationship, there is still that slight thrill there when you see them."

"Oh," she breathed, suddenly understanding. "I'm so sorry, Dennis."

He shrugged, although the shadows in his eyes and twitching of his jaw contradicted that gesture. "It was years and years ago, El."

At the restaurant, he asked about her resume. She was grateful for a lighter topic. "I updated it. Ready to send."

"Then how about we leave here and go work on the application. We can easily get it all sent tonight." He gave a nervous cough. "I mean, we can go somewhere like a library if.."

"It's fine. We can go to my place if you don't mind. I feel bad taking all your time."

"El, I was home watching Star Trek reruns. Summer is my slow time and sometimes... I would rather be busy. So, humor me, please."

Dennis was true to his word, and he went over the entire application process. Ella was a bit surprised and ashamed by how easy it was, how she could have done this long ago and not suffered at a job she was overqualified for. A job that left her miserable.

"They're changing our shifts. I'd have to work some evenings and weekends. Which is the last thing I want to do." She found it easy to confide to this man, this stranger. There was a level of intimidation, of becoming friends with this gorgeous creature and the electricity she felt on her end. It was not fear as much as feeling startled... uncertain and yet thrilled. But in terms of feeling safe, she had no reservations about leading him through her house. The one location that was her armor, her shell... the one place she felt most vulnerable when strangers like the plumber or electrician were there... and yet it felt right to have this tall, muscular form stomping through her small, delicate rooms. He felt almost familiar at the same time that he felt thrillingly new.

He leaned his hip against the desk, folding his arms and staring at her. "Then it's about time you got out of there, right?"

"Look, if I'm qualified then I'm qualified, but I don't want to be given any special treatment - "

"Special treatment?" Dennis scrunched up his face like an insolent toddler. "What? You have to be amazing at fishing to get any special treatment, and while you are okay...."

"Okay? Please! I saw your face when I pulled out that bass."

His expression melted into a grin. "Yes. Pretty impressive. But listen, I couldn't get you special treatment even if I tried. Their hiring procedures are by the books. But I can and will give them a head's up about your resume only because you have the experience and the skills that they are looking for. Deal?"

"Fine. Ice cream and a movie? Since you paid for dinner."

He seemed comfortable in her home. They settled in to watch a horror movie, an old cheesy film they both had seen before, and she was aware of every move, every word, and every glance. It was as if her body were on high alert. And yet, it felt as if they had done this before... as if this were one of several movies they had watched together. They fell into an easy dialogue, and by the time the movie was over, she had learned that he was one of three boys, the middle child, and that he was still close to his parents, who were older and needed more help around their house, in their life.

"There's nothing as helpless as seeing your parents deteriorate."

And she thought of her father and how it always surprised her when she saw him. He had been larger than life, tall and sturdy with a personality to match. A renowned photographer who now traveled to teach others the art. And on the rare occasions she saw him, she was devastated to find more wrinkles masking the large topaz eyes she remembered and the gray hair overtaking the thick brown hair of his youth.

It always made her stop and catch her breath. Time could be

a cruel prankster because Ella had been certain no one could ever take down her father. But age was rendering him weaker, more mortal... more human. He was her father... and yet not. The magic that went along with that title seemed to diminish as the years piled on.

And her mother...

"It's tough," she responded when she noticed the silence following his confession. And then, feeling a bit flustered, she blurted out, "My dad's coming to visit in a week. He just found out about the divorce. Impending divorce."

"Wait... he just found out?"

"He doesn't live close... he actually was in Alaska last time I heard, and ... we don't keep in touch, I guess."

"Understatement. Your mom?"

"Not in the picture."

Dennis raised his eyebrows but let the subject drop. And it was only after the movie was finished that he mentioned it in passing. "It sounds like you've been on your own for a very long time. I'm sorry, El. I don't know what I would do or where I would be without my family. But sometimes friends can help fill that gap. I'm glad I'm getting to know you."

Ella feared that one look up into those golden-brown eyes would render her a blubbering mess, so she glanced down and lifted a shoulder. "It is fine. I have my daughter. I'm okay." Taking a deep breath, as if gathering strength, she glanced up and chanced a smile. "Thank you for your help."

Suddenly that grin was back accompanied with a teasing glint in his eyes as Dennis leaned forward and whispered in her ear, "And thank you for that kiss." He stood upright and caught her gaze. "Fishing tomorrow?"

There was nothing to do but nod.

**

"Alex, not your business. Leave the house. Seriously, get the fuck out! I'm changing the locks." Ella opened the front door and glared at him.

Alex tilted his upper body forward, his teeth clenched so

that his words came out in forced hisses. "My business when my kid is living here. Do you not remember being beaten to a bloody pulp by one of your men? My kid was just across the lake. And now Connie tells me you're making out with another man in the middle of the sporting store!"

"My men?" Ella repeated slowly, her body trembling with a silent rage. "I went out on one date with that man. Not in any way my fault. You know what- you need to leave. Go. Now. I do not have to explain -"

"But you do! And you change the locks on this house before the divorce is final and everything is settled then you'll be hearing from my lawyer. Get your life together and act like an adult."

The rage radiating from Alex flipped her anger to fear. The ice-cold worry that someone was upset with her, that *he* was mad. It was instinct, built inside of her from years of dealing with the moods, the rages, of attempting to keep him pleased. But Ella swallowed some air and words of apology and instead growled, "I'll work on that, dear husband. But in the meantime, go home to your fiancé, you hypocritical moron! And tell that crazy bitch not to waste time spying on me when you're the one she should be worried about."

"You're a joke." He stepped outside and before he could sling anymore insults her way, she slammed the door.

Once the door shut, once she heard the bang of it closing, Ella felt her body grow lighter. She was not tied to his moods. Alex could try his best to destroy her in court, and although that scared her a little, she knew it would be worth being free. More and more, the fear and sadness over being alone were fading into the smallest bud of excitement.

Ella had not realized how imprisoned she had felt during the marriage. Somber moods she mistook for just average day blues had probably been festering from much more. She remembered a few years back, she had begged and pleaded with him to go to a concert. Concerts were not high on her list of favorite activities, but it was a singer she had revered since she was a child. It was probably his last tour, but Alex had not budged and insisted they could not afford the tickets. A month later, he had purchased wrestling tickets for him and his friends.

Some of it was her fault, of course. Ella should have stood her ground. She should have maintained a voice.

So, the flip side of having to give up the comfort of a long marriage was the thrill of discovering things she had been unable... or not allowed... to do before.

And Saturday night, she found herself in a loud, bright Mexican restaurant with four other friends she had known from high school. She had driven an hour to get to her hometown, anxious to see everyone. And they stayed talking and laughing long after they had eaten their meals.

Slowly the women cited families waiting and reluctantly left to return home. After three hours, it was only Ella and Leona remaining, and as if to prove her determination to stay longer, Leona leaned over her chair and waved down a waiter. "Another margarita, please? Ellie, for you?"

"No, just more water please. I have a long drive back."

She smiled at her old friend, feeling warm and content in the belly of the evening. This was how those feel-good fuzzy memories happened. Content flashbacks to a great evening. She had always been closest to Leona in high school, and they had kept in constant touch through the years. So, Leona knew better than most.

She tucked a strand of honey blond hair behind her ear and studied Ella. "You're doing okay?"

"Oh. I think so. Bad days, good days. I went fishing today."

Leona was a beautiful woman with round cocoa eyes and tiny features. She, however, was more interested in conveying her reactions through extreme expressions. Widening her eyes and curling her lips into a small O, she said, "I love fishing. But do you bait your own hook? I can't do that."

"Really? You were always the tomboy of our group. I'm surprised and a little disappointed, Leona. Of course, I bait my own hook."

Leona waved away her words. "Show off." She smiled her thanks at the waiter as he dropped off the large drink. "So anyway, listen. There's this guy I know that -"

"No! Don't finish that sentence. No way. I'm not ready to date. Especially not ready to be sold out by my friends. I'm fine."

Leona raised her eyebrows and looked to the side as she sipped her drink. Finally, she shook her head with that dramatic smile. "Okay. I just was going to say this guy I know owns a winery and has invited us there for a private tasting. He's actually already married so not sure if dating is an option. But I've already gotten us a discount so not asking you to help." She laughed as Ella's face reddened. "But damn girl, what's going on, because you are jumpier than usual about dating? Out with it. Who is he?"

Ella was awed by Leona's ability to home in on her motives, her emotions and actions. She loved that her friend knew her well enough to pick up on something new in her life.

"Not dating. No new guy. But…"

"Yes?"

"When I go fishing… I talk to this guy. Dennis. He was there… the morning I was attacked at the lake…. He is the reason I wasn't hurt more… he was there and saw and stopped…" She shrugged again. "Anyways, the guy is gorgeous, and I'm pretty sure he hangs around out of pity."

"Ellie! Stop."

"I'm being realistic. Okay? I'm a middle-aged frumpy woman that had her chance at anything remotely romantic long ago. I'm flattered at the attention, I'm enjoying it… but I know what I know."

Leona gulped some of her drink before setting it down hard. "Fine. Far be it for me to burst your safe little bubble and tell you that your life is just now beginning. You're far from frumpy. You're attractive and warm and intelligent. Don't you dare sell yourself short, whether this man is attracted to you or not."

"He isn't. It's just a matter of me not being his type. But he is an instructor at the campus and had me put my resume in for a job there. Editing, proofreading, some writing."

Leona leaned back in her chair. "Your ideal job. Good for you! If nothing else, he sounds like a good friend."

And that was just what Ella was afraid of.

CHAPTER 4

Ella's father Ted was like a faded memory standing in front of her. He seemed shorter, smaller... more transparent than she remembered. Even that booming voice seemed thinner.

"I told you! Ella, I told you from the very beginning that man was a bum! Sonofabitch!"

She shut her eyes and held up her hand, feeling exhausted within twenty minutes of her father showing up a day early at her front door. "Dad. Please. While I wholeheartedly agree at this time- at this point - that he is less than an ideal husband... we shared many years together. And a daughter. So-"

"More kids if you'd had your way. Thank God he had the sense to stop at one."

And she swallowed back the tears and bile. Because there was now more to her husband's love story. After years of refusing her more kids... Alex was now going to be a father again... to his soulmate.

She had found out in the most awkward, infuriating way. It seemed that Connie now frequented the same places Ella did. And this time, it was at the grocery store, across town from where Connie and Alex resided.

"Oh, you shop here? I told Alex we should probably go in the opposite direction, but I was craving that pecan ice cream, and this is the only place that sells it."

It was the longest she had even spoken to Ella, and to be polite, Ella gave a short nod and slight smile before turning her cart around.

"But I guess that's what happens with pregnancy cravings." Ella stopped, ice running down her spine. After a slight pause, Connie said, "Oh no, you weren't told? I told Alex to give you a head's up. I thought even Lila would say something to you. Oh dear. But now you can see why getting a divorce is more important than ever. Right?"

Too many things spun through her mind at once, and all she could think to do was turn, smile, and clearly respond, "Congratulations," before leaving her full cart in the middle of the aisle and walking out.

If she'd had her sense, she would have explained that Alex was the one holding up the divorce. He was the one finding the smallest things to fight about. She wanted to be free. But the mere news of her husband having a baby with another woman... she made it outside in time to vomit in the bushes, fighting to ignore the stares of passersby.

And now she was facing her father who seemed to know just how to dig into the most painful part of her soul.

"Dad. No. I can't. Can't do this. All right?"

"Hey, not all right! I'm your father!"

"Oh yeah? And where were you the past several years of my life?"

His face reddened, his wrinkles vanishing as his cheeks puffed out, and he shouted, "I was pushed out! I wasn't welcome in your life, Ella Grace. That's where the hell I was." He took a deep breath and lowered his chin to his chest, cursing under his breath. Then he looked up, the wrinkles back tenfold. "I'm sorry. Sorry for yelling, sorry for not being here, sorry for failing. But Ella.... I tried. You kept pushing me away."

"You punched Alex."

"And now looking back... don't you want to thank me?"

She laughed as her father shot her a self-satisfied grin. "Okay, I give."

"Kiddo, I want to be here. I want to be in your life. Not learning about it months after the fact. I mean, do you even have support around you? Have you... your mom -"

"No!"

He nodded. "So, doing all this on your own. You know what

this means, right?"

She rocked back on her heels, knowing that she had planned to refuse, to deny what had been her legacy... the sum of her childhood. She would refuse it, deny it, run from it... except now that she was in the moment, she would not. She would embrace it awkwardly.

"It can't be now." She spoke low, as if Alex were within earshot. Guilt washed over her.

"I know. It has to be once everything is finalized. We waited all these years. A little longer won't hurt." He studied her, and she caught a glimpse of that strong, sturdy dad from her memories. The one who was there when needed, who knew without being told. Who saved her from unspeakable horrors and from a mother who would never have saved her. "Listen, Ella Bella. This is your money. Yours. You earned it. You are still earning it. I just... you know why I couldn't let you have it. He would have taken it. He would have spent it all. Or found a way to take it with him. Right?"

"I feel this is wrong, dad. Underhanded."

"And he's not? Listen, I get the whole 'it was good while it lasted', but that scum - he blew the entire inheritance you got from Grammy. Right? And on what? Trip to the track with his buddies and gambling."

Her head whipped up. "How the hell did you know?"

"When it comes to my only child, I pay attention. I'm not just some oblivious photographer that doesn't get it, Ella."

"Never said you were."

"Oh, you think it. Anyway, that's why I never gave you anything before now. But Ella, you're going to be a very wealthy girl."

"Not for a while. He's dragging this out, dad."

He shrugged. "Do you have a good lawyer? I can get you the best. Let me help. I bet that ass isn't offering up any money to keep the house running. Right?" He sighed when she simply looked away. "How are you doing it then? Huh? Ella.... Ell, please. I can't let my daughter and granddaughter struggle.

Where are you working?"

It was then that she burst into tears. And it was then that there was a knock at the door, reminding her of why her father's early appearance was suddenly such an inconvenience.

Her father did not mince words when he saw Dennis. "Who the hell are you?"

"Dad! No! Not doing this. You're a visitor, not my guardian."

Dennis stepped forward, extending his hand. "Sir, I'm Dennis."

"Ted." He reluctantly shook his hand. "Her father."

He gave him a polite, curt nod and then turned his attention to Ella. "I brought the zucchini from my garden. I have tomatoes too. I apologize. I didn't realize I'd be interrupting-"

"No. Dad arrived a day early."

"I like to catch my daughter by surprise. It seems to be the only way I can find out anything about her life. How do you know Ella?"

"We fish at the same spot. Got to know each other a little. She's a great friend." He turned slightly away from Ted and mouthed, "Are you okay?" to Ella. She shut her eyes and nodded, horrified to realize there were still tears on her face.

"And what do you think of her no-good ex?"

"Dad!"

"Sir, I don't know the no-good ex. Anyone stupid enough to leave a woman like Ella, I have no interest in knowing. I do think this is a great new beginning for her. A chance to be independent and achieve some of her dreams." He never took his eyes off Ella as he addressed her father. And she cursed herself for that heat sliding up her neck, no doubt coloring her face.

It was not until she heard her dad clearing his throat that she realized she was staring. Dennis jumped, and then dropped the bag of goodies from his garden onto her kitchen table. "So, sir, it was great to meet you -"

"Stay for dinner," Ted insisted, motioning Dennis back into the room. Dennis hesitated and then stepped closer, glancing at Ella for some type of permission, and she could only stare. Her father could be a charming man, but when it came to anyone in his daughter's life, he was usually cautious... brisk. "I'm making my famous spicy chicken pasta. You'll love it."

And then suddenly it all closed in on Ella. The front door opened, and Lila's young, upbeat voice called out, "Mom, I got your text. Grandpa's here?"

Ted grinned. "Lila, get in here! Let your pappy see you!" He met her at the entryway and swung her around. "No! This can't be the little girl that was wearing band shirts and sulking. Three years has been too long. Are you driving yet?"

"Not yet, pap. But I have-" she stopped, glancing over her grandfather's shoulder and spotting Dennis. "What? Dennis? Oh my God!" She started to cry and before anyone knew her intention, she flew into the kitchen and threw herself into his arms. "Dennis, I've been wanting to see you. I never thanked you."

"Oh honey, it's okay." Dennis immediately went into soothing mode, his voice low and his arms holding the crying girl.

Ted stepped closer to them; his eyes narrowed. "Wait. What's going on? Thank him for what?"

Dennis shot Ella a questioning look, but before she could think up something to deter her father, Lila jumped away from Dennis and shouted, "For saving my mother's life!"

**

Chaos ensued.

Ella had always hated that phrase. Overdone, dramatic... and yet it described the scene in her kitchen moments after her well-meaning, impulsive daughter blurted out the news that Ella's life had needed saving.

Perhaps Ella could have brushed it off as her daughter simply implying Ella had needed a friend. That Dennis had saved her life by being a great emotional support. Because Dennis was not about to step on toes by explaining, and Lila seemed to have realized her blunder and was now close-mouthed. Ella could get away with lying. But she could not do it. How on

Earth could she even attempt to minimize what Dennis had done? All to save her the inconvenience of a guilty father's concern? No.

"There was an incident… no, that doesn't quite…" She drew in a breath, realizing her father was studying her, not about to let her off the hook. An explanation would have to be provided. "I was attacked, dad. This guy followed me to the lake. Fortunately, Dennis was there and … I'm okay, dad."

"You're okay? You're telling me you're okay… you were attacked to the point that my granddaughter breaks down when she sees the guy that… that saved you… I have a feeling this was more than just an incident." He paused and cleared his throat, and Ella could not ignore the break in his voice. "I may not have been in town, but I wasn't in some cave, Ella. You could have reached me within minutes. Text, phone call- hell, at this point, I'll settle for email. Something. I don't deserve this."

At that Ella snapped her head up, her eyes immediately darkening. "You don't deserve this? Sorry, dad. I'm not five years old. I don't just absorb the guilt you throw out. This happened to me. This. The divorce, the attack… me. I don't deserve this." She rubbed the heels of her hands into her eyes and then growled, "Just so there aren't any more surprises that can be blamed on me, dad, I'll update you thoroughly. Alex is going to be a father. He and his fiancé are expecting."

"Fiancé? Are you two even divorced?"

"No. But not my concern." She turned and focused on Lila, whose eyes were round and red-rimmed. "Sweetie, it's okay. You didn't do anything wrong."

And she felt herself being led out of the room. "Lila, catch up with your pap. Your mom's going to get some air."

The air was still and heavy, but it still felt more open than the air around her father. She breathed in, squeezing her eyes shut. "Thanks."

Dennis leaned against the railing. "You lost your color for a minute there. Deep breaths. Trust me, I know how parents can be. Mine still ask about any special girl in my life. I'm glad I have brothers to take the pressure off."

"Yeah, well, it's just me. Pressure on."

He kicked at an invisible stone before looking up to meet her gaze. "Ella, he's your father. Is he a horrible person?"

"No."

"Uncaring?"

"Obviously not."

"Then... do you think he might have a right to be upset? His only daughter has been having one hell of a year. Going through hell. And he was never told."

She gave a short, hard laugh. "A right? No. But should I have told him? Probably." Ella met his gaze again and sighed. "Look, our relationship is complicated. This... my life is complicated."

"You don't have to tell me anything if you don't want to. Not my business."

For some reason, his words infuriated her. "Then I won't!"

And then he grinned, as if her anger amused him. "Right. You're not."

"I was! I was just telling you! Don't laugh at me."

"Okay. Deep breath. I am sorry. And I know this is patronizing and sexist, but you really are cute when you're mad. Unfortunately, adorable. And no, you aren't telling me anything. You're giving generic answers. Every relationship is complicated. Life is complicated."

"Yep. Guess so." She spun around so that her back was to him and blinked back tears of frustration... perhaps tears of hurt.

And suddenly she was being nudged back around, his fingers pressing gently into her shoulder. "I'm here, El. Tell me what I can do. I can listen if you do feel like talking. What happened? What's going on between you and your dad?"

She raised a shoulder and then let it drop. "I got pregnant at seventeen." She paused, but he made no change in his expression, so she felt braver... more assured. "Dad was devastated. And I was bullheaded. I refused to get an abortion and insisted

I was marrying Alex. And I threatened. I told dad that if he didn't sign for me to get married, I'd run away and wait the last few months until I was eighteen, and he would never be allowed in my life again." She gave a short laugh, unaware of the tears until Dennis reached out and wiped one away. "I was a mean, spiteful teenager."

"As are all teenagers."

"Maybe. I was especially cruel. Dad was backed into a corner. And he finally signed. And we got married. And Brice was stillborn."

"God, Ella. I am so sorry."

"Of course, we're teens stuck in this marriage, and Alex felt trapped. We almost didn't make it past the first couple of years. And dad found out he was running around on me. I knew it though. I had already confronted him, and we both wanted to work it out. But dad shows up to my one-room apartment all dad-angry and punches Alex. And I was furious. My marriage, my business. So, I told him to get out of my life. When Lila was born, he started to come around again. But things were never the same. There were other bumps in the road, resentments festering. Rotting us from the inside out. And I know I'm standing in front of you a heartbroken woman. I know I'm getting divorced. But I still just… ugh."

"You still believe that your marriage… your business."

"Yes."

"Can I ask you something?"

She shook her head with a laugh. "I just unloaded all this icky personal stuff onto you. So yes. Ask."

"If it were Lila… if she were involved with a man that you knew did not treat her right, was not up to the standards you believed - "

"Don't do that."

He stopped, closed his mouth, and then in a low whisper, asked, "Do what, El?"

"Don't ask that question. Of course, I'd fight for my daughter. But this is different. There is a history I did not even begin to uncover for you. Things that happened, and no matter how fair or unfair, those events affect the rest of our lives. They color every conversation, they reshape each visit... the way things are for me and dad are not how things are with me and Lila."

"Okay," he answered. "Good enough." He studied her for a full minute before asking, "What can I do?"

"Nothing. I'm fine."

"El. You're not."

"In this moment, I'm not. But I will be. For God's sake, I'm going to be forty. I can handle my father. Right?"

He stared at her a moment before that grin appeared. "You can do anything. Even handle the father."

Lily peeked out the front door. "Mom, I'm so sorry. I wasn't thinking-"

"Honey, not your fault. At all."

"Well, listen. Pap promises to be good and not get too nosey if you come back in. He said double points if you bring back the guy that hates your ex. You hate my dad?" She stared up at Dennis.

He shook his head. "I don't." He motioned with his head. "Do you want me to join you for dinner, El? Or would it be easier if I left."

"I would like you to stay. Please."

Ted was true to his word and remained calm and pleasant as he cooked, talking to them about his adventures and classes. Dennis asked questions about his travels and then about his career. It was only a matter of time before he put it together.

"Oh, Theodore Barnes! Sir... I am a great fan of your work! The air shot of the jungle... the mist and ... I have that picture framed in my office."

Ella smiled softly. No matter what issues were between her and her father, she greatly admired his work and was proud when people recognized him. He had earned that. Ted smiled his thanks and then with a ball of dread dropping in her chest, she realized he was pointing to her.

"She is my greatest work."

"Dad," Ella growled his name in warning.

"What? I was nothing but a boy with a camera until that picture…" He turned back to the stove, stirring the sauce and avoiding her glare. "Hey, Dennis? Did you know our Ella here is a celebrity? Ever see the toddler holding the leash of the huge Mastiff on the advertisements for the dog food?"

Dennis's eyes widened. "Noooo! El? You? Ah, I can see the resemblance. Yes!"

She stood and walked over to the cupboards, reaching for a stack of dishes. "Oh, it gets better."

"It sure does!" Ted was obviously in his glory, bragging about his daughter. "Ever seen the ad for orange soda… the young teenager sitting on a wooden fence …"

"Of course, I've seen it. That ad is still shown. I'm beyond blown away, El. How come you've never told me about your fame?"

"She's modest. There are a lot of others. Those two just stick out because it was advertising. I rarely deal with that part of the business anymore. But her photogenic face… that's brought me a lot of notice."

"And Lila? She's her mother's mini-me."

Lila shook her head with a proud smile. "They both tried to rope me into it, but I don't want any part. I would be horrified to see my face up on some ad or picture on some stranger's wall. I don't want in front of the camera. I want behind it."

"Well, good enough. Your pap could definitely help with that. And we have excellent photography classes at the university. Do you have any pictures I can see?"

As Lila left the room to get the pictures, Ted commented, "I didn't realize she still had an interest. I honestly thought she was just saying that to pacify me the last time I saw her."

"Nope," Ella responded coolly, smiling up at Dennis as he took the silverware from her and helped set the table. "She's always been interested. She is really good too."

Dennis appeared genuinely impressed by Lila's work, as did

Ted, who raved about having another photographer in the family. After dinner, Ella shooed her father and Lila out of the kitchen, insisting they go out to take some pictures. She knew Lila was dying to get her grandfather's input.

As she cleared the table, Dennis followed suit, waving away her attempts to refuse help. As they started loading the dishwasher, he carefully began, "So... about your ex."

"Favorite topic," she quipped dryly. "What about him?"

"He's going to be a father again? I wasn't aware."

"Neither was I until just recently." She wiped down the counters. "Ran into Connie in the grocery store, and she had the pleasure of breaking the news to me."

"Ran into her- wait. Hey, hold up." Dennis gently caught her hands and forced her to meet his gaze. "I'm pretty sure you mentioned that they live even further away than I do. And ... I just keep thinking of that day she watched you in the sports store. Don't you find it funny that-"

"Yes. Of course. But I think she believes I'm the one holding the divorce up. So, she wanted to make a point."

"You lock your doors when you're home?"

"Yes. You know I do. But I doubt some pregnant woman is going to come after me."

"Really? Not saying she will, but I wouldn't put it past her." He leaned against the counter, releasing her hands. "Not the best way to get the news. I'm so sorry."

And she sensed that he was waiting, anticipating some confession, a purge of all she was feeling. Of course, he would expect that - today she had shared more than was necessary, more than she was comfortable with. It made her feel silly, grimy, and out of her league in speaking to this man towering in front of her. Finally, she said, "It's fine."

"I know that's a lie. It isn't fine."

"No. You're right. This past year, I've felt like I'm on one of those carnival rides that whips me one way and then the other way. I'm dizzy and confused and just trying to hold on and not fall out. But I can't talk about it. Okay? I just want to clean up the kitchen and then find another mindless chore until it's time to crash in bed." With a heavy sigh, she turned back to him, but kept her gaze down. "I'm sorry. I'm on edge."

"No. I'm sorry. I pushed. I just... sometimes I don't know when to stop. I don't realize I'm broaching on boundaries." He tilted his head with a small smile. "I'm going to go and let you just get some breathing room. It's been a day of it, I'm sure."

She lifted one corner of her mouth in an imitation of a smile. "Thank you. Good friend."

As she walked him to the door, he stopped and turned, his finger pointing toward her. "One of the reasons I stopped by - they're just now looking at resumes. Said they got behind, so that is probably why you haven't heard anything. Just... be prepared. Might get a call this week." He smiled down at her. "If you need anything, call. Okay?"

All she could do was nod.

And she almost did call later that night when Lila was at her father's and Ella's own dad was at a hotel across town. She felt restless, sad, and alone. She wondered if today had been too crazy for her new friend, and he was trying to forget all about it. All about her. She resisted the urge to text or call, knowing she was close to alienating him forever.

But just as she curled up on her couch for some mindless television, her phone rang.

"Listen," Dennis started immediately upon her greeting. "I know you have had a day of it. I know you said you just needed space. But I'm ... I'm sorry if I added to anything. I'm sorry if I overstepped."

"No! Dennis, you've been an amazing friend. I just hate... I don't like being in limbo. I don't like the drama infiltrating my life right now, and I'm embarrassed and upset and sad."

"Come outside."

She stood, her eyes skipping to the windows even though she knew the blinds were closed. "Why?"

"Because I'm out here."

She momentarily forgot about the sweats and t-shirt she

had on and stepped outside, grinning involuntarily. "Hey you."

And through the sharp moonlight, she saw him grin back. "Hey you."

"Oh, the stars. It's so clear." She sat down on the steps and tilted her head up.

"You're going to catch a cold. Hold on." He trotted to his car and then jogged back with a blanket. "Here." He swung the blanket over her shoulders, his fingers lingering. "So, you have to tell me, are we good?"

At first, she misunderstood. She took his question to mean what she wanted it to mean, what she feared it meaning. That they, as a couple, would be good. Then her senses cleared out the fog, and she understood. "Of course, we are."

"Okay. Because when I left, you just looked... and you sounded.... Defeated. And upset. I'm not always a good judge of when to stop. When to stay out of your business. I feel almost responsible for you because..."

And that sharpened her thoughts even more. "Oh. Because you had the misfortune of being there when I got myself into that situation? Is that what you're talking about? This is all because you feel sorry-"

"Ella, no! Stop!"

"No, you stop. I knew- " She whipped the blanket off of her shoulders and tossed it to him. "Take this. I'm not a child. I'm a middle-aged woman that doesn't need any type of pity. Trust me, you're not responsible for any of this."

He waited a few moments before responding in a low voice, "Ella. That is not at all what I meant. If you let me -"

"No. You need to go. Just like I told you earlier. This - this isn't me. Just blabbing everything about my life, letting a stranger see the dysfunction... the disaster... I'm mortified. And then to know that this... you being here, being nice and helping... it is out of some misplaced-"

"No! Listen-"

"You listen. Leave. Go do your usual Friday night stuff. I'm sure it involves dating and normalcy and having fun. Don't come here out of obligation to spend some pity time with a middle-aged, boring, frump of a woman -"

"Hey!" he yelled, his fist closing in around the blanket. He waited as she stared back in surprise. "Are you done yet?"

"Maybe," she hissed because she suddenly couldn't catch her breath.

He set the blanket down and then climbed the few steps before sitting down beside her. "Let's make one thing clear. I'm here because I want to be. And middle-aged? I'm older than you. By a decade. What I meant was I never want anything happening to you again. I can't even bear the thought. Frump of a woman? Honey, you have no idea just who you are, do you?"

Before she could ask what he meant, he leaned in and kissed her. Gently, hesitantly and then he drew back to study her. With a slight grin, a muffled curse, he kissed her again, this time with more urgency, hunger... as if he had been waiting to do just what he was doing.

Ella felt her body betray her by leaning into him, her arms lacing around his neck without her permission. She felt like she was made of air and yet could not sit up on her own. She felt his hands on her back, two hot spots that seared through her shirt and reached her racing blood. This was just some type of retaliation for her kiss in the store, she told herself. This was not real.

And then it was over. She felt cold, exposed as he pulled away, although his hands remained. "Dammit." He stared at her and feeling the pull, her gaze rose to meet his. He whispered, "I lied to your daughter."

"Huh?"

"Earlier, when I said I didn't hate her father. I lied. I actually do. I hate him for hurting you. But I am also grateful to him because he let you go. And I get to sit here and kiss you on your porch steps."

Ella sat there, her fingers touching her tingling lips. "This isn't what I meant when I said less drama."

He laughed. "No. I imagine it wasn't. And it was not what I intended to do, but you were sitting there so angry and ... that adorable thing... you know. Just..." He moved his hands to cup her face as he leaned in once again for another kiss. She was prepared this time and did not fight it. She melted, her body became this hot liquid being contained by Dennis, being controlled and protected... She heard a moan and realized it came from her, and it hit her that this was out of her control. This was not something she could take charge of. And that scared her enough to pull away.

"I can't think."

"Not supposed to right now. This is just ... impulsive. Two people sharing a kiss and forgetting everything else. Just for a minute." He studied her, his gaze dropping to her lips and making her think it might happen again. But then he blinked, as if leaving some type of daze that had held him captive. "Okay. I'm going. I just ... we're good?"

She decided to not try to guess the meaning as she nodded. "We're good."

CHAPTER 5

Do people start out with the intention of stalking? Connie often wondered this when she read the tabloids and saw some star was being followed, being stalked by a crazed fan. There was always that wording... the label of crazed... obsessed. But what if you were simply curious?

Connie had started out with just a stab of curiosity. The man she had fallen utterly in love with was married, and she had to see the soon-to-be ex-wife. She had to know about her. What had Alex seen in her? Did he still see something, because Connie feared that he was still a bit involved in what Ella was doing, whom she was hanging around?

Connie drove past their house several times before she caught a glimpse. And it fueled her interest. She needed to know what Ella did in her free time, how she dressed, what she was like. This was her fiancé's first love. His intense long-term relationship, hell, marriage. And she needed to know what made him choose her over all he had built with Ella.

She wanted to take one look and laugh. To feel self-assured. But actually, it was the opposite. Connie had always felt a bit plain. No figure. Just skin draped over bones, legs that were too long to be graceful. Boyish features. And there was this woman, this ex that came bouncing out of her house like a teenager. She was six years older than Connie, and yet she reminded her of a young girl. She seemed to hop with each step, twirl instead of turn, and her curves immediately sent Connie into a tearful bout of envy.

Ella's hair was thick and unruly, auburn waves cascading. When Connie had mentioned it to Alex, he had spit out, "Rat nest." She wondered about the emotional reactions he had to his ex. It seemed that he was angry, anguished... when he had been the one to leave. He spoke ill of her until she needed something, and then he flew out of Connie's house, racing back to his old home to rescue the bewitching Ella.

And sometimes, Connie found herself following Ella. She wanted to know what she was doing, what errands she needed to run or whom she needed to meet. If she knew a little about Ella's everyday life, she felt maybe she could minimize her to an average person. If Connie could be there to see Ella getting her eyebrows waxed or picking out toilet cleaner in a grocery store, then she could stop making her out to be some fantasy woman that could steal her husband back at any moment.

And that was how she ended up at the edge of Ella's yard at night, observing, obsessing... objectifying. The moonlight shed a silvery glow to everything but fortunately, she was hidden by the trees, and Ella was too distracted by her visitor.

That guy was there. That man that followed Ella everywhere with his eyes, with his entire being, it seemed. Connie had to admit grudgingly that they made a striking couple. But they were having a fight of some sort. She could barely hear their voices even when raised, but then before she could catch wisps of conversation, that guy was sitting beside Ella and kissing her. Kissing her like Connie wished Alex would kiss her. They were still new to each other, and yet Alex seemed preoccupied, almost angry. She knew he was still in shock and not entirely on board with the pregnancy, but he had told her he loved her. That they were soulmates. So why was he barely touching her lips when he leaned in for a quick kiss. Why was she left awake and feeling lonely at night even when he was lying right beside her?

Connie was relieved that Ella was preoccupied with another man. Maybe she would consent to the divorce and leave Alex alone. But she also felt a nagging irritation. She did not want Ella to be happy. She was already ahead. Cute and feminine, a mother, and she had been married to Alex for years.

Years. How could Connie begin to compete with the history... the memories? And now she was just going to skip along to another man? A man so good-looking, so full of raw manliness that even Connie, who rarely noticed such nonsense, had to stop and appreciate him. Not fair.

Connie waited until the guy left, waited for several minutes after Ella had practically floated back into the house before she ventured closer. She tried to see through the windows, but Ella had the blinds shut. Before she could stop herself, she ran up to the side of the house, hidden from neighbors by the strip of woods between them, and she pounded on the window before escaping into the dark camouflage of the woods. She watched as the porch light came on but felt deflated as soon as it went out again. Ella did not even venture outside. Was she scared? Was she shaking?

She waited thirty minutes before doing it again. This time she ran and hid for several minutes before running the three blocks to her car. No doubt, Ella would call the cops. And there was no way Connie could explain being in Ella's neighborhood.

As she drove home, she wondered what it would take to feel like she won. She already had the husband. She had the baby. Why was she so fixated on what Ella had?

**

"And you think - no, don't cast out there, you'll get caught again. So, the phone interview... you think it went well?" Dennis put down his fishing rod and walked the few feet between them. "Let me see it."

She grinned sheepishly. "Sorry."

"Not a problem. But after this, let's switch spots." Dennis focused on tugging the line until it gave. "Got it. So... Ell, what do you think?"

She stretched out her arms and wiggled her fingers until he handed her rod back. "It went great. I loved everyone. I thought the video conference would be weird, but it actually wasn't. But that's the problem."

"What's the problem?" He knelt down beside her chair, staring up at her patiently.

"I love it already, and I'm probably not going to get it."

"Why do you say that?"

She lifted a shoulder and kept her eyes straight ahead. "It's too good. Above what I deserve."

"Hey." He waited for a few moments and then reached up and nudged her chin until she turned toward him. "Stop that. Ella, I get that you've had a rough time of it, especially lately, but you have to stop basing your self-worth on what others say or how they act. You are amazing. I don't kiss just anyone."

"Yes, you do."

"What?" A laugh burst from his mouth. "What do you mean?"

She shrugged, hating that her face suddenly felt submerged in a heater. "I know your type."

His smile faltered. "Are you joking right now? I can't tell."

"Nope."

"Then tell me. What is my type?"

"Almost like a player but too much of a gentleman to entirely fit that label."

"A player?"

"Yes. I'm sure after you leave here, you go ... I don't know ... tennis ... where another woman is there waiting. Probably much fancier than me. Prettier. Younger, definitely."

Slowly he stood, his expression darkening and his voice low. "I understand you're preoccupied with your situation. I get that. But I did not think you were so self-involved that you saw nothing else. That's what you think of me?"

"It isn't like it's a bad thing. You're a handsome guy. Good job. Nothing wrong with playing the field. I see how women stare at you."

"What does that have to do with anything? Huh? I see how guys stare at you."

She laughed. "Now you're not being serious. Forget it. Forget I said anything."

"No. I can't forget. You're judging me based on what? My looks? The fact that I'm not racing into any relationship? That's a shitty thing for you to do."

"You're leaving?" She straightened up in her chair, her eyes wide.

"Yeah. Suddenly don't feel like fishing."

"Wait. No. Don't go. I … can we talk?"

He gathered up his rods and tackle box. "Don't feel like talking right now, Ella. I've been nothing but a good friend to you, and you repay me by labeling me some sort of chauvinistic playboy. I did nothing to give you that impression, so I think the problem is actually with you. Step out of your own world once in a while and notice others. Okay?"

Blinking back tears, she bent forward and started sticking items into her own tackle box. "Fuck you."

He stopped and watched her. "Your line -"

"Go away!"

"Your line's caught-"

She grabbed her rod and yanked until the line broke. Then she slammed it to the ground. "Don't want this shit anyways. I was just fooling myself. This isn't helping. This will never help." She heard him call her name, but she ran for her car and then drove off without looking back.

Ella had never been good at confrontations. And somehow this stung more than most. Dennis always came off as laid back and understanding. She had unwittingly hit a nerve. It just so happened to be the nerve that resonated with her as well. Because while she knew her place with this charming, good-looking man, there was still a part of her that hoped, daydreamed… imagined fitting into his life. Of suddenly becoming more than the frumpy friend he had in a way adopted. The little sister he felt the need to protect. But she had opened her mouth and blurted out things that got such a sudden reaction…

Going home was not an option. The thought of the empty house depressed her even more. She went to visit her father, surprising herself with the intense relief washing over her when Ted smiled.

"There's my girl. I was going to call. Can I take you out to lunch?"

It did not take long for her mood to resonate despite her attempt to laugh and chatter. Ted leaned back and watched her, setting his fork down on the plate. "Okay, Ella Bella. What's up?"

She stuffed salad in her mouth and shook her head. When that failed to divert his attention, she mumbled, "Nothing."

"Anything to do with that man that shows up at your house and hangs on your every word?"

"Dad, please. He's a bit... He doesn't want anything to do with me."

"Ah, still the same Ella. Listen, kiddo, stop selling yourself short. You do that, and you end up pushing forty and divorced."

"Hey! Not nice."

"I'm not saying it to be nice! I'm saying it so history doesn't repeat itself, and you end up with another asshole because you don't think you deserve a guy that'll treat you like the goddess you are. Listen, I know your childhood has a lot to do with the insecurities-"

"Stop-"

"No, let me say this. Please. I get that we messed up. Majorly. And that ex of yours, he's really done a number on you. But now you need to grow up a little and not be afraid of realizing just how fantastic you are. You deserve happiness."

She stabbed at her salad, spearing an olive and popping it into her mouth. "Moot point. Mr. Wonderful doesn't have any interest in pursuing anything with me. Even as friends."

"I don't believe that for a minute. But it doesn't matter. If not him, then another great guy will come along. You have to just be willing to see yourself as deserving of whatever it is you want and need in your life." He wiped a napkin across his mouth and then rocked back in his chair. "So... I'm making plans to move back here. Your grandma's house needs some work, but it would be ideal-"

"Not necessary, dad."

"Ella-"

"No. You're trying to make up for something that can't.... You don't need to prove anything to me."

He lurched forward, shaking his finger at her. "Not what this is about."

"Bullshit. You love traveling. Love your job. I'm not twelve anymore, dad. It's okay to have your life and not be buckled down by me." She knew it was a passive-aggressive move, to use his past words against him, especially when in the same breath she was assuring him it was all fine.

He sank back, his gaze steady but voice slightly shaky. "I wasn't the best father. I'm sorry for that. There's no excuse. But I want to be here now. Lila is growing up so quick. I'd love to be around for more. Anyways fixing up your grandmother's house does not mean I'm here forever. But I need a break from everything. I'm getting older, kiddo. I'm tired. Exhausted, actually. And I have this heavy, nagging feeling that I'm missing out on the best of life right here. So, this isn't all about you and making up for things already past. This is about me... not as happy as I thought I'd be at this stage in my life."

The evidence was right there in front of Ella. Her father's crinkled eyes and sun-damaged skin. The dragged-down tone his voice had at times. The hesitancy in his steps. He was aging faster than his years, and she understood it was that on-the-go lifestyle that was seeping the youth out of him. No stable home, no long rest... it would take the life out of anyone after so many years. She managed to smile at her father before offering, "Do you have the key to grandma's place? We can go check it out."

It had been years since she had felt as close to her father as she did on that afternoon. And it had been years since she has stepped foot in the one house that had provided a home for her. She had offered to come here, not realizing the intensity of emotions socking her right in the gut as soon as she crossed the threshold. Evenings on the floor in front of the crackling fire, treats of popcorn and milkshakes, homemade soups waiting for her after school. Sometimes Ella clung to the bad memories so much that she forgot the good. And walking into that house almost two decades after the last time… the good smacked her right in the face.

"Oh dad, the record player is still here."

He glanced over and absently nodded. "Most of their things are still… it all should be here."

By the looks of everything, she guessed her father had been militant about keeping up with the house. She knew there were many times he had called or emailed, letting her know he was in town. So many times, she ignored the contact.

It was not until she felt her dad turn her around and draw her to him that she realized she was sobbing. "Dad. I'm sorry. I'm so sorry."

"Hey, stop. Nothing to be sorry about. You were dealt a bad hand. That's on me."

"No. I had it better than I like to believe. I had you and pap and grandma…"

"True. But you have every right to be angry. I get it, Ella. I was young and stupid and sometimes I spoke without thinking. Because believe me, you were and are the most important thing in my life. Not my job or money or any of that. My beautiful daughter happy and safe. That was always my number one priority."

She gently shoved him away and swiped at her wet face. "I was a horrible child. Mean. Even meaner adult. How can you even be around me after everything I did and said?"

It seemed to get too overwhelming for her father. He was more sensitive than most men, but he hated breaking down in front of her. And as he busied himself with removing sheets off of furniture, she guessed that he was on the verge of tears. "You were a kid. And we hadn't been fair to you. You had every right to be angry. You deserved better. So make sure that guy - the one that shows up at your house with some flimsy excuse for being there... make sure he deserves you. That he gives you a better life than... well, you know."

The rest of the afternoon, she ventured through the house on her own, leaving her father to his own emotional journey. She remembered being an inconsolable kid, wanting her mother and yet fearing that life... being heartbroken over her father's obvious disappointment over where his life had ended up, stuck as a single father and forced to put his blooming career on hold... she remembered her grandmother doing her best to distract Ella with hugs and kisses and cookies and her grandfather awkwardly attempting some fatherly support. The confrontations, accusations... the rebelling in her later years and loose ends. She had never properly thanked her grandmother for everything. She had never told her she appreciated her love and her kindness.

Ted found her in her old bedroom, sitting on the bed staring up at the posters. "Funny to step in here. I kept it as it was thinking you'd be back. I could never... it was hard for me to see this room." He forced a smile and sat down next to her. "So, it's in pretty decent shape, the house. Won't take much to get everything ready to move in." He playfully elbowed her. "Ready for this? For your old man to be just a few miles away?"

Impulsively, she leaned against her father and rested her head on his shoulder. "I am."

**

Within fifteen minutes of being home, she heard knocking on her front door. And she was not surprised to see Dennis there. "Go away."

"Listen to me, wait. Don't shut the door. You hit a nerve. What you said.... What you called me. It hit a nerve."

She sighed and glanced up at him. "So you are. A player." Her heart sank because she had so wanted to be wrong.

"No! I'm not a player. But I avoid relationships. I never try to trick anyone. Ella, I don't... I can't... I lost my wife and ever since then... I just don't get invested. And I don't like that about myself. I feel guilty and shallow, and... I hate that you picked up on that. That you seem to see me in that light. I'm sorry."

Her throat seemed too small for the lump growing. So he was that man. He did not have relationships. And she knew the rule. You can't change men. She had learned that with Alex, hadn't she? After all the years of giving herself to their marriage and trusting him despite the rocky beginnings, he had not changed. He cheated. Again and again.

He jumped in, his words tumbling out when he was met with silence. "And I really respect your friendship. You're having a rough time of it, and I can't add to that. You get that, right? But you're - please don't ask me to walk away. Because you're becoming such a good friend. I look forward to talking to you, fishing and dinners and ... dammit, you know more about me than most friends I've had around for years. I'm not a talker. And here I am... talking."

His words tangled around her already crowded thoughts. He couldn't add to what? With what? Was he telling her he wanted nothing to do with her? But then he was saying she was his friend....

"I'm overwhelmed," she whispered.

"What? Ella... what?"

He peered into her face, and she focused on his cocoa-colored eyes. "I'm overwhelmed and tired and can't talk this out. I can't... "

"Hey, whoa!" Suddenly his arms were wrapped around her, and she felt herself being guided to the couch.

"Well, that was rather dramatic," she murmured, but the fog was enveloping her, and her eyes felt heavy.

The darkness swarmed around her, submerged her in a peaceful sort of nothingness that she had not experienced for a long time. No thoughts, no images, no puzzling questions... just quiet.

All too soon, the fog lifted, and she heard something in the distance. She was being pulled upward, it seemed, and the thoughts started to swirl like a wind tunnel just powering up.

The first thing Ella saw when she lifted her eyelids was Dennis studying her, his eyes narrowed and lips turned down. She sat up, realizing there was a blanket tucked in around her and a pillow dented from her head. "Oh! How long have I been asleep?"

"Few hours." He sat on the edge of the couch, reaching out and brushing hair away from her face. "How do you feel?"

"Sluggish. I'm sorry. I don't know what happened."

"What happened is you collapsed out of exhaustion. I noticed you've been... this past week ... have you slept at all, Ella? Because I'm seeing dark circles under your eyes, you're constantly yawning, and your words are slurring together."

"Maybe I'm a drunk."

And there was that flash of a grin. She almost regretted using humor because that grin could melt the iciest resolve. "Well, perhaps that's the case. You hide it well then." He sat on the edge of the couch and patted her leg. "Seriously. What's going on, Ella? Why aren't you sleeping?"

Rubbing her eyes, she shrugged. "Rough time, I guess. Overwhelmed."

"Yes. You've used that word. What can I do to help?"

"Can you stay for a little bit tonight? I don't feel like being alone."

He gave a short nod. "I can stay. Of course." There was a weighted pause, his eyes travelling across her face, searching. "What's going on?"

"Nothing."

"Bullshit." He sighed. "Fine. But to just basically collapse... that is not normal. That is exhaustion to the exaggerated degree. Have you eaten? I'm starving." He reached for his phone. "I'll order in. What are you feeling like?"

"Whiskey Sour."

He tried to suppress a grin. "You're a wicked woman. So, I'm guessing Chinese works for you?" He waited until she gave a sufficient nod of approval before placing the order.

Ella sat up, swinging her feet to the floor and tossing the blanket aside. She felt disoriented, as if she were not sure what time it was or what she should be doing. The heaviness of sleep was still bearing down on her, but she wanted to focus, to be alert and functioning while Dennis was there.

"Okay, they said it will be about -"

A sudden pounding on the window cut off his words with an abruptness that jolted any remaining sleep from Ella. He jumped and then swung his wide-eyed stare her way. "What the hell was that?"

She grabbed the mug of tea and sat back. "That is what has been keeping me up for the past damn week."

But he was already moving toward the front door. "Ella, come lock the door behind me. Don't open it for anyone but me."

She did as he asked, not having the chance to beg him to stay inside. The only consolation was if it happened to be someone or something that wished her harm, it would have done so by now.

After ten minutes, Ella threw open the front door and stepped outside. "Dennis! Hey, Dennis! You out here?"

She lost some of her bravado when a shadow moved along the side of the house, a dark spot moving among darkness coming toward her. Then a familiar voice, that sound that sent shivers through her weakened body, identified the shadow just as it sprang into view. "What are you doing, Ella! For God's sake, get in the damn house!"

The level of anger registering on Dennis's face caught her off guard, and that emotion looked so out of place on him that Ella started giggling.

His features relaxed and his shoulders dropped as he followed her into the house "I was going to ask if you were okay, but it seems you're handling this rather well." He turned and looked out the side window. "How long?"

"For the past week. Sometimes early evening. Sometimes one in the morning. Sometimes it is the front door, sometimes it is the basement windows. One time I was in the kitchen making dinner for the next day. I went to put it in the fridge and BOOM! One loud knock on the window. Lasagna and glass everywhere."

Dennis studied her and then walked into the kitchen. He came back, his fingers slicing through his long black hair. "So... there are no blinds on that window. Someone was watching you. Waiting to knock right when you had your hands full."

"Well... yes. Seems that way."

He cursed. "Why didn't you say something to me? Is it... did they -"

"No. He's still in jail. I checked."

"And Lila?"

"Happens either before she gets home, when she's asleep, or when she is at her dad's. So, she doesn't know. She just knows I'm not having a restful week."

"Alex?"

She shook her head. "Not his style. At all. And I was on the phone with him when it happened on Thursday. He heard it and asked who the hell was at the door."

"Not his style? He had his girlfriend spying on you not too long ago."

"Look, it's probably just some neighborhood kids. I used to do that when I was young. Running up to the house and then running away before getting caught."

"At one in the morning?" Dennis watched her reaction and then his expression softened. "Listen, I'm staying here tonight."

"Not necessary."

"Then you can stay at my place."

Ella locked eyes with him, ready to defend her independence, ready to shout her rights and strengths as a woman. She had waited years to be this strong, self-sufficient woman who had more important things to do than fear the dark. But the thought of being alone, another sleepless night waiting for another knock-

"Fine. You can stay here."

"Have you called the cops?"

"Yes. And I'm just a precious girl that hears noises in the dark." She dropped her shoulders. "Not much they can do until someone damages property, breaks in, or harms me."

"Dammit, Ella. You don't even have a working porch light."

"So, my fault?"

"No. But you need to be safe. To do what you can to eliminate this person's chances of getting away with scaring you every goddamned night." He tugged her to him, his arms encasing her in a protective circle. "It's probably nothing. It'll be okay. But let's just be careful anyways and take some precautions."

The nap and the reassurance of not being alone that night melted her exhaustion into relaxation, and as they ate and watched some mindless television, she revealed her father's plans to move back to the area. She also confessed her strong emotional reaction to being back in her grandmother's house. And it was nice to simply talk, to forget about holding back or worry that someone was not listening.

Alex had always pretended to listen, to nod every few beats and mutter some noise of agreement, but too often he would interrupt her mid-sentence with his own story, or his eyes would glaze over, or she would simply let her voice fade away, not finishing. And it gave it all away. He rarely truly listened.

But as she let the relaxed state affect her no-filter purge, Dennis was at rapt attention. He maintained eye contact, asked questions, and actually left her distracted when his finger brushed against her cheek. He sat close, and as she talked, he lifted her legs and put them across his lap.

She paused in the middle of telling him about her old bedroom and how it was kept the same. "Wait... I forget what I was saying. I...."

"Your bedroom, El. Posters." He leaned forward and pressed his lips against hers. Then leaned back. "I'd love to see that. Your teenage taste. Get an idea of who you were back then."

"An asshole."

He threw his head back and laughed. "You were not!"

"Oh, I was. But it was just a reaction to how I felt…" She shrugged and rested her head on his shoulder. Something about this … being close to Dennis sent electric shocks through her, and yet it was natural. Right.

"Why did you feel you had to be like that? El?" His voice was low, soothing. And it drew out words she had never spoken out loud.

"My dad- he wasn't happy. And I'm the reason he wasn't happy. He even told me. We got in this huge fight when I was twelve. And he said it. He said the very thing I'd always suspected. He told me he had never wanted kids. That my mom begged, and he agreed on the condition that he would be there, but she would do the child-raising. He wanted his career. To travel and live. And instead…"

"What happened to your mother, hun?"

"She just wasn't… she got sidetracked by another path. Dad wanted his photography, and mom wanted her freedom. Dad was infatuated with her and when she left… dammit, Dennis, I forget myself around you and just talk."

"Nothing wrong with forgetting yourself every now and then."

Ella was not sure who initiated it this time, but suddenly she was deep enough in a kiss that she felt dizzy, encased in his hold, suddenly on his lap. His lips were firm and fit against hers perfectly, his mouth was her new addiction, and she was suddenly awake, alert and still unable to form a coherent thought. His hair was thick and soft, and she knew this because her fingers were grabbing, tugging and then her hands found their way underneath his shirt… just as she realized his hands were against her back, fingers on her skin…

"Oh my God, Ella. What are you doing to me?" he groaned against her mouth. Then he reared back, his hands untangling from her shirt to grab her hands. "You're exhausted."

Although a large part of her wanted to beg him to continue,

another part was relieved. This was all so confusing. She still missed her ex on some nights, and now here she was making out on her couch? The very couch she had bought with Alex? It was too much. "I'm not exactly sleepy, Dennis." But she scooted off his lap, gasping when she brushed against the very proof of his arousal. She did that? She still had that kind of power?

"Are you okay?"

"Your kiss isn't that powerful, Reeves."

That flash of a grin slammed any type of coherency from her. "I meant... you're tired and stressed, and this probably doesn't help."

"Doesn't hurt. Distracts me." When she glanced up and saw his crinkled brow, Ella laughed. "I'm not five, Dennis. Please. Not made of glass."

Immediately he nodded. "I'm sorry. You're right."

They settled in, their attention on the television. There was no more kissing, but he kept an arm around her, and she rested her head on his shoulder. They spoke in low whispers, as if unwilling to break the bond between them, the certain kind of calm in the air. Hearing his whisper was like being caressed, being cared for in a way that had not happened to her in years, if ever. There was a gentle firmness to it, a protective quality. And when he urged her to get some sleep, she refused, afraid to leave this tranquil state with him.

"Can I ask you something, Dennis?"

"Always."

"What was her name?"

There was silence, and she wondered if she had crossed a line but then she felt his fingers brush back a strand of her hair. "Her name was Robin."

That was the last thing she remembered before sleep captured her.

CHAPTER 6

"I hope you told them that you have a super fantastic daughter that is almost all of your doing. That should get you the job." Lila practically skipped to the car, her arms full of shopping bags.

"Not yet." Ella opened the trunk and dropped her own bags in with Lila's. "I figure I'm just going to show them your picture, and that will be that. Anyone that could make such a beautiful, striking creature has to be top notch."

Lila crinkled her nose. "Interview advice. Don't use 'top notch'."

"Well, it depends on the age of the interviewers. 'Top notch' could get me an in with the university if they are as old as your mother. But any younger and then yes, chance shot."

"Seriously, mom, I'm so excited for you. Aren't you excited?"

"It's just a second interview. I don't want to get my hopes up." But she grinned at her daughter, a slight thrill ripping through her. The thought of working for the university, the benefits, the pay… the vacation time! It was her dream job, but she knew the competition was fierce.

They had called her earlier that day, while she was at work, asking for an in-person interview. She had texted Dennis and had not heard back, but she tried not to overthink that part of her life. Things were too confusing to worry about some guy responding. Some guy she had recently kissed…. Some guy that had made her skin sing with his fingers just by brushing them along her bare back….

Despite her resolve to not become an infatuated girl, Dennis managed to infiltrate most thoughts. He was becoming such a prominent figure in her imagination that she even imagined his car in her driveway. Until she realized it was actually his car. And he was there on a ladder propped up against the side of her house.

Charging from her car, she called out to him, and he glanced over as if he were expecting such a reaction.

"What the hell are you doing?"

"Motion detectors. There's a security system coming too. Hi, Lila."

It was the blatant, casual disregard for her reaction that perhaps sent her over the edge. She heard Lila calling out to her softly, a gentle warning, but Ella would have none of it. This was her house, her property. She had not heard from him in days, and suddenly, he was there on a ladder, making changes to her house. Her house.

"Dennis," she said in a tone so calm it surprised her. "Get off that ladder, and come here."

He took his time climbing down, and then he strolled up to her, wiping his hands on his jeans. "Can I explain?"

"Mom. He's doing something nice for us. You should thank him." She met her mother's tense glare for a moment before backing away. "Sorry, Dennis. I tried. I'll be inside."

"Thanks," Dennis called out, and then he returned his focus to Ella. He sighed deeply, his chest rising and falling with the effort. "I'm sorry. I should have told you and not just been here when you got home but -"

"Should have told me? Dennis... what about asking? What about -"

"What about respecting your pride? Dammit, Ella. You're forgetting that I was here the other night. I witnessed the fear on your face, the pounding on the side of your house. Bullshit, don't stand there and try to defend your independence when this has nothing to do with that. I've got no ulterior motives, I sure as hell don't want to take your freedom from you... I'm your friend, and I am scared that if we don't do something, this could escalate." He paused, his breath pushing his chest out.

"Unless I stepped on toes because you were about to get this done yourself."

The fight had left her after his second sentence, and she stared up at the porch roof, her face flushed and heart pounding. And she felt a hand on her shoulder, his breath warming her cheek as he stooped down to talk low, talk close... "El... I'm sorry. I should have approached this better. I just kept thinking of you and Lila out here alone... But can I show you? The motion lights? And a very, very basic security system-"

"What?"

"Listen. This is me. El, it's me. I'm not doing this expecting anything from you. I want nothing in return. I'm doing this because you're a friend who needs something in place to keep you safe. Look at me. Please tell me you aren't angry."

Her voice cracked as emotions she could not decipher, could not understand, overwhelmed her. "I'm not angry. Just feeling helpless."

He squeezed his eyes shut and then drew her to him. "That's worse. I'm sorry. I'm sometimes not good at interactions... friendships. El, my intentions-"

"I know. It's not that. Not entirely. It's just my life this past year. It's the fact that someone has been terrorizing me by coming around my house. I don't have any control."

"You do. You had control in the situation with your husband. You decided enough was enough. You have absolute control over your time- going out there and kayaking and fishing after... El, look at me. You've had so many people try to take that from you- and you didn't allow it. Ultimate control. Now, I'm usually the first person to respect boundaries and not force my decision on anyone... but you are getting these lights and security system. I'm sorry. You just are."

There was nothing she could think of to say, so she said nothing and followed him to the porch. He showed her the lights, asked which direction she wanted them aimed at, and explained the security system that would be installed.

And Ella knew he was doing his best to make her feel included; asking questions, giving her details, watching her expressions, but she could only nod, no longer feeling stupid and small, but feeling unsure.

Dennis focused on unwinding cord as he spoke. "I'm sorry I haven't called or anything. I actually took over a class for another instructor and -"

"No," she stated firmly. "You owe me nothing. Don't need to explain."

There was a long pause, and she glanced up to find him watching her with an undecipherable expression. When he caught her gaze, he softly insisted, "Whether I owe you anything or not... I do have to explain. I am compelled to explain."

Then Ella refused to break the contact. "Fine. Busy. You explained."

"El-"

"No! Don't be all intense, telling me you have to explain, and then just give me a shit reason of being busy. If you insist on being so damn chivalrous, then be honest. Otherwise, you owe me no explanation!"

They continued locking gazes until finally Dennis lowered his head, no words spilling out to deny. To assure. And her heart felt like it was splitting in two for a man who was a practical stranger. For a guy she had been sure had superior integrity, flawless morals. But he was standing before her unable to voice that he had not wanted to call her after they had kissed... after they had spent most of the night curled in each other's arms.

Before the silence could sink into her skin and poison her soul, she turned and walked over to her front door. "Show me where the camera goes."

Now that Ella knew where she stood, what kind of man Dennis could be... she knew distance was key. And although she was almost entirely determined to shoo him off her property before Lila could invite him to dinner, she realized he was giving her a top of the line security system. She had to at least feed him.

So when Lila came outside and shot her mom a cautious look, Ella nodded wearily. And she was only partly surprised when he immediately accepted the dinner invitation.

When Lila went back inside, he studied Ella. "I have a movie in the car. The one I was telling you about. Old, creepy..."

"Oh. Sounds great except I have to get to sleep early. I'm exhausted and if I stay up and then have to go in to work to-morrow-"

"No. I understand. Some other time." He lifted the corners of his mouth up to smile, but it came across as a strange wrangling of lips and cheeks. It gave her a glimpse into Dennis beyond the maturity... besides the confidence. He was vulnerable, and it was unnerving.

"They called me for a second interview," she revealed, breathless.

It took a minute for her words to take meaning, to sink into his distracted psyche, and then before she could prepare herself for his next action, he yelled her name, jumped forward, and grabbed her in a bear hug, swinging her off the ground.

"Why wasn't that the first thing you told me? Damn, second interview means you are definitely in the running. When is it?"

"Monday. Lila and I went out and found a dress."

His arms were still around her as he grinned and congratulated her... and as Alex's car swerved into the driveway.

Reluctantly it seemed, Dennis dropped his arms and stepped back. She shot him a smile, not sure what she was thinking. They had just established that he had not called her, and yet here she was grinning at him with gusto.

"Sorry to interrupt," Alex strode toward her, ignoring Dennis because he would rather intimidate someone unable or unwilling to strike back. "What are you doing to the house?"

"Security system," she answered curtly, turning her back to him. "What do you need?"

"Can I speak to you privately?"

Ella noticed Dennis shot him a dark look, but he said nothing as she walked a few feet away. When Alex motioned her further, she narrowed her eyes. "No. Just tell me what you want."

"I'm actually dropping off Lila's science book, but Ella... him? Really? Isn't he like really old?"

"And isn't Connie like really bitchy?" She shut her eyes and took a deep breath. "I'm sorry. Look, just give Lila her book and go."

"No. Wait." He shuffled his feet and averted her gaze until finally with a heavy sigh, he glanced up. "I wanted to talk... I know we messed things up... well, I messed things up. But could we do counseling or -"

She blinked. "Counseling? To co-parent?"

"To reconcile."

Her first reaction was to smile because she thought he was joking. But when he held that stony, miserable gaze, she realized he was being sincere. "Wait. What? No. What are you talking about, Dennis? Connie's pregnant!"

The color drained from his face. "Lila told you? I told her not to say anything-"

She folded her arms, tilting her head in angry disbelief. "Wasn't Lila, but great parenting to ask our teenage daughter to keep secrets. No, Connie herself told me. At the grocery store down the street. Just happened to run into her. Congratulations."

"This isn't what I wanted."

She widened her eyes. "But .... You wanted new, remember? And to not worry about paying bills. You wanted to live off some other man's money in his former home-"

"Go to hell."

"Lila's in the house," she called out over her shoulder as she walked away. "Drop her book off, and then you can go to hell."
**

Connie hated when Alex got like this. Avoiding eye contact, mumbling responses, fidgeting. They had started out with such passion, finding ways to sneak kisses, hold hands, ways to share their lives... and she had assumed that desire would roll on over into their true life together.

But Alex was moody. Quiet. Sullen. Even before she announced the pregnancy. But she had to admit, the pregnancy announcement had made things a bit more tense. What had Alex expected? She had told him the reason her marriage was not working was because her husband could not have kids. And Alex had always clucked his tongue in sympathy. Never once did he state that he had no desire to have anymore. Until she had told him the news. Then he had exploded.

Three weeks later, and things were still obviously divided between them. As she asked how his day was, he grunted a reply that she could only guess meant it was fine. But this was more than just his usual mood. This was angry. Because no matter how he felt or acted, Connie was in love with him. She knew his moods and thoughts before he could even hope to express them.

"So, are you going to come out with it?"

He rolled his eyes. "What?"

"What's wrong? Did I do something?"

It seemed she had punched in the magic words. He straightened and pointed a finger at her. "Did you talk to Ella about the... about your -"

"About our baby?" She blinked back the hurt that his inability to voice her condition caused. "Yes. I happened to run into her-"

"At the grocery store two towns over?"

Okay, so she had not thought it entirely through. Hearing it said out loud did make it sound bad. "Alex, you said you were going to tell her. I just thought-"

"Bullshit! You were trying to cause trouble."

"No! She has a right to know! She -"

"She doesn't have a right to shit! She's a whore!"

And as much as Connie clung to any negative thing Alex said about his soon-to-be ex, she felt almost personally offended by his words. "Whore? Aren't you the one that cheated?"

He jumped up and for the first time since they had started their relationship, Connie feared he would hit her. "She's a whore, and you're causing trouble."

Despite the fear, she refused to back down. "I wasn't trying to cause any trouble, Alex! But I wanted her to know that you and I are a real thing, and she better just sign the papers."

"Not your business."

"How can you say that? You and I are starting a life together-"

"This isn't what I wanted. Another kid on the way... more responsibilities, more of the same... no. Don't expect me to be all on board with this. And don't interfere with the divorce. Got it?"

She sat back and studied him. He did not belong with Ella. She knew that the first time she heard him talk about his wife. Uppity and educated. He needed a woman that was willing to throw everything aside for him. Connie had no desire to get a degree. No desire for a better job than one that put food on the table.

Finally, she spoke. "This was what you wanted all those months ago when you convinced me to leave Bob. When you told me that Ella wasn't any sorta wife to you. That she was fat and dumpy and snobby. This... me... that's what you wanted. And now that's changed?"

He sighed, rubbing his face before softly answering, "No. I just had a bad day. Went to give Lila her book, and there's Ella hanging all over that guy. Right in the front yard. Installing security lights and cameras on my house."

Connie flinched at the words "my house" and then the full meaning of what he said hit. Security lights and cameras. She could no longer go to the house, knocking and running. No more micro-glimpses into the life of her competition. But knowing that her actions caused such a large reaction made her feel like she had a part in Ella's life. A controlling part. And that gave her such a jolt, such a feeling of life when everything around her was uncertain and bleak…. She would have to find a new way to filtrate Ella's world.

**

Ella was impulsive. That was never a question. And when she had gotten that call, when she had discovered that her days at a dead-end job she hated were over, she did what any deliriously happy woman would do. She invited several of her friends to a dinner party the following Saturday. And everyone knew that half the people invited would not be able to attend, right? Not so. Every single person said yes. Ella had great friends, if nothing else. And not enough chairs for the ten women arriving in less than a week.

"When are you putting in your notice?" Dennis asked, dropping a bag of takeout onto the counter. He paused and looked up. "Are you giving notice?"

"Yes! Bad karma if I don't. Such bad karma." She stood on her tiptoes and peered into the boxes. "Wonton soup?"

He pulled out a container. "Of course."

Ella grinned and danced over to the drawer for a spoon. "I'm telling them tomorrow. Using a vacation day Friday. I sorta did something…. I'm going to need Friday off."

"What'd you do?"

She took a sip of the soup and shut her eyes in delight. When she opened them, she found Dennis grinning down at her, his fingers lightly skimming her shoulders. "What did you do?" he whispered before leaning down for a kiss.

"Do?" Her eyes fluttered as she tried to remember what her last thought had been. His lips had a way of clearing all thoughts. "Oh! Yes. I decided to throw a dinner party with some friends."

Dennis had returned to the food and paused as he laid out the containers. Finally, he glanced up. "A dinner party? Sounds fancy."

"Ten women. Eleven including Lila. Twelve including me. And I have at most, eight chairs. Eight. I don't even have enough chairs to seat everyone. I just kept inviting and inviting, and everyone said yes. Why? How? I can't just be happy with a new job. I have to punish myself with this dinner and -"

"Hey," Dennis soothed. He crossed the room and took her hands, smiling. "It's going to be great. What better way to celebrate a new beginning than with friends?"

"Eight chairs."

"I heard. Easily fixed. I have chairs you can use."

"And the cooking..."

"El, you're a great cook."

"Twelve of us! I am a mediocre cook for two to three people."

He put a plate in front of her and scooped out some rice. "Tell you what. I can help you plan a relatively easy menu. And I can help get it all started before anyone shows up."

She smiled as he slid his fingers up and down her tingling arms. "Thank you. But seriously, who invites a number of people and has everyone actually accept?"

He gave her an odd look, his hands dropping as he turned back to the containers of food. "Someone very special. Your friends obviously care a great deal about you."

"Yeah. Or maybe they are all about free food. Speaking of which, thank you. For the free food." She giggled. "Definitely for the free food. And for the help with this job."

"Well, listen. You are welcome for the information on the job. Everything else you did on your own. I spoke to Eileen, and she absolutely adores you. Thinks you're going to be a great fit with the team."

Ella noticed he kept a distance, his gaze flitting around the room, as if that touch, those kisses had gotten him too close to the flame. She wondered if it was seeing her, actually looking at her that caused him to come to his senses. She felt huge and plain in a cotton dress that made it easy to move around the still, humid air. But perhaps he saw her for who she was - just a simple old woman past her prime with nothing to show for it. No exciting love tale or courageous adventure abroad.

"You okay?"

She glanced up and saw he was in front of her, his eyes searching hers. "You suddenly got... this faraway sad look in your eyes and .... Where'd you go just now, El?"

He was close again, his lips near her cheek, and she stepped away, unable to keep it all straight.

"Don't know what you're talking about, Dennis. I'm right here."

"Seriously. What just happened? I thought we were ... What's wrong?"

"Dennis! I'm just following you... your mood. One minute you're here-" she sliced a hand in front of her face to indicate the closeness, "and then you can't get away fast enough." She spun around, picked up a fork, and then dropped it in frustration. "Forget it."

"El-"

"This was a stupid dress to wear!" she cried out.

Slowly, Dennis nodded. "Such a stupid dress to wear." And he was right behind her, his hands drawing her back against him. Leaning down, he whispered, "Because I can't think straight seeing you in that dress. You look young and beautiful, the color brings out the green in your eyes. The fabric is thin enough that all I can think of is how very little is between us when I am against you like this. And when the sun hits you just right... the dress... El, the dress is a little see-through."

She spun around, colliding into him, her large eyes seeking his in a panic. "What? Dennis, I was out running errands -"

"I know." His lips teased the tip of her ear, stifling her words. "And I bet all the men that crossed your path are still trying to recover. So, when I suddenly get quiet and move away, it's because I'm doing my best, El, to be a gentleman. Because something about you drives me crazy, and I forget myself. I forget how to be a civilized male, a proper adult." His lips were suddenly on her neck, and her knees buckled.

By the time their lips met, she was lost in his hold, entirely at his beck and call. Her mind swirled so that no thoughts could materialize, and all she could focus on was the desire for more... to feel more and know more... to get answers through his touch and the feel of him through her own fingers and lips. Suddenly she was sure that the only way to get any answers about Dennis was to encounter him without his clothes on. To know what his skin felt like against her skin. To hear his moan as she clawed his back....

"Oh shit!"

Ella heard the words, realized they did not come from her own mouth as it was presently pressed against Dennis's, but the meaning did not fully sink in until she felt Dennis jump away from her. Even then, she could not gather any coherent thoughts. It was not until he called out, "Lila!" Then he squeezed Ella's shoulder. "It's Lila."

That made her jump out of the fog quickly. She turned to see her daughter red-faced and grinning. "I was told to come home and eat. I would have stayed away if I'd known this was make-out central."

"Lila, stop!" Ella spun around to get Lila a plate and realized her legs were still a bit shaky. Feeling Dennis's hands steady her, she threw a smile over her shoulder.

"Mom, do you know your dress is see-through?"

"Apparently."

"I think she knows and wore it on purpose." Dennis slid his arms around Ella as she tried to steady herself. "All part of her ploy to seduce me."

"I believe it, Dennis," Lila quipped, motioning for more as her mother scooped noodles onto the plate. "Did she tell you about her party she's throwing herself? We don't have enough chairs."

"You women really are obsessed with chairs. You know they sell them down the road. Folding chairs- pretty cheap."

Ella laughed, feeling the color warm her face. She started to respond, to say a clever answer, but the words caught in her throat as the memory of his hands flashed through her. And she doubted that she would ever be the same, no matter what was to come.

CHAPTER 7

"You didn't wait," Dennis stated in a flat tone. He flung his hand in the air. "Told you to wait and not to move that patio table by yourself. Did you scratch up the floor?"

"No!" She jutted her chin out. "I lifted."

"You're going to hurt your back. Don't do any more heavy lifting unless you have help. I'm here. No need to risk injury or tire yourself out -"

"Dennis! I wanted to do this. I wanted to put the table where I wanted it."

He stared at her for a few moments and then let out a long breath, rubbing his face. "I get it. You... Ella, I just want to help. I don't want to take your independence away. Do you hear me? I don't want to stifle you or your plans or ideas. I want to be here taking orders from you. And keeping you from getting hurt. Hear me?" When she nodded, he pulled her to him. "Sorry I snapped. I didn't realize where this was coming from."

"I'm being dumb. I know."

"No. You're not. You have a great thing. Freedom. After years of being controlled and shadowed... you're on your own, and it's great. So, I understand. But listen, I'm not that guy. Let me help you. Not impede, not stop, help. Because you deserve tonight. The celebration and the friends. This is about you."

Ella clung to him, to his words, for a few moments before pulling away and nodding. Because she had always wanted to hear those words. She may not have known it, but she longed for someone to understand her need to be her own person. Ella wanted to do things on whim, to be spontaneous and to follow her interests and hobbies. And she wanted someone at her side that understood and even encouraged it.

Finally, she glanced up at him. "I did scratch the floor. The table got heavy."

He raised his eyebrows. "Where?" He bent forward and inspected the spot she pointed to. "Okay. I can take care of that. No worries. You did great. This dining room looks amazing."

Lila strolled into the room, grinning at her mom. "Did you see the scratched floor?"

Ella shook her head, and Dennis burst into surprised laughter. "You just missed the conversation. A little too late, but you, Miss Lila, are a tattletale. Has anyone ever told you that?"

She nodded with a proud smile.

"Have you helped your mom at all?"

"She dusted in the living room and dining room," Ella informed him, laughing when Lila wrapped her arms around her and squeezed. "And she's going to do dishes."

"Mom! Fine. But I get to sit by Shannon during dinner." Shannon had been in their lives since Lila was a toddler, and she had been appointed Godmother, although Alex scoffed at the very idea of a Godmother. Shannon lived out of state so visits were cherished, and Ella would never dream of trying to keep her daughter and best friend apart.

"Are you staying for dinner?" Lila asked, her arms still draped around her mother.

Dennis chuckled. "I don't think your mom would like that."

"What?" Ella shot a surprised look his way. "What do you mean? You're helping cook. Of course, you can stay."

"Let's see how it goes. These women might hate me and the thought of a guy crashing the party."

"Oh, I think they'll be fine with it," Lila teased. "Some are single. You're single, right?"

"Lila!"

Dennis just laughed. "Kiddo, your mom has already

turned my life upside-down with her smile. I won't be noticing anyone else in the room."

And for a moment, Lila was as speechless as her mom. Then she nodded slowly. "Okay. You get points from the daughter. That was good." She backed away, her lips slowly curing up. "And just for that, I'll go do dishes."

Ella could only stand there, perplexed and trembling. Her head tilted, and she chewed on her lip as she tried to think of something to say, something to ask. But before she could untangle her tongue, Dennis was in front of her.

"I mean it," he whispered. "I'm enamored with you."

"It was the see-through dress, wasn't it?" she whispered back, and they both started laughing, his hands landing on her arms with an intoxicating firmness.

"The dress didn't hurt." He pressed his forehead against hers, his eyes latching, bewitching, promising. "But listen... I get it. I know you're struggling with this new lifestyle and moving on past a life you had for over twenty years. So, no pressure. Right?"

And the exuberance she had almost allowed herself to experience dissipated. Right after the words had left his mouth, Dennis was quick to pledge no pressure. His interest in a middle-aged mother was just a short adventure. Something new to try after being bombarded with college girls and beautiful women. Forcing a smile, she nodded. What else could she do?

But it was almost impossible to stay in a dark mood. Her heart was hurting, but Ella knew it was just par for the course this year. Broken marriage, unrequited crush... but just being around Dennis brought a lightness to her step. Just hearing his voice and being the target of his smile... she found herself smiling.

Dennis had brought chairs and wine, food and plans. He knew his way around a kitchen and had a calm vibe about him. Ella found herself relaxing, trusting that things would get done. They worked well together, and when he suggested a certain dish, she agreed and showed him how to spice it up. They were so involved in what they were doing, they lost track of time. And Ella was almost disappointed when Lila ran through the house, announcing some of the guests had arrived.

"Ella," Dennis grinned down at her when she tried to stir the sauce. "Go enjoy your friends. I promise, I got this. Your night." He stepped away from the stove and brushed her cheek with the back of his hand. "Did I tell you that you look absolutely beautiful tonight? Having friends over suits you. A lot."

And it struck her how different he was from her ex-husband. Alex would have grumbled about the pain of it all- the inconvenience of having people in the house, of having to talk to her friends, trying to find a reason to leave. He never complimented her appearance and never suggested that she was happier with friends. Alex felt he should be enough. Their life together. Sitting together. On the couch. Watching television. Friends? Dinner parties? Absurd.

But here she was standing in front of this man she was wildly attracted to, and he was praising her for having friends, encouraging it. Dennis felt it was the sign of being a great person when her friends accepted her invitation to dinner. She felt proud at his compliment, she felt understood.

Sure, she missed being married. She even missed Alex. Having a husband, someone to come home to - that was a big comfort in her life. But Ella had missed out on a lot during her marriage. She had missed her friends, connecting with other women. There was a part of her personality that had felt under-developed during those years. Somehow, she had maintained friendships, but to help them truly flourish… that was next to impossible.

But she considered that Dennis was perhaps too encouraging because this was not his home. She was not his wife. If they were truly a couple, would he feel differently? Would he roll his eyes at the chatter and laughter and find a quiet escape? Would he periodically come into the room and yawn or turn the television up to an embarrassing volume?

As her friends continued to arrive, Ella became busy with greetings and excited chatter, noticing the women's curious stares as she introduced them to Dennis. He was charming, that wide grin and low voice winning them over immediately.

Her neighbor Therese arrived and after the introductions and some small talk, she observed, "I was going to come over the other week. I saw a woman running out of your yard and was going to mention it to you, but figured it was just some random… but then I noticed the security system and… I hope there aren't any issues. Should I have spoken up sooner?"

While Ella reassured her it was okay, Dennis turned away from the stove and asked, "A woman? Tall, maybe?"

Therese nodded. "Shoulder length hair. Couldn't tell much more in the dark. I was in our driveway so didn't catch more than a glimpse."

When Ella returned to the kitchen, Dennis cornered her. "Connie? Do you think it's been Connie coming around?" When she merely stared up at him at a loss for words, he sighed. "Let's not worry about it tonight. But seriously, this is getting a little ridiculous. She's stalking you, Ella!"

As everyone found her seat and introductions were made, Ella stood to grab some wine. But she felt a hand on her shoulder, anchoring her down, and glancing up, she was slammed with that incredibly sexy grin.

"Okay, ladies, we have bottles and bottles of wine! Let's get started! The food will be out in about ten minutes. There's some chips and buffalo chicken dip, some artichoke dip, some bread." Dennis went around the table and poured everyone a glass, smiling and talking and sneaking glances at Ella the entire time. She blushed, trying to shoo away the less than wholesome thoughts popping into her head.

Any worries about everyone getting along or finding something to talk about were quickly banished. The women's voices rose, and laughter soon filled the entire room. She smiled at Lila who was speaking to Marty about college and majoring in business. And then she got out of her chair and entered the kitchen.

"Ella…" Dennis warned, glancing over his shoulder.

"You're almost done! Let me please just help bring the food out. Please."

He handed her a platter of sandwiches, dropping a kiss on the top of her head. "It seems to be going great. You picked the right combination of friends. The conversations haven't stopped." She smiled her agreement and helped him bring out all the salads and sandwiches, soups and vegetables. While she had prepped a lot of the foods, Dennis had done the real work. And she was impressed with the feast in front of them. There was something for everyone, for the few girls that were vegetarians, for the picky eaters, and for the ones that loved anything and everything.

By the time dessert was brought out, she reached for Dennis and motioned at a chair beside her. "Please," she whispered, widening her eyes expectantly.

He nodded and sat slightly behind her, his arms wrapping around her shoulders and his lips pressing against her neck. She scooted away to fix him a plate, and the rush of emotions when he shot her a grateful smile left her momentarily speechless.

"How long has this…" Grace motioned toward them with a subtle smile.

"This is just friends," Ella informed her. "We fish at the same spot. So… about four months."

"And Alex… can I ask about him or am I sticking my foot in my mouth?"

"You can ask. He and his fiancé are expecting a baby."

Grace clucked her tongue, shaking her head. "Shitty thing for him to do, though. You're better off and got a better deal."

Dennis jerked his head toward Lila. "Thank you, but considering the man's daughter is sitting here, we should probably show a little more respect. Sometimes things don't work out, and it's better for both parties to just separate amicably. I don't know Alex, but I know these two ladies here have handled themselves with poise and beauty through a difficult, turbulent time in their lives."

Grace shot him a look of irritation. "No shit. But I have an ex-husband. I know it can be hell trying to co-parent. And I know Alex. Now Lila isn't a little girl. She knows the score. Her dad is her dad is her dad, but I think she is smart enough to know he was a horrible husband that betrayed his wife in the worst possible way."

"Grace." It was one word, spoken softly but with a firmness that put a stop to any further conversation. While Ella knew her friend was merely being protective after all she saw her go through, she did not want her daughter to sit there and hear her own father being demeaned. And that reminder from Dennis was enough to send her crushing even harder.

Shannon was the best at keeping conversations going and bringing others into the fold. She sat up straight, her eyes twinkling. "Okay. Best memory of Ella!"

A few friends spoke up, telling funny stories, laughing at the memories. "Oh my God, I remember the fights with her dad," Carla chimed in, sputtering out the words as laughter overtook her. "He was so large and scary! He was the type of dad that made us shut the hell up with just a look. But not Ella. When he found out she was dating Alex, he forbade her to go out. She just glanced up from painting her nails and said, 'Try and stop me, dad.' We were terrified, but Ella stood up, her 5'2" height barely making it to his shoulders, and she insisted calmly that she was going to do what she was going to do."

Ella giggled. "I was such a little shit."

"We tried to leave," Carla admitted, "But Ella made us stay, so we had to watch as her dad got angrier and angrier. She was the most rebellious nerd."

As the laughter finally died down, Tamarin blurted out, "Ella made a grown man cry at work."

Ella ducked her head as Dennis cried out, "Wait… what?"

"He was an idiot!" Ella cried out, bouncing forward.

Tamarin nodded. "Such an idiot. But you turned him into a crying idiot!" She turned to the rest of the table. "So, this guy started, and he was obnoxious. Swagger and all. Thought he was the shit. But he kept messing up. So, Ella would tell him to shut up and sit down and work. She would get frustrated when he got things wrong."

"Let me stress," Ella interrupted, "that getting things wrong at a trucking company means more work and worry. You have to be on top of things and at least attempt to get it right."

"So anyway, one night one of the guys goes into the men's bathroom and there's Wally standing there sobbing. SOBBING! Says he can't take it anymore. The guy says, 'Whatever you do, don't let Ella see you cry. It'll make it worse.'"

"Mom, you're a badass." Lila laughed.

"Mouth, Lila!"

Dennis wrapped his arms around her from behind, leaning forward in his seat. "I knew you were ferocious. The quiet act doesn't fool me."

Marty laughed. "She does try to trick people with that quiet personality, but once you get to know her or trigger that anger… forget it."

And she felt Dennis's gaze on her as he started to speak, his voice low and emotional. "I have a memory. I haven't known her as long as you all have, but… I saw her experience a rather difficult time. Something that would knock anyone else off their feet for a very long time. I actually never expected to see her again. Then one day I go to the lake early in the morning, and I see this vision out on the water. Just paddling in a kayak with the most serene, breathtaking look on her face. And although I had noticed her way before this, had been rendered speechless by her beauty, I knew on this morning that she was so much more than a pretty woman. She was the strongest person I could ever hope to know."

Everyone grew quiet as Ella turned toward him and rested

her forehead against his. She shut her eyes as his fingers pressed against her cheeks, relishing in his touch and his words.

For the next few hours, more stories were told, and more laughs were had. Ella sat back and enjoyed her friends, trying to be present in every moment. Because she knew that this was how memories were made. This was the type of night that she would store in her mind and bring out when she needed to smile, when she needed to remember that she was loved.

After everyone had left and Lila escaped to her room, Dennis hung around to help Ella clean up.

She gathered up the plastic cups and glanced over at him as he swept the floors. "You don't have to do that. You've helped enough."

"Are you kidding? You let me hang around. I got to hear stories about you from various phases of your life. Gold. The least I can do is clean up." He paused and gave her his full attention. "That was really fantastic, El. I know you now, and I know you've changed through the years, but a lot of the stories about you in your youth... that strong personality, the sense of humor... it's still you. And it seems everyone in your life adores you."

She smiled softly. "My friends are the best. They put up with me."

"Your teenage daughter loves you. That is quite the accomplishment." When she was silent, he continued, "It was weird. To hear about you and Alex. You guys have such a long history. I forget. It has to be devastating to lose that. To end such a central part of your life. Sometimes I don't think of that. I'm insensitive to it."

"Well, it isn't really your issue to be sensitive about." Ella moved slowly, avoiding his gaze, not sure where he was going.

"It is. It is my concern because if I'm pushing you into something you're not ready for, we're both going to get hurt. I'm not saying to end it all. But I am saying I'm not going to stay tonight."

She spun around and stared at him. "I wasn't inviting you,

Dennis."

He grinned. "No. I know. But I mean… we're not going to rush into anything. That's what I mean. Sometimes just being around you drives me crazy. But I don't want to jump into something you're not ready for and destroy anything that might happen in the future."

She rocked back on her heels and rubbed her eyes. "I'm too tired for this. Seriously, just leave everything. I'll get it in the morning."

"Just go to bed," Dennis insisted, walking up to her and rubbing her shoulders. "I'll make sure everything is locked up, and the alarm system is set." He nudged her so that she was facing him and then kissed her in a way that contradicted his words, confused her even more, and made her want to go back on her statement and invite him to stay.

But instead, she ended the kiss with a slight push and a flash of anger and then she left the room. She was exhausted, and he had her thoughts tangled like a fever dream. He did not want to stay, but he kissed her like he could not leave. And Ella knew that she would not have much willpower to stop anything from happening.

CHAPTER 8

The next morning Ella came downstairs and saw that Dennis had cleaned everything. Tables and chairs were put away, dishes were washed, and surfaces had been scrubbed down. And she realized she had been so exhausted that she had fallen asleep as soon as she let her head hit the pillow, not realizing Dennis was doing all the work.

In the middle of a sparkling clean table was a note from Dennis. "You deserve to wake up to a clean house and relax. Love, Dennis."

It was just another part of the puzzle. He had signed the note "Love". But that could mean so many things. It could imply friendship. It could have just been carelessly scribbled. It might mean he was simply toying with her emotions.

Lila was up soon after her mother, and she told her of plans to go hiking with her dad and Connie. Ella smiled and told her to be careful, meanwhile she was pushing back thoughts of hurt and bitterness. She wanted to be out of the darkness, not caring what her soon-to-be ex did. She wanted to be completely at ease with sharing her daughter. With no temptation to badmouth the man who helped raise her.

Dennis called mid-morning. "How'd you sleep?"

"Great. I didn't realize you were scrubbing down my entire downstairs."

His chuckled melted her anger just enough. "Don't exaggerate. I moved some of the tables and chairs so you wouldn't."

"You did more than that."

"So? El. Why is it wrong that I want to do nice things for you? Anyways, do you have plans today? You and Lila?"

"Lila is already gone. But I'm free. What's up?"

"Can I take you to lunch? Somewhere sort of nice."

A couple hours later, he was at her house. He stood at the bathroom door and watched as she curled her hair. "So, I don't think you ever answered me - did you put in notice yet?"

She nodded, unraveling the curling iron from her hair and inspecting the curl that bounced in its place. Satisfied, she backed up and glanced at him. "I did. Three weeks."

"Wow. Quite a notice."

"I don't start at the university until the beginning of the month."

"Don't you want some time in between? A week off?"

She unplugged the curling iron and set it on the sink. Then she grabbed a brush. "Sure. Wouldn't we all? But I need to pay my bills."

"I'm sorry, El. I wasn't thinking."

Ella inspected herself in the mirror and then turned to Dennis with a distracted smile. "It's fine."

"I just don't think … it can't be easy being a single mom and trying to make ends meet."

"Dennis… seriously, it's okay. I don't expect you to know all my hardships or to tiptoe around it all. I'm struggling just a little financially, but it is short-term, and it is worth every second of stress just to escape the marriage with my soul intact. So, it's fine." She squared her shoulders and lifted her face up to his. "Can we please just be normal? Please don't treat me like some charity case. Or some breakable china doll. Now. Does my hair look okay?"

It took a few moments to gather his composure, but he leaned down and kissed her. "I apologize. And your hair looks amazing. You look gorgeous."

Her lips slipped into a satisfied smile. "There. That's better. Where are we going?"

"It's a surprise."

On the car ride, they talked about the night before. They discussed her friends and whom Dennis favored and whom he thought was too quiet or abrasive.

Ella fully expected him to dislike Grace, but he surprised her. "I like that she speaks her mind. I don't think it was fully appropriate with Lila sitting right there, but at least you know where you stand with her."

"She's been a great support. She's given invaluable advice concerning lawyers and divorce proceedings. Rough around the edges, but as soon as I call her, she's here."

After a few minutes of silence, Dennis pleaded, "Please don't be mad for what's about to happen. Please. Just know I am sometimes very selfish and ... don't be mad."

Those words should have driven alarm through her veins, but Ella was simply curious. Because this was Dennis, and she knew instinctively that he would not purposely hurt her. With a light tone lifting her words, she asked, "What is it?"

"We are on our way to lunch. At my parents'"

She stared at him, but he kept his gaze focused on the road, his jaw twitching. "Dennis. Why would I be mad?"

"I didn't give you any warning."

"No. It would have been nice to know. Am I dressed okay?"

He glanced toward her with a teasing grin. "I would have preferred the see-through dress but yes, you look beautiful."

A laugh escaped her mouth. "Why didn't you tell me?"

"I thought you might refuse." His grin turned sheepish. "Sometimes meeting the parents is... I don't know. Intimidating."

"We're not fifteen."

They pulled up to an older split-level house, beautifully kept and landscaped with corkscrew bushes and flowers coloring the sides of the long driveway. Ella immediately imagined Dennis growing up here, riding his bike down the road, throwing a football in the front yard, sneaking out late at night. She suddenly wanted to know all about his childhood. She wanted to know all about him.

"Don't you dare get out of the car," he warned her with a devilish grin. "If my mom sees that I didn't open your car door for you, I'll never hear the end of it."

His parents, Ed and Shirley were older, mid-70's but looked great. Shirley's hair was a faded blond that just touched her shoulders, and Ed had salt and pepper hair and the same almond shaped brown eyes as his middle son.

"I hope you like sandwiches and pasta salad. It's too hot to make anything more than that." Shirley grabbed her hand and squeezed, smiling with her entire face, much like her son.

"I think that sounds great. What can I do to help?"

Ed loved to joke and immediately teased Dennis about bringing a woman to the house to meet his parents. Ella took a little thrill at seeing the blush creeping up Dennis's cheeks, and she added, "He did not even tell me he was bringing me here. Just said lunch and drove."

His parents both laughed. "Dennis! You know better!" Shirley admonished. "Oh, he's stubborn, Ella. Gets an idea in his head and... I hope you weren't too thrown off guard."

"Not at all. I'm happy to be here."

Ed leaned toward Ella and poked her shoulder. "He doesn't bring any girls around. You're the first since..." He nodded as if that said it all, and with a start, she realized he meant that she was the first since his wife had passed away... over twenty years ago. She tried to make sense of that, to digest the words... but Dennis quickly changed the subject, giving her a wink.

They asked Ella how she and Dennis met, and she told them about her fishing trips. Ed's eyes widened with appreciation, and he slapped his knee. "A girl that likes to fish? Tell you what, boy, you better hold tight to her. "

Dennis nodded. "Agreed. Hey, dad, I was going to see if you wanted to go fishing this week. I have Wednesday off."

"Sure do. Let's take your kayaks. I need to work my muscles."

"You have kayaks?" She waited until she had his attention, and when he nodded, she asked, "Why don't you ever bring yours on Saturdays?"

He leaned in close and whispered, "Because that's your

time. I never wanted to intrude." He took her hand and squeezed.

His parents were easy to talk to. Shirley mentioned that they had recently celebrated fifty-five years of marriage, to which Ella asked, "Tell me, how did you two meet?"

Shirley giggled as if she were again that young girl and motioned for Ed to tell the story. He inched forward so that he was sitting on the edge of his chair, anxious to tell a story Ella was sure he had told a hundred times before.

"We met at the local skating rink. I knew her sister. And her sister skated a certain way. Tilted her body to the left instead of forward, her arms pumping. It was just an odd way to skate. One day I noticed this young girl skating the exact same way, so I went up and said to her, 'You have to be Ruth's sister. You skate just like her.' She was sixteen, and I was eighteen. We got married one year later."

Dennis angled his body toward Ella with a conspiring smile. "And had my brother Barry six months later."

Shirley waved her hand at him. "He was premature."

"He was over eight pounds!"

Shirley giggled and shrugged. And when she led Ella into the kitchen, she turned toward her with twinkling eyes. "I'm not supposed to ask you any personal questions. I think Denny is scared I'll chase you away."

Ella set the bowl on the counter and turned to the older woman. "You can ask me anything."

"You're married?"

"I am. We have been separated almost a year. Waiting for him to sign the divorce papers."

There was no judgement in her expression. Only sympathy. "I am sorry to hear that. Never easy. You have a daughter?"

"Lila. She's fifteen, almost sixteen."

"I have four grandchildren. Barry, my oldest, has three, and Sam, my youngest, has one. Barry's divorced too. And Dennis... well, he was married. Married so young, and they didn't always see eye to eye. But bless her soul, Robin passed away before-"

"Hey mom." Dennis strolled into the kitchen, searching Ella's face as if uncertain to how she would take the current conversation. "Ella doesn't need to hear about that."

Shirley wiped her hands on a tea towel. "You're right. I forgot myself."

Leaning against the counter with an assuring smile, Ella asked, "What was Dennis like as a boy?"

Although she could hear Dennis groan, she knew the subject was a good one as Shirley's eyes lit up, and her hands danced through the air with her words. "Oh, he was a sweetheart. Always so helpful. A little more serious than Barry, but with more of a sense of humor than his younger brother Sam. He was rebellious, but he always apologized for it. More of a 'Sorry, I did that, mom. I'll probably do it again, but sorry for being a pain in the ass.'" She and Ella both laughed. "Out of all my boys, Dennis was the animal lover. When his yellow lab died, he didn't cry. He just walked out and didn't come home for hours. Not a word. And now… well, Sam comes to visit and tries to take over house projects. He means well, but he will stampede over our plans and drive Ed crazy. Barry will come stay and not lift a finger. But Dennis comes over and asks what we need done. He will make Ed feel like he is helping, not taking over. He knows that we are still capable. But he helps."

"You've done a great job raising such an amazing man."

In the car, driving away, Dennis said, "Thank you. You were great with my parents. I know they can be… they were a little overzealous about me bringing you there."

"Are you kidding? They're great."

He grinned. "Yes. They are pretty wonderful. I am lucky."

"You are."

There were a few beats of silence and then he asked, "Are you ever going to tell me about your mom?"

"Are you ever going to tell me about Robin?"

He clenched his jaw, his gaze fixed on the road in front of him. "She was my wife over 25 years ago. She died. Over 25 years ago."

"My mom was a bad mom and is no longer in my life."

His shrug belied his obvious irritation. "I guess we don't have the type of relationship to share such things."

"Guess not." She blinked back hot tears, angry and confused. This was not what she needed in her life right now. The day had been great, albeit a little odd that he just took her to his parents without a word. But now she was feeling guilty for not sharing... even though he had no intention of talking about certain parts of his life.

"I've got a headache. I'm just going to go lie down," she informed him evenly. "Thanks for lunch."

He reached out, touching her shoulder, his fingertips drawing her back. "Hey. El. I'm sorry."

"Sorry about what? Just not that type of relationship. Bye, Dennis." She took extra care not to slam the car door. She wanted to portray a calmness, although her screaming nerves and broken heart were anything but relaxed. And as he got out of his car calling her name, Ella kept her steps slow and even to the front door. It was only when he started running up the porch steps that she whirled around to face him.

"No. I said I was going to go lie down. Don't chase me. Don't follow - that... no!" The thought of someone, even Dennis, running after her made her blood run cold, and the memories of just a few months ago came rushing back.

The color drained from his face as Dennis immediately backed away, stepping down the stairs slowly. "Oh, I'm sorry, Ella. I ... I'm sorry."

She pushed open the front door and slipped inside, a firm shut telling him just what he could do with his apologies. And fortunately, she felt her entire body sag with an exhaustion that promised the sweet escape of sleep. It was as if she could not get to her bed fast enough. She even considered just falling onto the couch for immediate slumber, but she dragged herself up the stairs with the thought of her large, soft bed. There was nothing like it when she was tired. And after the preparation of yesterday, the excitement of last night, and the nervousness of today along with the stinging disappointment, she could barely keep her eyes open.

Sleep seized her for two hours. There were no dreams, no tossing and turning, just blissed unconsciousness as her mind and body tried to restore some semblance of energy and strength.

Waking was a slow, hazy process. Finally, Ella stretched and sat up, feeling that kind of contentment that only came from solid rest. She blinked a few times and slowly got her bearings, gradually understanding it was the middle of the day, and her mood was off. Because of him. Somehow, Ella had let herself get attached. Somehow, she had once again become dependent on her feelings …for a man.

She checked her phone, pulling the covers up as thunder roared outside. There was a storm raging, and it had probably kept her sleeping, soothing her to that unconscious state. Still blinking the sleep away, she saw she had texts from Dennis.

"I'm sorry. I was an idiot." "When you can, come outside." "I'm not leaving until you tell me I have to leave."

The texts had been sent over an hour ago. She assumed he had gotten the hint and left, the storm rushing him along. But glancing out the window, she saw his car parked in the driveway.

Something in her broke, the thought of a man waiting for her, sitting around in his car for hours just to apologize… she raced downstairs and threw open the front door, stopping abruptly when she was faced with Dennis, soaked and holding a bouquet of wilted wildflowers.

"What the hell are you doing? How long have you been standing out in the rain?"

He shrugged, trembling. "I don't know. About an hour. I had to tell you… Ella, please believe me, I am so sorry. I was a jerk. And then to know that I scared you-"

"Why didn't you wait in your car? Or in the house? You know the alarm code. I fell asleep, Dennis. I -"

"I saw that fear in your eyes, and it made me sick knowing I did that today. I put that uncertainty there. I'm not going to go into your home without your consent. And I wanted to be right here waiting. I wanted you to -"

The pounding of the rain was so loud, she had to keep raising her voice. "I'm here. I'm standing right here in front of you. Whatcha going to do? Huh? I've been standing in front of you for a while now waiting for you to make a move and -"

Suddenly he threw down the flowers and then cupped her face as he leaned in for a hungry kiss. For a moment, Ella wondered if she was actually levitating as his lips, his fingers.... as he took her to a different plane... She felt as if she were somewhere else, a place no one could reach them. It was safe and thrilling and scary. And she kissed him back with a desire that seemed to boil up inside her from the pit of her stomach to her mouth. As if all her wants and needs from the time she was just a young woman new to all the secrets and burdens till now had culminated to this very moment. She had to have him. And as they stumbled into the house, she realized Dennis felt the same.

By the time they were upstairs, she was in her bra and panties and he was in his boxers, and that was when the thoughts infested her mind, building doubt and tearing away at the harmony. Ella placed her hands on his chest, rising to her knees.

"Wait!"

Immediately, he backed away, reaching for her hands. "El?"

"I don't know how ... it's been a really long time."

His wet hair framed his face as he grinned, and she found herself falling even more. "Ella... honey... you've been doing great so far."

She found herself laughing, her insecurities fading as she saw him gaze at her longingly, his hands running over her curves as if he were trying to memorize them through touch. Then he drew back once again, his smile fading. "If you're not ready... El, I'll wait however long it takes."

"No, I'm..." Her gaze dipped down to his mouth, and that

was all he needed. He was slower, however, gentler. The frenzied makeout session smoothed into more savoring, a more tender approach. When Dennis caught her trying to cover up, his hands framed her face, and he whispered, "You're beautiful. Absolutely stunning."

And suddenly Ella was too mesmerized with his body, his moves to worry about how she looked. He was solid and lean, his shoulders broad and chest tight. She explored with her fingers, her lips, trying to slow down that rush of passion, the need for more… for it all. By the time he moved over her, she felt delirious with desire and was begging. Ella might have felt self-conscious if he were not scratching out her name in a low whisper.

And then she experienced such release, such jolting electricity whipping through her body as she made a sound equivalent to a howl. She clutched him, her nails ripping into his flesh, her teeth clamping down on his shoulder. In her 39 years, she had never been brought to such ecstasy, losing control to that degree and wanting nothing more than to be left in that paradise of exquisite pain and pleasure… to be dangling in another hemisphere where her nerves sang out, and her body convulsed in pure delight, raw vulnerable bliss.

Ella seemed to step back into her body, into the present when she heard Dennis whispering her name, cradling her in his arms. His kisses rained down on her body as she burrowed closer to him, feeling his strength and masculinity.

"Are you okay?" he murmured, his lips pressing down on the top of her head.

"Yes. I just… that was amazing."

"It was. You're amazing." His fingers tapped her chin so that she looked up. "I'm sorry for earlier. Sometimes I want what I want and just jump forward with questions or … I'm sorry. And I really hope that this was something you …."

"Yes. I did. I wanted this."

"We should talk about what this-"

She shifted so that there was space between them. He already wanted to make it clear that this meant nothing. And she could only flounder there, immersed in the afterglow of their lovemaking with stars in her eyes and hope in her heart. "Please. Can we just enjoy this? The moment? I don't want to dissect it right now."

Dennis studied her carefully before slowly nodding. "Sure, El. No analyzing. But I want you to know that this meant a lot to me. This meant so much."

"It did for me too." She slid the blanket over her naked body and glanced over her shoulder. "I heard my phone. I'll be right back." When she returned minutes later, she gave him a smile. "Lila is staying with her dad tonight."

And her resolve melted when Dennis reached for her. "So, does that mean I have a chance at spending the night with you?"

The blanket dropped from her shoulder as she half-shrugged. "If you feel that's best." She squealed when he nodded and reached out to tug at the blanket.

"It's definitely what is best."

There were still insecurities and awkwardness, despite the uninhibited romp they had just participated in, so she begged off joining him in the shower and waited until he was done before jumping in. She let the warm water soothe her, reassure her, and she smiled thinking of the night ahead. Ella would make a point to enjoy the moment and not worry about future days. Because this... this was worth indulging in... More of his touch and his words .... More of him...

Ella dried off and then panic started to set in. What should she wear? Anything? But she heard him rustling around downstairs so she assumed she should venture out of the room. Should she wear a cute ruffled nightie? Did she even have one? Finally, she chickened out of anything daring and simply put on the clothes she had been wearing previously.

And downstairs, she found the living room lit in candlelight with several bouquets of flowers placed all around. She froze and stared up at Dennis, who straightened from the plates of food he was setting down.

"I had a bunch of flowers in the car.... To apologize. Found the candles and... the food left over from last night. I thought we could maybe watch a movie. Have a nice night in..." and he threw her that devilish grin that gave her no choice but to smile back.

They made it ten minutes through the movie before they were once again distracted by each other.

CHAPTER 9

Lila tried to push her way through the crowd. The house was packed, which didn't seem possible because it was a rather large house. But kids were stuffed in each room trying to move enough to constitute dancing. And all she wanted was some air.

"Hey Lila!"

She sighed and stopped, glaring at a guy that slammed into her, almost dropping his cup of beer. Then she turned to face Brad. "What?"

It always caught her off guard when he displayed anger toward her in situations like this. Shouldn't she be the one that was upset? He dragged her here and ignored her requests to leave... to at least step away. "What the hell are you doing? You're being rude!"

Feeling flushed and closed in, she turned and shoved a girl that stepped on her heel. Turning back to Brad, she insisted, "Take me home! Take me home now, or we are done!"

"Stop being such an uptight bitch!" He leaned down and glared at her. "You're such a fucking baby. Find your own way home."

"Brad! You promised if we stopped out here, we would only stay for a little bit. I wanted to spend some time with you."

He rolled his eyes. "To what? Sit around and listen to you cry again?"

And Lila wondered what she ever saw in him. Sure, he was older and could drive. And he was freakin' hot! But the attitude and lack of intelligence made the attraction fade rather fast. And Brad knew he was good looking. He reminded her often that if she was not going to be what he considered the best girlfriend, there were plenty of other girls that were waiting to take her place. And now he was throwing her emotional state from the other night in her face. Nice. What a charmer. "Go to hell. Loser."

He grabbed her arm and tugged her toward him and then dragged her through the crowd. She tripped a few times before he finally released her. They were in the hallway where there was a bit more room, and she noticed his eyes were dangerously dark and narrowed. "You want to be a bitch? Huh?" He grabbed her face, his fingers squeezing like a vise. "Say it again. Go ahead. Say it-"

"Hey, asshole! Let her go!"

Brad stepped back, releasing her to face the intruder. Lila leaned sideways and saw a tall guy with wavy auburn hair and freakishly light blue eyes staring Brad down. Brad was just as tall but bigger, more muscular. This guy looked thin, almost scrawny, but he squared up his shoulders and met Brad's glare straight-on, his mouth set in a straight line and eyes narrowed.

After several tense moments, Brad reached out and shoved Lila. "Right, Finn. You take the whore home. I was done with her anyway."

And just as Lila did her best to block out the words and blink back the tears, the guy stepped up to her, his expression softening. "Hey. Are you okay?"

She dragged the heels of her hands across her eyes. "Yeah. I'm fine."

His eyes were wide, as if he weren't sure what to do next. But then he leaned in close. "Brad's a jerk. A total asshole. If you need a ride home…"

Lila glanced up and noticed his red, squinty eyes and his sluggish movements. "Are you even capable of driving?"

A slow chuckle came out of his mouth. "I haven't had a drop of alcohol."

"No, but you've had a few puffs of the other stuff."

Another chuckle. "Give me another half hour, and I'll be good to go." He held out his hand. "Finn."

"Lila."

"Lila, what's a gorgeous girl like you doing with an asshole like that?"

She managed a smile before looking around, the crowd close and tight. Finn noticed her discomfort and motioned for her to follow him. Within minutes of zipping and dodging people, they were outside, the warm night air refreshing, and she gasped as if she had been underwater for several minutes.

"Yeah. The crowd isn't really my thing either." His stare was intense, and Lila had to look away. "Are you sure you're okay? He really grabbed you."

"Fine. I'm fine."

"Does he do that often?"

"No." The truth was Brad had been getting more and more temperamental, yelling and grabbing and pushing. He always apologized afterwards, always held her close and gave her re-assurances that covered her like a thick, soft blanket. Her father was gone, starting a new family with a strange woman, and her mother was busy trying to rebuild her soul, her life. While they both loved her, there were things weighing heav-ily on her shoulders, and she needed that comfort, that feeling of being loved, sought out.

But Finn lifted a corner of his mouth. "You're a terrible liar. Look, not my business, but you're a beautiful girl. Don't waste time on scum like that."

She eyed him up with a small smile. "You have any weed left?"

**

It had been a week since their night together, and Dennis and Ella had not been able to spend any romantic time to-gether since then. Lila was home during the week, and they both worked. There were calls and visits and brief kisses, but nothing compared to the past weekend.

But it was Friday night, and Dennis had shown up with groceries, stating his intent of cooking her a fantastic Italian meal.

"Two more weeks of that horrible job," he reminded her, grinning as she laughed. "How are you feeling? Is it nice to go there knowing there's an end?"

Ella grabbed a strip of green pepper, popping it in her mouth. "Hell yeah, it's nice."

The front door opened, and Lila's voice called out, "You guys home? Dressed?"

"Don't be funny. We're in the kitchen." Ella stepped into the center of the kitchen and waited until her daughter appeared. "It's late. You're not staying at your dad's?"

"I am. I need my bathing suit for tomorrow. Dad's taking us out on -" she stopped herself, her cheeks reddening. "We're going fishing."

And Ella wanted to reassure her daughter. She had already learned about the pontoon boat purchase after conveniently running into Connie at the local gas station. But she leaned in closer and noticed Lila's eyes. "Hey. What's going on? Are you sick? Your eyes are red. Were you out with friends?"

"Mom! I'm exhausted. Going back and forth between here and dad's. I was out with Brad and a few others because dad said it was okay. What? Do you want me to stay here? Can't I see dad or -"

"No." Ella sighed. "I'm sorry. I washed your bathing suit. I'll go get it. Then go to your dad's, and get some rest."

Lila turned and watched her mom rush from the room. She kept her shoulders hunched; her body tilted forward as if ready to bolt. Dennis took a few steps closer and then said her name.

"Lila. Hey, look here." He waited patiently until she slowly turned. "What's going on? Huh?"

"Look, you're not my parent -"

"Of course, I'm not. So, I'm not falling for the 'Woe is me' act. I know that look. Your eyes are barely even open. Let's make a deal. You leave here and go straight to your dad's. You have a safe ride?" When she nodded, he made a noise of disbelief. "Give me your phone."

"What? No!"

He held out his hand, his gaze fixed on her. "Phone."

With a sigh, she pulled it out of her pocket and placed it in his hand.

"Okay. I'm putting my number in here. Listen, you ever find yourself in a situation you aren't comfortable with and you feel you can't talk to your parents, give me a call. Got it? Now, your parents love you, and you can go to them with anything, but if you feel you can't or don't want to chance it... then call me. And don't get in the car with anyone that's drunk or high." He handed her phone back, and she stared up at him, surprise registering in those bloodshot eyes.

"Thanks, Dennis."

"Yeah, well, this isn't a free cab service. This is if you're careless enough to find yourself in a bad situation. It happens. I get it. Just... be careful."

Ella appeared minutes later and handed Lila the suit. "Have fun, honey. I love you."

"Love you too, mom."

Dennis had returned to the stove, his full focus on stirring as he said, "Lila mentioned giving you a call when she made it to her dad's. Or was it that you should call Alex to ensure she got there?"

With a huff, Lila corrected, "I'll call mom. I said I'd call mom."

Once she was gone, Ella raised her eyebrows. "What was that about?"

"Nothing. She just wanted to reach out when she made it to her destination."

The expression of doubt told him that she bought none of his words. "I trust her. She goes where she tells me she goes."

"Hun... she's fifteen."

"Not your usual fifteen. She's different."

And Dennis smiled and turned his attention back to cooking. Because if she did not see, if she was not ready to truly look, then nothing he could say would make a difference. But he saw a young girl overwhelmed and hurt and confused and that meant that turning to something for comfort was the next natural step. For a lot of kids, comfort was found in any form of rebellion. From what he knew of Lila, she was a smart, good kid, but even good kids were vulnerable.

To change the subject, he lifted an eyebrow and asked, "Fishing? Thought Lila wasn't a fan. And bathing suit?"

"Alex bought a pontoon boat. I think Lila was trying to spare me the news, but I -"

She had his full attention. "But what? Huh?" When she rolled her eyes, he continued, "Why do I have a feeling I know this answer. You were already told, right? Where did you run into Connie this time?" When she still did not answer, Dennis gave her a half-grin. "Fine. But it's to the point you're going to need a bodyguard. You won't get rid of me."

Finally, she smiled. "Promise?"

**

There were days when Alex did not want to face the direction he had set his life. This was not supposed to happen. He had wanted some fun on the side, some attention from a woman other than his sometimes emotionally unavailable wife who, truth be told, had let herself go in recent years. How was it that men were just supposed to accept the extra pounds and house sweats and bad haircuts? Why was it expected that men lie down and play dead when their wives stopped seducing them? He could not remember the last time Ella had initiated sex. Or even thrown him a flirtatious smile. She had given up long before he had, just without the guts to say it.

But he had not wanted to uproot his entire life at 40 years old. If Ella had not been such a miserable untrusting wife, they could still be sharing a life together. But she had to get suspicious. Had to sneak around and check his phone messages. As if that were not enough, she had kicked him out of his own house.

But Alex was adjusting. Connie could be clingy, and her looks were plain, but she could be sweet at times. She adored him, and that was more than he had gotten from Ella.

And Connie was great with his daughter. Lila was still uncertain, still adjusting to the split, and he did feel remorse for having turned her life upside-down. The one thing he wanted to be in life was a good dad. Sometimes he did not know what that meant, how to go about achieving it... but his heart was in the right place when it came to Lila. So, the fact that Connie tried did not go unnoticed by him. She seemed to genuinely care for his daughter, and while the last thing he had wanted to do was raise another child, he was starting to warm to the idea. He had a feeling Connie would perform most of the parental duties. This time around, he could sit back and just enjoy the child.

The money was not bad either. Connie had been given a generous amount in her divorce settlement, and she treated Alex like a king. He was even willing to go fishing with her, something he was not crazy about, if it meant going in style in their new boat.

Connie and Lila were in the kitchen cutting out pictures from a magazine for a school project, and he reached in the refrigerator for a drink.

"So, I might get a new camera," Lila was saying, scissors gripped in her hand. "And pap said he can take me to that new trail for some good shots-"

"Wait... what?" Alex slammed the door and turned to face the women. "Pap? You don't mean my dad... he doesn't go outside. Which pap, Lila?"

His daughter dropped the scissors, her eyes wide. "Hey! Why are you yelling at me? I didn't do anything wrong."

"Do you mean your mom's dad? He's in town? They're... talking?"

"Yes." He almost apologized because she slumped in her seat looking miserable. But he was too fired up to comfort her.

Glancing at Connie, he said, "I'll be back." He waved her away when she tried to ask questions. But his blood felt hot, and his nerves were suddenly pressed against the inside of his skin. He had to go and get this straight. Ella thought he was a stupid man, but she had another thing coming.

The twenty-minute drive took him ten minutes, and before Alex could think anything through or take note of his surroundings, he was storming up to his old front door and pounding on it.

"Alex?" Ella flung open the door with that damned irritated expression he always wanted to wipe off her smug face. "What the hell are you doing?"

"Your dad is in town? Ted's here?"

"What business is it of yours?" But he caught that shadow crossing her face.

"You're a fucking sneak. You know that? You ran to your daddy, and now he's going to give you all that money, right? As soon as the divorce is final. Fucking sneak! Don't think you're going to get away with this."

"Away with what, Alex? My dad is visiting. That is not against any type of law. It is also not your business."

"It is! You're trying to keep money from me. We were married over twenty years. You get money, it's half mine! And this house, the alarm system and new locks, they're coming down. You have no right-"

Ella's voice was infuriatingly low and calm. "You moved in with your pregnant fiancé. The same woman that was seen lurking around my backyard pounding on my windows at night. So yeah, I had to get a security system."

"You're crazy."

"I'm not the one running around screaming about money that isn't even there. Not trying to keep your parents from you. So -"

"Does your dad know his precious daughter is already sleeping around? You wanted to cry around about my infidelity but from what I hear -"

"That's it!"

And it was then that Alex realized there was another person in the house. Dennis stepped out. "You really want to do this?

Because I know the laws regarding divorces. I also know what your divorce decree says. You want to come here and harass Ella about something as innocent as her father visiting? Then she'll get a protection order on you. As for your girlfriend, tell her if she sets foot on this property one more time, we will release the video to the police. Understood?"

"No," Alex moved forward so they were nose-to-nose. "You are not a part of this. You have no idea how this bitch can-"

The punch was unexpected, and Alex lost his balance, falling through the flimsy railing to the ground with a heavy thud. He heard Ella gasp and curse, and then he saw Dennis jump off the porch and loom over him, fists clenched and teeth gritted. "I warned you. Now get your ass out of here, and the next time you get the urge to try to bully a woman, think twice, asshole."

Alex felt himself being heaved up off the ground, and his back screamed in protest, but before he could try to pull away or say a word, Dennis dragged him across the yard. He gave him one final push.

"You're going to jail. Both of you," Alex threatened before climbing awkwardly into his car.

**

Ella could not catch her breath as she shook. Bending over and placing her hands over her face, she cried out, "Just go! Dennis, leave."

"Not until we talk. Look here. Breathe. El, you have to breathe." He knelt in front of her and rubbed her arms. "Honey, there is no way I was going to let that man stand there and degrade you like that! No!"

She sank into a nearby chair. "He's going to go to the police, Dennis!"

"Let him! I'm the one they'll come after. And we have video. He was aggressively in your face, pointing and yelling. I'm not going to tell you I'm sorry because I'm not."

"He's the father of my child!"

"Ella! Listen to yourself! What the hell does that have to do

with that man mistreating you? Huh? To come here screaming because your dad is in town? How is that okay? To call
you names, to insult you and beat you down verbally after he
already committed the ultimate betrayal... no! Please tell me
you're not this blind when it comes to abuse. Please reassure
me, baby, because I'm afraid that you've spent the majority of
your life in a relationship that's done nothing but beaten you
down-"

Ella's auburn hair flew around her face as she adamantly dis-
agreed. "It wasn't like you're making it out to be. He could be
a jerk but... right now, we are going through a divorce, so he's a
bit cruel-"

"A bit? Ella, I'm starting to think you mistakenly believe
you deserve this. That was not 'a bit'. That was nasty and abusive, and if I'm around, I'm not tolerating it."

Ella sprang out of the chair, her eyes wet and voice wobbly.
"You have no clue who I am. None. You don't know what I've
been through or what I believe. You only know that on nights
when you're horny, you can come here for a piece of ass."

He drew back as if hit. "What? Ella! No! That isn't-"

"Yes, it is. That is exactly what this is. I barely hear from you
during the week-"

"Bullshit!"

"You want to come here like some... Neanderthal and cause
me more trouble because.,.. What does it matter? I'm just the
weekend girl. Not really anyone of any -"

"Hey! Stop! I get that you're upset but don't-"

"Just go. Leave."

Dennis stared at her for a few moments, the silence dragging
out like an accusation. Then he asked softly, "I'm the bad guy?
He treats you like you're trash, and I'm the bad one?"

"He is my ex. We have a history and share a child. I was not
allowing him to treat me any way. I was not standing there
speechless. But my point is that this isn't about you. You don't
get to play protector only to leave here and not look back."

His shoulders sagged and face crumpled, but he tried one

last time. "You think that is what this is? Me coming here and then just leaving? Not looking back? You think that of me?" When she stared back unflinchingly, not bothering to say a word, he continued, "That's such bullshit, Ella! That's not fair!"

"It is fair! Because I hear from you on the weekends. I barely hear two words from you during the week, because you know there is no possible booty call. You're a hypocrite because you treat me just like an object. Like my ex did. So, you have no right to interfere and make judgements."

He stood there watching her... waiting, his chest heaving with heavy breaths and disbelief. Then with a short nod, he turned and stomped out of the house. And she resented him even more for proving her right and leaving.

**

Alex barreled into the house, hunched over and stifling groans. Lila and Connie stared up in horror when he stumbled into the kitchen. He almost started screaming, yelling out obscenities and threats regarding Ella, but he saw the look of pure fear on Lila's young face, and he swallowed the rage.

"Dad! Your face! What happened?"

"I fell. Hit my face going down. I'm okay. Back's out. Look, sweetheart, can you go upstairs?" When she started to protest, he added impatiently, "Dammit, Lila, I'm not asking. I'm telling you. Upstairs!"

He waited until her footsteps faded before he spun around and confronted Connie. "Tell me right now. Have you been sneaking around my house?"

At first her eyes widened and mouth dropped open, and he had his answer. Then she jutted her chin out. "Your house? You mean her house. Your house is here now.... Isn't it?"

"Dammit, Connie! Answer me! Because they are saying they have you on camera sneaking around the house. Do they?"

Connie wrung her hands together, staring up at him imploringly. "I just... no. I mean... it was before she had the motion lights and cameras installed. I think."

"What the hell are you doing going over there?" he exploded. "I can't even go to the goddamned police now because if I do, Ella will show them video of you trespassing! What did you do - go to the front door? Peek in the windows? What is that video going to show?"

"I .... I ..." She struggled for words, for air. "They're lying. I stopped."

"How did they know it was you then?" When she shook her head, he persisted, "What did you do? I need to know because if they take this to the cops..."

"I would look in windows and then.... Then I would knock and run."

He stared at her for a long moment before turning away and cursing. She got up and moved behind him, hesitantly... fearfully. "What happened, Alex?"

"He sucker-punched me, and I fell off the porch. That's what happened. That whore has that man staying there."

She put a hand on his shoulder. "Then maybe she'll give you that divorce, and we can-"

He slapped her hand away. "We can what, Connie? Huh? Live happily ever after? I have to deal with this and make sure they don't come after us. I am not worried about a divorce right now. You just made this a thousand times worse. Holy shit, my daughter lives there. You're going there to spy and ... I can't right now. I can't do this."

"Do what?" Her voice came out strangled as fear gripped her. "Us? This? It's a little late. I'm pregnant, Alex."

"I can't deal with this situation. I need to get my back checked out. Just... stay away from her. Got it?"
**

Being fifteen sucked. There was no other way to explain it. Lila was miserable. She hated school, hated what was happening to her home life, and felt like she had no control. No power in her own life. And then there was Brad.

Despite the disastrous party where Finn had driven her home, and despite meeting up with the odd boy a few random times during the week to get stoned and laugh and forget the tangled mess of her life, she and Brad were back to being a couple.

Lila was fifteen and was smart, so she understood this was not a forever relationship. However, at this time of her life, she was unable to resist him. She craved him. And when he stopped by her locker a week after their fight with that puppy dog look and those flowery words, she could only lean against him in silent surrender.

"You know how I get, Li. I'm sorry. And I tried to just forget you, because I was hurt you didn't want to hang out with my friends. But I can't get you out of my mind. I can't sleep. Please."

As they walked down the hall, hands in each other's back pockets, she passed Finn. He stopped in the middle of the moving student herd and simply watched in confusion and hurt. And she could only offer a sad half-smile. Finn was fun and cute, but this was Brad. He was on the basketball team, the debate team and was gorgeous. He was going places. Finn was going to a dark hallway to get stoned.

CHAPTER 10

Ella was not doing well. She felt as if she were physically falling apart, as if her skin could no longer contain her bones and guts. One crack and everything would come spilling out, and everyone would see that she was a fraud. Because on the outside she smiled and chatted, took phone calls from friends, and answered emails and texts. She declared her excitement for her upcoming new job, and she laughed along with co-workers when appropriate.

But Ella felt cracked and hollow, not real. The smiles and conversations… she was going through motions when all she longed to do was go home and curl up in her bed. The same bed she had shared with Dennis for those few ridiculously amazing nights.

The only times she truly forced herself to be present was around Lila. Because something seemed to be happening with the teenager. There were mood swings, tantrums, and tears. Everything Lila usually was not. And she wondered if Lila had been in her father's destructive path that fateful day. She had tried to tentatively inquire, to see if Lila needed to talk. To find out if her daughter had been unfairly put in the middle. But it had backfired, as Lila exploded and accused Ella of trying to pull information from her about Alex.

"Don't put me in that position, mom. I actually love going over there. Connie's great. I'm sorry if you don't like her, but she and I really get along."

Ella drew back in surprise. "What? No! I don't want information about them, Lila. I just wanted to make sure you are okay and that nothing happened there to … I wasn't sure if your dad-"

"Just stop, mom."

One more weak attempt. "I am okay with you getting along with Connie. That makes me happy and relieved that when you go there-" she stopped as Lila whirled around and stomped out of the room. And Ella was able to slump over and stop being present. Stop being there.

It was a week after the horrible fight with Dennis and a week until her new job started. She had not heard from him. And she had not reached out, although she felt intense guilt over what she had screamed at him. Ella knew she had been unnecessarily harsh and overly hysterical. The scene with Alex had sent her into a full-fledged panic. But she also knew some of the words she had thrown at Dennis were her truth. And his continuing silence merely confirmed it.

The day after the altercation, Alex had called to say he would not press charges if she would not go after Connie. She agreed with the added stipulation that Connie stop following her and never show up at her house again. And Alex assured her that was the plan.

And today Ella endured another mind-numbing day at her job, trying to cheer herself with the fact that it was almost over. There were better things ahead. But the thoughts of Dennis shadowed any joy, any attempt at life.

So, she got through another day, and she considered picking up food for dinner but remembered Lila was going to a baseball game and then out to eat with friends. And Ella could not really taste food.

The same scenery flew past as she drove the short distance home. The one thing about her new job was that she would have longer travel time... paying out more for gas. But Ella always loved long drives, so she was ready for the change.

It was not until she had parked in her driveway and was getting out that she noticed her porch was fixed. The broken railing had been repaired, and the porch had been painted the bright red she had mentioned wanting to Dennis. Slowly she walked over to the porch, seeing signs made in his handwriting that stated, "Wet paint."

Her hands shook as she got out her phone and texted Dennis. "Thank you."

It was only several moments later that a text came back. "The damage was my fault. My responsibility."

And Ella blinked back tears of frustration and hurt over the curtness that she read into the text. Feeding off that hurt, she texted back, "Damage, yes. The paint was a bit much."

Within moments, her phone was ringing, and she allowed herself a smile. "Hello?" she answered as if not knowing who was calling.

His voice was low and teasing, and she shivered as it washed over her after a long week. "I took the day off to fix the railing and even went the extra step to paint it the color you wanted.... In the heat... and you're going to say it was a bit much?"

"Day off? It's summer. You already told me your schedule is more flexible."

That deep chuckle rolled through the phone lines. "I've missed you. I know it's only been a week but... Ella, can we move past this? I'm sorry I lost control. It wasn't planned, wasn't something I'm proud of. I don't apologize for coming to your defense. But I am sorry for the way I went about it."

She shut her eyes, his voice warming her. Knowing he was willing to apologize, hearing that he missed her... "I'm sorry, Dennis. I said some things..."

"You did. But if that is how you feel then we should discuss it. It bothers me that I gave you that impression... Ella, can I take you out to dinner?"

She agreed and that evening, as they sat across from each other in a low lit, cozy restaurant, Dennis was the first to bring up their fight. So far, they had averted such talk with subjects such as the weather, her last days at her job, and how he was preparing for the fall semester. But then he cleared his throat, his gaze pinning her in place.

And suddenly she felt vulnerable and silly, afraid of what

he was about to say and ashamed of her behavior. "Dennis. I'm sorry. Can we just leave it at that?"

"No. There is no possible way I can just leave it at that, Ella. Because you mean the world to me, and to think that those thoughts even skimmed the surface... let me just say this... I was raised to respect women. Respect everyone. And I do my best to follow that. I don't consider women booty calls. I don't just use women. And you, especially you. Ella, I have immense respect for you. I admire how you carry yourself even when you feel your world is collapsing. You have this grace and gentleness, this glow that follows you. And for you to think I treat you or think of you in a certain way, a negative away, I was quite frankly devastated. I am sorry for ever making you feel like that."

"Please stop." She looked down at her plate, her throat suddenly closing up with regret and shame. "I was just in a panic. I was upset and scared, and I lashed out at you. I'm truly sorry."

"Ella, I think that you're thinking I'm angry at you for saying that. I'm not. At all. Any volatile emotion I'm feeling is toward myself. And I know you were highly emotional that day. But it doesn't change the fact that you said it, and I have a feeling that you really do see it that way... even if just slightly."

Ella sighed and took a sip of the wine. She could feel his eyes still on her, waiting for her attention to return to him. Finally, she glanced up, and he continued, "I respect you, El. And every moment with you... it means everything to me. You mean everything to me. I want to make that clear."

"Okay."

"Okay?" He searched her face as if trying to find the truth, to determine her feelings. "If ever you feel that you're not being treated fairly or this... between us...isn't working for you, I hope you can talk to me. You can always talk to me. There's no reason to be nervous or scared..."

"I understand," Ella forced herself to say, her lips twisting up. Because she did not understand. He was saying a lot of words, claiming respect and caring for her... but that could mean as a friend... with benefits.

He must have sensed her confusion because he cursed and shook his head. "It isn't coming out right. Just..." Suddenly he leaned forward, locking eyes with her in such a manner she would not have been able to look away if she wanted. "Just know that from the first day I saw you, I knew that you were not just some ordinary woman. That you wouldn't play just a passing phase in my life if I were ever lucky enough to have you in my life."

And just like that, everything Ella thought she knew about Dennis... about their relationship... was suddenly not clear at all. But after that talk, they seemed to pick up right where they had left off. They talked and laughed, and Dennis complimented her in that intense, sincere way he had that made her blush. Ella felt not so unsure, a little more cheerful. Perhaps there was hope in moving beyond a broken marriage, a cracked spirit. Perhaps there was such a thing as better days ahead, even at her age.

Dennis walked her to the door, and Ella motioned inside. "I have this scary movie we can watch. It's an older one and -"

"Sweetheart." She stopped, her eyes lifting to meet his. "There is nothing more I'd like than to go inside and watch a movie with you. But we both know what's going to happen if I do."

A slight blush crept up her neck as she struggled to understand the problem. "Well... yes."

"Right. And El, I'm not trying to ... I want to be sure you know I'm here for the right reasons."

"Dennis...," she drew out. "I already know-"

"I'll call you later." He kissed her forehead, his lips pressing there for a long moment before he backed away, the corners of his lips tucked in to form a small smile.

Usually the start of the weekend was such a relief, a reprieve from the stress and misery her current job brought. But the idea of a Friday night alone... her mood sank. She called some of her friends and while most were busy or unavailable, a couple made plans for the following night. And she realized that for the first time in as long as she could remember, she would be going out dancing. It made the lonely night ahead not so bad.

A few hours later, Dennis called, asking if she had time to talk. Ella braced herself, thinking he would say that he did not want to see her again, but it soon became clear that he actually just wanted to … talk.

There was something so soothing and at the same time playfully erotic about talking to the man that had made her toes curl and nails pierce his skin. To simply talk on the phone made her feel pursued and young. Like a teenager flirting with her crush. His voice was low and husky as he flirted back, and then he asked about her… about her life. Their conversation grew deeper as they discussed childhoods, and Dennis confessed to being closer to his father. He described their fishing and hunting trips and how he was the one out of three boys that liked helping his father with house projects.

Dennis explained that he appreciated his dad's strong silent personality. He could be talkative and had joked around with Ella when she met him, but when Dennis was growing up, he knew his father as a man that thought before speaking. He could stand and stare during an entire conversation, never once tempted to throw in his opinion.

"I asked why he did that? If he just didn't like to talk," Dennis described. "And he told me that of course he liked to speak his mind, but it was more important to listen and learn when you could. He said a lot of people just argue without knowing what they're actually fighting against. And I love that about him. He listens. He tries to understand." There was a pause on the line, and then he continued, "I had a rough time in school. I had trouble reading, got behind, and would act out by talking or fidgeting. My mom and the teachers would get frustrated with me. Thought I was just being difficult. But dad, he took me out to the lake for a fishing day. We sat there in silence for much of the day, and then he simply asked, 'What's going on with you and school? What's wrong?' He didn't accuse, didn't scold… he listened. And when I tearfully explained that I couldn't read, he nodded his head and said, 'Listen, we're going to fix that. Don't be upset.' And… he fixed it."

Ella was transfixed on his voice, his story, his love and gratefulness for a father that had listened to a boy troubled. "Oh, Dennis, that had to be so hard on you. But look at you now!"

"Well, I had to work harder than most when I was younger. And that sort of set the pace for me. I just worked hard, and any obstacles… I just found a way to get past them. You do what you have to, but you know that better than anyone, El."

She warmed under his voice and his compliments. She tucked her feet under her and rested her head back on the sofa. She remembered when she and Alex had started dating. They talked on the phone at night, and he wanted to ask her questions, wanted to get to know her. She felt so special, ready to share those secrets he was seeking, thrilled he wanted to know more about her.

And his first question had been, "What kind of underwear do you wear?"

Of course, he had been a hormone-driven teenager, clumsy with any type of emotional intimacy. This, however… this was different. This was not a ploy to trick her into bed- she had already made it clear she was willing and ready. This was a man who wanted to know her as a person.

It almost seemed natural, the flow of the conversation, for her to bring up her own childhood. It was easy to talk to him, and although she spoke of only certain parts, it was still a brave push ahead. "My grandma was my support. I had my grandfather and of course, my dad. But my grandfather was so emotionally unavailable. No hugs or affection. It was always about if I got chores done or homework. How were my grades? Why wasn't I wearing dresses? He loved me, and I knew it at the time but still… And my dad … he didn't want to be a hands-on dad. He wanted to be out on his adventures. He would try. He would take time off… but even as a child,

I could see the restlessness slowly settling over him. Day by day, his eyes would glaze over even more. He usually lasted two weeks, maybe three before he was charging off to somewhere much more exciting than at home with aging parents and a clingy kid."

"How long was he gone?"

"Months, usually."

"Wow, Ellie, I'm sorry."

She folded her knees under her chin. "Hmmm, no. I had gram. It's okay. She and I were close, almost like friends. We had our movie nights. We went for walks every evening. In the summer, we would wake up early and walk for miles looking for yard sales. Just pack a thermos of iced tea, and go."

"That sounds like some really special memories, El. How old were you when they passed?"

"Grandpa died when I was twelve. Gram passed when I was fifteen. Dad had to come back. That was a rough couple of years. He tried. He really did. But it was obvious he did not want to be there. I was holding him back from what he loved. From what he was born to do."

"No-"

"I'm not being dramatic. You've seen his work. You're a fan. You know he was meant to be a photographer. And that meant traveling. For two years, his career was stunted. And as angry as he was over the pregnancy and as much as he hated Alex... there was a shimmer of relief. He was free again. And the fight between us through the years... just one less thing on his plate of responsibilities."

"El. I am sure being away from you ate him up inside. Things are rarely black and white."

Ella stood to pace, wishing she had not gotten started on the subject. "I agree. Dad loves me. I don't doubt that. But his passion, his entire reason for living was photography. I could not compete with that." She rushed to change the subject, fumbling through words and struggling to find a relevant topic. She was grateful when Dennis swiftly followed her cue and graciously took over the conversation as she recovered.

By the time they stopped talking, it was almost midnight. They had been on the phone over three hours. Ella marveled at how quickly time flew when talking with him. She wanted to keep him on the line for another three hours, but she stifled a yawn just as Dennis suggested they end the call and get some rest. And as tired as she was, it was another hour before she could settle the thoughts in her mind enough to drift off to sleep.

**

The morning sun rained down on Ella as she practically danced through the house. The heat was already stifling at almost 7 in the morning, but she did not mind it. Summer was always her favorite time of year, and after last night's call, she felt like it was indeed a sunshine frame of mind. Everything was warmer and brighter, dazzling in fact.

The knock at the door startled her, and Ella quickly ran down a list of people it could be. Her dad, perhaps. Alex's knock would be more insistent, almost entitled.

"Dennis?"

He stood there, taking her breath away so early in the morning, his grin a little sheepish as he held up a thermos. "Iced tea. I know you're getting ready to go fishing but … how about we walk to some yard sales and then I take you kayaking on a lake about an hour from here?" He motioned toward his truck, and she saw the kayaks. And she realized he had truly listened. She had rambled on about her childhood and grandparents, and Dennis had heard every word.

"Have you ever gone yard saling?" she asked, as his hand covered hers and they began to walk, the sun warming her all the way to her curling toes.

He grinned. "Yard saling. Is that the official name for it?" He chuckled and then staring ahead, nodded. "Yes. When I was really young, my mom would sometimes get in kicks where she would like to go. She'd load me and my brothers into the car, and we'd drive around. You can imagine us boys hated it, so she'd bribe us. If we were good and waited as she browsed, and we didn't touch or disrupt, then she'd take us out to lunch. Ice cream. She'd get us a new video game. Anything if we would just stop roughhousing on people's lawns."

She laughed and made a face. "So, this must be torture for you."

"No! I was just a little boy with enough energy to want to be anywhere but stuck at his mom's side looking at grown up stuff I couldn't buy. Now...," he squeezed her hand, "there's nothing I'd rather be doing."

Within two blocks, they found a few houses with scrawled writing on colorful poster boards announcing a sale. And they took their time browsing, showing each other their finds, laughing at private, unspoken jokes. Ella felt a part of something. She felt as if they were an extension of each other, in a way she had never experienced with Alex.

Alex might have gone along with her at one point in their relationship, but he would have made it clear he did not want to be there by standing back, arms crossed and mouth turned down.

Dennis was at her side, inspecting items and checking prices. Soon she found a box of books and immediately began sorting through them, silently cheering at some of the author's names. She glanced over and saw Dennis rooting through a box of records, the same excitement lighting his face.

"Don't even argue," he warned when he took the box from her and added it to his own. "I think I can find a few dollars to pay for it all." He gave her a wink, the same wink he gave again at the next yard sale when he bought the bronzed sun and moon wall hangings he had caught her admiring. By the time they started back to the house, they were each balancing boxes and items, laughing as they stopped to pick up one fallen treasure or another.

The lake Dennis took Ella to was on the border of Pennsylvania, close to Maryland. It was a quaint campground with a large, beautiful lake that included a boat dock and kayak launch. As they dragged the kayaks down the dirt path, Dennis suddenly stopped and held out an arm to stop her from walking forward.

"Careful. Snake."

She breathed through her mouth, a high rush of air as she strained forward, seeking out the very thing most women ran from. "Where?"

He leaned so that his cheek brushed against hers and pointed. "See? On the right side, half on the trail. He's looking at us." He straightened and motioned for her to go. "Go around me so you're not close to it."

"What kind is it?"

"See the eyes? The pupils are round. He's harmless. But still... walk around me. Bites are not fun whether venomous or not." He took her hand and guided her to the left of him, watching the snake as he did so. Once she was a safe distance, Dennis walked after her, watching the path. "I forgot that this place is infested. Be really careful, El."

Once they had their kayaks in the water, they paddled around, a sense of serenity settling over Ella. She always felt relaxed, at peace, while paddling around, sitting close to the water and floating... drifting.... rocking. How could one not be relaxed? Even when they raced, the rush through the water was exhilarating. This was how she had found her way through the dark during the first days of separation from Alex. This was how she had found her contentment and powered through such dreary times. It was those mornings as the fog lifted off the water, as the birds chirped and the sun fought through dawn, that Ella was given a smidgen of hope that things would someday be better. That she would be able to breathe through the pain, dance through the storm... that someday she would not feel as if every inch of her was shattered beyond repair... beyond being loved.

And now here she was... laughing and screaming as Dennis reached for her kayak as if to tip it over. Here she was playing and breathing and enjoying... falling in love. She cursed that last thought as it slid into the front of her mind. Falling in love was not practical. There was a divorce still in process. Most of all, the man currently frolicking with her was not the type to fall as well. No. He had his fun. He was respectful. He was charming. He meant no harm... but he meant no lifetime guarantee either.

Dennis set his paddle down and studied her. "You got serious all of a sudden."

And Ella worked on paddling to the side, away from him. "Just trying to get steady. So clumsy."

Despite the doubt shadowing his face, he chose to drop it. "I packed some sandwiches. Drinks. Cooler's in the truck. Ready for a break?"

They sat on the dock and ate, chatting between bites. Ella felt the discomfort melt away, and at one point, when he put his arm around her, she leaned against him without hesitation. She once again had no control in her life. Even though this felt good, even though this brought a true smile to her lips... it was again a situation where she was left powerless. That part niggled at the back of her mind, replacing discomfort with an unidentifiable sadness.

"I'd like to take you to dinner tonight, El." Dennis brushed her hair out of her face, smiling at her before giving her a soft, quick kiss.

Ella blinked and smiled back. "Oh. I can't. I'm going dancing."

Dennis leaned back on his elbows. "Dancing? Really? Should I be jealous?"

His words stung as they sounded a bit patronizing. As if she were just a silly girl he humored with his company. But she forced out a laugh and answered, "A few friends and I are going."

"Good for you."

By the time they pulled into her driveway, Ella was exhausted. They had spent several hours on the water, paddling and racing. Then they had walked on a nearby trail, catching sight of another snake. And their conversation rarely lagged, but they both avoided anything substantial.

And part of Ella wanted to invite Dennis in, planned to offer coffee and then perhaps convince him to stay longer. She wanted to cancel her plans with friends and seduce him. But she also wouldn't mind if he left, and she had a couple of hours to sleep before getting ready for that night.

But as soon as they pulled in, she saw her father sitting on her porch steps, waiting impatiently. When her feet hit the ground, he was up and striding across the yard. "Just what is going on?"

"Dad?" She stared at him blankly, trying not to react to him.

Ted gestured toward Dennis who stepped closer to Ella, his own expression blank. "Lila told me that you're not speaking to this guy. That you've been sullen and cranky, you've been crying all week. Now I come here, I've been calling and texting and don't hear from you-"

"No service where we were at," she informed him briskly, brushing past him.

He followed. "And where was that?"

"To the woods where he could murder me, dad. Why the hell do you need to know?" She heard Dennis breathe her name under his breath and realized he was right beside her, his hand on her shoulder as if to calm her. Staring up at him, she sighed. "Dad, why are you listening to the fifteen-year-old about my love life- I mean..." she cursed, anger flaring up like flames in her chest. "I mean, personal life."

As she brought out her phone and turned it on, Ted stepped toward her, his hand outstretched. "Wait. You mean, you haven't checked messages... haven't checked your voice-mail?"

"Dad. I had no service. I shut my phone off. Why? Is Lila okay?"

"She's fine, but ... give me a chance to explain before you go listening to any calls. Wait!"

His voice vibrated with a panic that stopped Ella, and she jerked her head up to stare at him, noticing his pale complexion, his wet eyes.

"Dad?" Fear smothered out the anger, but her tone was still sharp and loud. "Is Lila okay?"

"She's fine. Worried about you. Frankly, so am I. Because you're back with this guy after -"

"Dad! What was Lila doing at your place?"

"She stopped to visit. Wanted to show me some pictures. She was with that boy. The one - Fig? Or Finn..."

"You mean Brad. Tall. Big boy. Brown hair."

"No. Finn. Wavy red hair. Goofy grin. Can't take that kid for long. He laughs like a damned animal. He drove her to my place before."

"Before?"

"Yeah. She wanted to show me some pictures she took while she was hiking up the mountain. She got some good shots. But today... she caught me off guard. She ...She met her grandma."

Ella's mind worked to make sense of the words... grandma... met... and her blood ran cold. "Dad. What the hell do you mean? Who did my daughter meet?"

"Your mom."

For a few moments, her vision blurred and throat constricted. She stumbled back and felt Dennis's hands clasp her shoulders. "Mom? Diana? Where?" When Ted said nothing, she shook her head. "Not at grandma's house? Right, dad. Right? DAD!"

"Yes! We've been... seeing each other. She's actually been staying with me."

She straightened, shaking off Dennis's touch. "Get off my property, dad. You hear me? I knew you were a bad father but to know you're such a horrible person... get out of here, and don't you ever contact me again-"

"Ella, stop! You know that woman is the love of my life. Don't put me in this position."

"Like I did years ago, dad? When I was seven? Is that what you mean?"

And something snapped in her father's expression. "Stop. The past is the past. People change. People make mistakes."

"You're calling what she did... what I went through...just some mistake? And you've been lying to me-"

"What do you call what you've been doing?" Ted yelled, and Dennis stepped in between them. Ted glared at him and then leaned to the side to once again address his daughter. "You've lied to me over and over, Ella. About your life, your choices. What's this? Huh? This guy? Another mistake. Another dead end. He'll keep breaking your heart and shattering your spirit, and you'll keep taking him back. So don't get all judgmental with me. I gave up everything for you. I gave her up."

"For me?" Dennis felt himself being pushed as she shot past him and was again face-to-face with her dad. "For me? I was seven! You know what they did. You know what I suffered-" She stopped and shook her head. "I would never put my daughter through that."

"Didn't you just find yourself in the hospital? Don't tell me what you would or wouldn't do. Because I'm staring at a mistake right now. And that money? Your trust fund? Don't think I'm going to hand it over when you're just repeating the past-"

"You've been hanging that over my head for twenty years. Tell you what, father. You take your money, and you shove it up your ass. Take your crummy parenting, and shove that up your ass. You were the worst dad. You get that? The worst and - "

"El...." It was a soft brush of a whisper, but it was enough to ground her, and she turned and tilted her head up to Dennis, a sob breaking through. His fingers grazed her elbow, and Ella noticed he was careful with his touch, hesitant and gentle. "Let's go inside," he urged, his voice low... soothing.

As he led her away, she turned and managed between the sobs, "Worst dad ever. Stay away from my daughter." And she noticed with a stab of satisfaction that he was silently crying, large tears rolling down his face.

CHAPTER 11

Lila motioned to Finn to give her a minute, and she answered her phone, her heart pounding. "Mom, I've been trying to call-"

"Lila, your pap said you've been showing up with a boy with red hair-"

"Finn."

"Who's Finn? What happened to Brad?"

"Finn's a friend, mom." She turned her back to Finn's hurt expression. "Nothing happened to Brad. I just don't hang out with him every day."

Her mom's voice was strained, and Lila suspected that she had been crying. "I have never met this Finn. You're fifteen. I -"

"Mom! Dad's met him. I'm usually at dad's when we hang out. I'll bring him around one of these times, but he's just someone I know. Anyway, mom, are you all right?"

"I'm fine." Her voice was curt, sharp, and Lila blinked in surprise. "Just.. what's going on? You go to your pap's without letting me know-"

And fear of her mother's disappointment and misery propelled her into an angry, defensive response. "What - am I not allowed seeing my pap now? Mom, I was visiting your dad. How is that being twisted into a bad thing? Huh? I didn't know he had your mother there. I'm just tired of being in the middle of you and dad and now you and pap. I can't do this."

"Lila, I don't put you in the middle-"

"You do! You're doing it now. Look, I'm sorry I showed up at pap's when she was there. I left as soon as he said it was her, and I tried calling you and texting you. I did. So, I don't appreciate being made to feel like I've done something wrong. I love you.

I gotta go. See you Sunday night."

She turned and saw Finn staring at her, his expression unreadable. Slipping her phone into her pocket, Lila hissed, "What?"

"Kind of mean to your mom. I mean, you said she would be heartbroken over the deal with her parents and ...." He shrugged.

Tears burned her eyes as she stared up at him. "I know. I kind of freaked because she was asking who you are and ... I know."

"Well... who am I?" He shut his eyes and shook his head when she narrowed her eyes in confusion. "I mean, you and I hang out a lot. But you're still with that asshole."

"We're friends. You and I. Friends, right?"

"Sure." But his stare lingered as if he was waiting for more, for perhaps a correction to her statement. Then he jumped forward, his eyes imploring. "Listen... Brad... he's an idiot. I saw him yesterday.... At your locker."

She dropped her gaze and kicked at an invisible stone with her shoe. "That was nothing. Really."

"He was yelling, Lila. You're beautiful. And amazing and smart. He is too stupid to see that."

"Thanks for the smoke," she said, walking toward his car. "But dad's probably wondering where I am."

She heard Finn curse behind her and then heard his footsteps as he jogged to catch up with her. "Hungry? We can stop at the restaurant and grab a bite."

Lila had to admit, for being a pothead, Finn had his act relatively together. He was a shift lead at a local restaurant and always had spending money. And he loved spending it on her. As a friend, of course. Because Lila had Brad, and Brad was everything she wanted. Everything. He was just always under pressure with school and friends and family. It would all get better.

**

Ella waved Dennis away, swiping at her cheeks. "I'm fine. I have to take care of the situation with Lila before I even think about my dad or that woman. Okay? I have to deal with this first." She turned away from him and held the phone to her ear.

"Alex? Hey, do you think I could come get Lila? She spent last weekend there and-"

Alex's voice was hard and biting, and she knew he was still smarting over the incident with Dennis. "What? We worked out a system for a reason, Ella. No. Hold on." She heard his voice at a sudden distance shout, "Shut the hell up! Let me talk, Connie!"

And then Connie's shrill tone managed to reach Ella's ears. "Why is she calling you, Alex? Tell her to text or go through Lila!"

There was some more back and forth before Alex returned to the line. "Hey, not getting her. We have to go by the schedule we both agreed on."

"But I let her stay on weekends that should be mine."

"That's on you. She's fifteen, Ella. She should be able to decide where she wants to go."

"Do you know about some boy named Finn? Dad said Lila's been bringing him around and not Brad."

"Not going to be questioned about what I know as a parent, Ella-"

"No! Not what I'm trying to do. I-" She cursed as she realized he had ended the call. And it was then she finally faced Dennis, defeat and misery draining her energy, her will to fight.

Dennis was right there, his hands clasping her shoulders. "Take a breath, El."

"I'm losing sight of everything. I thought I had a fantastic relationship with my daughter-"

"You do, honey. It's great."

She raised her eyes to his. "I don't know the kids she is hanging out with. Fifteen and just riding in cars with people I don't know. And my dad... I really let myself think this time would be different."

"Maybe give him a chance to explain. You don't know what happened between then and now. Maybe she's different or -"

And she stepped back, away from the excuses and the hopes. Ella suddenly realized that this was nothing she had imagined it to be. Just like she had dreamed her father would be that man she had needed when she was young, she had envisioned an impossible love story with the man in front of her. And he had just spoken words everyone else had said a million times over. Give her another chance. She has changed.

But Ella knew her mother. She had met the very broken soul of that woman when she was just a child and knew even then that there was nothing to change that character, that demented personality. But everyone always cheered for the mother. Mothers were naturally loving, right? Mothers had their children's best interests at heart. So, all of her life, people encouraged Ella to reach out to her mother and make amends. As if her seven-year-old self had a part in the nightmare that happened. As if she could have stopped it. Make amends. Forgive.

All her life, Ella had felt that her mother was more the victim in other people's eyes. Poor, poor mother could not get a break. She had had Ella so young, no chance to have fun and be carefree. A wife and mother before most people finished college partying. Of course, she was stressed. Of course, she would break. And now her selfish, ungrateful daughter was so bitter as to not allow another chance. Children could be so difficult.

Ella felt that blame, that misplaced responsibility over her mother's mistakes come at her full force, so she put distance between herself and Dennis and calmly said, "I need to get ready for tonight. You can go."

Dennis studied her as if he knew, as if he could read her thoughts and unnerved, she turned away. "El. You're upset-"

"I'm actually fine." With a sigh, she turned back to him. "I'll be fine. Just go. I'm going to go out with my friends and have fun. No sense in sitting around sulking."

"Are you going to be drinking?"

"Hopefully."

A brief smile passed his lips. Then he pointed a finger at her. "Do you need a designated driver? Don't even think about driving if you're drinking, El."

"I wasn't going to." But she knew her expression gave away that she had not thought that far ahead.

"Listen, I can drive you. Drop you off. Or call me. I'll pick you up from wherever you're at."

She shut her eyes and nodded solemnly. "Yes. I will. If I need a ride."

And for a few moments there was a strained silence until she opened her eyes and saw resignation flashing in his own eyes. He gave a quick nod. "Okay. I want to do more. I want to listen and fix this. I want you to open up to me. But I can't make you do that."

She sighed wearily. "I'm trying to just...it's all at once, and I still have to process it all, Dennis. This isn't personal. I'm not trying to..."

"What he said out there... Your dad... about me. About us. He's full of shit. He doesn't have a clue about what this is. Got it?"

She nodded because it was the only thing she could think to do. At this moment, she did not have the strength to reassure him, to believe his words and to hope. Those were luxuries for people with beautiful features, slim bodies, and a past full of loving, supportive families. Those were not for middle-aged frumpy women who had never known the comforts of true families.

**

The club was not too packed, and Ella was pleased to see it was an older crowd. There would have been nothing worse than stomping her way through a crowd of twenty-some-things that were still new to the idea of legal drinking. No, her time was better spent in a quieter place with her friends.

"Are you okay?" Leona asked, raising her voice to be heard over the music.

Ella motioned to the bartender, nodding. "Fine. Just want to forget the day and focus on having fun."

Carla popped up beside her. "Then let's do shots. And dance! Bill is home with the kids. I'm good to go."

Ella already felt the effects of the drinks she had chugged. But she waved on the shots, ignoring Leona's pointed stare. She could always tell her moods, sense when something was off, and while Ella appreciated that perception and depth of their friendship, she did not want to talk about it. Instead, she turned to Carla. "How is Bill? How are things between you?"

Carla burst out laughing. "What? Why? You know something I don't?"

"No," Leona leaned forward, waving an empty shot glass toward them. "She is asking because she's all into the new guy, and she wants to know how your second marriage is going."

The shots were taking effect, and all three girls burst out laughing. After catching her breath, Carla revealed, "It's good. He's a great guy, and I'm happy. I think because I was older, I had a better idea of who I was and what I wanted so this time around... yeah. It's good. And holy shit, this is the guy at your dinner party?" When Ella confirmed it with a nod, she continued, "Keep a tight hold on that one. He's ridiculously hot and was hanging all over you all night."

Leona wagged her finger at Carla. "She has a good point. You were so young with Alex. And we all knew ... anyways, this time around... do what is good for you."

Ella laughed, reaching for her drink. "You guys, I'm not even divorced yet."

It was not long before they were on the dance floor, giggling like young girls and not caring who watched. This was something Ella had not done during her marriage. Alex hated going out anywhere, especially to clubs. And he stressed the fact that married women should not be seen in such places alone. She had never argued, thinking she could live without a night out. Thinking she could live happily just staying in their cozy home being a happy family. But looking back, she realized she had not been happy. She had been numb. Ella had been willing to live in a muted state with dulled senses just to keep her family intact. And Alex had not been so willing.

With a jolt, she realized he had saved her from more years of living a shell of a life. He had cut that rope, or at least given her the scissors to cut and set herself free. They had not even really been friends by the end of the relationship. Just casual acquaintances passing each other in the hall each afternoon, nodding hello, trying to suck up enough energy to tell each other about their day. To communicate and get through another evening of their farce of a marriage. How had she mistaken that for a life? For happiness? Hell, she had not even been content except on the evenings he worked, and she had the house to herself. The days she and Lila went shopping or out to eat, the times she and her daughter took a road trip together. Those were the true glimpses into happiness, and she saw it now. Ella was fairly sure she saw it then too but was too scared to change anything. Growing up, all she had ever wanted was a family. That had colored her choices.

"Hey, you still with us?" Leona waved a hand in front of her and when she had her attention, grinned. "Feeling pretty good? Can't hear your phone ringing?"

Ella gasped, realizing that it was not part of the music. Moving off the dance floor, she wedged herself in a narrow space away from the noise. "Hello?"

Dennis's chuckle came through the line, and she relaxed, relieved it was not a crisis with Lila. "Hey you. I got your texts. I'm going to assume you've had a bit to drink."

"Why? What do you mean?"

Again, he laughed. "The texts made no sense, except for a few crude words. So where are you at?"

Ella forgot about the phone call until twenty minutes later when Carla grabbed her hand. "Your second husband is here."

"Huh?" She followed her gaze and tried to hold back a smile. "Don't call him that, Carla! He's just a friend."

"Right. Because friends just come all the way out here on a Saturday night to take care of their drunk friend. Sure."

She lifted her hand and called out, "Dennis! Dennis, she's over here." Carla grabbed Ella's arm and hissed, "Act drunk."

As the room spun, she fought the urge to insist no acting was needed. Dennis grinned as he strode up to her. "Well, look at this. Can't stand straight but still the prettiest woman in the room." He leaned forward and asked, "How are you?"

Ella took his hand and spun herself under it. "Great. Lila called me back and apologized. Said she would bring that boy up for me to meet next weekend. I told her I was going out, and she told me to have a great time. So, I'm better."

She stopped moving, and Dennis seemed to read her mind. "Want some water?"

He led her to a small booth in the corner of the front bar, and he motioned toward Leona. "She okay? Does she know that guy?"

Ella sat up and squinted. "Oh yeah. That's Razz. They sort of, kind of date off and on. It looks like right now it's on."

After getting her a plate of fries, insisting she should get something in her stomach, Dennis asked, "What's the plan? Are we staying until closing? Leaving now? Want me to go hide so you can have fun without me hovering?"

Ella's mouth was full of hot fries and after gulping down some water, she vehemently shook her head. "No! Why would I want you to go away? Can we stay a little longer though?"

"Whatever you want."

"Dance with me?"

"Of course."

By the time she had eaten the fries and finished the water, the nausea was gone, and she was more aware, sobering up. She led Dennis out to the dance floor, ignoring the girls' teasing glances, and although she was still a bit uncoordinated, Ella managed to follow his steps. It did not hurt that she hung on to him for balance.

And suddenly she straightened, her feet still, and he tightened his hold on her. She asked quietly, "How long?"

His voice was low, any humor gone. "Since I got here. I didn't want to worry you. You were having such a great time after the day you had..."

She pulled away and gave him a smile. "Can you give me a minute?"

"El, I really don't think you should-"

"I'm fine. I'm not going to cause a scene. I promise. Then we can go. Okay?"

His mouth was set in a grim line as he gave one short nod. She rose up on her toes and kissed his cheek, her own lips lifting when his face broke into a wide grin. "One minute," she repeated and then turned and made her way toward Connie.

Connie was flanked by two of her own friends, one a cute, short brunette, and one that was probably her sister. The second one was just as tall and shapeless and despite the makeup, had a plain look about her. Ella glanced down and noticed that Connie was drinking water, and for that, she was relieved.

Connie wasted no time confronting her. "Don't call Alex anymore. There's no reason to when you can text or go through Lila."

Ella smiled and waited for a few beats, letting Connie know she would not be intimidated or pushed to overreact. When Connie seemed to shrink back, she widened her smile and responded, "I will call him whenever I feel the need. Whenever I need to check on my daughter or get information about my daughter... I will call. I will not go through Lila. That's putting her in the middle. Don't worry. I do not want that man back. Do you see him?" She leaned to the side and pointed at Dennis who was still watching them carefully. "Why the hell would I go back to some cheating bastard when I have that waiting for me? So, here's some free advice, Connie. Leave here. Go home. Tell my no-good husband to sign the divorce papers. Have him show you, Connie, that I have signed them. They've been signed by me for months. Just waiting for him now. And despite what he might tell you - I don't want his money. I am not fighting visitation. I just want a divorce. And if you keep following me, let me make this abundantly clear. I will take action. Your baby will be born in a jail cell. Leave me alone. Make a life with my ex. Go be happy."

She managed to walk away without stumbling, and never paused when she heard Connie's friend mutter, "Fat bitch."

As soon as she reached Dennis, he grabbed her and tilted her back as he kissed her passionately. She heard Carla and the other women cheering loudly. She never glanced behind her to see Connie's reaction. There was no need. She felt the glare sear through her, and she knew this was far from over.

**

"Are you asleep?"

Ella became aware of the stillness, the lack of motion that had lulled her to sleep, and she opened her eyes and smiled as Dennis watched her. "Hey you."

"Hey you. We're here."

Connie's friends had tried to extend the confrontation, following her into the dance floor and yelling insults. When she and Dennis made their way outside, the brunette was right on their heels, screaming as if they had stolen her first born. Dennis paused at one point, but Ella tugged on his hand, urging him to just get her out of there.

And once they were in the car, they both agreed it was not a good idea for her to go home. Even the security system did not ease Ella's discomfort. Those girls wanted a fight, some type of drama that women that age should not crave. It made her uneasy, so it did not take much for Dennis to convince her to spend the night at his place.

She had seen his house from the outside before, when he had made a quick detour to pick up some fishing rods. At the time, Dennis had insisted his house was too much of a mess to allow her in. But now he led her in, his hand on her back as if to steady her.

His house was an impressive ranch style house with a large front porch that immediately drew her in. Tan with green shutters, warm and inviting. Inside, it was a mish mosh of large, soft furniture in neutral colors. There was not much on the walls. Not many personal items laid out for view. But it was neat and orderly, and she had to wonder if his house had really been too messy for her or if he had wanted to keep this private. To keep her at a distance.

"I'm not tired anymore," she stated softly, and he nodded as if he had expected that.

"We can stay up. I'll put a movie in."

Ella changed into a shirt and sweatpants of Dennis's, feeling warm and safe in the oversized items. And back in the living room, she sat close to him, resting against him as the movie started. Every so often she would shift to get more comfortable, a little closer, and he would adjust his arm around her, stroke her hair and ask if she was okay.

And perhaps it was the alcohol. Perhaps it was feeling sheltered in his clothing. Maybe it was knowing that Dennis was someone she could trust, hoping he was the guy that would listen. But suddenly she was voicing memories she had not said out loud in years.

"My mom broke my arm."

Dennis straightened, careful to keep his arm around her, his eyes taking her in with shock and sympathy. He reached out with his free hand to grab the remote and turn the sound off. "Ella… are you sure you're up for talking about this?"

She lifted a shoulder. "I don't have to if it makes you-"

"No. I'm here. You want to talk, honey, I'm here. She …. She broke your arm? How old were you?"

"Seven. She was …" She swallowed, realizing this was more difficult than she had ever imagined. This was the tragedy that had set the course of her life. It was the beginning of an ongoing nightmare that still haunted her. "My mom was having an affair. She would take me along on dates and to his house. They'd lock the bedroom door while I was out in the living room. I knew this because I'd get scared and try to find my mom. I'd hear noises...moans and it scared me more, and I'd yell and cry. She'd get mad and hit me. The guy would scream at me. And I told my dad." She sat up and moved away, needing space as the memories cascaded into her consciousness like a damaging waterfall. Dennis pulled his hands back, understanding flooding his eyes.

"I told my dad. I was the one to cut him off at the knees. I was the one to devastate him, to destroy his life. Because my mom… she was his life. I think she even came before his photography. And I was the person to just take all that away."

"Wait." Dennis edged forward, rubbing his face. "Wait. You were seven. She destroyed their life together, she pulled apart your world. Her child's world. Her actions did that."

"But if I'd kept my mouth shut."

"Bullshit! Honey, I'm sorry. But you know better. You know you did not do this."

Ella swung her wet gaze to him. "Fine. I know it. But I also know my dad thinks of it that way. I'm the one that told him his world was over."

"And your arm?" He almost looked angry, tense, and Ella knew it was simply his reaction to the thought of a child being hurt. But it still made her nervous. Somehow, he sensed that. "I'm sorry. I just… you were just a baby, El."

"I told dad. He was absolutely crushed, and he left her. Well… he left to go on a photography job. And mom was furious with me. She screamed and raged…. she moved the guy in immediately, and while she had never been the most doting mother, her demeanor changed drastically."

"Drugs?"

She paused, considering this. "Oh. That would make sense. Maybe. I don't know. But I know one particular night, she was upset and yanked me out of the bathtub. Threw me against the wall, and I landed on my arm… I screamed anytime I saw her after that. And dad had no choice but to take me in."

"Ella, you were his daughter. I'm sure-"

"He told me. When I was twelve, I mouthed off to him and he told me he had never wanted kids. That he only agreed to have me so mom would stay with him and now he was stuck with a kid he didn't want, and he had lost the love of his life.

He said that. And you can tell me he didn't mean it. You can assure me that the man loves me, and I'm sure that the obligatory love is there. But I'll always be the one that destroyed his life. Not my mom. Me."

And as if he could not hold back any longer, Dennis edged closer and drew her into his arms. "I'm so sorry. Ella, I'm sorry they let you down. And I'm sorry I ever suggested you should allow her back into your life. Knowing the story now, I get it. I understand."

It was the first time someone had told her that she was right in feeling as she did. The first time her feelings were validated, and it was as if years of struggle and anger melted away, and her body sagged in relief and exhaustion. And she slept solid until she woke up in his bed the next morning.

Shuffling into the kitchen, she saw he had the table set and was working on a stack of pancakes. "Don't you ever sleep in, Reeves?"

He turned and grinned. "Yeah. When I don't have drunk women to cook for. Speaking of which, is the smell of food making you sick?"

"What? No way. I'm starving."

"Ah. One of those. Good. Impressive."

Once they were seated, he sat back and studied her. "You're okay? I mean... "

Ella finished chewing and then narrowed her eyes. "Well. I woke up in your bed. So, I am trying to guess all that happened."

Dennis's mouth fell open, and he dropped his fork. "Ella Barnes, you are kidding, right? Because I slept on the couch. I would never -"

"I am kidding. Sorry. Just a joke."

Picking up his fork, he shot her a dark glance. "Well, not funny. Speaking of which... I'm feeling guilty because you told me some things... do you remember?"

"I was drunk. Not unconscious. I remember. And don't feel guilty. I felt like confiding in you. That's all."

"But I pressured you before, and maybe I should have-"

"Dennis. It's okay. I would have told you sober. Thanks for listening. Thank you... for everything."

His shoulders seemed to drop in relief as he exhaled and nodded. And while her words were sincere, Ella did her best to steer the conversation away from that. She wanted to be seen as more than a victim. She wanted Dennis to admire her for the woman she was, not the stuff she went through. But if he saw her as the woman she was, Ella feared he would not be around much longer.

CHAPTER 12

It was a few short weeks before classes started, and Dennis had a lot to get done. Too much, in fact. But Sheena had stopped by his office just as he had arrived, and her observations had him worried enough that nothing would get done until he got to the bottom of it.

Today was Ella's first day. She had rejected his suggestion of driving to work together, and he had not even had a chance to check in with her before her new boss was seeking him out.

"She's great, Dennis. Just great. Already hard at work. But I think something's happening. She got a call and came back all red-faced and flustered. We're all going out to lunch and invited her. She refused. Might want to check on her. Otherwise though, she's perfect. Already catching on faster than I could have hoped."

He thanked Sheena for the update and immediately made his way down the hall. Taking a sharp left, he walked a few more feet and landed right outside the large room that housed Ella's new office that she shared with her immediate supervisor Amber.

Knocking, he pushed open the door and stepped inside. Ella looked tiny in the large room, and before seeing it was him, she wiped tears from her face.

"Ella?" He was at her side in an instant, squatting so they were at eye level. "Honey, what is it?" He waited and when it was obvious she was about to break down, he stood and nudged her up.

Once they were safely in the privacy of his office, she broke down crying. "He took it all."

"What?" Alarm ran through him, and he had a slight inkling

of what she was going to say. "Who took what, Ella? Ella, who took what?"

"Alex was mad I told Connie about the divorce. He was upset because he didn't want her to know he was the one holding it up. And my bank account still has his name on it because the divorce isn't final. But he had already taken his portion of the money out when we split up, and we agreed... But today the bank called. I'm overdrawn. Because he took everything out. All of it. My bills are going to - I can't even-"

Her body shook, and Dennis pulled her close, surprised when she suddenly clung to him. Her strength was amazing, and he knew how scary this must be for her. She was a struggling single mother. It was already difficult for her because he knew she had little support. He already knew she would not ask her father for help. As she trembled in his arms, he felt her fear. How could she pay bills or buy food for her daughter? How would she get through the next couple weeks until she was paid again?

"Listen," he softly insisted, stroking her back as she hiccupped from suppressed sobs. "Listen, baby, it's going to be okay. I'll lend you-"

"No!" Ella flew out of his arms and shook her head. "No. I won't take your money."

Dennis waited patiently as she fussed and protested. Then when she quieted down, he continued, "I'm going to lend you money so your bills get paid, and you can live. It's fine, Ella. It isn't a big deal-"

"Yes, it is!" Her eyes were wild, and Dennis understood that she felt cornered. She was not the type to accept help. To be obligated.

"Okay. Big deal. That asshole took money that was yours, that was for your daughter. But listen, he's not going to win. Because you have friends. I'm a friend. And it's not a problem to lend you money. I promise it isn't. But we need to act fast and get money in your account so you're not overdrafting on all your bills. Okay? I know this is difficult, and I know you are so strong and independent, but right now, you need some help. And that's okay."

Dennis knew she would not honestly answer if he asked how much she needed, so he asked no such questions. He took charge and drove her to her bank, and within thirty minutes, it was taken care of, with precautions against her ex repeating the same offense. Then he convinced her to meet him after work at a lawyer's office, a friend of his. Because her lawyer was extracting money without doing much of anything. And this needed to change.

"I know you tried playing nice and keeping the peace, but he can't keep doing this. Ella, you need someone that can properly represent and protect you."

Dennis was shocked when she simply whispered, "Okay." It was then he knew how close she was to breaking. To succumbing to emotional exhaustion and sadness. And he once again felt an intensely strong urge to protect her. To show her that not everyone would suck her strength from her and simply leave. But he remained quiet, not feeling he yet had the right to promise such things.

Despite not knowing each other long, they knew each other well. Because as they left the lawyer's office, after she thanked him, she took his hand and softly insisted, "Don't go there."

"Huh?" he stuttered, thrown off guard because he had already been planning.

But Ella stopped walking and waited for him to turn and face her. Then she repeated, "Don't go there. Do not try to find Alex and ... please. I don't want to worry about you getting in any type of trouble. Promise me?" When Dennis sighed and ran his hand through his hair, torn between easing her mind and relieving his pent up fury at a man too petty to do the right thing, she stared up at him imploringly with wet eyes, and he half twisted around and cursed. "Dennis, please. Don't give me more to worry about."

"Fine. Ella, I won't." He reached out and pulled her to him, kissing the top of her head. "I promise."

And when she flashed her smile up at him, he relented with one of his own. It was the first time that day she had smiled, and there was something so consuming about knowing he was the reason for it. Frightening and exhilarating. Dennis did not know if he should run or profess his undying love, and that alone set off warning bells he tried to ignore.

**

Dennis knew it sounded corny and old-fashioned, but his favorite part of weekends with Ella - well, second to the obvious - was holding her in his arms. Because Ella was more relaxed and told him things she normally would guard from him. He loved the smell of her wild, tangled hair and the flush of her skin as they both tried to catch their breath.

And usually he ignored his phone. But it just happened to be within sight, and he saw the name of the person texting him. And with a groan, he sat up, unraveling his arms from her body.

Reading the texts, Dennis cursed and then leaned back against the headboard, staring down at Ella. "Honey. I have to go do something really quick."

Ella sat up, holding the sheet against her body. He had to smile at her modesty when what they had just finished doing was scandalously naughty. There was such a pure sweetness to her that soothed him, and for a moment, he forgot his mission. Then she asked, "Is everything okay?"

He paused. "It will be. I should be back. If I'm held up, I'll call. Okay? Can you keep the bed warm for me?" He inched toward her for a kiss, grabbing the sheet in the process and pulling it away, laughing as she squealed. But then he pulled back. "You trust me when I tell you that this doesn't… "

Ella gave him a smile. "Go do what you have to do. It's fine. I'm here."

It took Dennis twenty minutes to get to the address provided, and he bit back a curse as he saw the party spilling out into the yard, music pumping and people screaming. "Stupid kids," he muttered, slamming out of his car and marching across the street. There on the curb was Lila with a young boy sitting next to her.

"Are you okay?" Dennis asked immediately in mid-stride, seeing her tear-streaked face.

"I'm fine."

He stopped in front of the couple and pointed to the guy who immediately stood as he was addressed, his electric blue eyes wide. "And you are?"

"I'm Finn, sir."

"Finn. You were with her tonight and managed to drink to the point of not being able to drive?"

Dennis had to hand it to Finn, the boy stood straight and made solid eye contact. "Sir, I didn't drink. I'm really stoned."

He squeezed his eyes shut. "Not any better, buddy."

"But wait, I wasn't with Lila. Or I would have made sure I could drive her safely. She…" He stared down at the despondent girl who shrugged her indifference at what he was going to say. Finn looked back up at Dennis. "She was with Brad. They had an … an unfortunate disagreement, and he left her in a parking lot. She walked here. Just a few blocks. I don't feel safe driving her in this condition. I'm really, really stoned."

Dennis sank to his haunches and addressed the young girl. "Lila. Are you okay? Did Brad hurt you?"

She gave that half-shrug that her mother did so well. "No. He just yelled. Said some pretty shitty things."

"Pushed her," Finn exploded, his face becoming red.

"Finn!" She glared up at him. Then added, "He just sort of nudged me out of the car."

"Was the car moving, Lila?"

"No."

He nodded, trying to contain his anger. He focused his attention on Finn. "Do you need a ride home, Finn?"

"No, thank you. I'm going to crash here tonight. I just didn't think it was a good place for Lila to stay though."

Dennis stood. "Thank you for not driving her in your condition."

"Sir, if I'd known she would need a ride, I would have ensured I was capable."

"Well, it's a good thing you didn't try to drive. You kids did the right thing. Lila, ready?" He helped her to her feet.

"Thanks, Dennis. Can you take me to dad's? Maybe drop me off a block away so ... you know. Dad sorta hates you." She smiled so innocently that he chuckled and nodded.

In the car, he tried to broach the subject casually. To not sound like he was lecturing. Because he was a middle-aged man that had no children. He was not sure how to approach this. "Lila. Listen, not my business except you did have me come out here. But Brad... if that asshole just leaves you in the middle of nowhere... if he is saying shitty things to you... that's not right. It is not acceptable. Understand?" The more he talked, the more Dennis was determined to make her see. "You are to be treated with respect. Give respect, expect respect. Learn to do that now while you're young before-"

"Before I end up married and trapped with an asshole like mom was with dad?"

"Lila. I didn't say that."

"Did you punch my dad?" She asked with a curious tone, no malice. "He stormed out of the house the one day and came back with a bloody face and a fucked up back. He said he fell. On his face."

"Not discussing this with you, Lila."

"I know it was you. And I just want to know what he did or said to push you to that. Because you seem like a really calm, cool person."

Dennis gave her a slight smile, his eyes still on the road. "Thanks for the compliment. But still not discussing this with you. Not because you're not mature enough or intelligent enough. You obviously are. But because you deserve to have an excellent relationship with both parents and not be bogged down by anything trivial."

He could feel her stare, and he tried to smuggle a grin. Then she asked, "Do you like my mom?"

"Lila!" A laugh spilled out of his mouth. "What? Of course, I like your mom."

"I mean really like her. My mom's beautiful. She's the nicest, funniest woman around."

"Lila." He glanced at her with a solemn look. "You don't have to sell me on her. She's amazing."

"Right. I'm just saying I think she likes you."

"I'm glad."

"And you'd be cool to have around. If you stick around, I mean. You don't get on my nerves. But you've been single a long time and -"

"Hun, again, don't worry yourself about any of this. Okay?"

She sighed heavily as if he had said the dumbest thing ever. "It's my mom, Dennis. I worry."

Dennis pressed his lips together, not sure what to say to this precocious teen. Her intentions were the best, and he even wondered if maybe she was right to ask. This was her mother, and she had watched her go through hell this past year. Her point was obvious.

But still he avoided any answers. "Listen, you and this Brad…"

"He was just in a mood. He's usually-"

"Lila. Please, promise me you'll at least step back and evaluate the relationship." He wanted to add that she was so young, too young, to find herself in such a dark, restricting relationship, but he knew that would sound patronizing. And what age, exactly, was a good age for such a toxic experience? So, he merely added, "You don't deserve that treatment." When his words were met with silence, he simply hoped she would hear some of his advice. To both change the subject and get some information, he requested, "Tell me about Finn."

"He's just a friend I like to hang out with. He's funny and sweet. I don't have to worry about much when I hang out with him. I'm not being asked what I'm doing or thinking or why I said what I said. I don't have to be careful because Finn doesn't have a temper."

"He smokes a lot?"

"When he isn't working. He doesn't drink though."

Dennis bit his tongue because the last thing this girl wanted was a lecture. He threw some more words of caution her way as he pulled up just outside her father's house. He did not give a shit if the man saw him or not, but to keep the peace for Lila and Ella's sake, he did park so the large oak tree in the front hid him from view.

**

Lila threw her dad a smile that displayed her dimples. "Daddy, it's fine. I'm just going with Finn."

As predicted, his attempt at sternness melted faster than ice cubes in the mid-August heat. "Okay. Text me in about an hour or so."

And she knew even as she agreed with a kiss on his cheek that no text was necessary. Her father had his hands full with Connie and their baby on the way. While Lila liked Connie, she knew the woman played havoc with her dad's nerves. He did not want to add to his list of responsibilities or concerns so he was far less likely to reinforce any rules. And if Connie attempted to step in as a guardian, her father became resentful as if it were an insult to his parenting abilities. Lila was able to play this household like a violin, and after the disruption her own young life had suffered, Lila blocked out any guilt for using it all to her advantage.

"Was your mom's boyfriend mad?" Finn asked as soon as she slipped into the car.

"Nope. Worried, maybe."

"He seemed really nice."

She nodded absently. "He didn't yell when you admitted to being stoned out of your mind."

There was an infuriating chuckle as he pulled out onto the road. "Yeah. But how are you feeling? How's your ..." He reached out tentatively and when she made no move to stop him, he gently pulled her pants down just enough to show the severe brush burn on her hip. "Still looks so sore."

Lila flinched as the denim brushed against the broken skin,

and Finn put a hand on her shoulder in apology. She shot him a smile. "Thanks for helping to clean it out. And for not blabbing to Dennis what happened."

"That the asshole threw you out of a moving car."

"It was almost stopped, Finn."

He stared straight ahead as he drove, his jaw twitching. It was one of the few times Lila had seen him upset, let alone outright angry, and it was unsettling. She reached out and placed her hand over his on the steering wheel. "I'm sorry."

Startled, he glanced over at her. "Sorry? What'd you do?"

"You just seem…"

"Not at you. You know what has me mad." He exhaled and then his words were tumbling out. "That's not true. I'm a little mad at you. I am. Because he is such an asshole, Li. Such an asshole and …. Never mind. I don't want you to think you can't come to me. Because you can." He pulled into his driveway and shut off the car, turning to her. "Li. No." He leaned forward and awkwardly drew her into a hug. "Don't cry."

She sniffed, pushing away from him as she struggled for composure. "I just … you're a good friend. And everything is just… my parents and Brad and … I can't catch my breath. The last thing I want to do is make you mad."

She was surprised when he did not immediately reassure her. Instead, Finn advised, "Just be careful and use your head. If he's being a jerk, odds are he is just a jerk. And no amount of attention is worth spending time with a jerk."

"Not why I'm with him."

"Maybe not the entire reason." He sighed, raising his eyebrows. "Let's go inside and see if we can keep that from getting infected. Okay?"

And Lila knew that even a stoner like Finn would have his limits. She could only push people so far before they turned on her. And it was a sick sort of game to see just how far. Before she was completely alone.

**

The second week into the new job, and Ella was pinching

herself. The department of ten was beyond amazing and help-ful. Their boss took them out for lunches, and the job itself was gratifying. She was learning new things every day. There was little stress, at least as compared to her former job.

And Dennis was right down the hall. As she typed the last of the article she was working on, she felt someone behind her, and a grin bloomed on her face as his breath hit her neck.

"Do I get to steal you away for lunch or do you have other commitments?"

Carefully, she spun around in her chair and almost bumped noses with him. Still hunched over, Dennis stole a look around the office and then leaned even closer for a kiss. "Hey," she scolded gently. "Not here. You know that. And yes, I'm free."

As they walked the few blocks to a Thai restaurant, they talked about his classes and her job. They joked about see-ing too much of each other during the day to possibly want more, although they both knew they did. And when they were seated in a private corner away from the lunch chaos, Ella leaned toward him.

"Saw the lawyer. Asked about payments."

If she thought Dennis would be chagrined at being caught, she was wrong. He maintained eye contact and sat back. "Right. Just say it, El."

"You paid him?"

"He was my suggestion. So yes, I paid him. Take it for what it is."

"Charity."

Irritation flashed across his face. "Come on! Stop that. You are the strongest person I know. I'm just helping out a friend."

The word friend was enough of a slap in the face to shut her up. It was a way for him to avoid any type of twisted misun-derstanding. Friend.

With a forced smile, she pushed an envelope across the table. "Along the same lines, here. The loan. Paid in full." He tilted his head, and she confirmed, "I got my money back. He returned it."

"And you're sure you don't need this? For anything. House repairs, car payments... because it isn't necessary to repay so soon-"

With a gentle smile, Ella reached over and covered his hand with her own. "Thank you. From the bottom of my heart, thank you for your help with this. But I promise I am good now."

He lifted her hand to his lips for a quick kiss, his eyes never leaving hers. "Would you tell me if you weren't?"

"Yes."

And he nodded, releasing her hand to reach for the menu. "Did Amber tell you about my online course?"

"A little. You're requesting me to work on it? It's a bit much, Reeves."

He pretended to be offended. "What? Why, Ella, that's a bit presumptuous. I need a writer's eyes on this. You're the editor of the department, are you not? So yes, I requested the editor. Or are you too busy and important to help out a professor?"

"Now you're being mean," Ella snapped, her head tilted and fingers gripping the edge of the table.

"No. Just teasing." But his eyes seemed to glaze over, and his tone had an edge, as if he were suddenly a distance away. It was occurring more frequently, Ella noticed, and she could only hope it had nothing to do with her. But he surprised her when he said, "I'm going to miss you next week."

"It's only a few days. Right?"

Dennis had taken a few days off to help his father with a remodel of his parents' kitchen. His younger brother Sam would be in town to assist as well. "Yes. Taking off just three days. But I like coming to work. There's this unbelievably gorgeous woman down the hall from me that I keep requesting help from..." He grinned and dodged her balled up napkin. "Seriously, maybe I could convince you to come over to my parents' one of those days for dinner. You and Lila."

"Maybe. I might be busy. There's this professor at work, he can be such an ass. He's going to be out next week, and I'm sure he'll leave a shitload of work for me to do."

**

Lila found herself backing away from Brad out of pure instinct... fear. It was that flat tone, the forced words, and the snarl of his lips. She knew enough about him by now to know she was in the danger zone of his mood. Even worse, she was the cause of the mood.

"Carl said he saw you two together. Are you calling him a liar? Because I can call him over right now-"

"No! I told you we're friends."

"And I told you he's a freak piece of dirt that I didn't want you to go anywhere near! It's embarrassing to be told your girlfriend is hanging around some scumbag." Suddenly, Brad's body sagged. "You know what? You're not worth this trouble."

And that hurt more than anything physical. He wanted to simply toss her aside. Lila jumped toward him, her hands reaching for him. "Wait! No, listen. Just listen to me, he was just a friend. Not even that. Finn follows me around. If you don't like it, Brad, then I won't go near him. Okay?"

"I don't like it."

"Fine. Then I won't-"

"You know what?" Brad raised an eyebrow and smiled. "That freshman with the dark curls... Josie? She seems like the type that wouldn't mind keeping me happy. She gives great blowjobs too-"

"Fuck you!" Lila was all for playing along until he wanted to make an ass out of her. She'd heard the rumors about him and Josie disappearing into a closet at the party the other night. She had heard and chosen not to believe but now-

"What?" He lunged forward and grabbed her arm, twisting it so that she was on her knees in an instant. He shoved her then grabbed her hair. "Listen to me, Lila. Don't you dare fuck with me. I'll ruin your life. Got it?"

Lila curled into a ball, not sure if the rage was over, if her punishment was over. For a few minutes, she heard his panting, the exertion pushing him to exhaustion. That's what she did, she drained people of their energy. She robbed them of their bliss. And now she tried to curl up and disappear until she heard Brad say, "Okay, stop it, Lila. Stop overreacting. Just get up."

He would not make eye contact, as if he were ashamed of her. As if she were so ridiculous as to force him to act that way. To lash out. It suddenly occurred to her that this was his issue. His temper.

Lila did not have abusive parents. Her father might snap at her out of impatience or frustration, but never did he come at her and strike fear in her. And her mother was practically a saint when it came to parenting. Ella rarely raised her voice to her daughter. She had, however, perfected that stern tone and intimidating stare-down.

But they never struck her or screamed. She had seen her father lose it around her mother. The worst things she saw were her father yelling and swinging, his glare scarier than anything ever directed at her. But those times had been few and far between, and again, she had never been on the receiving end of it.

So why now? As she slowly rose to her feet, avoiding eye contact with Brad as much as he was with her, she wondered how this was now a part of her life. Infatuation? Need for attention? Fear?

"I'm going to call dad for a ride," Lila informed him softly, rounding her shoulders as if it were a shell she could hide beneath.

Brad heaved a sigh and stared upwards, his eyes suddenly glistening with unshed tears. "Dammit, Lila. Don't! Please ... just... I'm sorry. I am sorry. I love you, and when you say shit like that to me, I get so mad. Please-" He reached for her, and she flinched before finally allowing him to pull her close. "I'm really sorry, Lila."

It was all she could do to keep from crying herself. Because the emotions behind his words seemed so sincere. So raw. And she hurt for him. He was desperate for her forgiveness, and Ella knew it would be a night of gifts and affection. A good night. When she did not have to worry about an angry, confused father or a crying, devastated mother. For a night, life was good.

CHAPTER 13

Dennis stepped between the counter and Ella, and she stepped back, tipping her head up with a fiery expression. "El, don't lie! I saw you! I was two cars behind, and I watched you text on your phone."

"Fine. I texted."

"Right. You did. And I'm asking that you don't do that any-more-"

"Right. Okay. Got it."

"Hey. Hey you," his voice got softer, and he reached for her, lowering his face so they were forehead to forehead. "Just worries me, El. You were swerving. Be careful out there, 'k?" When she nodded, he pressed, "Okay?"

She opened her eyes, staring straight into his cocoa brown eyes and for a moment, lost her breath. Then she smiled. "Okay." With a nod and kiss to her forehead, he stepped to the side, resuming his task of chopping vegetables. "What if I'm stopped at a traffic jam?"

Dennis tossed down the knife. "Ella! No. I'm going to demand your phone anytime you go anywhere in your car."

"Pfft. You want to look through my phone. That's what this is about. You want to know who I was texting."

And his serious face suddenly broke into a grin. "You know me better than that."

"Oh?" Her eyes widened. "You don't care who I'm texting?"

"I trust you."

"Because I keep hearing your phone go off."

There were a few moments of silence, and then Dennis gently asked, "Is that what this is suddenly about? You're feeling threatened by a few beeps of my phone?" He reached into his back pocket and brought out his phone. After pushing a button and swiping, without glancing at the screen, he held it out to Ella. "Here. I don't even know who's been texting but I sure as hell don't have anything to hide." When she tried to wave him away, Dennis insisted, "I want you to look. El... I want you to know there's nothing to fear when it comes to me." He walked over to her and put his arms around her from behind, holding his phone in front of her. "There. These are the texts coming through. These are all the texts and calls from the last week. Do you see, honey?" He pressed his lips to the top of her head.

She leaned back against him, her heart pounding and eyes watering. "Silly man. Go call your brother. He made it to your parents' house."

"Yeah?" He held the phone up and looked at the texts. "Oh, so he did. First time he's ever been early. But listen, El... "

"Thank you. And no more car texting."

"Seriously. No more. I can't even stand the thought of ... it's my biggest fear."

And it was then Ella saw the pure vulnerability and fear stamped on his face. Dennis had lost someone he loved, and of course, that affected his life going forward. Of course, it would track him to every encounter, every relationship, every time in life he had to give up control. And the fact that it scared him terrified her.

**

Ella pushed her old car to its limit, passing other cars and checking her phone, despite knowing there was nothing to show since the last five seconds she had checked. Nothing. No answer to her calls or texts, to her frantic pleading.

Dennis was missing.

He had been missing for a day. And Ella had not even known it until Amber told her he had cancelled his classes for the rest of the week. His father had died unexpectedly. And Ella was ashamed to admit that her first reaction was hurt that he had not immediately sought her out, not even a text.

But now his family was looking for him. His oldest brother had called her at work asking if she had seen him. The conversation had been short, and she had to tell him that she had not heard from him, let alone seen him, but she would be in touch if she found him.

His family was in pain, and Dennis was only adding to that. Ella was not sure how to feel about that. This was not the strong, unbreakable man she knew. This was not her hero, the man that never hesitated in jumping in and stopping her attacker and then racing across the lake to save her daughter. This was not the man who kept her safe by installing a security system.

She had to face that he had his own demons. This was his father, the man he admitted was his own hero, had been his role model while growing up. His dad was his best friend, and suddenly, in an unexpected instant, he was taken from him. Of course, this was not the man she knew. This was a lost little boy trying to deal with death at its cruelest.

And that was when it hit Ella. She remembered Dennis's mother telling her about the death of his dog and how he had disappeared into the woods for hours. How had she not thought of this first thing?

There he was, sitting at the edge, no fishing rod or chair, no jacket. Dennis was very still, and Ella did not even think he knew she was walking toward him, until he called out in a gruff, raw voice, "Go away."

It startled her, and she jumped back before drawing in a deep breath and continuing forward. This was Dennis, her friend, more than her friend, and he was hurt beyond words. "Honey, your family, they're looking for you. Dennis... I'm so so sorry."

He picked up a rock and wailed it into the water, his jaw clenched and bicep bulging with the effort. "Barry wasn't even helping dad. He was sitting on his ass just watching. Dad had a heart attack. Doing all that goddamned work. I told him to wait. I had to finish my class in the morning then I'd be free to help. But fucking Barry just -"

"Dennis." She reached out to touch his shoulder, but he jerked away. "He didn't know. Your mom even told me that Barry never helps. Your dad knew. This was no one's fault."

"The hell it wasn't! Don't try to tell me that! Don't try to make this all better by turning a blind eye. You do that. You just live in some fantasy world where everyone has good intentions and-" He stood and walked a few feet away, cursing. Then he said, "He has specific instructions that there isn't to be a memorial of any type. And mom's just going to follow that. We're just to bury him quietly and move on with our lives. No real good-bye. How? How does one do that?"

"I don't know," she answered weakly, her heart breaking for this man in front of her.

Suddenly he turned toward her. "What the hell are you even doing here, huh?"

"Dennis. I'm here... I'm here because I love you, and I'm worried. I want to be here for you-"

He sneered. "Love me? What the hell do you think you love? Who do you think you love? It ain't me, darling. You're not ready for anything even remotely close to love-"

"What? What are you talking about-"

"If you think you are ready then you're delusional. You're still married. You haven't even moved beyond that -"

"I have! Dennis-"

"Listen closely," he growled, and she involuntarily stepped back, blinking back tears. "If you think there is anything between us other than just acquaintances with a passing attraction, then you sure as hell aren't ready for anything. You can't even see this, see me, for what I am. That's how bad off you are, Ella. That's how delusional you are."

Ella was shaking her head, as if that could ward off his words. "You're upset. You don't mean -"

"I do! This is nothing. It means nothing. I need you to not - oh my God, you come out here like some starved puppy that can save me from my grief over my own father. You aren't some Juliet. I sure as hell am not your Romeo. Stop being so gullible. Stop allowing people to just take advantage. Stop it! Just stop!" He was yelling, and she straightened, forcing herself to take charge of her emotions, to not show the utter devastation.

Forcing herself to meet his glare, she paused for a few moments, then spit out, "Call your family. Your mother is heartbroken enough, she doesn't need to worry about her grown assed son running off like some insolent child."

She whipped around and started marching to her car, willing her composure to stay intact. And when he called for her, his own voice breaking, Ella continued walking, never stopping. His voice grew louder, fighting the wind and his tears as it wailed out her name, like a broken song. And her steps grew stronger, fighting her heart and all she had hoped in the last several months. Like a silenced song.

**

Ella had never considered herself particularly strong. She had endured a lot in her life, but she cried a lot. She leaned on others when she was able. She avoided confrontation. Sure, she had kicked her husband out, but it was after almost twenty years of infidelity and indifference.

There was the childhood she had survived, but it was not like she had a choice. She'd had to survive, had to muddle through. Just like millions of others with a not-so-stellar homelife. That was nothing extraordinary.

But now Ella knew the meaning of strength. To carry on after losing the man she thought she had started to love... the man she thought was the answer to all that was... Those words he had thrown at her so viciously reverberated through her head almost constantly, shaming her and reminding her that she was on her own. And that was fine as long as that meant she did not have to go through such a painful, embarrassing ordeal ever again. She had let herself forget who she was. She was Ella Barnes, ordinary and old, nothing worth changing lives for. Nothing worth a happily ever after.

Ella blocked Dennis's number. It was two days later that he showed up on her porch, the same porch he had recently painted for her. And she knew strength was flowing through her when she opened the door and stepped out, not jumping into his arms. Because he looked good. Tired, miserable... but good.

"Ella," he breathed. "I .... I tried calling and texting but you... my mom wanted to thank you for the flowers you sent."

"Of course," she answered, surprised by how steady... and strong... her voice sounded. "Please send her my regards. You didn't need come all the way out-"

"I miss you, Ella. I love you."

Something in her snapped. Because this man thought he could crush her very soul one day and then come declare his love the next. How dare he play with her emotions like this! How dare he utter those words for the first time after screaming such hateful words! Tilting her chin up, Ella informed him, "It's the grief talking. You're reaching out because you're hurting. That's all."

"No. Listen, I was blind with grief. My best friend - " he choked on a sob, "He died. He's gone. I miss him so damn much." His body shook with sobs, and Ella led him to the porch stairs, holding him as he cried. She murmured words of sympathy, cradled his head to her chest, and put aside her own misery for his. Because this man meant everything to her despite it all. And he had just experienced the greatest pain.

"I need you," he stated once the sobs subsided. "Ella, I got scared. I lost someone, and it made me terrified of losing anyone else. I -"

"Look, you don't need to explain. Please... don't explain."

Dennis eyed her warily. "But ... I want to explain. You deserve that."

She stood, stepping away. "I deserve a hell of a lot. But I don't want an explanation. Dennis, I am really sorry about your dad. Truly sorry. But you're right. I'm not in a place that I can pursue any type of relationship-"

"Hun, you are. We are -"

"We are nothing. The fact that you can say what you said to me... we are nothing. And I'd appreciate it if you don't contact me again. Please."

She walked into her house. She shut the door.

That was strength.

**

The chatter and laughter filling the kitchen soothed Ella's frayed nerves and consoled her beaten soul. After the disaster of a week, she was grateful for some quality time with her daughter. It was Lila's sixteenth birthday. They had gone to the movies then out to eat, and now Lila and Brad were in the kitchen making guacamole. Ella sat at the table and watched them with a smile, basking in the glow of their young love and naive ideals.

"Brad!" Lila sputtered out between laughter. "Don't stir it! You have to mash it. Mash!"

He dropped the spoon in exasperation and sent Ella an imploring look. "Can we make brownies instead? That's more a birthday-type food. At least a dessert."

Ella waved a hand in the air. "You can make whatever. But I'm not sure my daughter will relent on the whole guacamole thing."

One hour and three recipes later, Brad declared it was time for him to leave. As Ella made sure to send him home with some cookies, brownies, and dip, he gave Lila a quick kiss and wished her a Happy Birthday.

"Thanks for stopping over," Lila said, smiling up at him, and Ella noticed how her daughter's eyes sparkled at his attention. "And thanks for the earrings. I love them."

Once they were alone at the kitchen table, Ella smiled between bites of cookie. "You two seem to be getting along lately."

"Yeah. Well, he's been in a good mood lately. Hasn't been getting mad."

"Mad?" Ella set down the remainder of the cookie and

stared hard at her daughter. "What do you mean? What does he do when he gets mad?"

Her daughter stared back without flinching. "Don't be so dramatic, mom. I just mean he gets moody sometimes. And we're teenagers so sometimes we fight and storm off. That hasn't happened recently. All I meant."

Ella smiled, her body sinking in relief. For a moment, she thought she had seen something in her daughter's eyes, a familiar spark of fear... but as she watched her daughter happily read the card her boyfriend had given her, she knew she was simply projecting her own experiences and fears onto her.

"Is that the door?" Ella glanced at Lila who shrugged. "Hold on. I'll check."

Somehow, she knew upon seeing the stranger, the young boy with gorgeous eyes and wild hair, that he was Finn. She smiled politely. "Hello. Finn?"

"Yes, ma'am." He jumped forward and shook her hand. "Is Lila home?" He lifted the gift bag in his hand. "Birthday surprises."

More curious than anything, she led him into the kitchen, and Ella noticed how her daughter straightened, guilt flashing across her face.

"Finn!" Then as if remembering herself, she turned back to the bowl of guacamole. "You just missed Brad. We baked brownies and made guacamole."

It was impossible to miss the pure heartbreak stamped on the young man's face, but he forced a smile and lifted the bag. "I brought you a birthday gift. I waited for you at the restaurant..."

When Lila ignored him, Ella stepped forward and addressed her daughter. "Lila. Did you have plans with Finn?"

"I forgot!" She had enough sense to show some regret. "I'm sorry, Finn. It was chaotic today and..." She waved her hand in the air as if that just explained everything, and Ella wanted to shake her until she realized how much she was hurting this kid.

"I figured. So, I thought I'd bring this to you." When she made no move toward him, he set the bag on the table and reached in. And suddenly Lila was giving him her full attention as he pulled out a bag of her favorite chocolates, then a six pack of her favorite orange soda, and then he pulled out a large wrapped gift.

Ella tried to appear busy, wiping down counters and the stovetop, but she was just as curious as Lila, and when the young girl squealed, she gave up on all appearances and went for a closer look.

Her eyes wide, Lila gasped, "A record player? Finn, this is fantastic! Look at these records! Where'd you find them? They're so old rock!"

And Ella shot her daughter a curious look. Because Lila loved classic rock, 70's hippie style music, but she had made Ella promise to never bring it up in front of her friends and especially not Brad. So why did this guy know? How close were they?

Because the initial impression Ella got was that Finn was almost a nuisance to Lila. A boy crushing on a girl that could not care less. But as she continued to watch the couple from a safe distance, she noticed the blushes and quiet stares, the gentle touches and mirrored movements. It startled her, because she had thought Lila and Brad were a close couple as far as teenagers go. But seeing Lila with Finn.... Warning bells went off. This boy could be dangerous. He could become so much more than a high school crush. More than a cute suitor. This boy was fire. Ella knew. She had experienced much the same at that age. She realized that was not true. She had experienced it recently... with Dennis.

**

The job was amazing, and Ella was adjusting to the laid-back atmosphere. Instead of having to be at work at a specific time, she could arrive whenever she wanted to in the morning. Her schedule was flexible.

Instead of the constant stress of phone calls and drivers at the windows and planning trucks on routes, she worked at her own pace with easy deadlines and a calm atmosphere around her. Instead of a thirty-minute lunch at a specific time, she could go to lunch anytime for as long as she wanted. No one was keeping track.

There was freedom and joy and career growth. But there was also Dennis.

"Ella."

She grew still, her fingers pausing over the keyboard as she tried to swallow back the lump that formed upon hearing his voice, at remembering... it was torture to try to get through the day knowing she would not be seeing him or talking to him after work. This was hard enough without Dennis standing behind her, his breath on her neck as he stooped over to whisper.

"You have me blocked from calling, and I just want a chance to explain and -"

"This is my work," she stated in a flat tone, staring straight ahead.

"What? Yes. I know. I just want to talk to you, Ella. Five minutes. Let me explain. I was crazy with grief and thought I could walk away from you, so I didn't get hurt but the truth is I'm in more-"

"My work." She turned slightly, still avoiding his gaze. "I am here to do a job. This is my haven. My escape. I get lost in my work. There is not a big gaping hole when I'm here. Are you going to make this impossible for me?"

"No. No, please, I just -"

"I have to work with you. Part of the job. I need to know we can do that without letting this... I can't do this, Dennis. Please. I need to be here and not deal with this. Okay? I can't..." She blinked and turned away.

Something seemed to register, and Dennis straightened and stepped away. "No, I... I'm sorry, Ella." His voice cracked, and he cleared his throat. "Of course, this isn't going to be a problem."

"I can't come here and work with you if-"

"Of course. I'm sorry."

She waited an agonizing five minutes after he left before she walked out to get some air. Unfortunately, she had to walk past Dennis's office. His door was open, and she caught a glimpse of him sitting at his desk with his head down.

And as if there truly was some freakish type of connection, he lifted his head and stared right back. Her feet stopped working, and she felt planted there, trapped by her own misery, hope, and desire. Trapped by some bizarre kind of hold he had on her.

"Ella?" He whispered, his voice cracking. "Please let me explain. Five minutes. Because this - I can't just walk away from you. I-"

"Dr. Reeves."

Ella whipped around and saw a young blond in her early twenties smiling widely at Dennis. She moved around Ella, almost as if she were unaware that Ella was standing there, and practically danced into the office, her long tanned legs moving lyrically with each step.

Backing away, Ella felt bile rise in her throat, realizing that this was a sign. She was not young, and she had never been this type of stunning blond young. Ella felt large and shapeless, matronly.... Silly, and she spun around and raced down the hallway and then pounded down the steps, anxious for air.

"Ella! Please."

She stopped, knowing Dennis was much faster than she was.

"That was a student of mine."

"I.... I know." She gulped for air and composure, choking on both.

"You came to my office-"

"I was walking past. I have to walk past to get outside."

"But you stopped. I was hoping you were ready to -"

"Ready to what, Dennis? Give in? Play your game again? I can't."

He backed up a step as if to give her the space she had

secretly been needing. To give her air. "To talk. To let me explain. No game. I just... when dad died, it took me back to that dark time in my life. I lost someone when I was so young. Then I lost dad, and this fear just gripped me, the darkness came back. How could I get close to anyone, how could I fall in love with you, when there's a chance I could lose you? And Ella, that terrifies me. Not just losing someone else I love but you... You. I can't catch my breath at that thought. My throat burns, my chest tightens .... But what I've realized is there is something scarier than that. And that's not even taking a chance with you. You're all I think about. All I dream about. Those days you would go fishing, those tears down your cheeks. I knew even then-"

"Dennis."

It was a muddled whisper, but he heard it. "Yes?"

Ella gripped the railing, feeling light-headed and nauseous. "Do you remember when we were in my kitchen arguing about how I texted while driving?"

"Yes."

"You-" She stopped and cleared her throat, blinking back tears. "You told me that with you, I had nothing to fear. Do you remember?"

"Of course, I remember."

"And yet less than a week later, you shattered my heart."

"El- please listen. I was out of my mind with grief and fear -"

She shook her head, her wavy hair flying against her cheeks. "Doesn't matter. I mean, I am so sorry for your loss. I am. If I could take that away from you, I would. Because not only do I have feelings for you, but I sincerely like you. But Dennis, you said something that day - you said that I wasn't ready for a relationship. And while you might not have meant it, you were right. I'm not. I am not emotionally strong enough for this. I ended a marriage. A twenty-three-year marriage. And I was attacked. I'm not in a place where I can help you heal."

"Let me help you," Dennis insisted, but his voice was weak. He knew where this was going.

"No. I have to do this on my own. I can't rely on anyone else. That gets me hurt more. Every time. I don't want to hate you. I don't want to blame you for anything. So, I'm going to go outside to catch my breath. You're going to go back to your office. And when we need to work together, it's going to be polite and professional because we are both good people capable of that." She stared at him and then nodded, as if agreeing with herself before she turned and ran down the flight of stairs.

The tears fell when she realized she heard no steps behind her.

Later that week, Amber stopped to talk and tapped her fingers on Ella's desk. "Pretty serious?"

"What?" Ella broke away from her computer to regard her supervisor with curiosity.

"Whatever has you and Dennis fighting." When Ella started to shake her head, Amber waved the denial away. "Let me tell you something. I haven't known you long, but I've known you long enough to know you're a little mopey lately. And Dennis... in the seven years I've worked with him, he has never come close to displaying any type of negativity. Until today when he snapped at me." She gave her a sympathetic smile, leaned down and confided, "For what it's worth, he looks worse than you."

Ella gave a weak smile, but once again, tears threatened. They were always underneath the surface. When Alex left, she had cried a lot. Just streams of tears down her face, sometimes without her knowledge. She could be talking to someone, and the person would stop in mid-sentence, step back, and then point out the tears.

And she cried now. But it was not the same. The pain was deeper, more agonizing. It crept along with every move she made, it punctuated every breath she took. But the tears were not as prominent. This suffering was more to herself. It seemed to diminish what she felt by putting it on display, cheapening the ache by sobbing. Instead, she moved through the day. She woke up and made breakfast, asked about Lila's plans for the day, and went to work.

It was not always possible to avoid Dennis. They seemed to show up at the same time each morning, mumbling greetings and rushing to their separate parts of the building. If she had a question about his course, she warned him with an email that she needed to speak to him, and he politely offered times she could come see him. Little eye contact and words only relating to work got them through each encounter.

At one meeting, he reached out and touched her wrist. "You know, I don't go there anymore. I know it's important to you, so I stay away."

"What?" Her mind was still focused on how her wrist burned from his touch. Her heart slammed against her chest as if demanding more.

"The lake. I don't go there anymore. I know fishing was therapeutic for you so… if you wanted to go… you don't need to worry that I'll be there."

She nodded and walked out, not bothering to tell him that without him there, she saw no need to visit the lake. What she had considered at one time to be comforting was now a gut-wrenching reminder of what she had felt. A nudge of a memory of feeling alive and young and crazy with emotions. A time she could not wait to wake up, anxious for more of their story to unfold. And she could not yet bear those memories knowing that is all they would ever be. The thought of never feeling that - panic enveloped her, squeezing out her air.

Fortunately, being a mother forced Ella to perform as a human. She had to celebrate her daughter's 16th birthday, had to get her ready for her junior year. This was an important time in her daughter's life, and she could not let that fade to the background.

Lila got her driver's permit, and her friendship with Finn seemed to dissipate or at least reside in the shadow of her relationship with Brad. Ella got the impression that the two guys did not get along, and she wanted to know more, but she knew by asking, she risked being shut out completely. So, Ella focused on teaching her daughter to drive, hoping she would talk when she needed to.

Her daughter seemed to be more settled, calmer. She even spent some weekends with her. They went to the movies and out to dinner, and Lila confessed that she missed Dennis.

"Mom. I've never seen you that exuberant. It was like you were finally yourself."

And Ella had nothing to say to that, so she simply forced a smile and patted her daughter's hand and continued to talk about turn signals and parallel parking.

CHAPTER 14

Dennis drove with the intention of turning around at the last minute. Because she made it clear. Ella had told him over and over that they were finished.

Even after a month, she was not budging on that. He knew he had blown it, and every day was just another reminder of that. If he had been honest with her from the start perhaps or had voiced his fears. If he had been honest with himself...

He pulled up to Ella's house and saw her car was gone. Perfect chance to turn around unnoticed. But Dennis did not seem to have the knack lately for doing the right thing. So, he parked and got out, content to wait. To confront.

It was less than ten minutes when the familiar, somewhat beaten down car, pulled into the driveway, and he grinned as he noticed Lila behind the wheel.

The young girl flew into his arms with her usual enthusiastic abandon. "Dennis! We've missed you so much! Did you see me driving?"

"I did! Congratulations."

"Just a permit. I take my test in a month. And thanks for the gift card! It came right on my birthday."

He asked her about her class schedule and her friends, and he listened as she eagerly chatted away, noticing Ella standing just in range, wrangling her hands in her nervous way.

"I'm glad you're doing well, Lila. Want to give me and your mom a few minutes, please?"

The couple stared at each other as Lila reluctantly dragged her feet into the house. For a few more moments they locked eyes until Dennis shook his head. "Really, El. I see all the cameras are down."

He had to hand it to her, she never flinched. Did not look away. "That's right. They came to take them when I cancelled the service."

"Was that really necessary-"

"Of course, it was," she hissed in an uncharacteristic manner. "You think I'm just going to continue accepting all your charity?"

He rocked back on his heels, willing a calmness to counter her agitation. "Was never charity. I always thought we were friends above anything else." Dennis paused, and then added, "And the lawyer too? How are you going to protect yourself in this divorce? Retaining another lawyer is just going to cost -"

"Well, it isn't your problem anymore. Okay, Dennis?"

He closed his mouth, her words stinging even more than he had prepared himself for. Finally, he pleaded, "It's been a month, El. Can we go talk? Can I take you out to dinner? I miss you."

Ella immediately shook her head. "I was in a marriage for many years. Trapped and miserable because I couldn't change the man. I couldn't make him happy with me. I'm not about to venture into another relationship with a man who's already broken my heart. No. So if you'll wait right there, I have a box of your stuff to give you."

**

Lila stepped back and crossed her arms defiantly. "Brad, this isn't - no. I didn't even look at Jim. He's your friend, you made us stay there when we were supposed to go to the movies."

"I saw you! You two were practically all over each other. You laughed at everything that motherfucker said."

"You're being crazy. You sound like every other jackass that -"

And before she could prepare, could try to block it, he slapped her so hard that her head snapped to the other side, her neck screaming out in pain. "You want to call me crazy when you're nothing but dirt! Just some ratty looking whore." He reached out and grabbed a handful of her hair, yanking her back when she tried to escape.

"Brad! OW! My neck! Let me go."

He gave one more yank and then shoved her away from him. "Then go. Get away from me. I tried. I did everything, and you still embarrass me and break my heart." He paused and added, "You're still seeing him."

And Lila forgot for a moment about escaping and instead turned back to him. "Who? Finn? I'm not. We're friends. I'm not seeing him." A sob forced its way out of her mouth. "You just... dammit, Brad. I thought we were past this. I can't do this. I'm sixteen and -no."

"We're not past this. You said you'd stay away from him. You act like you're the total victim but you're playing me."

Lila started to answer, but she saw that dangerous gleam in his eyes, and she escaped before he came at her again.

There were not many places she could go. She could not admit to her parents that her relationship was out of control. They would never let her go anywhere ever again. They would not trust her to make any type of decision regarding her own life.

She and Finn had fought the night before over her inability to break free from Brad. Finn confessed that he felt used and stupid for allowing her to play him. Those words left her defensive as she tried to explain to him that she just couldn't leave Brad. She only managed to upset Finn further and to her horror, tears sprang to his eyes.

"Do you even realize, Lila, how self-involved you are? I've been there for you for months, and it makes no difference."

"So, you've just been nice to me in hopes of getting more? Huh?"

"I always put our friendship first. Always. I ignored my own heart just so you could have someone to turn to. But even our friendship - you just ... "

She had left soon after. But now she called him, hoping he was not holding a grudge.

"What?"

Okay, so Finn was not yet over their fight. As tears wobbled her voice, Lila pleaded, "I need a friend right now, Finn. Please."

There was a pause and then a heavy sigh. "No. Lila, no. I can't keep going through this."

She started to explain that there was nothing further to go through, but he had already hung up.

She felt low and alone, without any type of support. There were a few friends she could call, but they were all involved in their own drama, and she had isolated herself with Brad and then with Finn. She was not as close to her old group. And the girls would gossip with any information she gave them anyhow. Because they were teenagers, after all. It was what they did.

"Lila? Are you okay? Is your mom okay?"

The panic in his voice set off her hysteria, and she burst into tears, the side of her face now throbbing. She managed to sputter out, "Mom's okay. I'm... I don't know who to talk to."

Dennis paused and then asked, "Where are you?"

Fifteen minutes later, he was out of his car and rushing over to her. "Lila! Your cheek. What happened?" He led her to a nearby bench. "Hon, talk to me."

"You have to promise not to tell mom."

Regret filled his face. "I can't do that, Lila. You know I can't. If something is going on, she should know."

"She'll overreact."

"About?" His eyes searched her face. "What's going on? Who did this?"

The concern was too much for Lila to handle, and she hunched over shaking with sobs. "I'm such a horrible person, Dennis. Mom would hate me."

Dennis let her cry, his hand on her shoulder. He was quiet until he noticed that she started to settle down, the hysteria leaving her. Then he held her gaze and slowly asked, "Who did this to you, Lila?"

Sniffling, she asked, "Haven't you heard anything I've said? I'm hurting with more than just a bruised cheek."

He gave her a gentle smile, trying to mask the fury he felt that a boy might have struck her in anger. He reminded himself he did not know the entire story and flying into a rage would not convince this lost little girl to confide in him. "I've heard every word, Lila. I want to address one thing at a time. Who hit you?"

And just like that, he saw her eyes look right through him, her shoulders grow rigid. "I was upset and walked right into the edge of the door."

"Lila," he breathed.

"It's true."

"Your mother will never hate you. You can tell her any-thing. What did you do that you feel is so bad?"

The sniffling stopped, the high-pitched tone dropped to a more normal level, and she heaved a sigh before answering, "I took advantage of a good friend. I knew he was attracted to me, and I used that to get what I wanted. His time and atten-tion. I liked feeling that control."

"Lila. That's normal. Especially at your age. You've had a very turbulent year with your parents splitting. Your mom's attack. You're not a bad person. Quite the opposite. In fact, I think you're so careful not to offend your mom that you get overwhelmed with that responsibility." He paused and let his words sink in. He watched as she chewed her bottom lip, the same habit her mother had when she was thinking. Then he gently asked, "Finn? Is that who you've upset?"

She nodded and he pressed, "Did he do this? Your cheek?"

Her head flew up and her eyes widened. "Oh God, no! Finn would never do that!"

"Brad?"

"I knew it was a mistake to talk to you. You're like dad and mom. You don't listen-"

He managed to remain calm, showing no response to

her frantic words. This was a little girl that was trying to push her way into adulthood too soon. A little girl that was seeking out love and acceptance with boys that could not grow up enough to recognize the beautiful woman she would soon be. And Dennis wished she felt safe enough to go to her own father or mother and express her fears and disappointments. But he worked around young people enough to know that they rarely felt comfortable confiding in anyone, let alone parents.

"Lila, I won't ask any more. But I will say this. If someone is putting his or her hand on you in anger or in any type of unwanted contact, then you need to stop all communications with this person. You need to get away. Because this is that person's issue, not yours. And I think you know this isn't right."

"So, no one is supposed to hurt me. But I hurt Finn. Doesn't that make me a bad person?"

Dennis realized she wanted to punish herself. He sighed and gave her a small, reassuring smile. "You're a good person, Lila. Maybe Finn expects too much. If he has a crush on you, and you don't reciprocate that... That isn't on you. Be careful with his feelings but don't feel obligated." He studied her and seeing that she relaxed a bit, he ventured, "Finn obviously gets high, Lila. Are you-"

"No! And it's just pot."

"Listen. Be careful. Okay? And my offer still stands. If you need a ride, no questions asked."

She nodded, her lips turning up in a ghost of a smile. "Thanks for coming out here. I ... just thanks. And hey." She lifted one shoulder, another trait of her mother's. "I'm really sorry it didn't work out with mom. I liked having you around. I never saw her so happy."

"I'm sorry too, Lila."

He tried to smile back, but the air felt knocked out of him. Because he wished it had worked out with her mom also. He hoped as he left Lila that she would heed some of his advice, that she heard at least half of his words. But she was young, and the young did not always want to listen to adults' words.

Dennis was older, and he had met a variety of people from all walks of life. It was not difficult to formulate a plan. Because if he had confronted Brad himself, he could not guarantee he would maintain control. And being charged with assault of a minor was not something he wanted.

But he was not willing to simply pretend he had not learned that Brad had a problem pushing around women. He could not ignore that at all. So, Dennis reached out to some connections, and he hoped that Lila would learn to use some caution when it came to the people she let into her world.

**

The hot air was simply a reminder that summer was not giving up so easily. Despite the leaves changing and the days getting shorter, the air was heavy and relentless. Connie felt huge, her stomach starting to swell and her body becoming a heater as it worked to nurture the baby growing inside of her.

She sat up when Alex walked into the room, his steps quick and his smile forced. Things had been strained, and Connie was not sure why. But then he strode up to her and shoved a letter under her nose. "Look!"

His forceful tone tightened her nerves to the point that she was sure she could hear them humming, and her focus refused to sharpen enough to understand the words. "What?"

"Read it!" he insisted, shaking the letter at her.

Startled, she glanced up at him and then took the letter, trying to comprehend the language. But it might as well have been foreign to her, and she shook her head, dropping the letter. "What?"

Alex eyed her with disbelief. "Are you crying? Dammit, Connie, what's wrong with you? I was just teasing. It's the divorce. It's final."

"Couldn't you have just told me that?"

"Just trying to be a little funny," he murmured, bending to pick up the paper. "Trying to lighten the mood around here. I think I'll frame this. Celebrate my escape from that lunatic."

Connie ventured a weak smile, her hand floating to her stomach. "So that means we can plan our wedding!"

He squeezed his eyes shut, his hand shooting out in front of him as if to block the words. "Can I breathe for a minute before you nag me? Jesus, Connie, I just got the notice that my twenty-something year marriage ended. And wedding? Oh no, I'd do something like go to the courthouse. I already had one wedding in my lifetime."

"Not with me. I have never had a wedding." She watched helplessly as Alex sighed and shook his head before storming out of the room. And she wondered where the fun had gone, when it had stopped being so damn glorious to be around him. Connie used to shiver when she saw him walk into a room. And she remembered how his eyes lit up when he saw her. How he followed her around, begging for some stolen moments, some shred of hope for a shared tomorrow.

And now he sulked around the house, and he rolled his eyes at the sound of her voice. There were harsh tones and hurt feelings. The more Connie tried, the more she felt like a failure.

She loved this man, had loved him from the start. Connie was not proud of breaking up a marriage, no matter how much she told herself it was already over. But Alex... she could not just walk away. She had been so sure it was true love, it was the romance like the books she read. Being with him when they could find time to be together .... That was happiness. And wasn't happiness worth fighting for no matter what obstacle stood in the way?

Well, there were no obstacles now. Yet the happiness had seemed to leak out, dissipate. Connie could not understand it. They had the green light. He was free. Shouldn't he be running into her arms, promising her the world? Shouldn't he be thanking her for sticking by his side? Where was that romance that had snagged her in the first place?

Alex walked back into the room and tilted his chin at her. "Want to go grab some lunch?" It was as if the earlier conversation, his cavalier manner of ensuring her he was not necessarily committed to her and the relationship had never occurred. When she merely glared at him, he mimicked her expression and snapped, "What?"

"Nothing." She hauled herself up from the chair. "You go do what you want, Alex. I'm going to lay down."

"What's wrong with you? What did I do?" He spoke in that defensive tone that always put her on edge. As if he could not fathom what she had against him *this time*.

"Stop. Okay? You've made yourself clear. I got it. Now just give me my space so I can take care of myself."

Alex stopped following her and cursed. "What the hell are you bitching about now? I just said I wanted a moment to breathe before we start planning anything."

She paused at the door to their bedroom. "You're right. We definitely need to just stop and not make any decisions before I figure all this out. Not sure this is exactly what I want." The last thing Connie saw before she shut the door was his stunned expression.

**

Lila slowed her steps when she saw Brad pacing, his face scrunched up in anger. This was not how it went, she thought, alarms ringing in her head. He would lose his temper, they would fight, he would shove or slap or scream vicious, vulgar things and then they would not talk for a day or week. Then he would write her a long text begging for forgiveness. Sometimes he would send flowers or her favorite chocolate, and her mother always oohed and aahed and gushed about what a great boy he was.

She would give in and meet him at this spot, this playground that was almost always empty, and he would push her on the swings or lie with her on the ground to watch the clouds. This... the tension... was not part of the scenario.

"Brad?" She tiptoed up to him, and he swung his body around in a jerky motion. "What.... What's wrong?"

"Cop came to see me today."

"What? Why?"

"I guess someone turned me in for roughing up a woman."

Lila's blood ran cold, and she fought to keep her expression neutral as she stuttered, "What? What do you mean?"

"I mean," he snarled, "that someone went to the police and reported me for abuse. This cop came out to the house and asked to speak to me. Thank God, my mom wasn't home. But he said that if he hears of any other incidents, he's taking me in to the station and - I'll be tried as an adult."

Lila took a back step, her mind whirling. "Was the cop tall with dark hair?" Because she would die if Dennis had impersonated a cop to scare her boyfriend.

"No." He flung his body away from her and cursed. "That bitch Josie is going to pay for this!"

It took a few moments to catch her breath, to realize just what he was implying. "Josie? What?"

Brad flung his hand up in the air. "Bitch was mouthing off to me. I just slapped the voice right out of that cocky bitch."

"Josie? So... you and -"

"Lila!" Brad cried, gripping his hair. "Shut the fuck up about me and Josie? Alright? I have the cops knocking on my god-damn door, and you want to make some deal out of a whore that I don't even talk to now?"

Lila watched as he paced in front of the swings, and it hit her. This boy assumed it was Josie, because he knew Lila would never stand up for herself enough to get cops involved. She would just take the abuse and keep coming back.

Brad would never change. He was not going to suddenly soften and stop pushing her around or stop running around on her. Maybe someday he will grow up, mature and get help for his violent tendencies, but until then... was she willing to waste her youth ducking his angry swings and crying over his roaming attention?

"See you around, Brad."

"Hey!" He turned toward her in agitated surprise. "Where

the fuck are you going?"

"Away from here."

A moment later, she felt herself being yanked around. She glared right into his eyes and slowly advised, "Get your hands off of me, or you'll have a second visit from the police."

Brad let go. "Crazy bitch."

And she realized as she rushed away from the boy she still loved, away from the humiliation and heartbreak, she realized she was sprinting in fear. She was afraid he was behind her, going to grab her at any moment. She lost her breath and stumbled, catching herself and lurched forward, smacking right into an obstacle.

A scream tangled with a sob as she clawed at the object, and then she heard a familiar, soothing voice snag her out of the hysteria.

"Lila! It's me. It's Finn. Lila, are you okay?"

She swung around to ensure Brad was not behind her, and then she sighed, her chest heaving as she tried to catch her breath. As Finn frantically called her name, she held out a hand and bent over, managing, "One second."

When she could breathe and speak without a mouthful of sobs, Lila straightened and shook her head. "I'm fine. Sorry. Something…. I was just caught off guard and -"

"Lila." Finn leaned forward to meet her gaze. "You were running as if someone were -"

"No. I … What are you doing here?"

He suddenly appeared sheepish, splotches of red staining his cheeks. "I … I came to talk to you. I wanted to say I was sorry for… then I saw you, and I followed… I knew you would come here to see him so I hung back waiting to see if.. Are you okay?"

Lila nodded, and Finn led her away from that spot. They walked toward her house in silence, and every now and then he touched her back or smiled down at her as if trying to assure himself she was there, and she was okay.

And Lila was numb. The sudden, intense fear had escaped

her as quickly as it had come and left her feeling exhausted and drained. At the same time, she felt as if she were waking from an incredibly long slumber. She was awake and could see reality from the dreams that had settled in among the cobwebs of her good sense and confidence. She could see the way that boy, that fraction of a man had used and humiliated her. Lila had stuck around in the name of love, but that was not love. It was the ego of a guy that only cared about his urges and his reputation.

"I parked over there." Finn's voice was soft as he studied her. When she offered no words, he continued, "About the other day... I'm sorry. We're friends, and I should have been there for you."

"No. You were right. I was being unfair to you. I'm sorry. You're a good friend. I just," she took a deep breath and one last time, glanced over her shoulder, "I am really messed up."

He cocked his head with an uncertain smile. "You mean, like, high?"

"No!" She swallowed a sob, tears burning her eyes. "Like I let a guy just push me around and treat me like shit. And I need to just figure things out."

"Figure out if you're going to stay with him?"

"No. Figure out why I'd do that. Why I stayed with him in the first place. I... "

His eyes grew rounder as the meaning of her words sunk in. "No. I get it. Aw, Lila, I understand. Just friends." He jumped forward when Lila burst into tears, pulling her to him. "Lila, don't cry. Please don't. It's okay."

And she clung to him, relieved she had a friend she could turn to.

**

The office suddenly seemed too small, the air scarce as Dennis pulled a chair up to Ella's desk and pointed to her screen. "That's the problem. Building quizzes from the question bank. I tried to form groups, and it's still telling me I don't have enough questions to pull from. But there are twenty questions!"

"All right." Ella felt the corners of her lips tilting up. When she caught Dennis's hurt gaze, she held up her hands. "I'm sorry! I'm so sorry, but you sound so dramatic."

A grin broke out on his face, and he ducked his head. "Okay. I'll try to tone the urgency down."

"Hellooooo!" There was a knock on the door and then Steve Finch, a professor Ella worked with often, peeked his head in. "Oh, I didn't mean to interrupt. Hello, Dr. Reeves."

Dennis tipped his head and smiled. "Dr. Finch."

Steve stepped into the room. He had wide eyes that made him appear constantly surprised and long skinny arms marked with age spots. But his easy laugh and good nature made him one of Ella's favorites. He dropped a small packet on her desk. "Sunflower seeds. I see you like plants." He motioned toward her feeble attempts at a green thumb. "But don't try to grow them in here. Not enough sunlight. Plant them at home, away from any shade."

"Oh wow!" She smiled up at him. "Thank you so much!"

As soon as he disappeared behind the closing door, Dennis sat back with a wide grin. "Someone has a crush. Bringing you flowers… or flower seeds."

"Oh, please."

"Are you blushing? Ella Banks- you're blushing! Do you like being given seeds from him?"

"Stop! He's like really old."

Dennis's grin grew wider, and he pointed in her direction. "Ella! He's only a few years older than me."

Jumping forward in her seat, Ella burst into laughter. "What? Really?"

"Yes. He's mid-fifties."

Her shoulder lifted, her auburn curls tumbling around the movement. "You don't seem that age. Definitely not in his range."

"Ah, thanks. But I doubt I can compete with sunflowers."

"Stop. He just was being nice." She turned her focus back on their work and for the next thirty minutes, they discussed the issues, and she was able to show him how to create and store quizzes. In the short time she worked there, Ella had caught on and learned so much.

After thanking her profusely, Dennis leaned back in his chair and studied her. "How have things been, Ell?"

She felt her shoulder rise almost involuntarily as she considered his question. How have things been? Things have been out of whack, as if a part of her was dying each day she was not in his arms. Things have been dark and panicky, almost as if she were on the outside looking in with no way to warn or help. She wanted to tell Dennis that things were not good. Her life was in order. New job was great. Her daughter was starting to be more like herself again. And yet... she woke up in the mornings, and there was a second she felt great. Grateful to be alive. And then she remembered. He was not there. So, he wanted to know how things were?

"Things are good," she answered with a soft smile and slight tilt of a shoulder. "Divorce is final."

Ella felt a glow under his reaction of elation. "Really? Aw, Ell. That's great. Congrats. I mean, on at least the technical part of it being done." His smile faltered slightly, and his hand moved as if to touch her arm and then he pulled back. "How... how are you really? I mean, no matter how you feel about him specifically now, this represents an end to ... you shared a lot with him, a lot of years."

She blinked, her arm tingling from the anticipation of his almost-touch. How did he do that? How did he reach into the deepest part of her thoughts and just pick out the very words she would have used if she would ever be brave enough to describe how she was feeling? "Um... yeah. Not easy. But ... not as difficult as I imagined. I've learned there are .... other things much more difficult... to get over." The words were out of her mouth before she even realized what she was saying, and she lifted her gaze to his and saw the surprise registering on his face and what looked like hope. He started to talk, but she rushed to speak first. "And, uh, Lila, she's been home more. Her attitude is better. But you... how are you? Your mom.." Her voice automatically softened, and she tilted her head. "Is she doing okay?"

There was a beat of silence, and she glanced down, unable to meet the intensity of his stare. "She's actually doing okay. Thank you for asking. It's not easy. But she has her friends and church groups. She's keeping busy." He paused, and Ella noticed that he glanced down and swallowed, as if nervous. Then he looked up at her. "Actually... I wanted to talk to you. About Lila."

"Okay."

"She called me the other day. Needed someone to talk to. An adult who wasn't a parent, I'm thinking."

Panic flooded through her as she imagined her daughter upset and afraid to talk to her. But Ella squared her shoulders and met his gaze with determination and calmness. "And?"

"And... we talked. I didn't want to keep this from you, and I've been going back and forth on ... she's your daughter. I get that. I don't want to overstep boundaries or upset you."

"Dennis... is she okay?"

He paused, his eyes searching hers. "She will be okay. I'm sure of that. But I don't want to break her confidence. I'm sorry, Ell, but if she has someone, an adult, that she feels safe coming to, don't we want that?"

"Yes."

"I mean, I've never had kids so I'm no expert but... I promise you, if things escalate... if she is in danger, I will come to you. I will tell you. I would never play around when it comes to that. But for now... I mean, do you trust me, Ell?"

With a ghost of a smile, she nodded, just a slight tilt up and then down of her head. "I do. When it comes to this, I trust you."

There were shadows in his eyes as her words registered, as he realized that she did not trust him in other areas. Finally, he spoke, "I am so sorry about that day. The things I said. I was out of my mind with grief and fear. But this... I'm glad you and I can talk and ... "

"If something more happens with Lila and she goes to you... you'll tell me?"

"Yes. This isn't... I'm not using this situation to get closer to you, Ell. Please tell me you know that."

"I know that. But she's okay?"

"Listen to me." He grabbed her hands and leaned forward, his gaze drilling into hers. "The very fact that she came to an adult tells me she knows the rights and wrongs of the situation and just needed to hear it echoed back to her."

"And you did... echo it back?"

He grinned. "I echoed. Listen, you're a fantastic mom. The best. You're doing a great job with her."

There was something about his soothing tone and that infectious grin that caused her to straighten in her chair and blurt out, "Want to get some lunch?"

Maybe it was the weeks of misery she had endured or the dreams that had him close to her, the dreams when finally she felt good again... maybe it was knowing that this man was the one to set off all the sensors in her body, all the nerves in her mind, everything turning on and reacting whenever he was close... whatever it was, she needed it back. She wanted him back.

But as soon as she asked the question, his face fell. "Aw, Ella... you know I'd love to but-"

"No. It's okay. It's just that time of day and -"

He glanced at the computer screen and jumped to his feet. "Oh, shit. I have to go. Listen.. raincheck?"

"Sure."

Ella sat there for several minutes, willing the tears back. Of course, he was busy. She had asked him last minute. He was at work, for Christ sake. There were meetings and conferences and office hours for students. After calming herself down, Ella walked out into the hallway to stretch her legs and grab a coffee on the first floor. As she neared the end of the hall, she heard Dennis apologize to another instructor as he cut their conversation short.

"I'm so sorry, Gwen. I have to go. Plans and I'm already late."

Gwen laughed and waved him away. "Go! It's that hot date you've been talking about. So, go, we'll catch up later."

Ella ducked into an empty office before Dennis could see her, and she bent over, clutching her stomach as tears fell. He had moved on. Of course, he had. Ella was just an average, if not below-average woman, that had pushed him away. He was not going to pine away for her.

Her own father had not waited around. There were more interesting things, more enticing adventures than to parent the ordinary.

And suddenly a memory hit her. She had been six or seven, small for her age, and her grandparents had taken her and two of her cousins to one of those outlandishly expensive and indulgent amusement parks with rides and shops and best of all, the one thing she had stayed up all night imagining, walking and breathing characters! Characters come to life from her favorite cartoons!

Ella had been up earlier than anyone, dressed and waiting at the tiny table of their miniscule kitchen inside the suite. Breakfast? Impossible. She could not eat, her nerves would simply toss back any attempt.

Finally, the rest of the group woke, and it seemed like agony as they muddled through their breakfast. Ella felt all the pent-up frustration of a six-year-old when her grandparents insisted she eat something. She managed to swallow down some toast and then stood by the door as everyone else stumbled through the rooms searching for shoes and money and a lucky rabbit's foot that had been popular back in those days.

Ella had raced through the park, only slowing down when her grandfather lost his usually unending patience and snapped at her to stay with them. Her cousins Meredith, ten years old, and Brendan, eleven years old, seemed impossibly composed, even bored, and Ella resented them for not racing and yelling and bursting with excitement. As she joined her family and walked with them, she felt her body vibrate with the bliss, the pure joy of what was to come.

And not even ten feet inside the park, she saw a group of characters greeting children and posing for pictures. Her grandmother, after instructing the oldest cousin to keep an eye on them, motioned for them to go.

Ella's short legs meant she lagged behind because suddenly the cousins seemed to catch her enthusiasm. They raced ahead and soon were being engulfed in hugs and giving high fives. She waited for her turn and then stepped up to her favorite character, the bear in all the cartoon movies that she watched over and over. Adorable and happy, that was him. She loved to sing along to the songs, loved to watch his antics as he tried to sneak food that wasn't his or crashing parties he wasn't invited to… because he was a bear.

So, she stepped up to this come-to-life character and smiled up at him…. Just as he turned away and hugged another child.

"Ella! Don't lose your cousins!" her grandfather scolded, apparently not seeing the soul-crushing scene or the tears welling up in her eyes. Afraid to anger her grandfather even more, somehow sensing that three kids on a trip was overwhelming to the older couple, she ran to catch up with her cousins. But the trip was already set, the damage done.

CHAPTER 15

"Excuse me, ma'am?"

Ella gave a little jump and glanced at the time. It was already early afternoon, and she had little work to show for the day. She had to focus. She had to forget about some guy that never had the intention of taking her seriously, and she had to aim her attention on things that mattered.

Still dazed, she glanced up at the man waiting for her attention. He was tall and broad shouldered, a bit husky. Sandy brown hair that curled at the ends and soft blue eyes. He had fat lips, a square chin and a large nose, but there was something oddly beautiful, delicate about his looks. She blinked. "Yes?"

His smile was disarming, a friendly yet sheepish gesture that made her smile in return. "I was here visiting a friend and … I'm lost. I need to leave. I need to go, but this building… it won't let me."

A laugh spilled out of her mouth, and she scooted her chair back. "I can show you. Are you parked in the main parking lot or in the back?"

He shrugged. "I parked in the parking lot in front of the door I came in."

"Helpful. Hmm," she stood, her eyes lifting up as if she could find the answer in the ceiling. "Oh, okay. Did you park in the parking lot that has the booth?"

"Oh yeah!" He wagged his finger at her. "There was this woman in the booth. She gave me the meanest look."

"Yep. That's Vinnie. She isn't mean. Just her expression."

He gave her a doubtful look. "She rolled her eyes when

I asked if I could have a ten-minute pardon. I don't see why I have to pay by the hour if I'm only stopping in for a few minutes."

"And she rolled her eyes? Unbelievable." She rolled her own eyes and then motioned him to follow her. "I'll lead you out if you promise not to enter the maze again."

He caught up to her. "I'm Owen by the way."

"Hello, Owen."

"And you are?"

"Ella."

"Like that character in the kid's movie?"

Ella stopped walking long enough to send him an exasperated look. "That's Elsa. I'm Ella."

"Well, Ella, now that I have your attention, may I be so bold as to tell you that you are the most beautiful woman I've seen in a very long time. You have amazing eyes."

She took a breath and then started walking. "We're going to go down this hall and then we're going to turn left. The elevator will take you down to the first floor - push 1 for that to happen. And then you're going to exit the elevator, turn right, and the door to the parking lot will be right there."

"I'm sorry." He gave a half grin, tilting his head. "I sounded like a loon just now, didn't I? I'm sorry. But you really are beautiful. Can I take you out to dinner tonight?"

"Excuse me?"

"Too soon? What about tomorrow night?"

"No."

"Married?"

"No."

"Living in sin?"

"No."

"I'm too grotesque to endure an evening with?"

A laugh sputtered out as she widened her eyes in surprise. "No. You actually have very nice features."

"So... let me take you out."

"No. I'm sorry, but I don't know you."

"Isn't that the point of going out on a date?"

And the laughter left her slowly, air leaking from a balloon. "I - I don't work that way. I don't go out with strangers."

"Aw, I see. Okay, but listen, I'm a cop, so if you're safe with anyone, it would be me."

"You?" She giggled. "You're a cop?"

"Yes."

She shook her head and then pointed to the elevator. "First floor, go right, then door."

"Hey, you don't believe me?" He stood there with a helpless look on his face as she waved goodbye. "Ella. Who lies about being a cop?"

Smiling to herself, Ella returned to her desk and finally got some work done. It was freeing to lose herself in the work, to have her attention be solely on the right words to use or the requests to be added to an online course. There were so many things on her plate, and she relished that. Keep that plate full, she thought, this is my life raft.

**

Dennis found a break between classes and students and instructors to go back to Ella's office. By then it was late afternoon, but the morning meeting they had had was fresh in his mind. She was ready to start again, to forgive him and move on with him. This is what he had been waiting for, what he needed. Because the constant reminders of her, a whiff of lilacs or a glimpse of bright green like her eyes, and he wanted to simply fold up and cry. Yes. A grown man, a man well past the age of any foolishness, wanted to shed tears over this woman. This creature of beauty and grace.

"Ella."

She glanced up and then her expression hardened. "Dennis. Something wrong with the course?"

"Uh, no." He was caught off guard by the flatness of her tone and the narrowing of her eyes. Was she just stressed? "I thought maybe we could go grab a bite to eat."

Her eyes remained focused on the screen in front of her.

"Busy."

Dennis shuffled uncomfortably. "Is... is something wrong, El?"

"No. Just busy."

"Are you upset about Lila? Is that what -"

"No. Just... I think it is best if we limit time together to unavoidable work interactions."

Dennis frowned and leaned against the side of her desk. "El, you asked me to lunch. You. So why the sudden change?"

Frustration seeped through her so that her joints stiffened, and blood raced. "No shit. I know what I asked. It was a mistake, Dennis. Okay? Thankfully, you already had plans, so it didn't happen."

"Hey, if this is-"

"Please go. Just…. Just go."

He paused for a moment before pushing away from the desk and giving a curt nod. "Very well."

Dennis made a point to smile, although every muscle in his face fought against it. But no matter what, he knew he was to blame for Ella's demeanor. He was the one to screw up. To push her away. She had already been through so much, and even now, he saw the pain flashing in her eyes paired with a twinge of fear. Standing up to him made her nervous, afraid, and that broke his heart. So he smiled. And then he left.

**

There were times that Ella got so caught up in her work, so soothed by the tapping of the keys as she typed, that anything outside of that rhythmic world startled her. And as Amber called her name, she jumped, spinning around with her hand over her heart.

"Sorry," Amber dutifully apologized although they were both accustomed to the reaction by now. "But you have a visitor. He asked for 'Ella, not like the kids' movie.' Hope you're not in trouble."

She threw her boss a confused look, but Amber merely motioned outside of the office. It had been a long, confusing day, and her heart was hurting, but she forced a smile and stepped into the hallway. And despite herself, Ella found herself grinning when she came face-to-face with Owen, completely decked out in a police uniform.

"Didn't I tell you not to re-enter the maze?" she teased, feeling herself warm under his stare.

"You gave me no choice. You didn't believe me. So here I am. In uniform. In my working uniform."

"Owen, anyone can get a cop uniform. Any costume store." She shrugged when he whipped out his badge for her to inspect. "You're showing me a badge. I'm just a regular citizen. I don't know what's real and what isn't."

"Ella!" He laughed. "It's against the law to impersonate a police officer."

"Right! So, either you are a cop. Or you are a very bold criminal. So, you see my dilemma."

He smiled at her, and she noticed the crinkling at the edge of his eyes. He was a good-looking man, adorable. "Okay, Ella. I won't keep you. I did want you to see that I am who I say I am. I had to at least try. It was good meeting you."

She shook his hand and watched as he spun around in a full circle, his neck stretched as if by simply looking, he could figure his way out. With a laugh, she motioned him to follow her, and she again led him to the elevators.

Owen thanked her, his lips stuck in a slight grin, and impulsively, she jumped forward and blurted out, "One dinner couldn't hurt, right? I mean, I'd meet you there at the restaurant and... that should be okay."

And that smile widened until it seemed his entire face was glowing. "Can't hurt one bit."
**

Diana watched as her husband - she still thought of him as her husband despite being divorced from him for over thirty years - stood in the doorway of what had been their daughter's room growing up. She saw his body sag, the grays in his hair seemed to multiply, and the wrinkles around his mouth deepened.

"Hey, honey," she called out softly and despite the gentleness of the whisper, Ted jumped and spun around. Then he gave her that sad small smile and reached a hand toward her. She returned the smile and stepped forward. "Call her, Ted."

He turned back to the bedroom and slowly shook his head. "No. What's done is done. I was horrible to her. When she was just little... I was such a bad father."

"I was an even worse mother."

"Eh. But you had issues you were fighting through, Diana. You had your reasons. I was clean and sober and just... just a shitty parent. I blamed a child for my life. I let my work control me..." His voice cracked, and he covered his face, breathing deeply, trying to get control. Trying to come to terms with having achieved everything in his career, re-uniting with his true love, and yet, failing utterly as a father. Hurting despite all the positive because the one area in his life could never come together. No, that was inaccurate. It was be-cause he had never tried hard enough. Ella had needed him. As an emotionally traumatized little girl, an angry teenager, and a lost young wife. She had needed a paternal guidance he had never wholeheartedly given her.

Ted had yelled and ordered, threatened and bribed, thrown his hands up and run. But he had never actually parented her. He wallowed in heartbreak and self-pity and healed himself with his work, his passion. As a way to excuse his behavior, he managed to convince himself and those that were part of his world at the time, that being raised by his parents was much better, much more stable for Ella than to be raised by an eccentric, moody father. The truth was his daugh-ter needed her parents, whether together or separate, she had needed them both. And both had failed her.

Suddenly he was overcome with remorse and heart-ache. She had been so young, so scared. Her mother had betrayed Ella, as well as him, and then put her in such a dangerous position. No matter the reason, that had to have traumatized her. And what did Ted do? He worried about himself. His broken heart, his photography... he had essentially abandoned her as well. And that poor baby girl grew into a confused, sullen teenager that took up with the first boy that showed her a charming smile. Ella had been so hungry for that love. His parents were great, but he knew they had been older and old-fashioned, affection not really part of the parenting skills they possessed.

And suddenly Diana stepped up beside him, her posture straight and rigid, but her eyes leaking their own sadness. "Maybe we were bad parents. I know I was horrible. But can we make her see that we can give her now what we couldn't back then?"

Ted turned to his soulmate and simply shook his head, all hope draining fast from his aging body. He had returned to this town to repair his relationship with Ella. That was his focus... and yet he had been communicating with Diana off and on for a couple of years... in between assignments, during lonely spells... and he had had an inkling that returning to this town would mean seeing her again. And he also knew that seeing his ex would mean falling victim to that intense ache and need to be near her.

She had felt the same. Clean and sober for several years, Diana was once again that natural beauty with a fresh personality and mesmerizing smile. Her laugh often repeated in his dreams and her soft, lilting voice raised him up from the depression threatening as he adjusted to a much more stagnant life. This was the woman that had beguiled him when they were young and naive, and the woman that had promised him the world and all that lay beyond with just a flirty tilt of her lips.

Diana. Ted understood his daughter's fury. His wife had slayed them both with the ultimate betrayal. But he also understood forgiveness. He only hoped his daughter learned that as well.

**

The autumn air was crisp and chilly, but it was still warm enough to go to the lake for a quick morning of fishing. But Ella feared losing that bubble of bliss she had been feeling lately. If she ran into the very man that could remind her of what her days were missing, what her soul still lived without, the day would not be as glorious as it felt right now.

So instead of getting some last-of-the-year fishing in, she cleaned. And Ella hated cleaning. But the sunlight streaming in and the music playing cheered her up. Sometimes things happened for a reason. Sometimes one did not get the ridiculously good-looking knight that came riding in on the horse Sometimes that knight showed up only to ride off without her. And that was okay.

Because sometimes what one did get was steady and dependable and enough to make her stomach flip when he smiled at her.

Owen might not have been one to make her speechless or weak in the knees, but she was growing fonder of him each time they saw each other. And truth be told, she was beginning to develop a small crush on him. He was invading her thoughts when they were apart and monopolizing her attention when they were together. Four weeks and five dates, and she realized that she was waiting for that text or call asking her for the next date.

Dennis was busy with his classes and some traveling. If he needed assistance, he spoke to someone other than her unless it was unavoidable. One time they had passed each other in the hall, and there was enough stuttering and fumbling between the two of them to make them both take different routes to the bathrooms to avoid the discomfort.

And tonight... tonight Owen was cooking for her... at his place. Four weeks into what was now a relationship, and Ella knew what that meant. It meant she would take extra care in getting ready, in preparation for a man to be up close, a new man. Her mind had to be mentally prepared to accept someone's touch other than Dennis's.

That thought slipped into the front of her mind so quickly, so naturally, that she had no choice but to acknowledge it, to handle it gingerly, inspect it, and react. Because this would not be Dennis touching her, loving her. It would be Owen, and she already knew her responses to him were different. There was not an explosive, mind-blowing reaction to his presence, but maybe that was for the best. It was nice, and it was slow. Easy. Ella had a chance to breathe near him and consider her emotions in the moment.

But knowing that tonight might mean a new turn in their relationship, Ella had to consider the difference. Could she give herself to a man in that emotional and physical way, knowing it would not fill her soul, would not light her up from the inside, as had happened with Dennis? Could she be satisfied with less?

Of course, she could. Perhaps Ella would even be happier with less. No fireworks? Good, because with the fireworks, she had always been left to wonder if he'd be there after the sparks burnt out. With Owen, he was dedicated and vocal about his intentions. His heart was on his sleeve, so to speak. That was a warm comfort, like hot chocolate on a snowy afternoon. Or sand between one's toes. Pleasant. Solid.

Ella managed to chase the melancholy thoughts away and smiled as she remembered their first date. Owen had jumped up out of his car and jogged over to her when she had parked at the agreed upon restaurant, opening her car door and murmuring compliments as his face flushed. He was endearing right from the start.

She learned he was also divorced. He had two kids with his ex, the oldest was a twenty-three-year-old son who was living out of state and newly married. And a daughter who was in college.

"Things just didn't work out between us," he had explained with a small smile that did not reach his eyes. "We were good while the kids were young, busy and happy, and then the older they got, the more we were left staring at each other twiddling our thumbs. What now? She wanted to move further south, I didn't want to... and it was almost natural, you know? The growing apart and then ending things. Natural and friendly."

He had walked her to her car and asked for a hug. Endearing.

He had texted her to ensure she had made it home safely. And then checked in with her the following day. So endearing.

The jarring buzz of the doorbell caused Ella to jump and curse, her warm thoughts scattering and bringing back the cold realization that he was not Dennis. Could not kiss like Dennis or smile like Dennis. No matter how endearing he was, Owen could never begin to fill the shadow of Dennis. And that was the unfortunate truth, no matter how Ella spun it.

Glancing at the clock, she saw that it was hours before her date. Lila was with her father on a trip to some historic battlefield Ella had always begged him to take them to when they had been married. There was no one else she was expecting.

The first thought that trampled over her nerves as soon as she opened the door was that the person at her front door was not Dennis. Some secret, dark part of her had been hoping... wishing.

The second thought... well, it was a string of silent alarms and exclamations as it registered who this older woman was standing in front of her with a somewhat bewildered expression mixed with a bit of resolve.

"What the hell are you doing here?" Ella spat out at her mother.

The years had not changed her mother all that much. The hair was shorter, there were some wrinkles around her eyes and mouth, and she seemed smaller... shorter. But she was ultimately the same as the last time Ella had seen her. And the last time had been her high school graduation. Diana had been hiding in the back of the crowd, but Ella had still spotted her. It had almost made her cry ... actually, she had cried. Because her father had not attended. Her grandparents were dead, and there was only her husband who was just a child himself. So, the only family member who had been at her graduation was the one family member she would not speak to.

Now she was at her door. Jumping forward, Diana held her hands out as if to stop her from rejection. "Please. Hear me out."

And in that moment, Ella despised herself for the weakness that held her in place, the old tugging need to have her mother's love that kept her from stepping back and slamming the door shut. In that moment, Ella hesitated. And Diana took advantage of that slight pause.

"Ella, please listen. I know I was a horrible mom. I don't deserve to be in your life, although I would give everything to just be in a small part of it... but your dad. You're killing him, Ella. Slowly but surely, you're killing him. Please don't shut him out."

"Oh, that's rich. To tell me I'm killing him. You know what, get off my property."

"That came out wrong! I meant that not having a relationship with you, he's not doing well. Listen, Ella, honey, you are his world-"

"No. His work was his world. You were a close second."

Diana stepped forward, bracing her hand against the front door. "He didn't choose sides, Ella. He stayed away from me up until this past year. No one's taking my side, not even me. I was ..." Her voice caught, and she swallowed. "I was a disaster of a mother. And I need you to know that I regret that every day. I have nightmares about losing you, about making those mistakes over and over-"

Ella did her best to keep her expression blank. "Am I supposed to feel sorry for you? Because, mom, I have nightmares too. I have nightmares of trying to find you, of hearing scary noises in that bedroom of that man's house. A stranger's house. Of suddenly moving and that strange guy being there all the time. I dream of the yelling and the crying. Of the pain surging through my arm. Do you know my arm never fully healed, and it aches right before it rains?"

There was a slight satisfaction in seeing her mother shake with sobs. A sick kind of joy in knowing she did have that effect on her. She was not invisible, not a forgotten memory. But she straightened and squared her shoulders and in her iciest tone, ordered, "Get off my property and stay away from my daughter."

The door was almost shut when she heard her mother hiccup, "No!"

Ella swung the door open and stared at her incredulously. "What did you say?"

And it seemed her mother could straighten and square her shoulders just as well, although her voice was wobbly from leftover tears. "I said no. I didn't come here just to … you want to dish it out, Ella Barnes, then do it. I deserve it. I'm not going to tuck my tail between my legs and run. I did this to you. Yes. I am so sorry. And I'm sorry your dad wasn't the father you deserve. But please, I'm here to beg you to give him a chance. I'll stay out of it."

"Will you stay away from my grandmother's house?"

Diana met her daughter's gaze. "No. I love your father. I will leave if you come over. If that's what you want."

"I let you talk. Now what I want is for you to leave. Okay? Please go. I heard you out. And it makes no difference."

This time the door shut.

CHAPTER 16

There was an unsettling silence after Ella's rant, and she slowly sank back into her chair, tossing her napkin onto the plate. "I'm sorry. I'm being a buzzkill."

"What? No." But Owen sighed. "I just didn't … it's a bit of a heavy topic for what I wanted tonight. That's all."

Ella's face flushed, and she stumbled for words. The trauma of her mother's visit had weighed heavily on her throughout the day and when she had shown up at Owen's place, the story had poured out of her. He was right, of course. This was supposed to be romantic, fun. And her issues had destroyed that.

"I'm sorry. I just… her visit caught me off guard."

"I realize that. But it's your mom. Not some monster. Just talk to her."

She bristled at those words. "Talk to the woman that broke my arm?"

"Sounds like it was an accident. Listen, I'm not excusing her behavior. But her affair, it was between her and your father. She was not doing it to hurt you personally." He shook his head as if to shake out the very conversation. "Look, can we talk about something else?"

"Of course. I'm sorry."

"No. Just… let's focus on better things."

She forced a smile and nodded, trying to hide the fact that her chest was tight, and her throat burned. She felt disappointed and humiliated. There were rules to dating. Don't overshare. Don't attempt to garner sympathy. Have some mystery.

Unfortunately, Ella had never been good at rules.

She helped Owen rinse the plates and load the dishwasher, and then she backed up a few steps, clearing her throat. "I think… I'm going to head out."

"What?" His shoulders dropped. "No! Ella, if it's because I asked you to -"

"No. It's nothing you did. I just … I'm tired and have to get up early."

The disappointment seemed to smother his features, and she wanted to cry. Cry for herself, cry for the embarrassment of her behavior, and cry for him. She was sure he thought of this as a new beginning. And Ella had simply stormed through here with her over-told, sad story of parents who were less than ideal, catching him off-guard, throwing off his attempts for a perfect, romantic night.

Owen tried again to change her mind, but Ella knew the mood was killed. It would be an evening of awkwardness and over-trying. That overwhelmed her. Just the thought. Pure exhaustion.

Twice she had to pull over because of the sobbing. She realized this was probably payback from the joy in seeing her mother cry. This was the Karma she deserved. The second time she pulled over, she tried calling Leona, but the call went straight to voicemail. And she was relieved because somehow, in some warped train of thought, that gave her permission to call him. Dennis.

He answered on the first ring and when she could only cry in response to his greeting, he immediately demanded, "What happened? Oh my God, are you okay? Where are you?"

"No, no. I'm fine. I'm not hurt. Just… I'm pulled over on the side of the road right before the Tyeville exit and -"

"Stay there."

It was less than ten minutes before she saw headlights pull up behind her. She rolled down her window. "I'm sorry. I shouldn't have called you. I- I'm okay now."

Dennis leaned in and studied her, his eyes pinning her in place, locking her in with the intensity of concern and the richness in their color. "Bullshit. You can barely talk right now." He sank down to his haunches and waited as she fought to regain her composure, struggled to stop crying.

When she could finally speak, she revealed, "My mom came to my house."

Dennis's eyes widened and then he cursed under his breath. "My place is closer. Can you drive?"

And she nodded, although she knew she should decline. But the pull was there, the need for his comfort, his words, and his closeness. This was Dennis. She needed him, even if it was just temporary.

Ella sank into the familiar couch and smiled up at Dennis as he covered her with a blanket and brought her a cup of cocoa. He ordered a pizza, and then he sat beside her and rubbed her back as she recounted the scene. He gave her the sort of attention she had longed for with Owen. This was what she had wanted. To be heard.

"Was it at all healing to hear her apologize and take responsibility?"

Ella considered his question before shaking her head. "I don't know. I'm still reeling from it all."

"Understandable. But you said your mom showed up this morning. What happened now? Because I know you, Ella, and you weren't driving around in your car for hours just crying. What's wrong?" Ella stared down at her hands on her lap, swallowing as the words to tell him got stuck in her throat. With a noise of understanding, he added, "New guy problems?" He waved away her concerned expression. "Sheila made sure to tell me that you've been going on dates with a new guy. I think she wanted me to move in quickly, as if I had a chance of sweeping you off your feet and away from any other suitors." He gave her a sad smile. "So, what does new guy have to do with this?"

"I told him. I said my mom had stopped by, and it shook me up. I told him the history with it all. I just word vomited everything onto this practical stranger's lap. He basically told me to get over it, talk to my mother, and to change the subject to something a bit more cheerful."

Dennis flinched. "Ouch."

"Right. But he had a point. I mean, I don't really … we don't know each other that well to just blurt out everything. It had to be a little overwhelming."

"Sure. But we're not kids. We're adults with adult problems and issues. If he wants a relationship, if he wants to know you, he has to be willing to hear about this. To want to know. Don't you think? I genuinely want to know your past, your concerns, what makes you sad so I can avoid ever doing that. What gets you irritated to the point that your nose scrunches up and those lines appear between your eyebrows. What makes you get all distant-looking. I want to know what makes you laugh, what makes you want to get up in the morning… and most of all, Ella, I want to know how to make you look at me the way you used to."

Ella did her best to avoid his stare. One look and she knew she would not be strong enough to resist that hold. Dennis was playing his usual game because he knew she was seeing another man. He was trying to win some messed-up game no one else wanted to play.

"I should go."

And just like that, Dennis stood and nodded. The intensity gone. "Okay. Are you better now? Okay to drive?"

She nodded, although her head was spinning. What was that? How did he turn it on and off like that? Ducking her head to hide the tears threatening, she followed him to the front door. Mumbling a thanks, she tried to brush past him, but he blocked her way, his hands landing softly on her shoulders.

"Can you at least look at me, Ella? Please?"

"Dennis. Stop."

"Fine. But there is a reason you called me. Honey, there's a reason I'm the one you sought out when your world came crashing down today. And there's a reason, a very clear, very good reason I came running the minute you did." He leaned down and pressed his lips to the top of her head before moving aside.

And she ran to her car. Before she lost all senses and ran back to him.

The rest of the evening was long, blurry as if in a fever dream. Ella felt restless, uncomfortable, and it seemed she kept replaying the day's events over and over until her mind screamed out in protest.

There were a few missed calls from Owen, but no texts or voice messages, so she assumed he was relieved to not get in touch with her. There would probably be no next date, and a part of her was disappointed but another part was relieved.

Dating at her age was equivalent to teaching that old dog new, complicated tricks. Ella was unique in personality, quirky and probably confusing to a lot of people. She had no desire to change. She had had to mute her personality for years. Now she was free to behave as she wanted. And if it was too much for a guy, if it was not what the other person deemed as appropriate, then she could walk away.

Finally settling her nerves and mind with a light, fun movie, Ella almost chose not to answer her phone when she saw it was Owen. But it would not be fair. He did not deserve to be avoided. He really did nothing technically wrong.

"Ella, I've been trying to call." His tone was tinged with concern, not accusation.

"I had my phone on silent."

"I'm sorry. I'm not good at this. My ex will tell you that I suck at listening and giving advice. I didn't mean to … when I get focused on something, I can't think of anything else and I was just focused on giving you the best dinner. I wanted to impress you. In case you haven't noticed, I'm crazy about you, Ella."

Ella squeezed her eyes shut and breathed in sharply. Because all she could think about was Dennis whispering in her ear, his eyes seeking her out, his hands on her shoulders. There was a man telling her everything she wanted to hear… and it broke her heart. "Owen, I just got divorced. And maybe I share too much, and I'm sorry about that, but I do think you should know that I recently ended a relationship that … I'm not so sure I'm ready to try again so soon."

"Give me the chance to make you forget him. Please. Can I see you again?"

"I'm not good at this either, Owen."

"Then let's just suck at this together. Please. Let me take you out tomorrow."

There was a beep to signal another call coming through. "Um, okay. I actually have someone calling in so … tomorrow."

She glanced at the phone to see who was calling, and her heart jumped.

"Dennis, it's late-"

"Yes, I know. That's why I didn't knock on your door. I didn't want to startle you."

Dropping the phone to her side, Ella strode to the front door and flung it open, the light from the motion detector spilling out and illuminating Dennis. "What are you doing here?"

But the teasing expression she had expected was gone, and in its place was a look of misery she knew all too well. "I wanted to check on you."

"I'm fine. It wasn't fair of me to run to you."

"But you did." When she did not respond, he continued, "Can I ask you something?"

"What?"

"Did you really tell this new guy all about your mom? Are you that comfortable with him?"

"Dennis." She sighed, the pain from his words seeping through her skin. She did not want to admit that this man in front of her had feelings. That she could trigger such emotions in him. It was much easier to think of him as the man who had broken her heart.

But that damn shine in his eyes proved he did in fact

have emotions. "It all had just happened. I was overwhelmed, and I wanted some feedback. That's it. Don't read too much into it." She had to lie. Ella could not very well admit that she had been trying to force some closeness with this new guy, try to trigger the same type of wild attraction she had felt for Dennis. In her mind, she thought if she confided the same things Dennis had wanted to know, then she and Owen would somehow bond. She would feel closer to him.

Dennis stared at her for a few moments before giving a short nod and walking away.

**

There was something comforting about the whir of the mixer, that deep hum jumping to a louder whine the faster the hand mixer spun through the batter. Lila watched as Connie focused on smoothing it out, and she realized that she felt at ease, at home with this woman. It was not as cozy and familiar as with her own mother, of course, but she loved that her soon-to-be stepmother treated her as her own. Lila felt content and cared for, but along with that came guilt because she knew her mother had been betrayed by this very woman.

"What are you smiling at?" Connie asked with a growing grin of her own. "Are you making fun of my discomfort?"

Connie's stomach made it difficult to get close to the counter, and having her attention drawn to that, Lila giggled. "No. But that's pretty funny."

Connie directed a warm smile at her and almost instinctively patted Lila's shoulder. When Lila's dad had left and moved in with Connie, Lila wanted to hate her. She did everything in her power to be miserable when she was near her. But now she adored Connie. She knew Connie was not so nice to her mom, but she treated Lila with such tenderness that she enjoyed being in her company.

Connie was still watching her with a curious smile, so Lila shrugged and elaborated, "I'm just happy that I'm here."

With those words, Connie glanced down at her own hands. "Well... why don't you stay here more? During the week sometimes."

"Oh, I... it might -" she fumbled for words, for an explanation that while she loved being here, she enjoyed her own home more, her mother more. Because her mother was the ultimate source of comfort and love. But Connie did not want to hear that. Although she was careful never to say anything negative about Lila's mother, Lila instinctively knew it would disappoint Connie to hear her speak lovingly about Ella. "It's probably better if I hang out at home during the week. I can visit here some evenings but mom... she has been in a funk ever since Dennis..."

"Oh?" Connie started scooping the batter onto the cookie sheet, pausing to offer Lila a taste. Almost as an afterthought, she murmured, "They're not together?"

"No. Not for a while now. Mom's dating some new guy. I haven't met him yet. But I don't think she's as into him. She still... she seems upset... sad. I know she misses Dennis."

"Aw, that's a shame."

"It is. And she tore down the security system he put up. So, it must really be over. I don't know." She knew she was blabbing everything her mother did not want her to blab, but Connie just listened to anything she said, so she wanted to keep talking, to keep that maternal attention directed at her. "Anything he got her is put away. But she's dating, so she's good," Lila rushed to add, wanting her mom to be seen as resilient and brave.

"Who's dating?" Alex strolled into the kitchen and ignoring Connie, smiled at his daughter.

Lila shook her head, but Connie answered, "Seems your ex is dating another man already."

Alex's eyes widened, and he whistled. "What? Lila, your mom is getting around!" Seeing his daughter's expression, he chuckled. "I'm kidding. Lighten up. Seriously though, should she be bringing all these men around you?"

"I haven't met him. I - I'm going for a walk." She avoided Connie's apologetic stare and her father's urging to grow up and take a joke and made her way outside. Tears burned her eyes, and she fumbled for her phone, feeling betrayed and alone. Lila felt ashamed for thinking such great, loving thoughts about a woman that not only was the reason her family was in pieces, but who didn't so much as blink before spilling all the information Lila had confided in her.

Finn answered on the second ring, his voice hushed and hurried. "Lila? What's up?"

"I just can't be here anymore. Finn, I need to get away." She choked on a sob. "Please, can we go somewhere?"

There was a pause. "Li, I'm at work. Middle of a shift. I can come get you at 6 tonight."

She did her best to stifle a cry of frustration, her voice coming through high and broken. "Okay. It's fine. Tonight."

There was another long pause and then a sigh. "No, I'm sorry. I'll be right there."

"No, Finn, don't, please. I don't want you to get in trouble."

"It's okay. I can get Sadie to fill in for me. Where are you?"

It was not long before they were settled in their private spot in the woods, sitting on a few rocks by the creek, smoking a joint. The sobs had settled into silent tears, and when Finn wrapped an arm around her shoulders and pulled her close, she relished in that feel of comfort and attention.

"Look, Li, they're wrapped up in their own stupid lives. Sometimes adults just ... they suck. You know you can count on me, right? I'm here."

Lila turned and locked gazes with Finn, his electric blue eyes mesmerizing and his earnest promises intoxicating. That was all it took before they were kissing passionately, arms entwined and expectations mounting. She knew, sensed it deep down in her gut, that Finn would walk through fire for her. It was a power she was not used to, a heady sensation that she was not sure what to do with. For the first time she was in control, and the raw energy from that knowledge overpowered the thrill of his kisses. This was hers. He was all for her.

**

Ella slept with Owen on a warm, Autumn evening after a quiet, if not clumsy, dinner and awkward conversation. They were both nervous, but it seemed for different reasons. Owen wanted everything perfect. Ella just wanted it to be not a disaster.

And it was not. It was the same as his kisses, the same as how she saw Owen himself. Safe and attractive... a comfort in a time she thought her heart could never bounce back. But a strange sort of homesick sensation overcame her as she lay in his bed afterwards, the wind blowing leaves against the window, the night sky overpowering with no moon as a reprieve. Owen's room was small and musky, damp as if it were clogged with sweat and shadows.

"That was amazing," he announced, pulling her closer. She felt her lips pull up and hoped it was convincing enough to not hurt his feelings. But she counted the minutes until she could escape the dark, dank room with the man she felt she barely knew.

The next day he sent flowers to Ellie's work, and she did her best to hide them from view, but mid-afternoon, she glanced up from her computer to see Dennis standing a few feet behind her, staring at the bouquet. He gave her a tight smile as he widened his eyes before leaving. And it irked her that Dennis seemed to be judging. He had no right. He had no claim.

When her phone rang several minutes later, she was still feeling distracted. Owen's voice came through, low and gentle, a good-tempered bear. "Hey you. I can't seem to stop thinking about you. Last night..." He gave a low whistle.

And she felt herself flush and swoon. "Owen, thank you for the flowers."

"The flowers are part romance.... Part apology."

"Apology?"

"Our dinner tonight... I actually forgot I had made

other plans with a buddy of mine...he's actually who I was visiting when I met you."

"Oh." She sat back, staring at the bright red roses on her desk, a soft, unguarded smile playing on her lips. "It's okay. We can go out another night."

"Ellie, you're such a sweetie, but that isn't ... no. I still have to see you tonight. I can't not see you after ... No, what I'm asking is if you would mind if he joined us for dinner."

"Oh." And she realized with a start that they were at that stage now. She would be meeting his friends, then his family... she would be expected to introduce him into her world. "Sure."

"Thank you for being so understanding. You're going to love him. I'm glad he is the first of my gang you're going to meet. Shorty might not scare you away so fast."

She forced a laugh, although her throat was dry. Was she ready for this step? Sure, she had slept with the guy, but to meet friends... Ellie was not sure she could stomach a relationship. Not after the year she had had. It was almost one year ago that her husband had left. Now she was divorced, had been attacked, and had lost the love of her life and she was expected to date? Not only date but meet friends? No.... She tried to think of a way out of the dinner. But she glanced at the flowers and remembered his tone when she had agreed to the plans for that night.

After work, Ella went home to check on Lila, who already had plans and was rushing out the door. She had asked Ella about working at the small restaurant in town, and Ella assured her that if she kept her grades up, she could. It would be a great experience to earn some spending money, and if everything went according to plan, Lila would have her license in just a few weeks.

"Mom, I'm going to go tonight. Just like an hour of training but then the manager said I can start on Monday evening."

The sudden interest in employment struck Ella as odd, so giving her daughter a sidelong look, she casually asked,

"Does Brad work there?"

"Brad? No. Why would he? And I don't really talk to him anymore."

"Oh?" This news both surprised and alarmed Ella. She sat down and gave Lila her full attention. "What happened? And when? Last I heard, you guys were still getting along."

Lila rolled her eyes. "I'm sixteen, mom. Don't think I'm going to find my forever-after sitting in English class." She shrugged, shoving her books into her bookbag. "We just... grew apart, I guess. He's pretty obnoxious."

"He always seemed nice when he was around me."

"Then you go out with him, mom! God! Shouldn't you be happy I'm not so serious with a guy? Why is it I suddenly feel I let you down because I'm not dating the damn quarterback?"

Ella sat back and exhaled, studying Lila carefully. "Are you done, Lila?"

Lila rolled her eyes. "Forget it. Look, I'm going to study after training so I might be home later than usual."

"Studying? With whom?"

A cry of irritation penetrated the room. "Just say who, mom. Grammar police aren't around. Who. Who. Sound normal."

"Why are you so nasty lately?"

"Sorry. That just freakin' gets to me. I'm studying with Finn. He works at the restaurant. He's actually the one that got me the job there. He's good at math, and I need help in it."

Before Ella could question the arrangement, ask if there was something about Finn she should know, Lila was skipping out the door. Ella knew damn well she should be grateful her daughter wanted to work. Not many teenagers voluntarily went out and got a job. But something nagged at her. There was more to this. She knew her daughter, and although they were not as close as they used to be, she could sense something was off. And by the level of hysterics she emitted when questioned about Brad, Ella was willing to bet he had a lot to do with it.

Of course, Lila could just be trying to keep busy after a heartbreak. Job and school and .... And Finn. Ella tried to sum up what she knew about the boy, and she realized it was not much. With Brad, there had been little mystery. He was an ideal student with parents well-known to not only Ella, but the community. Smart, athletic, and respectful.

The only thing Ella could hope was that if Finn was becoming more prominent in Lila's life, whether as a friend or more, then her daughter would bring him around more.

Ella had agreed to meet Owen at the restaurant so he could have a drink or two with his friend first and catch up. And it suited her because the last couple of times he had picked her up, she had been running late. Owen had paced the living room, trying to hide his annoyance with a smile. She felt rushed, as if she were putting him out.

One particular time, she had asked if they could just wait a few more minutes because Lila was on her way home, and he answered, "But she isn't going with us, is she?" When she had confirmed that her daughter was not joining them, he had answered, "Then do we need to wait around? I haven't met her yet and don't feel like the first time should be when we are rushed."

So now she took her time. She curled her hair and took extra care with her makeup. Without an impatient man sighing and stomping in the next room, Ella actually finished early and felt calmer. She felt more prepared. Perhaps she would suggest meeting at the destination more in the future.

The restaurant was crowded for a weeknight evening, and as the hostess led Ella to the table, she felt good. She felt pretty and light, and her reservations and fears over meeting his friend evaporated. She could do this. A new relationship - that was exciting. Who knew where it would lead? Down the road, she could possibly develop a more passionate feel... in time, she might forget -

"Ah, there she is!" Owen stood and stepped toward her, his hands reaching out, but she could only stare past him, her mouth open and eyes wide.

Because sitting at the same table was Dennis, his expression full of amusement.

"Oh," she managed, tearing her gaze from Dennis and glancing up at Owen. "I - you have - "

Owen laughed. "Surprised? We thought you would be. Here, sit down."

Ella fought for her composure as he pulled her chair out, and she sat with a smile, doing her best to avoid Dennis's pointed stare. She giggled as if she were just as amused as Owen. But her mind was racing as thoughts whirled and fought to fall into place. What was going on? Where was Owen's friend, and why was Dennis sitting across from her, staring with an intensity she was positive Owen would feel?

But instead Owen grinned at her. "So, you already know Shorty."

Ella managed to tilt her head with mild curiosity and repeat, "Shorty."

"Yeah. I used to play basketball with some guys I knew. That's how I met him. We called him Shorty because he's tall... get it?" Owen snorted and hit the table.

"I get it," she answered with a forced smile.

He opened his mouth to say something else, but his phone buzzed. Glancing down, he groaned. "Hey, it's work. Sorry, guys. Be right back."

As soon as Owen was out of view, she focused her glare on Dennis. "What is this? Huh? What kind of game are you two playing?"

Dennis scooted forward, holding his hand out as if to ward off her fury. "Listen. El, I did not know. Not until we were sitting at this table, and he told me your name. And then he saw my expression and immediately caught on that I knew you. I didn't tell him anything except that we met while fishing, and I mentioned the job to you, and you applied and got it. That's all."

"You couldn't give me a head's up?"

"How? It would seem a little obvious if I whipped out my phone and started texting. I was in shock, just like you are." He leaned back and studied her. "He's a good guy, Ella. And he's crazy about you. He told me... he said he is falling for you."

"What?" She shook her head as if to clear out such a thought. "We barely know each other." And then she gasped, her head jerking up, and her eyes taking in Dennis with shock. "That day - the hot date you had - it was Owen. She was joking."

"What?" He studied her intently and then nodded slowly. "Yes. It was Owen... Ella, what are you saying? Is that why you suddenly- you thought.... No. Ella, there was no one but -"

"Sorry about that!" Owen's voice reached them before he turned the corner and reclaimed his seat beside Ella. She sat there avoiding Dennis's miserable stare, afraid to consider his words, what he had been about to say, what it all meant. Because it was too late. Wasn't it? She shifted in her seat and stared up at Owen who flashed her a beaming smile. And she knew it was too late. Too many things had happened. Too many things were in the way.

"Everything okay with work?" Ella asked, having to clear her throat before the words could escape.

"As okay as they can be. So, what's everyone ordering? I'm supposed to watch what I eat, knock off a few pounds but this is a celebration, right?" He focused his smile on Ella once again. "Are you going to start being one of those girlfriends that lectures me on what to eat?"

"No, of course not." She knew Owen was excited, amped up on nerves over his new romantic prospect meeting his best friend. So, she tried to be patient and kind, laughing at his jokes and nodding along to his comments. But she wondered how he could not sense the tension. How did he not notice the red blotches on her chest or Dennis's stony silence? How did he not feel that wave of sexual familiarity flowing between them? She almost felt naked, definitely vulnerable.

"So, you two played basketball together?"

Owen leaned back and grinned. "Yes. Five years ago. I wanted something to do outside of ... well, I was going through the divorce. And I met him through this basketball league. We ended up going out after practices and games, and he was just a great support."

Ella pulled her lips up in a semblance of a smile. "He does have a way of doing that, doesn't he? Being a support to those going through a rough time."

And she felt small and shallow for feeling hurt that she had not been the exception. It seemed Dennis was everyone's support. It was just who he was. A great guy.

As Dennis stared right back at her, Owen cleared his throat, a tight smile on his face as he answered cautiously, "Yes, he does. And I'm forever grateful he was there during that time. True friend. I owe him."

The words seemed to sink through Dennis's reverie, as he finally broke his stare from hers and change his expression to mildly amused. "Stop with that. You owe me nothing. I seem to remember a few favors I've called into you."

The awkwardness dissipated just enough to let natural conversation flow. Ella heard stories of their basketball games as the men reverted to boys with competitiveness and bragging. She learned of Owen's sprained wrist and Dennis's injured knee and the camaraderie formed between the teammates. And she glimpsed a side of Owen she had not seen or bothered to notice before. He always struck her as the average man, shying away from emotional displays or confiding anything too personal. But now she saw that he was just like her in the regard that he had been hurting. He had sought out some comfort in the form of friendship... in the form of Dennis. Owen was not some stereotypical grunting caveman of a guy. He was simply awkward at feeling and showing those emotions. He was uncomfortable with the sheer volume of misery divorce brought forth.

At one point, Dennis folded his hands and leaned forward, an over-the-top jovial tone spilling out with his words. "So, tell me. How did ...." he waved toward them, "happen?"

Owen beamed, sneaking a glance over at Ella. "I was leaving your office, got all turned around on the shit directions you provided to get out of the maze, and I walked past this room where this ... this beautiful woman was sitting. There was no way I could just walk past and not talk to her. She wasn't very nice at first."

A short, surprised laugh shot out of Ella's mouth. "What? I was ridiculously nice to you!"

He winked at her with a devilish smile. "You accused me of lying."

"Right. I didn't think you were really a cop. But I wasn't mean about it."

"Ella! You ignored my explanation and just walked away."

"You started out the conversation by telling me I was the most beautiful woman you'd ever seen. That was a bit intense."

His grin softened, and he gave a short nod. "I see your point. I was quite honestly caught off guard. You're very striking."

She blushed under his blatant exaggeration and rushed to change the subject. "This restaurant is nice. I love the corner booths. Cozy."

"Have you ever been here before?"

It was an innocent question, almost so automatic and casual that she was not sure a response was even necessary. But the truth was she had been there once before... with Dennis. And she panicked.

"No. Never."

Ella saw the slight jerk of Dennis's body as his head shot up and eyes took her in with wide disbelief. She jammed a forkful of salad into her mouth and murmured, "Mmm. This is good. How's your burger, Owen?"

But before he could answer, his phone started ringing. Glancing up apologetically, he mouthed, "Work," and rushed from the table.

Ella held out her hand as if to stop the rush of words that might come out of Dennis's mouth. "I know. I know we were here. The corner booth over there. I remember. But I … he asked, and I didn't even want to think thoughts of you when we … there was …. My expression would give it away and -"

"Ella."

One word. Her name. Soft but with enough power in the tone to cause her to immediately stop talking and stare up at him. He gave her a small smile. "I get it. It's okay."

She felt her shoulders ease down from the hunched-up position, and she sighed. "Okay. I just didn't want you to think I was being purposely cruel."

"I'm glad. El, I'm glad you weren't trying to be cruel. And I understand."

Owen jogged back to the table. "I'm so sorry. I have to go."

"Is everything okay?" Ella managed to drag her gaze away from Dennis, the realization that Owen was leaving registering slowly, as if dragging through sludge and fog. He was leaving for a job that was dangerous. She had to focus.

"Um, yes. Nothing to worry about. Sorry about this." He waved their server over and pulled out some bills. "This should cover our dinners-"

"No!" Dennis jumped up, lifting his own wallet from his back pocket. "This is on me."

"No way, Dennis. I got this-"

"No. I invited you two."

The tug of war over who would pay for dinner, including hers, made Ella more than a little nauseous. Grabbing her purse, she lifted the correct amount of bills and threw them on the table. Smiling up at the server, she purred, "That should cover my part of the bill while these two fight over who can pound his chest the hardest."

By the time she reached her car, Owen was sprinting up to her, calling her name. "Hey, Ella! Wait up. Don't run off."

Calmly, she turned toward him, her gaze floating over his shoulder to see Dennis not far behind. "I'm not running. Just came out to wait for you."

"Look, are you mad? I'm not good at guessing these things. And if you are, I have no idea what I did. Is it because I have to go back to work?"

Her eyes widened and she tried to ignore Dennis who was now just off to the side, watching. "What? No! I wouldn't get upset about something like that. I just didn't want to sit there any longer and watch helplessly as two men fought over the bill. It made me feel… like an object."

Ella saw Dennis hang his head in understanding, a sigh heaving his shoulders. She knew he got it. But when she looked back at Owen, he was staring at her with a confused look. And she knew he did not get it. But instead of arguing, he smiled sweetly. "Hey, can I give you a call after I'm done? I'm sorry the evening got cut short."

She nodded with a slight smile. "Of course. Call."

Before Ella could know how to react, Owen pulled her to him in an uncharacteristic display of passion. After a longer than usual kiss, he let her go, his hand sliding over her rear. "I'll call." He pulled away and nodded toward Dennis. "Dennis. Thanks again, bud. I'll talk to you soon."

She did not see or hear Dennis's reaction. She simply stood there, watching Owen jump into his car and drive off. But she felt him. She felt Dennis's stare, the surprise, and as if she were connected to his thoughts, she knew before he inched up to her, before the hot, deep whisper stung her ear.

"You're sleeping with him?"

"Not your business." She remained still, staring straight ahead.

"Not my - you sat there, Ella and -" he stepped back, and when she turned to face him, she saw his eyes were blazing. There was a look she had never seen come from him. Full of rage and disappointment. "You sat in there and said you didn't even know him and things were moving too fast. Like you had no control. You know how you get control, Ella? You don't go sleeping with a man you don't want to jump in a relationship with!"

"Hey! Not your business, Dennis! At all. Got it? I was caught off guard tonight when I saw you sitting there. But you're right about one thing. Owen is a great guy. Wonderful. I never have to worry if he will be mature enough for a relationship or use his past as an excuse to be a player."

The color drained from his face, and she instinctively stepped back, knowing she had gone too far. Knowing that she had pushed a button that would set it all off. But then Dennis leaned away from her, taking a deep breath, and she assumed the rage was over. He had calmed down. Until he hissed, "Right. I guess I misread you all this time. I thought you gave more than a second's consideration about who you opened your legs for."

There was no air. There was no breathing. Ella found herself wanting to double over, to gasp and claw. Because those words coming from the mouth of the man she had thought herself to be in love with, had thought to be her hero.... Those words took the life from her. She was left an empty, struggling shell. In a parking lot. The irony almost afforded her enough air to laugh.

But it was not until Dennis cursed and whispered her name that the air seemed to return to her lungs, surging through and pushing out grinded up words through sobs she had not realized were seizing her body. "I hate you. I wish, I absolutely, truly wish I had never met you."

Ella saw tears splashing from his eyes, and it rooted her to the spot, stunned. But then she remembered the words, his words, and she escaped into her car, trying to breathe, trying to forget, trying to deny that the thought that leaving him behind hurt more than his words ever could.

CHAPTER 17

Ella noticed the door was unlocked and sighed, hastily wiping at her wet cheeks. Either Lila had forgotten to lock up, or she was here. As soon as she stepped into the house, the answer came in the form of a bouncing, smiling Lila. When she saw her mother, however, she grew still. "Mom? What's wrong?"

"Nothing's wrong."

"Mom, you've been crying. Did that guy do something? Owen?"

And Ella saw the fear, the memory of that attack flashing in Lila's eyes, and she quickly shook her head, knowing she could not leave that question lingering in the young girl's mind. "No, no. Owen is great, honey. I just got caught off guard. His friend joined us for dinner. And his friend happens to be Dennis. We were both surprised, and at the end of the night, words were exchanged."

Lila's eyes grew round, and Ella was sure she was awed by the fact that adults also have drama. "You mean between Owen and Dennis?"

"No. Owen had to leave, and Dennis and I... I'm just ...feelings hurt, honey. That's it."

"Dennis was mean to you?" Her expression was one of disbelief. Lila was taking this personally, a betrayal that included her. Dennis had been her friend, an adult that she trusted.

"Listen, Lila. It is not clear-cut. We hurt each other. Just... it doesn't matter now because... he isn't a part of my life. So, listen, what are you up to? How was your first night of work?"

She shook her head, still eying her mother warily, as if she knew she was not telling the entire truth. "Boring. Was going to study with Finn, but he had to take someone's shift. I thought maybe you and I could go driving."

"Yep. That's a great idea."

Having her daughter need her helped Ella focus on something other than her tangled obsession with a man that obviously thought less of her than she had hoped. A man that played with her emotions just enough to disrupt her life, her healing process, her very soul, and then had nerve to condemn her for moving on.

But now Ella was questioning her own actions. She had explicitly stated things were moving too fast, and she wanted to slow down. She had confided that to Dennis. So, it must have stung when he realized they had begun an intimate relationship.

Ella understood that. She could empathize with that, of course. But his words.... His insinuations that she was nothing more than a cheap whore... it was more than a slap in the face. During their short time together, Ella felt as if Dennis could understand her better than any man she had ever encountered. He seemed to know the innermost secrets of her soul, how her mind worked, how her emotions played out. Sometimes he sensed before she even knew what she was feeling herself. So, it should not have surprised her that just by watching her interaction with Owen, he had correctly guessed the level of their intimacy. But the pure disgust and viciousness he displayed toward her had nothing to do with whatever connection they may or may not have had. No, that was something else entirely. It was as if just knowing her shamed him. Angered him.

"Are you sure you're okay, mom?"

Ella sat up and glanced out the windows, recognizing the back roads they were on. With a smile, she nodded and pointed straight ahead. "Turn down this road. We'll take the long way home. Get a good long drive in. How do you feel? Do you feel you're prepared at all?"

Lila shrugged. "Sort of. Parking and turning scare me."

With a nod, Ella agreed. "Yes, you take turns too slow and wide. Stop being so afraid. That's what will hurt you. We also have to get you on the highway. Maybe in a couple weeks. Okay?"

Once home, Ella ordered takeout, grateful for her daughter's company. They talked about school and what would happen once Lila had her driver's license. They spoke about getting her a used car.

"If you are working... save up. If you put a thousand toward the car, I'll match it."

"Maybe dad will match it too. You think?"

With a gentle smile, Ella answered, "Maybe. That's for you to discuss with him."

"Hey, mom?"

"Hmm?"

"Are we going to have to move?"

"Probably." She wanted to reassure her daughter, wanted to promise her anything she wanted, but she knew that would only cause mistrust when the very thing she feared happened. All Ella could do was be honest and promise that no matter what, they would be okay. "I think I'm putting the house up after the holidays." She skirted around the table and sat beside her daughter, who had started to cry. "Lila, listen to me. We'll be fine. I just think this is too much house for the two of us. I don't want all the money to go to the mortgage. And there are some cute houses in the neighborhood. I don't expect you to move schools. This will be fun. An adventure."

"Mom, that's what you've said all year since dad left. I am so sick of adventures. I just want... I want the chaos to stop."

"I know. I do too. Soon it will. But honey, you have to understand that life is just a series of changes. Just as soon as you get used to the routine.... It is ripped out from under you. So, we adjust. We'll find a cute small house in the area, and it will be great." She took a deep breath and continued with a careful smile, "You thought the worst thing would be for me and your dad to separate... but honey, you love going over there. You get along with Connie. It worked out. And you'll have a new brother or sister. That's exciting."

"Exciting? Mom, I'm not ten years old." But she smiled back at her mom. "Okay. It might even be fun looking for a new house."

**

It was one of those rare nights that Lila and her mother got to hang out together. She knew her mom was not happy, knew that something had transpired between her and Dennis, but she also knew that tonight, together, they had fun. Her mom was better to drive with than her father. Her father just yelled. Constantly. And clutched the dashboard. But her mom sat back and softly corrected when needed.

Lila knew it was shitty of her to complain when her mother was the one who had been so horrendously betrayed, who had her entire life shaken up and spit out by several people and things this past year. And yet, here she was smiling at her daughter, cooing words of support and comfort. Her mother looked so young and hopeful, not at all like a woman about to be forty and just newly divorced. She deserved the best.

"Food's here," Lila called out to her mom.

"Money's on the counter."

Lila swung the door open, counting the money to ensure the right amount and then glanced up to see Dennis standing there. "What the hell do you want?"

If her words surprised him, he did not let it show. With a small, apologetic smile, he asked, "Is your mom home, Lila?"

"You know what, Dennis? No, she's not. Okay? So just turn around and leave." She sighed, unable to contain all the emotions stirring in her. The anger, sadness, missing this almost father figure. "She came home crying. Don't you think she's had enough misery this year? Can't you understand that my mom deserves so much better? When the hell did you turn out to be such a creep?"

"Lila!" A soft hand fell on her shoulder, and she turned to see her mom staring down at her. "Lila, go inside. It's okay."

Ella knew her daughter adored Dennis, so to hear her speak to him in such a manner let her know that her emotions were ridiculously visible. She had to work on that. She had to become a stronger figure for her daughter. Tough year or not, she was still a mother, and that was what mattered.

But now she had to face him. Face the man that made her heart jump out of her chest, squeezed and punctured by just a few of his words. Ella squared her shoulders and stared up into that face and tried to steady her breathing.

"Before you kick me out, please let me just say that I am sorry for what I said. I said it out of jealousy. Pure, irrational jealousy. Because I thought it was the most horrible thing to imagine you with some other man, some imagined guy... but I was wrong, El. The worst thing is to see that man, to see your reaction to him. I felt like my heart was being torn from my body. I felt like there was an anchor dropped on my chest."

"Listen," she interrupted in what she hoped was a cavalier tone. "I'm glad you stopped by."

"What?"

"I said I am glad you stopped by. I wanted to chat with you. Ask that this...." She moved her fingers back and forth between them, "Doesn't get out. I mean... Owen... he's the best, Dennis. He's there for me. I don't want to hurt him, and I don't want to hurt what he considers to be a great friendship. So, if we can play nice if we have to encounter each other ... let's play nice. Can I ask that of you? To not tell him details?"

Dennis straightened, his composure returning, although his expression was full of misery. "Yes. Of course. Anything you want, Ella, because what I -"

"And you were right. Before. When you said I didn't know what love was if I thought I was in love with you? So right. Because looking back... I'm not sure how I ever, ever fell in love with a man that could say such horrendous things to me. Thanks for making that call to break things off with me. Dodged a motherfuckin' bullet. Now.... get off my property."

**

The next morning, Owen showed up on her doorstep with a bouquet of roses. Ella ushered him in and unceremoniously introduced him to Lila. They regarded each other with mild curiosity as they murmured polite greetings, and then Lila raced outside to a waiting car, her weekend starting with a boy and a day off.

"Cute kid," Owen acknowledged, but there was something in the vagueness of his tone, the blankness in his expression that disappointed Ella. Her daughter was her world, and while she never expected a guy to fall into the father role, she did expect some interest in her world, her heart. Her thoughts involuntarily jumped to Dennis, and how he seemed to find that perfect balance between trying too hard and having no interest whatsoever.

"I think so. Thanks for the flowers."

He followed her into the kitchen as she searched for a vase. "So last night..."

"Yes. Last night." She turned to face him, staring up expectantly.

"I have to ask. Is there something... between you and Dennis-"

"What?" she interrupted, trying to control the temperature to her face, to stop the color from giving it all away. "No! We're friends. That's it. I was just surprised to see him."

He broke into a wide grin. "You misunderstood. It seemed to me that you disliked him. I wasn't sure if there some sort of history..."

"Dislike? No. He's a great guy. The kindest man... no. Nothing negative."

Owen nodded. "He really is. And don't worry. I never thought there was anything between you two. That wouldn't make much sense."

"Why's that?"

He did not seem to realize he was falling right into a trap. Didn't he know that when women asked such a question, he should tread lightly? But he chuckled, oblivious. "He's a bit ...

listen, he's been single forever. He has no interest in relationships, and you... you seem-"

"Not attractive enough?"

She was relieved that Owen at least had enough of a clue
to recognize that blatant trap. With wide eyes, he shook his
head. "No! Ella, I think you're pretty enough for any guy out
there. You know I can barely look at you without losing my
train of thought. But Dennis just ... I really don't think there
is a match for him. I think he's pretty much set in the bach-
elor life. So, he dates women that aren't in it for the long haul.
That's what I mean."

Ella struggled to breathe, to function without breaking
down into a puddled mess of tears and regrets. But she knew
her emotions were on the surface, and she also felt that this
man in front of her deserved a version of the truth. Something
to understand just what he was stepping into. "Listen, we
didn't tell you the entire story."

And in a gesture that communicated more sensitivity than
she had given him credit for, Owen leaned closer and touched
her arm. "What is it?"

"I ... I don't want to get into too much detail because
frankly, it isn't something I like to remember. But I did meet
Dennis while fishing. The divorce was so hard on me. I felt
blindsided, my old life just ripped from me. I started to fish to
relax. Dennis and I would talk and fish... it was a great distraction. I had started to date, and .... Let me put it this way. Dennis was at the right place at the right time and basically saved
my life and then saved my daughter from harm's way. So, I'm
indebted to him."

Owen searched her face, his gaze intense and fingers closing
protectively around her arm. "Ella... what happened?"

"I can't. Please... can we just leave it at that? I'm okay. I
learned my lesson in meeting new people and dating and ...
just please don't ask me to relive it."

He exhaled slowly, creases appearing between his eyes.
"Shit. And I came on so strong when I met you. I didn't real-

ize... I should have. Cop's instinct, right? You were jittery and ... I thought it was the divorce-"

"Owen. I never expected you to guess. It's okay. But I did want to give you the history between me and Dennis. And explain why this - us ... I can't go fast. I can't promise you any type of commitment."

There were a few beats of silence before his voice came through low, like a hum. "Are you breaking things off with me?"

Tears sprang to her eyes, and this time, she could not hide them. "Owen, I just am not in a good place to start a relationship."

"Is it me?"

"No."

He took her hands with such gentleness, she jumped. "Honey, if it isn't me and this is just uncertainty, then we can deal with that. I'm not asking for you to marry me anytime soon. If you want to take things slow, then we will go slow. I'm sorry if I rushed you in any sort of way. After my divorce, I really thought I'd never fall for anyone again. And then I saw you. And I just want a chance. If it doesn't work, then I will at least know I can feel that way again." He paused, squeezing her hands. "One chance? Let me take you out to dinner this week. Nothing more."

The truth was that Ella did feel an attraction to Owen. When she was able to clear any thought of Dennis from her mind, she could feel herself falling for this new man. This steady, uncomplicated man who had no trouble professing his feelings for her. He intended to pursue a relationship with her, he made no secret about that. But to also be willing to step back without any questions and go at her pace... that counted for a lot.

And yet as she tried to summon sleep that night, Dennis invaded her thoughts and dreams, and she felt that she was simply leading Owen on. Even though she and Dennis had no future, Ella's heart was not the same. She was not the same.

Was it fair to give Owen a chance when she knew it was just a way to kill time? A way to slip into denial and pretend her very core was not crushed?

As sleep took over, images of Dennis and Owen and distorted views invaded her mind…. Nightmarish sounds and confusion… and as she woke up in a cold sweat, Ella had to wonder if this was going to be her future. Restless nights and uncomfortable reflections.

**

Her boss stopped speaking long enough to give her a long, searching look. "Is this okay? I mean-"

"Fine," Ella chirped, pulling her lips up in what she hoped was a convincing smile. After an awkward pause, she sighed. "Really. It's okay. I have no problem working with him."

But later that afternoon, she was not feeling as brave as the time for her meeting with Dennis approached. Since that fateful dinner almost two weeks ago, their contact had been limited to passing each other in the hallway at work, a short nod if eye contact happened by accident.

Thinking neutral ground would somehow make things less tense, she booked a conference room. Larger than their intimate, small offices. More professional. She arrived a half hour early to go over her notes and questions, to fine tune the rough draft of a presentation she was to work on with him.

"Ella."

It was impossible to stop her body from reacting to that voice, to the knowledge that Dennis was in the same room. Keeping her gaze fixed on the screen in front of her for a few beats longer than necessary, she worked on her composure until finally she felt prepared enough to glance up and work a smile on her face. "Hi, Dennis."

Nope. She had not been prepared. And perhaps her imagination was triggered by the jolt of being near him, but Ella thought she caught the same tangle of emotions in his fluid cocoa eyes. That combination of misery and hope, confusion and struggle to maintain control. But then it was gone, and his expression was guarded, his eyes giving no more away.

He set a pile of folders and his laptop on the table and sat across from her. "I apologize if this is unpleasant for you. I tried to get help from elsewhere, but it seems..."

This caught Ella off guard and her head snapped up. "You're not happy with my work?"

"What? Ella. No. That's part of the reason we have to suffer through this. You're the best I can find, and this presentation is really important. I can't trust just anyone with helping. I just meant..." He paused, his hands spread out as if the answer were written on his palms. "El, this isn't easy."

"Because you're mad."

His eyes widened. "Mad? Absolutely not. I'm ashamed of myself. I behaved abhorrently, and said things that... I treated you with disrespect, and there is no excuse for that."

Ella took a moment to let his words sink in. Dennis had made her feel ashamed and guilty, and it had triggered an equally destructive reaction from her. "I want to apologize for my part in it too."

"You have nothing to apologize for."

"I do. Dennis, I lashed out and said I wished I had never met you, but that is far from the truth. Despite everything... I don't regret it. And if I hadn't met you, I might not have survived that day, and I'd probably still be at that miserable job so..." She cleared her throat and pushed her laptop across the table. "Anyway. Can you look at what I have so far? It's just a bare bones outline for now, but I wanted to be sure I have the right idea for the main focus."

Dennis took her cue and focused on the project. They spent the next two hours building up the outline. He was easy to work with. He listened to Ella's ideas and was quick to praise them. When she was stuck on a particular point, he filled in the missing information. Dennis had no problem working with anyone. His generous spirit and easy-going nature, along with his intelligence, made him a dream to partner with. What had started as an intimidating project ended up being a task Ella was excited to continue.

Dennis sat back and stretched. "I'm starving. Feel like pizza?"

"Pizza's good. Let me go get my purse."

"No, El-"

"If you say my treat, I'll seriously scream, Dennis. If you want to split a pizza, then I will pay half."

Dennis met her gaze unflinchingly, no amusement leaking into his eyes as he gave a short nod. "Then half."

When Ella handed over her half, he took it with a nod and a quiet thanks. It was not awkward and not a sore spot with him. She loved and missed that about Dennis. He truly seemed to understand her need to be separate, independent. In fact, he always appeared to appreciate that part of her. Celebrated her newfound freedom and assertion with her. Ella admitted to herself that she missed the abundance of understanding and encouragement.

Sometimes Owen seemed dumbfounded by her actions and demands, as if she were simply being silly by wanting to pay her own way or be the one to drive when they were together. He did not argue or fight, but he would chuckle or shrug. Sometimes he would even be dismissive to her requests.

They ate in silence for about ten minutes, and then Dennis cleared his throat, threading his napkin as he stared down at the table. "So... I ... how's Lila?"

Ella set down the slice of pizza she held and sighed. "She's good. Dennis... she didn't mean what she said to you."

"She meant it. And I understand. El, I do. You're her mom, and she is fiercely protective of you. And I was stupid enough to ruin any chance with the first woman I've had any type of real interest in in years. I deserve whatever she can throw out."

And something snapped inside her. Truce be damned. "Right. It is really easy to say those things when you know it's over. So easy to declare things you know you don't have to back up."

Something in his eyes solidified as he held her gaze. His

voice seemed caught in his throat, escaping through a narrow tunnel of jagged gravel as he informed her, "Ella, honey, you say the word, and I will back up every single word that's left my mouth just now."

Ella swung her gaze away, trying to break that hold, to escape that feeling of overwhelming desire. "Anyway, Lila is good. She seems to be better, actually. So, thank you for your part in that."

"No. I did nothing except listen." He turned his attention back to the food in front of him and once again, they ate in silence.

They worked on the outline for another hour after lunch and then scheduled meetings for the following weeks. This would be the main focus of her job for the next few months. Ella just hoped that her excitement over that realization stemmed from the task itself and not working so closely with Dennis.

But as she turned to walk down the hallway to her office, she sneaked a glance over her shoulder and when she saw that he was gazing back at her, she could not deny that thrill shooting through her.

**

Lila sipped her soda, smiling her thanks at Finn as he pulled sandwiches out of the fast food bag. "Sort of funny that we work in a restaurant and still go across the street for food."

She lifted a shoulder. "Food is a relative term. This delicious bounty probably can't be considered food. Fast food is questionable."

"Right. That's why it is so good." He sat across from her, his electric blue eyes combing her face, as if memorizing each feature carefully. "Are you upset about the fall festival?"

"I'm not happy," she responded evenly, her gaze fixed on the table.

"Lila."

She put her hands out in front of her. "I know, Finn. I'm not mad. Just not happy."

His stare seemed to pierce through her, and she had no choice but to look up and get lost in that mesmerizing sea of blue. He waited for a few moments before answering, "I know. You've been great, Lila. Really. And I know it sucks. But my car is literally - literally falling apart. I need to take as many shifts as I can to save up for a new car. I am sorry. I know you were looking forward to going."

"I know, Finn. I just... I miss you."

Finn tilted his head and raised his eyebrows. "You miss me?" he asked softly, his lips curving up. She nodded, smiling as he stood and leaned across the table for a kiss. "I miss you too. Even when we're both working here - when you're in the dining area, and I'm in the kitchen... I miss you."

She giggled. "Don't be an ass."

"No." He grinned back at her as he sat down. "I do miss you. I love you, Lila."

She blushed. It was a hesitation, a slight hesitation she hoped he did not notice. Because this, Finn, was not supposed to be a love story. He was meant as a distraction. Perhaps a support. But to her surprise, Lila realized he was indeed her love story. "Oh. Finn. I love you too."

"Yeah?"

She bit her lip and nodded. "Yeah."

Somehow Lila had fallen for the stoner boy, the guy she and her friends used to laugh at during parties, used to look down on for his baggy clothes and constant chuckling. And now, she smiled when she thought of him, blushed when she was caught staring, and sought him out when they were apart. This boy who was nothing like Brad. He was not popular or the textbook definition of good-looking. He did not come from a great family, and his future was hazy at best. But Lila now saw through all that. She noticed his kind heart and brilliant blue eyes. She saw his attentiveness when she spoke and his awesome work ethics.

And yet as they sat grinning stupidly at each other, she wondered about Brad. Why had she not been able to hold his attention? Was she not good enough? Did Brad somehow sense the defects in her, the flaws she tried to hide from everyone? Why had she triggered his temper enough to become one of those pitiful girls in corny movies that were known as victims? And was it just a matter of time before Finn followed suit?

Lila felt as if her happiness were cursed. Anytime she felt that carefree feeling, that contentment, a dark shadow fell over her and wiped out any type of sunshine. Things were great with Finn, but she knew it could not stay that way. She was not the type of girl that was allowed such joy, such love. No. It just was not for her.

CHAPTER 18

There are a few certainties in life. Taxes and death. Stress. Aging. Sunny days eventually. And the fact that if someone in a relationship claims he or she is okay with going slow.... That person will sooner than later rebel against that sentiment and demand more than the other person can possibly give.

And that was where Ella was at the moment. Standing in front of an exasperated Owen as he rescinded on all the promises of patience and understanding.

"I mean, Ella, how wrong is it that I want to spend the one free evening I have with you? How is that making me a bad person?"

She paused to ensure it was indeed her turn to respond. "You are far from a bad person, Owen. I don't remember ever indicating that you were."

"I am just - where is this going? Huh, Ella? Am I wasting my time here?"

Ella groaned and then tried to breathe, to get some air and let her thoughts loosen up, relax so that the tension did not leak into her tone and throw the conversation into an argumentative spiral. "Please don't do this. I thought you were willing to take this slow-"

"And we have been."

"For three weeks. I wasn't aware there was a time limit. Okay. Three weeks of slow and then what? I'm not supposed to go out with my friends?"

Owen sighed and turned away as if to compose himself. When he turned back, she noticed the effort to remain calm. The slightly longer than usual blink, the clenching of the jaw, and the slow, steadying breaths. And yet his tone was like a stretched wire vibrating with agitation. "Don't twist my words, Ella. Please don't. I did not say I would keep you from your friends. I said I was a little disappointed that you did not want to see me the one night I was off."

Taking a cue from him, Ella lowered her voice, doing her best to appear calm. "We had plans for two nights this week. Both nights you were called into work-"

"That's part of the job. Sometimes I have to go."

"And I understand that. But I had already planned this night with my friends. There are five of us and to get a night that we were all available and plan... I'm not backing out of that."

He leaned back and regarded her silently before adding, "Right. At a club."

"Yes," she drew the word out slowly, staring back at him cautiously. "And... what? You don't approve?"

"I'm not into that whole scene, no. I just assumed we were a little too old for all that crap. It's basically a meat market and -"

"Whoa! No, that is not what that is about. I want to hang out with my friends and dance. I don't care how old I am. I don't give a shit if I'm the only one over 25. I'm not there to impress anyone. I - you..." She cursed and blinked back tears of frustration. "My friends and I aren't wild or scoping out guys. Some of the women are married."

Owen rolled his eyes. "That doesn't make it better. Makes it worse. That is not the place for married people."

"What?" Ella stared at him wide-eyed, trying to determine if he was joking or exaggerating.

Shaking his head, Owen held his hands up as if to surrender. "The point, Ella, is I was expecting to spend some time with you this week. And it didn't happen."

"Because you got called into work!"

"I did. Yes. But when that happens, I want to make time for you on the days I don't get called into work. And I want you to want to make time for me."

"I do. I want to make time for you. But I don't think it is fair that you expect me to cancel plans to do that. No."

"So, we're not - I'm not some kid, Ella. I am truly falling for you, and I don't feel like being jerked around while you figure out if you want to party like you're a college kid or if you want a real relationship."

"I don't want to rush -"

"Into things. Yeah. I heard you. And I'm not here demanding that we set a wedding date or plan out the next five years. But I am standing here in front of you..." He paused with an imploring look that seemed to penetrate her very gut. "And I'm asking that you give me a chance. A true chance."

Ella forced herself to take a few cleansing breaths to prevent the impulse to simply agree. To fall over and allow this man, this handsome man, to charm her out of her instincts. When she trusted herself, she asked, "Do you mean like we have been? Because I'm giving this a chance."

"No." He shook his head with a sad smile. "You're not. You're holding back. I feel like I can't break through this wall you have up."

"Ugh. Owen. I have to go slow. I just got divorced. I just got out of a rebound relationship. I can't -"

"Can't what? So, I'm wasting my time? Huh?"

There was something almost taunting in his tone, and although Ella knew Owen was anything but arrogant and rowdy, it brought to mind her ex. And Ella toyed with the idea of breaking things off. This was a man who was getting attached. And while her feelings were strengthening toward him, Ella did not want to lead him on. She did not want to utter promises she did not fully mean. But she found that she did not want to lose him. Her reservations stemmed from the misplaced affections for Dennis, the insane attraction to that damned man. But she knew that was just a heartbreaking disaster waiting to happen if she dared try to pursue that again. Dennis was a good guy with heartfelt intentions, but she knew he could not settle down. And she wanted that. With him.

Instead, Owen stood in front of her ready to give her all

she wanted and more. He was infatuated, she could tell that. The way his eyes lingered on her with hope and imploring. The way he tried to overcome his gruff tendencies and lack of understanding when it came to women. He was a good-looking man, and his attention was flattering, if not confusing. Why was he wasting his time with her when she was sure there were other more attractive, nicer women willing to give him all the promises and dedication he seemed to need?

As if reading her thoughts, Owen sighed and admitted, "This comes down to wanting more. I'm really falling for you, Ella, and if there is no chance, then just tell me."

"I would. But I thought we agreed to go slow. You told me -"

"Yes. And we did."

"Right. For a whole three weeks. Oh. So, you expected me to fall at your feet within ... what? A week? Maybe two?" The deep breaths were no longer working, and she found her voice rising in irritation.

He narrowed his eyes and shook his head. "No! But I kind of want to know that this is going somewhere. That I'm not just following you around like some damn dog. Because at the end of the night, I get basically a handshake and a thanks for time spent."

"Ah. So, this is about sex."

"No! I mean... sure. Because sex is one part of a committed relationship. And I'm not saying marry me tomorrow, but if we're going to continue dating, I would like some type of indication that we are more than just buddies."

"And I can't give you that. I like you, Owen. A lot. But I'm just getting to know you. I was in a long marriage, and I was spun around and thrown on my ass by the ending of it. I can't just trot off with you into some fabricated sunset as if I'm not still reeling over my life this past year. I can't. And frankly, I resent that you promised me patience and played Mr. Nice Guy only to show up on my doorstep too early on a Sunday morning demanding more! No. I'm sorry I am unable to give you what you need. But now what I need is for you to go."

He stormed out without so much as a backwards glance, and Ella slammed the door, surprised at the emotions washing over her. She had been hoping for a nice guy. A calm, predictable romance. Not this. Not the nice guy stomping out her door, and Ella feeling as if she were making the same mistake Dennis had made with her.

**

This was what the business world would call a conflict of interest. A company would install boundaries and rules to ensure it did not happen. But this was not the business world, and Dennis was not at work. This was personal. Feelings were involved. Lies were being thrown around, and secrets were in full force.

And being asked to meet Owen for dinner so Owen could vent about his love life… which happened to involve the love of Dennis's life… was not an ideal situation to be in. He considered cancelling, making an excuse, telling him that he was ill. His classes were a mess, and he had to work through the night… the week. But Dennis hated lies, and he hated the fact that one of his close friends was being kept from the entire truth, and yet… he hated even more the thought of betraying Ella.

So, he arrived at the diner to find Owen already seated, picking at a side of fries. He sat opposite of him, and he noted the wrinkled shirt, the pale face and sunken eyes, and he tried to deny that his heart skipped a beat. That for a flash of a moment, he wanted to jump and shout in joy that his friend was no longer dating Dennis's soulmate. But he quickly composed himself with the reminder that Owen was a good man. And currently, a heartbroken friend. Dennis knew that feeling. All too well.

Owen wasted no time. "I need advice."

"No." Dennis could not cross that line. He could not trust himself to be fair. "Please, don't count on me for advice. I'm terrible with relationships."

"Then just … I need someone to listen. Please. I can't eat or sleep. I went crazy, and I think I shocked her -"

Alarms went off in Dennis's head. "Wait- crazy how? What'd you do?"

"I demanded more. She wanted to take things slow. So fine. Haven't had sex since that first time. I call and plan dates. Listen to her when she talks. But it isn't enough. I need to know she's mine."

Dennis drew back and regarded his friend in surprise. Just then, the waitress appeared. "Coffee, please. Thank you." He waited until she sashayed away before continuing, "What? Owen, are you crazy? You've known her a matter of weeks-"

"And I already know-"

"She just got divorced. What are you thinking, man? You're going to scare her off."

"Right. Already did." He sighed, twisting the coffee mug around in his large, callused hands. "I hadn't seen her all week. Kept getting called into work. The one day I had off, she refused to change her plans. So, I told her I need more, need to know this is going somewhere -"

"You what?"

"And she seemed annoyed. But if she is at the bar, to me, that just means she is trying to pick up guys."

Dennis dropped the fork he had been mindlessly twirling between his fingers, sputtering words that would not seem to escape his open mouth. Finally, he took a breath. "Okay. Wait. What? Owen, what's with you? Huh? I've known you to stop at the bar for a beer or two after a long shift."

"Right. And I know what goes on there. How guys think. And this wasn't like some small bar people stop to sit and relax. This was a club. She's like older, so what's she doing dancing around like some kid?"

"Oh, Owen." He rested his head on his steepled hands, feeling sick to his stomach. "Please tell me you didn't say that to her."

"I said she was a little old to be running around in bars." Suddenly the righteousness drained from his face, and he slumped forward. "I royally fucked up, didn't I?"

"Yeah."

"Tell me how to fix it. I'm not smart when it comes to this. My wife Susie was … when we started dating, she was the one to chase me. She knew what I wanted before I did. And after we divorced, I had no interest in any of that. Dating, trying to understand women. Too busy. But then Ella just … dammit. I can't think straight."

"Why can't you give her space, Owen? Apologize and then give her space. She's had one hell of a year."

"I know." He glanced up. "She told me that you saved her. From some type of situation."

"I did." He jerked his chin toward him. "You're a cop. I'm sure you found out what she was talking about."

"Yeah."

"So, you have to consider that. And yelling and making demands is just going to push her further away."

"I know. I know this and sometimes I just can't …I'm not myself."

Dennis felt cornered. He did not want to give this man advice to help him win back the very woman Dennis found himself obsessed with. Yet this man was his friend, and he could not purposely attempt to sabotage the relationship through bad advice. And a third side of this was that he could not silently sit back as Owen pushed Ella beyond her comfort. That was the side that won out. Because this was about Ella, and he would do anything to protect her world.

"Look. She's my friend. I witnessed that woman go through something no one should go through, and she survived. So please forgive me, Owen, but I can't sit here and listen to you complain about your feelings and your inability to stand back and give her space. She suffered. She had her dignity and privacy, any joy left over from an already tough year just ripped from her. If she is asking you for space, give her goddamned space!"

The two men stared at each other, both jolted by Dennis's

outburst. He sank his head into his steepled fingers, breathing deep and preparing himself for Owen's realization that his feelings sure as hell ran deeper than simple friendship with Ella. Much deeper.

But Owen surprised him. "Ah, man. Dennis, you're right. Absolutely right. I knew I could count on you to put it into perspective. I've been selfish. Susie always said I was clueless when it came to feelings and ..." He sighed and then spoke the words that made Dennis sick to his stomach. "I really need to do this right. I ... I'm in love with her, Dennis. I love Ella."

**

The silence was not the usual easy silence that they worked in. This was tense, making the air heavy and time slow. As Ella reached for a pile of papers with their ideas outlined, she asked, "Something wrong? You seem... distracted."

She was surprised when Dennis answered immediately. "Actually yes. Something is wrong. I need to talk to you." He glanced up and continued, "I met Owen for dinner yesterday. He wanted to ask me advice. Turns out it was about you."

Ella hung her head and bit her lip. This was getting ridiculous. Her latest failed relationship wanted to seek advice from the failed relationship victim before him. How did she get into these life situations? Finally, she sighed. "I guess you both had a grand time venting about how crazy I am."

Dennis shot her a look of disbelief. "Why do you do that, Ella? Have I ever given you reason to think I'd badmouth you to anyone? I might have screwed us up, and I take full responsibility for that, but I've never ... dammit."

"Sorry." She shook her head and sank down into her chair. "It's just... this is weird. What did you say?"

"I tried to tell him I'm not one to get advice from. I almost want to be honest with him, but I'm afraid he wouldn't understand."

Ella bit her lip, mulling over his words. "I'm sorry I put you in this position. He's your friend and .... To keep this from him-"

"You're my friend too," he stated firmly. "And none of this is your fault. You had no idea... none of us did. And I didn't really put up a fight when you suggested we not tell him about our... history." Dennis set down the papers in his hand and moved around the table, sitting next to Ella. "Hey. Are you okay?"

Her eyes were round and unblinking as she tried to ward off the threat of tears, and avoiding his gaze, she stared at the laptop. "Yes."

Because there was no self-respecting way to tell this man that he had somehow become her every thought and every breath. That working so closely with him was messing with her head, and now they were discussing a man she might or might not still be dating. When all she really wanted to do was ignore all the cautions her mind threw out and jump into Dennis's arms.

It did not help that Dennis seemed to sense the very thing she was thinking. He returned to the other side of the table as if to give her the space she needed to think coherently. But he continued to watch her, study her, and Ella squirmed in both excitement and dread. Because he was the last person she wanted to read her thoughts. And yet, he was the only one that could.

"It's supposed to be unseasonably warm tomorrow, Ella. Maybe if you go fishing to clear your head - to -"

"No."

He waited for a moment, his gaze softening. "Why not? If it's because of me, I won't go. You love to go fishing. It was always your comfort."

"Well, it isn't now. It reminds me, Dennis. And I don't necessarily want to go there alone to be miserable with the memories, and I sure as hell don't want to go there with someone else. Just... I'll be fine." She studied her laptop, blinking back tears and sensing his persistent gaze before repeating, "I'm fine! Can we please get back to work?"

And as she knew he would, Dennis gave a short nod and turned away.

CHAPTER 19

"Are you okay?"

Lila buried her face in the crook of Finn's neck and nodded. She felt him shift and pull the blanket up around them, and then he rested his hand on her back, brushing her skin lightly in soothing circular motions. "Are you sure? Lila, can you look at me?"

She reluctantly lifted her head. "I'm okay, Finn. I'm just overwhelmed. This... you... it's wonderful but a lot to take in." It was as brutally honest as Lila was willing to get. Because truthfully, she was overcome with emotions, and it took everything she had not to burst into tears from the sheer intensity of it.

It was not as if this were her first time. But it was her first time with Finn. And sex with Bradley had been much different. It had been mechanical, awkward, and sometimes a bit rough. She had not understood the appeal at all.

And now with Finn... she had reacted to his touches, was drawn to his kisses, and something inside, a sort of instinct, had nudged her toward the knowledge that this would be different. Finn was different.

As if to prove that, when it became obvious their affection was taking on a new level, when it became difficult to pull away from one another, Finn told her, "Lila... hey, Lila, wait... baby... if we're going to do this... if you're ready, I don't want to do it here."

Lila had pulled away and smiled at him. "Mom won't be home for another hour."

"Right. But ... not here. I don't ever want to put you in that position. We can go to my place. My dad's out of town. This,

255

here... I don't want you to sneak around, hoping we don't get caught and you get in trouble. This is your bedroom, your place. If you're sure, Lila, then we can go to my house."

And she had been sure. It was so different with Finn. There was a gentleness in his touch, consideration and protectiveness that had been missing with Brad. Finn watched her reactions, whispered reassurances and declarations of love, and held her. For the first time in her short experience, sex had felt good.

But it was impossible to work up the nerve to say all that. Instead, she ducked her head and tried to stifle a gasp when he pulled her close. "I love you, Lila, and I get it, you know? I get that this is all a lot. Do you need to relax? Wanna smoke a bowl?"

It was all so different than with Brad. She felt safe and alive and joyful. They smoked some pot and watched a movie, and during that entire time, Finn was attentive and affectionate. Even though he had already gotten sex, he still wanted her near him.

"I think you are the most beautiful thing I've ever seen," he whispered against her cheek at one point, and she got goosebumps. How could this be happening? She had been so sure that Brad was the one, the person she desperately needed to be with... and now somehow, she was here...in Finn's bed, his arms, blissful and loved.

Loved... this beautiful boy with his electric blue eyes and auburn hair, the infectious chuckle and insatiable appetite for life - he claimed to love her. And she was now lying beside him in an average body with plain looks and a dull personality.

Lila saw herself as nothing special. While Finn was fascinating with adorable quirks, she was bland with annoying habits. How could he love her? What made him want to bring her along on his ride through life? Why wasn't he searching for some wild woman that could hold his interest and make him laugh? Someone who was confident and brazen. Not a timid wallflower trying too hard.

But then again, maybe he was searching. It was easy to say you loved someone when they were the only person there. Hell, she said it to Brad enough times, and she easily moved on to Finn.

"Lila. Are you okay?" Finn asked, turning down the volume on the movie they were watching.

"I'm fine," she lied.

**

It was less than a year ago that Ella had bemoaned the fact that her evenings were less than thrilling. She missed those times. She truly craved an uneventful week at this point. As she glanced at the long text full of misspelled, scattered words from Owen, she longed for simpler times. And also, she felt her heart jump at the sight of his name on her phone.

She missed Owen. Somehow, somewhere along the short line that was their relationship, she had grown fond of him. And now, reading his apology and sincere attempt to back-track on all he had said, she found herself smiling. Owen was not good with words, he was only charming in that he did not know how to purposely flirt, and he sometimes was clueless in how to make her feel special... desired. But his raw honesty and boyish impulse to please was winning her over.

"Hello?" He answered the phone in a rushed, surprised tone. "Ella?"

"Hey you. Got your text."

"Yeah. I miss you. And I'm sorry. Can we meet somewhere? To talk?"

Despite her attempt to block any thought of Dennis out of her mind and despite her resolve to focus on Owen as he spoke ... Ella could not help but think that when Dennis had wanted to talk to her, he had camped outside her house in the rain.

But this was Owen. And with a soft sigh, she agreed. "Pizza place on 5th street?" It was his favorite spot, and it was a short drive.

An hour later, she sat across from Owen as he smiled into her eyes and melted her heart just a bit more. "Not the best week," he admitted, smoothing his wrinkled shirt with his hands.

"No. Not my best week either."

And Ella saw his struggle, his fight to find the words that did not come naturally to him. And she appreciated it. "Ella, listen, I am sorry for rushing you into something. I'm sorry I went back on what I said. But...I can't take it back. I mean, I'm not willing to lose you, I can't lose you, so if you can't give me anything back, I'll have to just accept that. But I'm not going to lie and say I'm okay with no commitment."

"We barely know each other, Owen," she gently insisted. "We need to give this time."

"So... you're willing to give it a try?"

A bubble of frustration rose in her chest, and despite Ella's initial joy at seeing him, she now felt cornered. Why couldn't this just be easy? An escape? "Owen. I'm willing to get to know you better to find out if we're even compatible."

She tried to ignore the shadows crossing his face as he attempted a smile. "You make it sound so mechanical. Isn't this supposed to be fun? Romantic? Ella, this could be the search for a soulmate."

The very thought of Owen, macho, practical Owen, thinking of soulmates almost struck her as funny. But the irritation crossed out any humor the situation might have herded in. And she almost denied believing in any type of romantic nonsense, but somehow, deep down, she knew that would be a lie. Because the very thought of Dennis, of her instinctual reaction to him... that was more than simple, everyday attraction.

Instead, she sighed. "Slow. Owen. Just ... really slow. That's all I can do. I want to see you. I can give you that. I missed you."

"I have a surprise for you."

Ella held her breath, hoping he did not pull out some piece of expensive jewelry or other trinket she would be uncomfortable taking. Instead, he held up a laminated license. She blinked and then leaned in closer. "Oh! Fishing license!"

"Yes. I know fishing is the one thing you love doing, and some of the guys at the station were saying tomorrow is going to be unseasonably warm and perfect for fishing so… I don't have to go into work until late afternoon. I thought we could go fishing. I haven't gone in years so I don't know the good spots or really… anything. I did buy a fishing rod."

She leaned back and regarded him with a small smile. It was presumptuous of him, perhaps it could be considered pushy. The very type of action that seemed to suggest he knew better than she did when it came to them, the relationship. But Ella understood that Owen was not being intentionally manipulative. His eagerness was sincere, and she could only smile and agree.

**

The morning was sunnier, warmer than had even been forecasted, definitely milder than mid-autumn is expected to be. The weather boosted Ella's mood and gave her hope that this was the right decision. That she and Owen had a fighting chance. Who could resist romance on a beautiful sunny day?

Owen seemed to be of the same mindset as he gathered her into his arms as soon as she opened the front door for a kiss that caught her off guard. She stumbled over her own feet and hoped Lila was not watching out the window.

"I waited all night to do that. Dreamed of it actually." He grinned, staring into her eyes, oblivious to her clumsy moves. Moving back, he took her in. "You look gorgeous. I have a cooler filled with your favorite soda and some snacks. Thought after we were done, I could take you out to eat somewhere."

And she found what he said to be true. The cooler had her favorite drink and snacks. Ella had not realized Owen was that in tune with her and not entirely clueless. This man was paying attention. Maybe it was time she started to also.

"So, are you going to take pity on me today? Maybe give me some pointers?" he asked as he turned the car where she instructed.

She smiled, feeling her cheeks warm. "Of course. But I'm not really that good."

"At this point, darling, you're better than me. I think the last time I went fishing, I was ten, and my dad took me during his weekend visitation."

"Did you have fun?"

He lifted a shoulder casually, but Ella noticed how his eyes lit up and his lips curved naturally. "Actually, I did."

"Well, then you're due for another good fishing memory." She paused and then reached out to touch his arm. "Owen, thanks. For this."

Owen moved his gaze from the road to her, his smile bright and sincere. "Of course. I mean... it's you, Ella. I'd do anything for you."

Their chatter continued as they gathered the necessary equipment and the cooler and started on the short trail that would take them to her spot. The spot. Because she did not really have time to think of where else to go, what would work for fishing. She was on autopilot, just as her life seemed to be. Going through the motions, feeling brushed along, pushed along.

As they turned the corner, she tilted her face up at him and laughed at something he said before turning back to seek out her spot.

And she saw him.

Dennis.

Standing with a fishing pole in his grip, his expression frozen as he stared at her.

"Oh, hey! Dennis!" Owen's face split into a wide grin, oblivious to the sudden, thick tension. He dropped the cooler and backpack a few feet away from Dennis and then turned, winding his arm around Ella as she worked on setting down the camping chairs and rods. "Beautiful day for fishing! Should have known you'd be out here. Did you know, Ella?"

"N-nno." Her voice cracked as she pulled the chairs out of their carriers and worked on pushing them into even ground.

"I didn't."

"Last minute thing." Dennis's voice was huskier than usual, his expression guarded. "Figured I'd get some fishing in before the cold weather sticks around."

"Yeah, great minds think alike. I actually just got my fishing license. Thought I'd better learn quick to keep up with Ella." He gave her a smile, and she forced her lips up in return, avoiding Dennis's stare.

There was a slight pause, and then she heard Dennis, his voice still low. "Yeah. She has a knack for fishing. That's for sure." She glanced up and saw him reeling in. "I'm actually going to pack up and go-"

"What? No, don't leave. We have enough food and drinks-"

"I appreciate it, Owen, but I've been here all morning. You two have fun. Enjoy the beautiful weather." After a few clicks of the tackle box and snaps of the folding chair, he straightened, his eyes seeking hers. "Goodbye, Owen. Ella."

She mumbled with a semblance of a smile as Owen stepped forward to slap his shoulder, promising to meet up for lunch soon. And Ella wondered how Owen could not see, how he could not hear Dennis's somber tone, the flat notes and blank expression. How was he so unaware? Or was it just that Ella was hyper-sensitive to everything Dennis?

The moments after Dennis walked through the clearing and disappeared from her sight, Ella felt a heavy sensation in her chest, darkness invading any bit of light that might have sprouted in her world. And panic seized her. She had to explain, had to tell Dennis that this was not planned.

"Owen?"

He turned and gave her a smile. "Yes, hun?"

"I forgot; I have a question about a work project for Dennis. I'll be right back."

"Okay." He was so trusting that she felt a twinge. But the pull to make things right with Dennis overwhelmed anything else.

Ella tried to appear calm and happy until she knew she was

out of Owen's line of sight, and then she ran to the parking lot. "Dennis!" she cried out when she saw him at his truck.

He grew still but did not turn toward her. She jogged up to him, swiping her hair out of her face. "Hey. I - he surprised me by getting his fishing license and -"

"Not my business, Ella."

"Okay, but I know I told you I wasn't ready to come here with a guy and-"

"Right. This isn't my business."

"But you're mad!"

"No. I'm not."

"You are."

"Ella!" His tone finally betrayed his turbulent emotions, but when he turned toward her, his face was composed into that stoic expression. "I assure you, I'm not mad. I'm just... I'm over this. I'm done with this back and forth, one or both of us getting hurt-"

"Dennis-"

"Tell me one thing, Ella. When I messed up, and I pushed you away... did you feel just a little bit victorious because that was what you'd been expecting? You wanted me to mess up to prove your point that you couldn't trust any man. You wanted me to mess up, so you didn't have to take that chance on falling in love." She started to shake her head and speak, but he interrupted, "Before you tell me that I'm being ridiculous, just stop and think. Okay? I'm not looking for assurances, I'm looking for the truth. You were waiting for me to mess up. Right?"

There were a few seconds of silence, before Ella sighed through her tears. "Fine. I was. I was waiting."

"Right. We were both just waiting for that other shoe to drop. For a reason to push away before we were pushed. So, we were doomed from day one. I can't do this, Ella. I can't keep chasing after a woman that doesn't want a relationship with me." He paused and in a softer tone, added, "I went through that once already, and once is enough in a lifetime." Then he got into his car and was gone, even as the tears streamed down her face. Even as she struggled to call him back. Even as she realized that she might have made a mistake in chasing away the best man she had ever known.

"Did you get the work thing taken care of?" Owen called out as she made her way back to their fishing spot. He stood from the cooler and turned to her. Immediately, he set down his drink and rushed to her. "Hey. Ella? What is it?"

She choked out a few sobs, unable to stop the torrent of emotions. Owen's eyes were wide, his hands firmly encasing her arms, and she sunk into his support. "I just... I messed up at work and ... just stressed."

"Oh baby," he drew her to him. "I thought something really bad happened. It will be okay."

The day would have been perfect if Dennis had never figured into the picture. Because Owen was trying. He was attentive and gentle, and even his cluelessness was endearing. It was obvious that in his marriage, his wife had led the relationship. She had given him all the answers, had set the pace and tone, and had never given him a chance to explore his own opinions or questions regarding his emotions.

And it seemed that was what Owen was comfortable with. Having to pursue Ella and face everything he felt was not within his realm of ease. Leading them both was new territory, and even immersed in her own self-pity, Ella could appreciate the challenge for him.

**

The texts kept coming through, and it was all Lila could do not to stare at it in front of Finn. Instead she put her phone on silent and stuffed it back in her pocket. The texts would read more of the same though. Brad claiming he missed her desperately and asking for another chance. Promising her that he was better for her than some stoner who was probably too high to even notice her.

And as Lila focused on Finn, she wondered if Brad was just a little on point with his observations. "Finn."

He glanced up from the papers in front of him. "Lila, I'm

sorry. Test tomorrow, and I need to use my breaks to study."

"Then why am I here?"

At this, Finn's lips quivered into an amused smile. "Well. You're working, Lila. Kinda have to be here."

Feeling foolish, she slammed her palms flat on the table and stood. "Not funny. I meant sitting here. With you. But forget it."

Finn was out of his chair and in front of her before she reached the break room door. "Hey. Lila. Wait, I'm sorry. I was just trying to joke you out of your mood. You're here because I love being around you even if I have to do stupid schoolwork. Okay? That's why."

Frustration boiled up inside her, but she pushed it down. She wanted his attention, wanted him to be so enamored that he could not keep his eyes off of her. After sleeping with him, Lila thought that is how it would be if he were as in love as he claimed. But the past few days proved trying as Finn worked and studied nonstop. Where was the fun carefree boy that had won her heart? Where was the adoring, puppy-eyed guy that promised her the world? Already gone.

"No. Listen, You're busy. I'm probably getting in your way."

"Not true." Calmly, Finn folded his arms and leaned against the wall. "I'm not the one whose phone keeps going off. Do you need to go take care of something, Lila? Call someone?"

She tried to keep her face even, tried to stop the flow of warmth from flooding her cheeks. "No! Just - just Andrea bugging about some sale going on."

"Okay." But his eyes were locked onto hers, as if studying and waiting. "Then let's just sit down and relax. I do have to study. I can't afford to start failing tests right in the beginning of the year. Did you bring any work with you?"

"No." The truth was she could get away with the bare minimum of effort and still escape with Bs and some Cs. But she grudgingly took his outstretched hand and allowed him to lead her back to the table. And as he studied, he talked out loud. He read to her from his notes and reviewed things with her.

And when Finn reached out to tuck a strand of her hair behind her ear, Lila felt herself melt, felt the frustration ebb just a little. It was not his full attention, but it was enough that she felt like she mattered. She felt like she was not some child in the middle of her arguing parents. Was not unseen in the back of the classroom. Was not pushed aside for her dad's new girlfriend or her mom's latest date. She was noticed.

**

Glancing up at the sky lights, Ella saw dark, angry clouds. How fitting. How absolutely corny for weather to match a mood. But it was what it was.

She tapped her fingers on the table and waited. She gathered her notes and opened her laptop and waited some more. Dennis was rarely late for meetings.

Ten minutes after the scheduled time, the door opened and in bustled a young, distracted man juggling a backpack and phone. "Heya. Sorry. Last class let out late."

"Who are you?" Irritation scraped at her tone, and the young guy stopped and glanced up.

"Oh. Mr. Reeves didn't tell you? I'm just giving you his latest edits and notes and stuff for you to go over. He said this project is far enough along that you can finish it." He brought his knee up and balanced a notebook on it as he searched. Then he pulled out a few sheets and handed them to her. "Also sent you a link to an online copy of his latest draft."

"Wait. Where is he?"

"Dunno. Just delivering the message. Gotta go. Have a class in five."

And she was once again sitting alone, confused and embarrassed. This was how it was going to be? Dennis was going to lash out because she was dating someone else? He was just going to send some gangly college student to deliver messages?

Ella gathered up the papers and closed her laptop, hoping no one noticed as she left the conference room alone and flustered. Charging through the building, she tried to steady her breathing and hush the panic. This was just a misunderstanding. She would make Dennis understand that she needed to meet with him and not just get his notes through a messenger. This project was too important.

Stopping at his office, she noticed the light was out. He was not there. Of course not.

Lila went back to her own office and busied herself with tasks. She usually could get lost in her work, and this time was no different, except that every now and then, she remembered. She thought of Dennis. The betrayal swimming in his eyes. The hurt coloring his face. And now he was making her pay.

That thought drove her out of her chair. He was back by now. She knew his schedule and knew he would be teaching his 2 o'clock class. It was on the west side of the building, and the emotions sweeping through her, the desperation to make him understand drove her through the busy hallways and pushed her through the necessary doors.

Before Ella paused to think anything through further, she shoved open the door to his class. He stood in front of a filled room, his voice booming and confident, and each student transfixed. But as she opened the door, he stopped and turned, his eyes widening. There were whispers cascading through the room, gasps and giggles, but as soon as she saw she had his attention, she stepped back, out of the line of stares.

"Ella?" Dennis followed her out and shut the door behind him, concern softening his features.

"You couldn't even come to the meeting today? You hate me that much?"

"The... the meeting?" Realization wiped his expression clean, and slowly he straightened. "That's why you're here? Ella, listen, I've given you all the information I have. We brainstormed for weeks on this, and now it's time to put it into solid form. That's how this process works. There's no need for me to be there now-"

"You're trying to punish me-"

"Stop! When have you ever known me to be vindictive? Maybe you're not the only one with emotions, Ella. Maybe you're not the only one who needs distance. I get that you've been through some rough times, but you are not the only one that feels."

Ella stepped back and opened her mouth to speak, but nothing came out. But even her obvious surprise didn't slow him down. He leaned forward and hissed, "And the moment you pleaded with me to not invade your workspace, I obliged. Work is off limits for personal drama, right? Remember that, Ella? And yet here you are, interrupting my class! I guess my day, my work just isn't as important as yours, just like my feelings don't count. I need to get back to my job, Ella. I need to get back to my life, and I'm asking for the same respect that you demanded. Is that okay with you?" He stared hard at her and then without waiting further for an answer, stormed into the classroom, shutting the door firmly.

It took several moments for Ella to break through the shock and move away from the door, hastily wiping the tears before anyone saw.

**

Dennis tried to shake the image of Ella's expression out of his head; the misery, the slight fear, the surprise. He made his way to the front of the class, glancing up and snapping, "Quiet!" The noise ceased immediately, and he continued with his lecture as if nothing happened. As if his heart had not shattered and temper had not boiled over. As if he were not constantly seeing the love of his life walking with his best friend to go fishing, to enjoy the day together. As if he had not just thrown everything away.

**

The kitchen felt stifling. The walls seemed suddenly too close, and Ella looked around for an escape, a relief, but there was none.

Owen leaned against the counter, regarding her with impatience and disappointment. "We're back to this?"

"Back to what?" She blinked long and hard and sighed. "Making plans with my friends? I get the impression you want me to apologize and cancel the plans but... Owen, be reasonable."

His eyes widened, and he lurched forward. "Reasonable? I'm asking you to meet my children. And you'd rather go out to a bar and drink."

She eyed him coolly and paused, letting his words sink in, giving him a chance to hear himself. Maybe he would hear what she was hearing. The demanding tone, the ridiculous expectations, the broken promises of taking it her speed. Finally, she calmly corrected, "I made plans with my friends. As you know from before, we make these plans like a month ahead to ensure everyone can make it. We go to the one club because it has great seating and an awesome dance floor." When he lowered his head, she sighed. "How about I meet you and your children for dinner and then after dinner I go meet up with my friends? Huh? Can we do that compromise?"

"I wanted us to relax and for you to get to know them, you and Lila both. Not have you rush off to some bar like a horny kid." He immediately held up his hands and squeezed his eyes shut. "I'm sorry, that was uncalled for. But you know my feeling about bars." He stepped forward and then stopped. "Ella?"

The feeling of being trapped was taking her breath, stealing her words. She knew Owen was watching and waiting, but it was several moments before she could swallow air and find her voice. "What do you want me to say, Owen? Huh? I'll cancel with my friends. I am just feeling that I'm not heard in this... in what we have. I'll cancel."

"Dammit. You know, I feel I'm not heard either. Meeting my kids, having dinner with them... it doesn't have to mean we're on our way down the aisle. I just wanted to show you my world. I wanted to show them... show them my heart."

They stared at each other, confused and hurt and not able to see each other's side clearly. And despite herself, Ella could not help thinking that Owen's brooding expression, his mouth set in a straight line and arms folded across his chest, it was a little sexy.

"Hey mom!" Lila's voice called out as the front door flew open.

"In the kitchen."

Lila raced in, smiling and breathless. "Hi. Hi, Owen."

He smiled, unfolding his arms. "Hey Lila. How are you?" She started to answer, but his attention was now on Finn, who had loped in after Lila. His eyebrows rose, and he stepped toward the kids, his tone light but gaze heavy. "Oh, Finn, it's been awhile. What are you doing here?"

And he had Ella's attention. She looked from Owen to Finn, and she noticed the boy's unease, the discomfort that had him shrinking back and staring at the ground. But then he took a deep breath and answered, "I'm here with Lila. We're dating."

"Really? I hope you've been on a better path since the last time we saw each other."

The young couple wasted no time in leaving. Once they were gone, Ella turned to Owen. "What was that about?"

He narrowed his eyes, his head tilted slightly. "How long have they been dating?"

"Not long at all. Actually, I thought they were just friends until this week. How do you know him?"

"Because I'm a cop. And he is a troublemaker. Always high, hanging out in parking lots. We have to run him and his friends off - caught him lighting up a joint once so took him in for that."

"Wait!" Ella's blood ran cold. "He gets high?"

"Yeah. I'm not Lila's parent, but Ella, I would strongly caution you against allowing her anywhere near that bum. Seriously, he is trouble."

CHAPTER 20

"What the hell, Lila, your mom's dating a cop?"

Lila noticed the whiteness of his knuckles, and she wondered if he was angry at her. She remembered Brad's outbursts, and she prepared herself. She slid as far as she could against the passenger side door, and when she spoke, her voice was soft and trembly. "Off and on. I didn't think it was something I had to mention."

"No. But that guy is just a pain in my ass. He's probably telling your mom all sorts of things about me and - hey, Lila? Hey, look here. Are you afraid?"

Before she could respond, he pulled into an empty lot and reached toward her slowly, gently touching her shoulder. "Baby, hey. What's wrong?"

"You're upset and .... "

"Right. But not at you. Lila... honey, I am not going to hurt you. This isn't your fault. And even if it was, I wouldn't... no. I'm not him. I'm me. I'm Finn, and you have nothing to worry about with me."

When he drove her home, Finn insisted on walking her into the house. Despite his insistence that he be with her to face her mother, Lila could sense his nervousness. But still, he marched into the house with his back straight and gaze strong.

As expected, her mother rushed into the room. "Lila, I told you to get your ass home. We need to talk."

"And I told you I would be home before curfew. Just because your flavor of the week tells you -"

Ella turned toward Finn, her eyes narrowed and hard. "He told me you get high, Finn."

"Marijuana, mom. Calm down."

"Right. Marijuana. So, if you're hanging out with him, I guess I can deduce that you're also smoking it."

"No, mom, you can't deduce. You don't know. That guy doesn't know either. You can't just take the word of some guy just because he is on some sort of power trip. You don't even really know him."

Ella remained calm and let Lila have her outburst. Then she continued, "If you're not, then you won't mind taking a drug test. Because I went out and got one."

"Mom! That isn't fair-"

"No!" Her composure slipped, and her tone rose. "What isn't fair is lying to me and running around with a guy that has a reputation for being stoned most of the time. And he's driving with you in the car."

"Ma'am, I love your daughter-"

"Finn, no offense, but my sixteen-year-old daughter is not equipped for love at this point in her life, and she is also not equipped, it seems, to make decisions that keep her safe and keep her on the right track. So that leaves me. I have to make her choices for her. She can't see you anymore, Finn."

"Mom!"

"Ma'am, please hear me out." He paused and when she did not interrupt, he continued, "I do love her. More than I've loved anyone or anything. I'm willing to do anything. I'll never smoke again. I won't. I choose your daughter."

"I need you to leave."

"Mom!" Lila shook Finn's hand off her arm. "No, mom, I'm not going to stop seeing him. I'm going to dad's."

"No. You're staying here."

"Mom! NO! You said I could see my father anytime I wanted. You can't KEEP ME FROM MY FATHER!"

"Lila." It took everything Ella had to stay calm, but she knew the edge of her tone trembled with emotions. With fear and anger and sadness twisting inside of her, she had to bite out every word, so she did not scream it out. "I am not about to let you play your dad and me. If you're in trouble here, you can't run to the other parent to escape. It doesn't work that way."

But there was no reasoning with the hysterical girl. She grabbed Finn's hand and spat out, "No! It works that way when I want my dad. Just because you don't know what that's like-you can't punish me by keeping me from the other parent. That's abuse!"

And with that, her daughter was out the door. Her very soul and heart just walked out the door without an "I love you" or "We'll talk when we are calmer". There was no sad glance over her shoulder. Just huffing and stomping and slamming. The connection, that steel-strong bond they had shared for so many years was nowhere in sight. It was as if they were strangers.

Was Ella wrong? She was second-guessing herself. Perhaps she should have sat Lila and Finn down and talked about her concerns. Maybe she should have remained calmed and not issued ultimatums.

But she knew how she was at that age. She remembered the rebellion... and the results from it. And while she would never wish it different, she definitely wanted better for her own daughter. She wanted Lila to experience a childhood, to take her time and learn and grow and be free. The last thing Ella wanted was for Lila to find herself in a situation where she was trapped, her options limited.

The only reassurance she got that night was from her ex-husband, who promised that Lila was there and resting. He convinced her to let their daughter spend the night and cool off. Ella did not like it entirely, but she understood it was probably for the best. They needed a slight break after the explosion between them.

Suddenly the years parted like a curtain, and Ella saw her daughter as a stumbling, laughing toddler. She and Alex were distracted enough by this miraculous tiny human and their attempts at playing house to ignore the differences between them, to pretend that Alex was not going stir-crazy and that she, herself, was not disappointed. Lila had been their link, the glue that they clung to in the name of normalcy. Ella still remembered Alex grabbing Lila's hand and walking with her to the store on the corner that sold the penny candy.

And it was a time that her daughter adored her. Lila mimicked her movements, copied her words. Ella remembered one night she and Alex belly laughed for a good hour when Lila stood on her tippy toes and pointed her finger, shouting nonsense noises and sounding just like Ella in lecture mode.

There were good times. And Ella caught herself wondering if Alex remembered it that way. Or if for him, it was all simply false.... A cover... painted scenes for some play... They had Lila as a connection, so was that real? Was any of it real to him? Tangible? Did harsh words and pregnant girlfriends wipe it all away? Make it less than it was?

Ella did not want her ex-husband back. But she wanted the family. The baby girl that was innocent and trusting. The husband that helped instead of fought against. She wanted support and unconditional love, stability and strength.

"Excuse me, Ella? Hey, Ella..."

Ella jumped in her chair, jumped out of the thoughts that had been plaguing her since the night before. Work was not getting her full attention. But as she spun around in her chair, Ella was faced with Dennis standing awkwardly in the doorway, and she realized that everything she had thought she wanted in the last 24 hours was not so.

Sure, she wanted her daughter to be easier, to be nicer, smarter about choices. But she did not want that family back. It had been real to her at the time, but now she realized it did not fit. The husband that was never fully there, that had one foot out the door, one eye on another woman... she no longer wanted that.

This... in front of her... she wanted THAT.

The thought was there before she could shut it out. She had not seen or talked to Dennis since she had so boldly and rudely interrupted his class. And now staring up at him, Ella found herself at a loss of words.

Moving his gaze away from hers, Dennis cleared his throat and held out a folder. "I printed out some... for the project. I realize there might be some redundant information but... I also wanted to check if you had any questions."

She stood and reached for the folder, smiling absently. "Yes, thanks. I mean... no questions but thanks. This ... I appreciate your help."

"My help?" His voice grew huskier and instinctively, she leaned closer. "You're the one saving my ass by doing all the work. Thank you." There was a slight pause, and then with the slightest nod, he turned to leave. He started to turn back to her, and Ella caught the look in his eyes, the question and concern and knew he was about to ask if she was okay. But then he stopped himself and walked out the door.

Owen was waiting for her when she got home. She tried to smile as she got out of her car, but the energy had seeped out of her, and all she could manage was a tip of her lips.

"Hey, pretty lady." He approached her and gave her a kiss on the cheek, reaching for her bag. "I wanted to come and say I'm sorry for yesterday."

There was nothing more to do than invite him in. Ella found herself edgy, her nerves right at the surface of her skin. She had wanted to deal with the situation with Lila, not this. Not now. But he had shown up, and she very well could not throw a tantrum and order him away. Not right away at least.

Owen sensed her reservation and gave her a half smile. "So, I might have been a jerk. You were willing to compromise. Can I please retract my initial reaction and accept the compromise? Dinner with me and my kids before you go out with friends?"

Her nerves settled down. "Of course."

That break on her anxiety was short-lived. "I have a question." When she threw her head back in exasperation, he narrowed his eyes. "Just a question, Ella. Don't be like that."

She moved so that the kitchen island was between them and rubbed her nail over an imaginary speck. "It's been a long day at work, and I still have to talk to Lila about... everything." Ella heard her words, her tone, and flushed with embarrassment. "I'm sorry. What? What's the question, Owen?"

"You mentioned before a relationship. After your marriage broke up. Is that why you're finding it hard to move on? Was it... were you in love?"

"Yes." She had expected there to be hesitation...some shroud of mystery, but her mouth opened, and the word spilled out. The truth escaped.

He nodded, but his face was pinched. "And are you still in love with the guy?"

This time the truth got stuck in her mouth, and it rolled around her tongue until she was able to garble out, "I ... it's over, Owen."

"Not what I asked. Are you still in love with him?" He studied her face as she avoided any eye contact, and softly, he continued, "Ah, that answers that." Owen stared down at the floor, his expression so openly pained that it took her breath away. For several moments, they seemed frozen in the misery of miscommunications and lost chances. The silence was agony and at the same time, a blessing. But then he broke that spell and put them both out of their misery by pushing away from the counter. "I need to get to work."

"Owen-"

"No. I ... I need to go." He took a few steps and then stopped, twisting his upper body in her general direction. "I have strong feelings for you, Ella. And I know this isn't your fault-"

"I'm not trying to hold on to him- to that. I want to move on, Owen."

He nodded, still not looking up. "I'll call you later. Have a good night, Ella."

The last thing she thought she would cry about was another man. And yet this one somehow found a way to bring such a reaction. Perhaps it was the accumulation of drama from the past few weeks. Or perhaps it was Owen, himself, walking out the door.

**

It was the third day that Lila did not come home. The third day her ex tried to push her concerns and pleas aside. In fact, Alex hung up on her when she insisted they sit down to talk.

It was the last day that Ella would allow this to continue. It did not matter that Owen had not called or that Dennis avoided her at work. This was her daughter. This was Lila, and nothing came before that.

As soon as Ella pulled into her ex's driveaway, Alex stormed out of the house. She was surprised by the vibrations of hostility she could feel emanating from him as he came toward her. Slowly she got out of the car and tilted her head in confusion.

"No, Ella! You can't just come here demanding what you want!"

"Huh?"

And to add to the circus that was becoming her life, Connie shot out of the house and screamed from the porch, "Get that tramp off my property! GET OUT! You can't come here!"

Ella widened her eyes and faced her ex-husband. "I have every right to come here to get my daughter."

Alex started to speak when Connie continued to scream out more obscenities, drowning out his words. Squeezing his eyes shut, he swung around and snapped, "Connie! Get inside the house! All right? I got this." He waited as Connie shot one more dark glare Ella's way before stomping awkwardly into the house. Then he gave Ella his full attention. "I already told you. She is staying here."

"But... Alex, I don't understand. She's dating a guy that's gotten into trouble with the law, smokes pot, and all I want to do is put boundaries down. Rules. I thought we'd be on the same page with that."

The fire in his eyes told Ella of a different story, and she braced herself. Too late she realized this had been a trap. This had been brewing behind the scenes, behind her back, for the past few days, and she had unwittingly walked right into the storm.

His voice was heavy with emotions. "She told me every-thing."

"Alex! She is a sixteen-year-old girl that thinks she is in love, so yes, she will tell you anything to get out of being grounded. But you have to communicate. What is she telling you?"

"She told me you're dating a cop. That you were seeing him, then you weren't, and now you are again, and you're letting him parent our daughter. Telling her who she can and can't see-"

Whom, she thought irritably. "That's not true. He merely told me he knew her friend from all the times he had been in trouble. That set off alarms, as it should for you too-"

"What sets off alarms is that my ex-wife is jumping from guy to guy, all in front of our daughter, and when this guy that you barely know snaps his fingers and barks orders, you follow them. You put our daughter in a bad situation! She told me that this cop, he was best friends with your ex-boyfriend, that tall, old guy. Is that right? You started sleeping with his best friend? Ella, who are you? I don't even know you."

Ella's face burned with humiliation and frustration. Lila was confiding these things to her father? "That is not quite what's going on. And it's not your-"

"Don't you dare say not my business, Ella! My kid is my business. Your behavior around my kid is my business-"

"Let me talk to Lila!"

He backed up, his gaze sweeping over her with disgust. "She's not here. She's out with Finn."

"Really? You let some stoned kid drive her around? Why- to get back at me for some invisible resentment you have against me? You wanted this, Alex-"

"I NEVER WANTED THIS!" he screamed, causing her to jump back. "You kicked me out, remember? I didn't want this. Stop claiming that I did!"

Ella looked past Alex and saw Connie in the doorway, her face white. And Ella cursed and started for her car. Because this was not what she wanted. As much as she disliked Connie, as much as she even blamed Connie for the demise of her marriage, she did not want to add stress to the expectant mother. No matter what, she and Alex were over. There was no need to destroy his relationship with his girlfriend.

"Tell Lila she wins," Ella wearily called out as she got in her car. "If she wants to live here so badly, then fine."

She drove off before waiting for a response.

**

Connie stood rigid as Alex walked in, and to her utter disgust, he barked, "Don't! I can't deal with it right now."

"I didn't say one word, Alex."

"No, but you're going to."

Suddenly she straightened, her hands going to her stomach as if to shield the baby from any impending harsh words. "I can't believe it. I just heard you tell her.... You lied to me. You said you left her. Then I find out you lied. She kicked you out, and I was the only remaining option. And now you have nerve to come at me like this is all my fault."

"No. I'm just sick of you taking everything and making it all dramatic. I was going to leave her. You know I was. We talked about it. But I wanted a plan in place. All right? You assumed I left, and I just wanted to avoid a fight."

With a shake of her head, Connie started to walk away. "I am beyond caring at this point. The lies are just-"

"Hey! Don't you dare accuse me of lying."

"Not accusing. Outright telling you that's what you do. You lie. Just... stay away from me. All right? Sleep on the couch. Oh, right. Like you do anyways."

**

There was barely time to take a breath and shake that visit off before Ella heard a car outside. She sank into a chair and rested her head on her fingertips, not ready to face whomever it might be.

But then she heard Lila call for her, and she slowly stood, bracing herself.

"Mom." Lila stepped into the kitchen tentatively. "I wanted

to grab some clothes."

Ella wrapped her arms around herself and stared at her daughter icily. "Then go grab some clothes."

"Mom. Don't be like this. I just want a break-"

"Lila. Go get your clothes. Go."

Her eyes widened as she stared at her mother. "What?"

"What do you mean 'what'?" And suddenly, the dam burst. Ella felt like she was outside of her body, unable to control the reactions, the words, spilling from her. It was as if something had control of her and all the frustrations and betrayals she had felt lately were being pushed out, right onto her daughter's feet.

"You're standing there, Lila, looking surprised. Like some baby deer caught in headlights, and that is pissing me off more than anything. I very reasonably wanted to parent you. But what the hell are you telling your dad?"

Lila's face flushed, and she stammered, the guilt radiating from her. "I ... I just said I didn't think it was fair-"

"No, Lila. You told him everything about my private life and then some. You said Owen was parenting you? What the hell? What is wrong with you? What happened to you? Huh? I can't turn around without your damn father screaming something about my life, my personal world. You run to him and that whore and tell them everything. But if I so much as ask how things are with them, if I make casual conversation, you huff and puff and accuse me of being nosey!"

"Mom, that isn't true!" She was shaking her head back and forth, tears splashing onto her cheeks.

"He had the girlfriend, Lila! He's the bad guy, and yet I'm the one whose life is scrutinized. Whose daughter has to run and gossip to her dad and that woman and judge me just for trying to move on! Stop it! Stop telling them about my life! Stop making me the asshole when all I've done is try to be there for you! So, you can go ahead and get what you need and go to your father's. I'm making that choice for you. Until you can respect me and my privacy."

She stopped and gasped for air, gasped to be understood and forgiven for her tirade. Already Ella was regretting her outburst, but she merely stood there, unable to take back the words and rage, unable to draw her daughter to her. Because she still felt the hot stab of betrayal, and she needed Lila to hear her, to understand the pain and humiliation.

But Lila was only sixteen years old, and no matter how angry she was at her, Ella was her mom and her sanctuary. She looked as if her puppy had been kicked and thrown out the window right in front of her.

For a solid minute, the mother and daughter stared at each other, both shocked and wilted and disillusioned. For so long, their relationship had been one of love and respect and even friendship. It was a connection that other mothers and daughters envied and strived for. And now it seemed to be gone. Not even broken. Not damaged. Just gone.

It was finally Lila who broke the gaze. With a crumpled cry, she turned and ran out of the house. Ella started to call for her, but she only managed a strangled noise, rushing to the window in time to see her jump into Finn's car, covering her face as he bent over the front seat to gather her into his arms. She must have demanded that he get her out of there fast, because Ella saw him nod and pull back, putting the car in reverse and taking her away.

Minutes later, Ella was in her car, determined. Somehow this volatile outburst had cleared her head on other long-lasting issues. As soon as the angry last word had dropped from her mouth, Ella had had a realization, and although she wanted to make things right with Lila, there was someone she had to see first. There was a matter she had to confront after years of avoidance and silent stewing.

Diana opened the door, her eyes round when she saw Ella. Too exhausted to exert any hostility, she merely leaned against the door jamb and softly requested, "Dad. I need dad." With a short nod, she turned and disappeared into the belly of the house.

Moments later, Ted was in front of Ella, whispering her name and gathering her into his arms.

"I get it, dad," she sobbed, letting him lead her into the kitchen, sitting in the chair he pulled out. "I get how you said what you said. About not wanting to raise me."

"Ella, I never meant-"

"I know. I just did it, dad." She lowered her head into her arms, lying there as if the darkness could encompass her whole messed up world and not just her sight. When she lifted her head, she saw Diana in the doorway, purse in hand, giving Ted a small wave. And just as subtly, she left.

"Ella," he murmured, reaching out to stroke her hair. "Slow down, and tell me what happened."

"I lost it. I was standing there, dad, and I just lost it. I said some pretty nasty things. I had to physically stop myself from saying worse. I called her stepmother a whore. I told her that her dad was the asshole. I told her to go live with him. And she did. She just walked out." He continued to listen as she gave details about the events, about what drove her to the breakdown.

And as she cried, Ted held her, soothing her as she had always wanted her father to do. When she was seven years old and mourning the mother she had known and then lost, she had wanted to feel safe and loved from her dad. She had wanted to know that she was more important than his own heartache.

"Hey, pumpkin, you hear me, and you hear every word. Are you ready? You listenin'?"

Ella sniffed and nodded, but that word just brought to mind Dennis. He always said "listen" as he spoke when he wanted her to pay attention to his words. It was a charming habit, never said with any aggression or as an order. Just simply a word used as a highlighter. And now her father was sitting in front of her, using that same language. "Yes. I am."

"Good. Because this is important. You, my baby girl, are so much better at parenting than I ever was. I said harsh things to you because I was frustrated at my own shortcomings."

"Dad, it's okay-"

"No! It isn't! But when I said I never wanted you- that is the farthest thing from the truth. I didn't want kids, that's true. But Ella Marie, the moment you were born, you were wanted. I wanted to be your dad. And I did a shitty job. I hid behind my marriage and then my job because I knew I could do those. I knew I could be a good husband. I knew I was excellent at taking pictures. But being your father? That's a mighty heady type of thing. I have always wanted to tell you this. Either I couldn't find the words... or you wouldn't hear anything I had to say."

"I'm sorry I've been so stubborn."

He reached out and grabbed her hand, giving it a squeeze. "Don't apologize. You were just a kid. All of this, it was unfair to you. And yes, I said things out of anger that I didn't mean. And you did that today. It's human. It isn't right, it sucks, but you've been through hell and back lately. I'm sure Lila will see that for what it is. Eventually."

Ted continued to comfort her, to talk and explain, listen and advise. And Ella was grateful that while she was willing to hear his words, to take in all he had been wanting to say for so long, he did not try to bring up Diana. Ella was not there yet. She was not ready to face the woman that had shattered her childhood and ripped apart her confidence.

Her father, after almost four decades of fumbling and disappointing, was now reaching out in a sincere, humble manner. No showboating or bullying to have her see things his way.

"Lila's becoming an adult," he stated in a soft, deep tone, his eyes searching hers. "And as much as it hurts, you have to give her space to make her own decisions. This kid... Fiddler-"

Ella laughed through her tears. "Finn!"

"Not much better. Finn. Is he disrespectful? How is he around you?"

"Polite. But you know kids. It could be an act."

"Absolutely. But at least he has the sense to act polite.

Right? How does he treat her?"

With an agitated shrug, she answered, "He seems to adore her. His eyes follow her everywhere, he opens doors for her, he asks how she is…"

"Okay. I don't like the fact that he smokes pot. I understand why you're upset. But when you cool off, when Lila calms down… talk. Don't make my mistake and just order or ignore. Don't do it. Because I've missed out on so much. Can we work on it?"

Ella nodded, using a crumpled-up napkin to dab at her wet cheeks. "Yes."

By the time she made it home, Ella was so drained, she was not sure she could lift her feet up enough to make it through the front door. It seemed that drama was becoming a ping pong game. From Dennis to Owen. From Lila to Alex and back to Lila and then to her father. Ping…ping…ping. Just thinking of it made her eyes heavy. She needed to sleep. For a long time. And as her phone made a series of beeps and lit up to show that Owen was finally reaching out, she simply put it on the bed-side table and vowed to read the texts after a sufficient nap.

CHAPTER 21

Owen came back into her life after a few days of sulking. The return was quiet and humble, as if he were embarrassed for trying to make waves, for expressing his heartbreak, but Ella knew what that felt like. She had recently felt her entire soul shatter from rejection, so the last thing she wanted to do was bring more attention to it.

So, she allowed him back just as quietly, as if she had never glimpsed into his anguish, never saw the watery eyes dull in realization. A part of her wanted to resist, to talk it out with him and explain further because it seemed Owen wanted to pick up where they left off... or rather, pick up further down the line. As if they were committed and fully in love. But she held back.

Without much fuss, she joined him for dinner with his kids. His son Evan, Evan's wife Laura and Owen's daughter Penny. Evan and Laura were polite, even interested in conversation, asking her about her job at the college and her interests. But Penny was sullen and uninterested in making friends with her father's date.

Ella understood. She had once been a young girl whose father would sometimes date. It was not often, but she remembered a few awkward encounters with these strange women, feeling out of place and in the way.

So, she was not insulted by the lack of interest. She tried to keep a distance but also did not want to seem like she did not want to know her. So midway through the evening, Ella turned to Penny and with what she hoped was a sincere smile, said, "Your dad says you are a junior at college. What's your major?"

Penny had enough decency to make eye contact and answer in a clear tone, "Graphic Design."

"Oh!" Ella lifted her eyebrows and informed the girl, "My daughter is interested in that. Maybe you can give her some advice."

She gave a half smile and a shrug. "Um, sure. Go to college. Take classes in that area."

"Penelope," Owen growled. Ella whispered his name in a plea not to make a big deal out of it.

But Penny immediately stared down at her plate and murmured an apology. Then she glanced up. "I just thought ... I thought it was just going to be us, dad."

Ella scooted her chair back. "Penny, I think your dad just wanted us to meet. But I actually do have to get going. You guys can continue your visit. It was lovely meeting everyone." She saw the grateful smile Penny shot her, but then she noticed Owen's annoyance, and she braced herself as he walked her out.

Fortunately, he did not try to stop her from leaving. "Hey, I'm sorry about Penny. Sometimes she can be..."

"No. She was fine, Owen. I promise. They're great kids. Thanks for inviting me. I know it means a lot for you to let me meet your kids."

He gave her a small smile. "It really does, Ella. He reached for her hand, lacing his fingers through hers. "Text me when you make it home, no matter how late just so I know you made it safe. 'K?"

"'K." She grinned as he pressed his forehead against hers.

"And if you drink, call me. Don't drive."

"I am not going to drink, but okay. If something impairs my ability to drive, I'll call."

Although the club was crowded, it was a calm, happy time. Ella felt she could breathe and simply dance with her friends. There was no worrying about daughters or exes, being in love or letting a guy down easy. It was the music, her friends, and the dance floor. And halfway into the night when a young man tried to dance with her, she waved her hands in front of her, as if that could make him disappear. Amidst the screaming and laughter of her friends, Ella managed to shoo him away.

At midnight, Ella glanced at her phone and grimaced. Carla peeked over her shoulder and made no attempt to smother back the giggles. "You sure as hell never reacted that way when it was Dinner Party boy texting you."

"Yeah, well Dinner Party boy did not demand a response and throw a tantrum because I was out past ten o'clock." She held her phone out so Carla could see the several texts full of exclamation points and capitalization and the missed calls.

"What the hell?"

She stepped outside, breathing in the sharp, chilly air, the sound of music blowing out every time the door opened, people laughing and yelling as they climbed the hill to their cars.

"Hey!" His voice came through unnaturally high and rushed. "You didn't call me. I was worried!"

Ella bit back frustrated words and waited a moment for her breathing to even out. In a softer tone than she had thought she could muster, she responded, "Owen. You asked me to let you know when I made it home. I am still out with my friends."

Silence followed for several seconds, and she wondered if he had disconnected the call. But then he spoke in a tone that she knew he also had to work at keeping even. "It's after midnight! I thought we were going to the festival later today?"

"We are."

"I'll be on call. I wanted to get there early."

"Owen, I promise you, we will get there early. We already agreed at 10 AM. Plenty of time for me to get some rest. I'm not staying out much later."

There was a pause and then his tone came through more re-laxed, almost relieved. "Okay. Good. It'll be fun. I haven't been there in years. I just thought... I thought you were only going out for a couple of hours, and you'd be home by ten at night.

Not midnight."

"Owen. I never said I was going to be home by ten."

"You left the restaurant at 7. Three hours isn't enough to see your friends and dance a few songs?" He sighed and continued, "I'm trying here. Just… text me when you do make it home. Just so I don't worry."

"I will, Owen. Thanks." And she was infuriated with herself for thanking the man that lectured her on how long to stay out. She was impatient that the old familiar relief was released through her body and mind once he deemed it okay that she was still out. Where was her independence? Where was her resolve to be that stronger woman?

Where was Dennis?

**

The sun blasted through the windows as Ella rushed to get ready. The early November day was masquerading as a gorgeous summer day, and it was perfect weather for a festival. Ella thought of the fried pickles, the hot sausage sandwiches, and the homemade soups, the crafts and crowds, and she felt her stomach dip in excitement.

"It's after 10," Owen called from the living room, and she heard the impatience creeping into his voice.

Stopping to close her eyes and breathe, Ella answered, "There is no set time we have to be there, Owen. That's what makes this so great. Our day, our speed."

Cursing under her breath, she heard the chair squeak as he got to his feet and came into the kitchen. "I know there is no appointment, honey. But we agreed to get there by 10 AM. Not 11. Not 12. 10. I warned you about the late night because I knew this would happen -"

The doorbell cut him off, and he rolled his eyes. Ella felt helpless, his mood draping over her like a black curtain. "One second. Let me answer that, then I just have to grab my purse, and we can go. Okay?" She leaned forward and gave him a quick kiss, relieved to see him smile softly. She did not bother mentioning that she could not locate her purse and that was what was holding them up.

Her mind preoccupied with all the possible places her purse could be, she swung the door open and stared at the person on the other side, not immediately placing him. Then the wheels started turning, and with a jolt, she realized her daughter's boyfriend was in front of her. "Finn! Is everything okay? Is Lila all right?"

His eyes widened, and he stepped forward, his hands out in front of him as if to stop her panic. "No! I'm sorry. She's fine. Lila's okay. I didn't mean to alarm you. But... I mean, she isn't really okay. She's safe and physically .... But she doesn't know I'm here."

"Okay." Why was this boy standing there when her daughter would not even come home? "Then what can I help you with?"

"Ma'am... I'm here because I love your daughter. I would do anything for her. And right now, she's upset. I'm hoping I can convince you to talk to her."

"Ella." Owen came up behind her. "We need to go."

She half turned. "Owen. Give me a minute-"

"I'm not sure what this kid is doing here, but can it wait-"

"Owen! This is about my daughter. Please give me a few minutes."

He stared at her in surprise, as if her outburst came out of nowhere. Then he turned his glare on Finn, who met his glare with a calm, unflinching gaze of his own. "I'll be in the living room waiting."

Ella returned her full attention to Finn. "I appreciate your concern, Finn. But if she is so upset, she can come here and talk. And while I don't know a lot about you, but I know enough to be concerned."

"Ma'am. I would never put her in danger-"

"You did by introducing her to drugs!"

"I've been clean since the day you confronted me. You can test me. If that's what it will take for you to trust me and trust Lila, then I won't smoke again. I won't. She means that much to me. Please. I'm asking for a chance to get to know me, to not just judge based on that one part of my life. I'm willing to sit down and answer any questions you have. Just... please talk to Lila."

Ella was taken aback by the courage and maturity Finn was displaying. There was something about the desperation in his eyes that drew her in. But things were chaotic. There was a man impatiently waiting for a festival, there was a sullen daughter that was not speaking to her, and there were feelings and thoughts she still had to sort out. With a small smile, she assured him, "I'll reach out to Lila soon. Okay? The rest I can't promise."

Finn hesitated, as if there were so much more he wanted to divulge, more he wanted to do to fix things, and somehow Ella sensed all that. She had this intuition that his intentions were sincere. This was not some monster standing in front of her. He was a lovestruck boy.

But as soon as the front door shut, Owen was there to remind her just what this boy represented. "I'm telling you, Ella, he is bad news. If Lila is really that serious with him, you might want to see how far gone she is-"

"Can we just... can we go? I need to find my purse."

Owen squeezed his eyes shut and pinched the bridge of his nose. "Find your- what? Ella, we had this planned for weeks. You couldn't be more prepared? I told you that staying out so late wasn't a good idea. Dammit!"

Ella turned and stared at him in surprise. The pure power behind his frustration put her on guard. "Listen. It will just take a few minutes to find it. The funnel cakes and the home-made pot holders will be there whether we arrive at 10 am or 8 pm."

"I just ...we had a set time and sometimes it drives me crazy how you procrastinate. I'm on call and wanted to see as much as possible before I get called into work."

As she searched for her purse, Owen suggested she find a designated spot to put it so this would not happen again. She nodded numbly, not having the energy to explain that there was a designated spot, but sometimes she got home, and things happened. She wanted to get dinner ready or had to use the bathroom or someone was calling. She usually found her purse within minutes... when there wasn't a man standing over her nagging.

The tension seemed to dissipate, at least on Owen's end, as he drove them to the festival. Ella started to warm up as he chattered about the bands that would be playing that day and the different booths he wanted to visit. She was surprised that he was into local art and could name several of the artists. It was a side to him she did not know, and guiltily, she knew it was because she refused to see him as anything but one-dimensional. To see more would put her in danger of becoming more involved.

The blocked-off streets were packed as people crowded in to see the blown glass vases and the paintings of rock stars. Ella gravitated toward the holiday crafts, reminding herself that if she bought anything, it would be one more thing to pack up when they sold the house.

But when Owen was not interested in the same thing, he was on to the next booth, grabbing her hand to pull her along. A few times, she had to verbally stop him, and in those cases, he waited off to the side, arms crossed and foot tapping.

They both ran into people they knew, and when Owen introduced her, he pulled her close to him, beaming proudly and assigned the term "girlfriend" to her without any hesitation. She could only smile and shake the hand of whomever was in front of her. When she introduced him, it was simply, "This is Owen."

It was after an hour of browsing that they both started making noises about finding some food booths and as they rounded the corner to the next row, they almost ran right into a very pregnant Connie.

"Oh!" Ella jumped back just as Owen stepped forward to steady Connie.

"Ma'am, are you okay? We're sorry. We didn't see you and-"

"I'm fine. Ella. Aren't you going to introduce us?" There was a flush to Connie's cheeks that Ella guessed was from the heat of the crowd and walking so far with the awkward bump in front of her. She forced a small smile Owen's way, fully expecting Ella to be uncomfortable.

"Oh, sure. Owen, this is Connie. Connie, Owen. Connie is Lila's stepmom. Or … I guess, soon-to-be stepmom."

Her words caught Connie off guard. "Oh, I… yeah. Soon-to-be. We're planning but want to have a beautiful wedding. Alex said he wants this wedding to be extraordinary. He's around here somewhere." She made a point to swivel her head back and forth searching for the man that Ella realized was not even there.

"Is Lila nearby?"

Connie started to speak, her expression pinched and lips pursed, and Ella imagined some spiteful sentence about to tumble out. But she seemed to change her mind because she blinked slowly, and her face relaxed. "Not right now. She's coming later."

"We're just about to get something to eat," Owen smiled warmly. "You and your fiancé can join us if you'd like."

Connie smirked. "Don't know where Alex has run off to, but I'd love to."

"Actually… we wanted some time alone. You understand, right, Connie?" She paused and added, "I could always stop by your house and have dinner with you if you'd really like my company. You and … Alex."

"Well, Owen, it was nice meeting you. I hope you come to your senses soon though."

Owen's stare drilled into Ella until she widened her eyes. "What?"

"Sweetheart, you were a little rude."

The fact that he used an endearment before insulting her caused her nerves to stretch and hit the inside of her skin with such force, she had to give her body a little shake. "Owen. That was my ex's girlfriend. The reason we divorced was because he was cheating ... with her."

"I know who that was. But unless you're still harboring feelings for him, you should let it go."

"This isn't about any type of feelings. This is about how she has behaved and disrupted my life since. Showing up wherever I am, prowling around my house-"

"Okay. Got it. I won't ask her to eat with us ever again." He jabbed her shoulder good-naturedly with a teasing smile. "I don't want in the middle of any cat fights."

"Wha-" She swatted his hand away and glared at him before stomping away.

By the time they got their food and found a spot to sit, Ella was cranky and sweaty, her stomach rumbling, but the food on her plate as appetizing as mud.

It seemed her irritation was seeping through to Owen. He stared at her for a full minute before prompting, "So now you're not going to eat? For God's sake, Ella, I just said the lines anywhere else were too long, and we'd lose each other. If you want something else, go get it!"

Ella blinked back sudden tears, his harsh tone cutting and the day a wash. "No. Forget it. I was waiting for it to cool down."

For several more moments he watched her, his expression softening. He opened his mouth to say something, but then she watched as something behind her caught his attention.

Turning, Ella saw Dennis a few feet away, holding a plate and looking frozen to the spot as his gaze flitted around, as if debating whether to flee and claim never having seen them, or surrender.

"Dennis!" Owen called out, waving him over.

Dennis waved and then looked around as if to find another place to sit. The picnic tables were all crowded, Ella noticed with satisfaction, and feeling a little stab of meanness, she called out sweetly, "What? You don't want to sit with us?"

Recovering quickly, a slow smile spread across his face, and he made a beeline for their table. His long legs slid over the bench with ease, and he settled right beside her. "Of course, I want to sit with you."

Owen shot Ella a chiding look. "Just ignore her. She seems to be in a mood today."

"What? Ella? No."

"Oh yeah. Invited a pregnant woman to come sit with us. She was here alone, and Ella shot that down right in front of her. Like some jealous child."

Ella could not believe the words coming out of Owen's mouth, and she felt her face grow hot as Dennis gazed at her. She felt his hand nudge her under the table, to give her support, perhaps sympathy.

"Connie?" When she nodded, Dennis addressed Owen, "That woman has been harassing Ella. Owen, she follows her and-"

"Well, maybe she is just a little curious."

"She would show up to my house and pound on the windows and walls."

"Right. That pregnant woman came and ran all around your house tormenting you. Why would she do that, Ella? She has the guy. She got him. I think you're being dramatic. And looking at you, I have no doubt you'd win in a fight against her."

She slapped away Dennis's hand and leaned forward, "Wow, Owen. Not exactly a comforting statement coming from a cop!"

The amusement left his face immediately, eyes narrowed and cheeks reddened. Just as he was about to respond, his phone went off. "Work," he mumbled, jumping up and moving a few feet away as he answered the phone.

"You all right?" Dennis asked in a low voice, his mouth dipped down to her ear. She gave a short nod, and then he lifted the edge of her tray. "Barbeque? You hate barbeque." Without waiting for her response, he shoved the tray away and slid his plate between them. "I can't finish all of this anyways."

She eyed the pierogies and with a sigh, speared one with her fork. Because she was starving. Although, as Owen so generously pointed out, her frame was large enough to announce her the winner of any fight with a skinnier chic. Lovely.

"Hey, I got called in. Just like I suspected. That's why I wanted to get here earlier than we did." Owen shot her a pointed look before turning to Dennis. "Can you give her a ride home?"

"Owen," she stood and started to slide out from the picnic bench. "I can just go with you. Drop me off home."

"No. I can't. Going in the opposite direction."

"Then I'll-"

"What? You don't want to hang out with me?" Dennis teased with a straight face, and suddenly she found herself smiling.

"Fine."

Owen walked briskly around the table and leaned down for a quick kiss. "Sorry. Call you tonight?"

She nodded, but he was already walking away. Dennis came up behind her. "Hey, can you save my spot? I'll be right back."

Assuming he had to go tell some woman that he couldn't spend the day with her, she sat back down. After several minutes, she wondered if he was even going to return. Maybe he had other plans, and the thought of helping out a woman that made his life miserable for a short period of time did not appeal to him.

"Okay. Here we go." He set down a tray with sausage sandwiches, potato soup, and cheese fries.

She grinned. "Does this mean you don't want to share your pierogies?"

That flash of a grin lit up his entire face. "I'll share."

"You didn't have to do this. But I am so glad you did. I need to keep up my fighter figure. Big girl can fight off stalking skinny girl anytime."

"He didn't mean it that way." He sighed. "He's not good with words or ...or expressing himself even." Ella focused on the fries, not giving any type of sign that she heard and understood. "So, listen, what do you want to do after we eat? What didn't you see yet? They have these posts with solar lights on top and our university logo on them. Might be something you like."

Finally, she looked up, a small smile displaying her gratitude. "Thanks, Dennis, but you don't have to do that."

"Do what?"

"Stick around. You can just take me home."

"What? Are you kidding? Listen, Miss El, I have not even been to the honey booth. Or the petting zoo. Have you been to the petting zoo yet?"

"No."

"They have a baby pig this year. And goats. I know you love those goats."

"I really do."

True to his word, Dennis led her around the entire festival. They stopped to watch a magic act, laughing as the guy fumbled through the tricks, and the kids stared in awe. They tried samples of homemade ice cream and got their caricatures done. Sometimes Dennis walked ahead to another booth, but he let her browse, never tried to rush her along. "We have all day," he murmured as he leaned forward. "Take your time. I won't be far. Promise."

She shopped at a booth that had baskets of hot peppers. When Dennis joined her, Ella stared up at him. "I want to make a sauce today with these peppers. But… will you … he's working, and Lila isn't at home any-- will you stay for dinner? Or is that too- never mind." She turned away and shook her head as if trying to clear the silliness from it.

Gently, he nudged her toward him. "Hey. Hey, El. What do you mean Lila isn't home? You mean today or…"

Forcing her lips up, she lifted a shoulder. "You know how it goes." She sighed when his stare persisted. "We're going through a rough spot."

Slowly he nodded. "I would love to have dinner with you tonight."

The afternoon passed in pure bliss. Ella could not remember laughing that hard in a long time as they fed and petted the goats and then tried tying balloons into animal shapes. Dennis convinced her to go on a hayride, and as they bounced and got jerked around, surrounded by smiling kids and tired parents, she felt young and carefree. For a few brief moments in time, Ella allowed herself to forget about the man that broke her heart and remember the man that had saved her and had become her friend. She lost herself in the moment. Laughter was freed from that knotted up tension inside, and when she glanced over at Dennis and saw that smile, she guessed he felt the same.

"Hey, El." His voice sailed out to her softly, part of the breeze caressing her cheek and automatically, instinctively, Ella turned, grinning to find him right in front of her, his hands out, reaching. He jerked his head toward the band playing on the sidewalk right beside them. "Isn't this our song?"

With a good-humored eye roll, she took a step back. "We don't have a song."

"Ella!" he chastised softly, persistently keeping his hands up, ready to take hers. "I'm disappointed. We do too have a song. That night. Out in your yard. Sunburnt from a day of fishing. Full moon shining down like a spotlight. Your old radio playing this song and some static…. C'mon. Really? You had on that top… it billowed out and you said you felt you had wings…"

Finally, she surrendered a smile. "I remember. Of course. But-"

"Just a dance. C'mon. We're in the middle of a crowded street. One dance."

She had no choice. The memory of that night flooded out any willpower. The smell of the grass. The cool night air chilling her burnt skin. His calloused fingers brushing against the backs of her hands and then her shoulders. She was transported back to that as soon as they moved together.

The stubble of his cheek soothed her as he bent to press his face against hers and whispered, "This is a little dangerous." She did not have to ask what he meant. She did not want to ask. For a few blissed minutes, they were fused together, swaying to the song.

The last notes of the song lingered in the air, and they continued swaying, even as the tempo changed, a fast, loud beat filling the air around them. "Do you trust me?" Dennis asked, moving his hands from her back to her arms that were draped around his neck.

As her hands automatically fell into his, she whispered, "Yes."

Suddenly, but smoothly, he spun her away from him and then pulled her back. Laughing, she twirled around and let him lead, trusted him to be her anchor. The music had livened up the crowd, and Ella heard people singing, hollering, but she could only focus on the man in front of her. She knew they were not the smoothest dancers there, and they were probably far from one of the good ones, but she was almost positive that they were having the best time. And that they were the only ones in their own world, only seeing each other despite the crowd. All too soon, the music died down, and the band declared a break. And the spell seemed to break between them, as they remembered where they were and just whom they were with.

Breathless, Ella tried to laugh off the experience. "Thanks for helping me get in my cardio."

With a small smile, Dennis reached out and moved a strand of hair out of her face.

By the time they went to her house, it was early evening, and their arms were full of goodies from the festival. Dennis followed her into the kitchen and started to pull out the necessary ingredients for their dinner, not needing asked where anything was or what she was making. He just knew.

"So Lila…"

With a sigh, she tilted her head up and squeezed her eyes shut. "We … I lost my temper. Really lost it, Dennis. I screamed at her. And she's dating a guy that does drugs."

"Finn?"

Her eyes grew round. "You know him?"

"I met him once or twice when I ran into Lila. Look, for what it's worth, he seems like a good kid."

"He gets high."

Dennis nodded slowly, his eyes never leaving hers. "Yes. He does."

"I don't want Lila around that."

Again, he nodded. "Okay. Fair enough."

"I mean, one minute my kid is running around with a good crowd. Has a decent boyfriend and then-"

"Whoa. You mean Brad? Because listen to me, Finn is no angel, but you see his faults out in the open. Just because Brad seems okay on the surface, just because he comes from money and a well-known family in town doesn't mean he is free and clear of any troubles."

"Hey! I didn't say I liked him because he had money. Far from that. He is in sports and .... And well, yes. He comes from a good family."

"Ella." He waited until she was calm enough to stare up at him. "And Lila comes from divorced parents that are struggling financially. And I'm willing to bet she's smoked pot. Does that make her a bad kid?"

"She smokes pot because of Finn."

"Right. That has to be it." He sighed and gently rubbed her arm. "I'm sorry. I know this is a sensitive subject. You have a very valid reason for not wanting her to get serious with Finn. But don't trade one devil for another one better disguised. When it comes to your daughter, listen, pay attention. Be alert."

She knew Dennis was trying to tell her something behind the words. There was a bond between him and her daughter, and she knew he was privy to more about her life than Ella was at the moment. So, she knew to take what he said seriously. With a curt nod, she returned to chopping.

"I said some really harsh things to her, Dennis. I told her to stop running to her dad about my life. I said she could get out if she couldn't keep her mouth shut." Much to her dismay and horror, tears fell from her eyes. "And she got out."

"Aw, hun, listen. Hey, listen to me. She will be back. You're allowed to lose it every once in a while. Hell, the year you've had, I'm shocked it didn't happen sooner. She knows you love her, and yeah, maybe she needed to hear that. To give you respect. She's a kid, and they take full advantage of the ones closest to them. Remember that."

"Earlier today, Finn showed up. Asked me to talk to her. And he said he would quit drugs because he loved her. I mean, they're so young, but that is sweet."

"It is."

They worked in mostly comfortable silence. Chopping vegetables, stirring the sauce, setting the table. Their movements were in sync, and Ella felt that familiar zap of energy every time they were close.

"I want to tell Owen the truth. About us. Our history."

"Okay."

"But I don't want to do that if it in any way hurts your relationship with him. Or if you'd rather I didn't."

He grabbed the bowl of pasta and brought it to the table. "Ella, I always wanted to tell him. Do you want me to be with you when you do? Or I can tell him."

"No. I'll do it. I'm sorry- for putting you in this position-"

"El. No one's fault. I just want you to be okay with whatever you do. I'm not worried about me."

She smiled her thanks, unable to talk, unable to squeeze any words around the lump in her throat. What was she doing? The very man that had thrown her universe into a dark, stormy pit was sitting at her kitchen ... because she had invited him. Ella still could not hold a fishing rod in her hand without tearing up, and yet she was serving him dinner with a blissful smile on her face.

"You're thinking too much."

She reared back as if struck, his ability to simply reach in and pull out her thoughts unnerving. "Huh?"

"That look on your face. I know it. This is just two friends having dinner." Dennis studied her and added, "You're so cautious. And that's not a bad thing, Ella."

There was no protesting when he insisted on helping to clean up. But she felt some tension between them, actually radiating between them like some invisible strength, a static sizzling and shocking. He became silent, almost brooding, and Ella tried to think back to see when the disconnect had happened.

"Now you're thinking," she softly acknowledged, and his eyes raised to meet hers.

"I lied to you when we first started talking."

"Oh?" Then she shook her head, moving back to the sink, to the dirty dishes she knew she could handle. "It doesn't matter now."

"Robin." He waited until she threw down the dish towel and turned toward him, placing one shaking hand on the counter for support. "I said I knew that love existed because I'd experienced it. But I led you to believe I was talking about my wife. I wasn't. I was actually referring to you. How I felt about you the first day I saw you. And each time after that."

She pushed off from the counter and rolled her eyes. "Stop. Okay? Just stop."

"I'm not giving you a line. You know me better than that. My marriage? Ella, I was a college kid that didn't know the first thing about love. We were miserable."

As tears sprang to her eyes, she clenched her fists and cried out, "Stop! This isn't fair!"

And suddenly they were nose to nose. "Not fair? No, it isn't. None of this is. Meeting the woman of my dreams when I'm still just a messed-up individual isn't fair. Finally getting to the point that I can let my guard down after years of blocking any type of deep emotions only to have my father, my best friend, die and drag me back to that dark place- that sure as hell ain't fair. And losing you because of my own fears and issues. That isn't fair. But I'm going to do this, Ella. I'm going to tell you what I should have told you from the beginning. It was not fair to lead you on and not share with you my past. My demons."

"Lead me on? So, you never intended to see this through?"

"Wrong choice of words, El. All I wanted since I first saw you in that camping chair, rod in hand, crying silently, all I've ever wanted was a life with you. But if I'm not honest, and you don't know me and my past, how's that going to happen? Even if it's too late. I want you to know. My marriage wasn't …. We weren't happy. We were naive kids that were in over our heads.

"She wanted to do the right thing. She wanted to split up. Divorce. But I thought of my parents, and I thought… I thought if we just stayed together and worked at it…I was afraid of being that failure I was as a kid that couldn't read. The way I overcame that was by working. So… I ignored her pleas. I insisted we work at it. And … I mean, she had other issues. She suffered with depression all her life… But no matter what, I loved her. Maybe not as strongly as I should have. We shouldn't have married. But she was my partner. My friend. First love. And I came home from class one day. She killed herself, El. And…" He took a deep, shaky breath and squared up his shoulders, "I'm not telling you this for sympathy. But because I kept a large part of my past, of myself, from you. And you need to know what I did to you… it stems from that. Nothing about you or what you did. It is my fear and my… my grief."

She wrapped her arms around him and hugged him to her, hearing a sob escape before he gulped for air. And Ella realized how terrifying it would be for Dennis to find himself responsible for another person's well-being. Because that's what relationships were about. And she understood.

Thirty minutes later, Dennis paused at the front door, staring down at Ella with a look she knew all too well. "I want to kiss you, El. But I won't try. I'm going to give you space. But this has been agony for me. I want to stop the back and forth, and I want us to be together."

A fiery streak shot through her belly, and straightening, Ella asked, "And what about what I want?"

Suddenly that grin flashed on his face. "That's why I'm giving you space. So, you can figure it out."

And then he was gone. And she felt the absence.

CHAPTER 22

Lila tried to take a breath and make sense of how she got here. How she got behind a line of booths, nose to nose with Brad as they flirted dangerously past the point of it being innocent. She moved slightly away and searched for the group of girls she had come with, but there was no one past the blue flaps of the booths.

It would be easy to blame Finn. His grueling work schedule left them little time to simply hang out, to be with each other. And especially today when she needed him.

Because the festival was usually the thing she did with her mom. She remembered years past, skipping beside the most beautiful woman there, her stomach full from the candy and soda. Lila remembered visiting the petting zoo, her mom always buying her a cup of feed for the animals. Or getting a balloon in the shape of a giraffe. They always ran into people her mother knew, other adults that squealed and hugged and promised to get together soon, although soon probably meant in a year, at the next festival.

Last year had been the first year Lila went with friends and not her mom. It had been such a turbulent time. Her parents had been fighting constantly, her mother had always been so sad, and Lila had a secret she did not want to keep... but had to. It was one of those toxic secrets that would destroy everything and everyone if she told. So, she had been stuck with it, and it had eaten at her from the inside out. Nights of lying awake, crying, and worrying. Filled with dread that her world as she knew it would simply unravel. Everything would change. Everything was such a lie.

This year did not seem much better. The world had unraveled. And now she was standing in front of Brad after calling him... after feeling the need to test the waters... to see if she could still keep him interested.

But as he stood in front of her, his hands pulling her closer as his warm wet breath invaded her face with what he thought were romantic lines, she had a change of heart.

"Wait. Brad."

"What the hell!"

She jumped away from Brad in time to see Finn standing just a few feet away, his face red and eyes narrowed. It was not the Finn she knew. The anger radiating from him broke her heart.

Brad chuckled beside her, reaching out to slap her ass. "Sorry, Finn. She knew the good thing she was missing."

Before she could register what was happening, Finn stormed up to Brad and landed a punch that knocked him right to the ground. Finn then stared at her, his expression melting into anguish.

"I... not what it looks like."

"Save it, Lila. You know, I left work early. Even after promising to stay the entire day, I felt guilty about leaving you here alone. Imagine that." He motioned toward Brad, who was writhing on the ground. "He's all yours. That's what you want? Some dumbass guy that cheats and pushes you around? I was willing to give you anything, Lila! I was willing to be anything. All for you."

"Finn! Wait!'

She stepped around Brad who was slowly getting to his feet and chased after Finn. Reaching out, she grabbed his shoulder. "I didn't - he was here and -"

Finn stopped suddenly, and Lila bumped into him. "Did he corner you? Huh? Because it looked kind of like you wanted to be there. Well, did he?"

"No, but-"

"Were you in any kind of danger? Did he force you back behind the booths and not let you leave?"

She whispered his name through the tears and when he repeated the questions, she shook her head. "No."

"Just one more thing for my own curiosity... was this planned? Or did you happen to run into him?"

"Finn, let me explain," she insisted through choking sobs. "I want to tell you-"

"And I don't want to hear anything except the damn answer. Was this planned?"

"I was curious. About why... what it was about me that - I knew he was going to be here, and I mentioned just meeting up to talk. But I would never... that was not going to go anywhere. FINN! You have to believe me-"

He stepped back when she tried to touch his arm. "You were curious about what? Why he treated you like shit? Well, congratulations. Because now that's my question. Why wasn't I enough? Why did the girl I love with everything in me just throw it all away for a guy that never deserved her?" His voice cracked, and to Lila's horror, she saw tears stream down his face.

"I love you, Finn."

But he was already gone.

**

Ella could easily have reheated the Cajun pasta she had made the day before. But considering what she had to tell Owen, she did not feel it was right to serve him the leftovers she had made for Dennis.

So, she made roast beef and mashed potatoes, glazed carrots and banana creme pie. All morning she spent preparing and chopping and measuring. The air was noticeably chillier, more seasonable than the day before, but she still found herself sweating in the kitchen, trying to get everything perfect. Trying to make it all great for him. She was not sure if this was out of guilt, or if she wanted to try to prove to herself that Owen meant just as much as Dennis did. That in some way, she could love Owen, and she could be assured that he would be loyal, and he would be steady. That was assuming he would stick around after she told him.

When Owen walked through the front door, there was no mistaking his elation as he drew her into his arms and pressed his lips into her hair. "Ah, Ella, I missed you. I'm so sorry about having to leave yesterday."

She found herself winding her arms around him, sinking against his sturdy frame. "It's okay. It's work. I understand."

"Well, it smells amazing in here." He walked into the kitchen. "Candles? Are we having a romantic evening?"

Unable to answer, she ushered him into a seat and poured him a cold beer. Perhaps romantic was the wrong setting to go with. She did not want to catch him completely off guard.

"Hey. There is something I wanted to talk to you about."

Ella snapped her head up, feeling a bit frazzled that he had taken her line right from her. "Huh?"

Owen leaned forward, resting his elbows on his knees as he held her gaze. "Lila. I know you haven't seen her and ... do you want me to go talk to your ex? Man to man? Maybe if I go there, he would be more willing to listen and ... I know this is killing you. Having her gone..."

Ella smiled gently. "Thank you. But no. I do appreciate the offer. Lila will come back when she's ready." She knew Owen did not like drama. He knew the law, enforced it, but he did not like the personal side of family conflicts. That was one of the first things she had learned about him. But here he was willing to forgo his own comfort... for hers.

It was not long before she had dinner on the table, and they were digging in. As he raved about the meal, she sat back and breathed in some courage. "Owen. I wanted to talk to you. There's... there's something I need to tell you."

He wiped his mouth with his napkin and set it down, his eyes narrowing in concern. "Ellie? What is it? Huh?" He started to get up to go to her, but she motioned for him to stay. "Is it that bad?"

"No. Listen, it isn't bad. It isn't good. It just is. It's something I thought you should know before we …" she choked on the rest of the sentence. Before we go further, she thought, but an image of Dennis appeared in her mind, and she knew she could not make any promises about the future.

"Okay." He waited for a few seconds and then gently urged, "Just tell me, Ella."

She placed her palms flat on the table and straightened, maintaining eye contact although she felt herself trembling. "Remember I told you about the guy I dated… before you?"

His expression fell, and he slowly leaned back. "Yes. The one you're in love with. Hard to forget that."

"You know him."

The statement was followed by silence, and she saw Owen try to process the bit of news, to think and guess and analyze in the span of seconds. "Wha - someone I know? Someone on the force or -" His eyes widened and cheeks plumed with color. "Oh shit. Dennis?"

"Yes."

"Son of a bitch!" He pushed his chair out from the table but stayed seated. "Seriously? Oh my God, you're who he meant when -" He stopped, his stare drilling into her. Ella longed to hear him finish that sentence but knew she couldn't be so shallow as to insist on hearing what her former lover had said about her. "Why didn't you- why the big secret? Was it some joke between the two of you?'

"Absolutely not! Owen, we didn't even realize until the night at the restaurant when you wanted me to meet him. I guess you'd said my name to him, and he realized right before I got there. And then I asked him to not say anything because I figured it was … he and I were over, and you - I was just getting to know you-"

Suddenly he gave a sharp laugh and covered his face. "Oh Christ, I just sent you off with him yesterday too. Just … holy shit, I'm such an idiot-"

"No. You're not. You had no way of knowing. He and I are still friends and -"

He straightened and locked onto her gaze. "Friends? But you still love him. Right?" When she merely looked at him helplessly, Owen cursed. "I went to him for advice. Told him everything. And that asshole was-"

"No! He wanted to tell you from the beginning. He wasn't comfortable with this. It was me, Owen. All me."

"He was one of my best friends. He sat in front of me and tried to convince me to leave you alone. Don't tell me he was innocent in all this."

"He was! Neither of us had ulterior motives. We didn't know the connection at first. But I'm the one that pleaded with him to not say anything. And I did that because I didn't want to hurt you or make you feel... I don't know... weird about all this."

Rubbing his face, Owen sighed. "Yeah, well. Weird."

"I know. And I'm so sorry. But I need you to know that this wasn't malicious or deceitful. It was an awkward situation. I was blindsided by finding out you were his friend, and my first instinct was just to not say anything."

Throwing his hands up, Owen sighed. "Okay, fine. You told me. Now what? Huh? Am I expected to compete with him for your love?"

"No!"

"So, he's out of the picture?" He paused for just a moment before leaning toward her. "You know, he mentioned you. He was in a dark place. He told me how he pushed you away. Said it was the worst mistake of his life. He wants you back, Ella."

Ella's head spun as she tried to keep her expression blank. "If he is telling you he wants me back, it is because he wants to win. The chase. I don't think you have anything to worry about when it comes to him. You said yourself, he dates a certain kind of woman. That isn't me."

He studied her, and she wondered if the nervousness shone through. As if he could see the wishing and hoping and the heartache that Dennis caused just by the mention of his name. Instead he jutted his chin out. "We could work, Ella. You and me. You know I adore you. I'm in love with you. I can give you and Lila a good life. I'm not rich. But I can provide you with everything you need and want. I'll never be unfaithful. I'll never hurt you. I would never lay a hand on you in anger." Without breaking his gaze, Owen scooted his chair closer to her and grabbed her hands. "Honey, I know your ex-husband did a number on you, but I will make up for all of that. I'll show you what a good husband is. And I may not be romantic. My ex can tell you I suck with finding the right words or remembering anniversaries, but when things get rough, I won't push you away. And that's what he did. That's exactly what Dennis did. He had you. He made you believe this was it. Then when he was hurt, he made sure you were hurt. That isn't me. I'm here. I want you to understand that. I'm so in love with you."

She let him draw her close, and she shut her eyes as her head rested on his shoulder. "Will you dance with me?" she asked, trying to blink back the memory of Dennis's hands on her as they moved slowly together. That had just been the day before. Why did it seem so far away... so out of reach?

"What? Dance with you? Where? Here?"

She placed her hand over his chest to feel his heart. To feel connected. "Sure, here. Anywhere. Just...if music is playing, will you stop everything and dance?"

He kissed the top of her head, his voice low and gravelly. "Sure. If you wanted to dance, I'd dance."

And for some reason that answer irritated her. Ella was not sure what perfect words she was looking for, but that was not it. And it was unreasonable to expect this man to know what she was thinking or what she wanted. He had already made himself vulnerable and spewed out all the words he could think of that had the slightest romantic overturns. And yet... it was not satisfying. Not quite right.

Owen did not seem to notice the frustration as he was already onto a different topic. "So yesterday, after I left... did you stick around the festival?"

She sat up, smoothing down her hair as she met his gaze. This was not casual conversation, she got that much. "Um, yeah. We walked around. I got some hot peppers for the pasta I made us."

"You made us roast beef."

"I mean... me and Dennis. Yesterday." Because why not? Having secrets made Ella uneasy. She always managed to slip up and say something that revealed everything and made her look sneaky and untrustworthy.

"You made him...pasta yesterday?"

"Yeah. I mean... he was nice enough to drive me home, and I didn't have anyone to cook for -"

"Ella. I'm not comfortable with this."

The conversation made Ella nervous, but Owen was calm and matter-of-fact. Breathing in, she tried to think through her words. "I am sorry you're not comfortable. But he is a friend. I get that the situation is now different for you. I'm trying to respect that. But Dennis - he saved my life, Owen. And then he helped me get the job at the campus. We're not together, and nothing happened yesterday other than two friends eating dinner together."

"Okay. All I can do is tell you that I am not comfortable with it."

And Ella understood that to mean the subject was not resolved. Not even close.

**

Lila clutched her books to her side and rushed to catch up to Finn. "Please. Can you just hear me out?"

He made no move to indicate he heard a word. He stared straight ahead, his jaw clenched and strides long. When she started to reach out to touch his arm, Finn jerked away, still never glancing in her direction. He nodded toward Ollie, his best friend and called out, "Ready to get out of here?"

Ollie's gaze slid past her, and slowly, he nodded. "Let's go."

"Wait, Finn. Please!" She stopped and choked back a sob, and she saw him hesitate, saw his feet slow for a millisecond before he charged forward without so much as a glance over his shoulder. "I love you. And I need to explain-" But he and Ollie were already turning down the main hall.

Finding Sherry, she convinced her to skip the afternoon classes with her. To drive her away from the school before Brad found her. She had already been ignoring his calls and had managed to avoid him that morning. But she knew he would be stubborn and angry over being humiliated by Finn. And she was the only one he had to take it out on.

Fortunately, Sherry was one who asked few questions. She willingly followed Lila's directions to the nearby hiking trail where they could hide away from the general population and get stoned. Where no ex-boyfriend or parent or past mistakes could find her. Sherry was a little ditzy, so she did not take notice of Lila's mood. She was in it for the weed and adventure. And that was perfect for Lila.

But as soon as Lila returned home, life bounced back in her face. Her father was home from work earlier than she had anticipated, and with a sharp icy fear, she stepped back as he bolted out of his armchair and stomped over to her.

"You skipped school? Where were you? I had to leave work early to deal with this. I looked everywhere for you."

"Dad! Stop screaming. It isn't good for the baby. You'll have Connie all stressed out."

Connie struggled up from the couch, her lips quivering in her attempt to not laugh. "Don't get me involved in this. You listen to your daddy, Lila."

As Connie left the room, Lila and Alex continued to stare each other down. Finally, Lila sighed and stepped back. "I don't do it often, dad. Usually I'm an obedient girl, and I stay in school all day. But today - just a really, really bad day."

The hitch in her voice eased the anger from his face. His body sagged and eyes softened. "What's going on?"

"Just guy stuff, dad. I don't really want to get into it. Can I stay home from school tomorrow? Tell the school I'm sick. Please."

He studied her before nodding. "Sure. Just tomorrow, then you go back. Look, I know about needing a break. Really. I get it. But you have to fill me in. And what's going on with your mom? Talk to her lately? She still infatuated with that cop or has she moved back on to the college teacher?"

Every nerve bristled as he took on a mocking tone. "Dad. Stop. I'm going to talk to her. Apologize. I wasn't nice to her. But I'm going to ask her if I could stay here for a while. I just think she and I need a break from each other."

"You mean she needs time with her men-"

"Dad. Stop."

"Fine, but if you're staying here, then she is going to pay support. She's not getting away with-"

"Dad!" She squeezed her eyes shut and clutched at her hair in frustration. "For God's sake, are you serious? Are you fucking kidding me?"

"Hey!"

"No! Listen, that's not even- she didn't ask you for support. She didn't ask you for alimony. Do you not want me here? Is it too much to ask that your daughter stay here for a little bit, or am I just in the way, dad?"

Alex blinked as he reached for her. "Lila, what? No. No, you know I love having you here. You'd never be in the way. You're my little girl."

"Then stop. Just stop. She's my mother. She may be your ex. She may be your enemy, but she is my mother. And I can't... I can't keep hearing about all she does wrong. I can't keep feeling pressured to give you good gossip just so you'll love me or be proud of me. She's my mother, and I'm part of her. Do you hate that part of me?"

"What are you talking about? I joke around, honey. But I don't... I never meant... I won't take her for child support, Lila." He bent forward so that he caught her gaze. "You are my most important thing in life, and I am sorry I made you feel bad. I wasn't thinking."

Feeling a surge of courage, she lifted her chin and admitted,

"I had to keep your secret, dad." Sobs overcame her as she struggled with the rest of the words. "I had to lie for you. To the most important person in my life. And I can't... I can't get over that. I can't forgive myself. I can't look my mom in the eye anymore."

"Oh, honey." He gathered her into his hold. "I'm sorry. Lila, I screwed up. I'm sorry. You never should have been a part of that."

After escaping to her room and trying to call Finn to no avail, she finally broke down and called the other person she needed to make amends with.

"Lila!"

"Hi mom." She started to cry, silent tears but she sniffled and caught her breath. "I'm sorry. I'm really sorry, mom."

"Hey you. Lila, sweetheart, I know you are. I'm sorry too. It's okay. We are okay."

"Can I come see you, maybe tomorrow after school?"

The sound of her mother's warm voice coated her inside and wrapped around her outside until she felt cocooned and safe. "Baby girl, you can come here anytime. This is your home."

"I think I might want to stay at dad's... the baby is coming, and it's closer to school and work and -"

"That's okay, Lila. I understand."

"And mom, about Finn... he's such a good person and ... I think I screwed things up with him, but if there's a chance he'll forgive me, I want to - I'd like you to get to know him. Please."

There was a small, light sigh, and she wondered if she had gone too far, as she usually did. But then her mom responded, "Okay. We'll talk and work on it. Doesn't mean I'll always agree. Please don't worry about us, you and me - we are fine. More than fine. I love you. I'm sorry I lost my temper. Bad mommy moment."

Lila's mood was boosted. And once again, she tried calling Finn.

"Stop calling me, Lila."

She froze, not expecting him to answer, but she realized he was not hanging up, so she sputtered out, "W-wait! Finn! Listen, please. I am so sorry. I was stupid. I realized that as soon as Brad was in front of me."

"Yeah, well, I realized the moment I laid eyes on you that you were the one. I didn't need to test that by humiliating you or breaking your heart!"

"I know that. Finn, I get that you're upset, and you have every right to be. But I'm not as smart or as introspective as you. When I was standing there with Brad, all I could think of was how to get away from him. How to go home and wait for you to be done with work. I couldn't get you out of my head. And I promise, Finn, I promise with everything I have that I realize now what you mean to me. I won't ever let anything get in the way of that. I love you."

There were a few moments of silence, and Lila knew that was better than an immediate hang up. But then he spoke, his voice low and wobbly. "I can't ... I would have done anything for you. And when I saw you... I - don't call me again, Lila."

Lila's mood plummeted. She might be mending things with her mom and dad, but she destroyed Finn. The one person who consistently had her back, who worked to pull her out of that low esteem pit she had fallen into. In return, she had stomped on his heart. On his goodness.

It bothered her that her mother never got to learn what a good person he was. Because she knew her mother was fair and would have eventually sensed that he was full of compassion and kindness.

Most of all, she regretted not trusting her instincts and allowing herself to be loved. She knew the past couple of years with her parents and their separation had gotten to her. The fights and lies and secrets had messed with her belief in love and view on relationships and men. She adored her father but witnessing his affair and selfishness had her believing that guys were not trustworthy. Lila guessed that she wanted to hurt before being hurt.

It was the middle of the night, and Lila was wide awake, lying in bed and going over every mistake she had ever made in life. She was scared and overwhelmed and sad. Finn invaded her thoughts over and over like some type of fever dream, and when there was a tapping on her window, she immediately knew it was him.

Without even checking, she threw on some clothes and raced as quietly as she could through the house to the front door. Because it was Finn out there waiting, accepting her apology and believing her sincerity. Because finally, there was someone that was all about her and her words and thoughts and feelings.

The night air was sharp and cold and wet as she tentatively stepped outside and squinted through the darkness. She heard a sound, a muffled, "Hey," and she took a few steps further into the yard, squinting to find him.

When her eyes adjusted to the shadows and moonlight, her heart dropped down to her suddenly queasy stomach as she realized it was Brad standing in front of her.

"I've been trying to call you. Tried to talk to you at school."

"Brad, look, I don't really want to talk. The other day, talking to you, asking you to meet me at the festival, it was a mistake."

It was dark, but she could still tell that his face was reddening. The anger was pumping through his veins. "You're a liar. You're just scared that dopehead will find out you want me instead of him."

"Sorry, Brad."

She turned to go back to the house, but before she could even lift her foot off of the ground, he grabbed her arm. She had anticipated that move as she moved away from him and yanked her arm from his grasp.

"Bitch!" His grip grew tighter, and he tugged her forward before she could make another escape.

"Hey! HEY! Get the fuck away from her!"

The porch light flooded the yard, and as she tumbled to

the ground, she heard her dad yelling as he ran toward them. Rolling out of the way, she got to her feet and stood helplessly to the side as her father swung at Brad. His fist landed on the side of his head, and Brad spun around in a half circle before dropping to the ground.

"Dad!" she screamed, as Connie yelled for him to stop. "Dad, don't. I'm fine. Just- he's not eighteen. You'll go to jail."

Alex straightened and faced her, the moonlight highlighting the rage swimming in his eyes. "You think I give a shit how old he is? He was pushing you around, Lila. Is this how you let guys treat you? Huh? Has this happened before?"

"Did I-" she stumbled backwards, choking on her tears. "Yeah, dad. I let him. I let him just like mom let you push her around whenever you had a bad day, or she said something you didn't like. We just let it happen, I guess."

"I never beat your mother! Lila!"

But she ran back into the house, pushing past Connie, pushing past her life and struggles and heartbreak.

CHAPTER 23

Ella took the plates to the sink, wondering if she had enough time to wash them. She wanted to get to work early.

But Owen was there. She had to find a way to shoo him out the door so she could finish getting ready. He had shown up at her doorstep at 7AM, offering to make her his "famous" pancakes. She knew what this was about. It was about his insecurities now that she had told him about Dennis. And Ella feared her future held many more unannounced visits and insisted time together when sometimes she just wanted to relax alone.

"You're not even ready?" he asked with a teasing smile. "Damn, Ella, how do you even have a job? You can't get anywhere on time."

"That's not true. Don't say that. I'm running late this morning because I wasn't expecting company and a full-course breakfast."

"Hey, but if you went to sleep at a decent hour and then woke up early enough, you'd be prepared for life's surprises. Right?"

Before she could argue, the doorbell rang. Muttering to herself, considering taking a sick day, she trotted to the front door. "Oh! Dennis!"

Dennis's somber expression coupled with his heavy steps put Ella on alert. She ushered him into the kitchen, and he gave a short nod to Owen. "Morning, Owen."

Owen stuck his chin out and growled, "Hey, Dennis, go fuck yourself."

Hearing Owen use such language caught Ella off guard, and she glared over at him and hissed his name. But Dennis waved it off. "Don't worry about that. Not now, El. There's a situation."

And immediately, he had her attention. Because Dennis always tried to keep things calm. To not worry her. But his eyes were narrowed, and his skin was pale. "Remember I told you I would tell you if there was a reason to worry about Lila? It's time to worry." He noticed immediately that her legs became wobbly and ignoring Owen's intensifying glare, he led Ella to a chair. "I saw Finn this morning, and I stopped and asked if Lila was with him. Because I'd thought about what you told me." His gaze slid to Owen before resting back on Ella. "About Lila. And I wanted to talk to her. See if things were... anyway, Finn said they're not together anymore. He caught her with Brad."

Owen cursed. "You come over here to gossip about some teenagers? Not really subtle-"

Without taking his eyes off Ella, Dennis barked, "This is dealing with the same guy I had you go threaten. Remember that, Owen? This isn't about gossip." Lowering his voice, he continued, "Brad's not a good kid, Ella. He has a bad habit of pushing Lila around."

"What?"

Owen's eyes widened. "Wait. That was ... he was - that had to do with Lila?"

Again, Dennis's attention never wavered from Ella. "I never saw it happen. And she never admitted it outright. But she called me in this frantic mood, and when I went to see her, her cheek was red, and ... it was bruising."

And Ella remembered that time awhile back when she had asked Lila about the slight bruise on her cheek. Lila had spouted off some excuse about bumping into a door, and she had done it so casually, so effortlessly, that Ella had not thought twice about it.

Dennis seemed to know where her thoughts were heading. "It was impossible to know, El, because she did not want you to know. She is such a smart girl and a strong girl, and I think she was fighting to get herself out of that situation. But now... we need to intervene."

Slowly, she nodded, her gaze glued to his, trying to find that calmness, that stellar of strength that could root her in a pool of peace. She found it. "Okay," she breathed. "I'll leave work early and go talk to her when she gets out of school."

He nodded along with her, his tone low, like a warm blanket wrapping around her. "Good plan. Do you need a ride to work?"

"She can drive herself," Owen snapped.

Ella shut her eyes for a long moment before answering, "Dennis, I'm fine. I'll see you at work."

She was left with the silence between her and Owen, until he grunted and stood. "I guess that is that."

Ella snapped her head up and stared at him in surprise. Then she nodded. "I'm sorry, Owen."

"I knew." He gave a short laugh. "I couldn't put my finger on it, but you're very jumpy. If ever I would lay a hand on your arm or reach for your hand when we were walking, you'd jump. And then I realized... when you're around Dennis, you don't jump. There was one time he leaned in close to you, his hand falling on your shoulder, and you actually leaned into him."

"You know, this isn't his fault. At all. I would hate to think your friendship would... he wanted to tell you as soon as he knew." Owen merely nodded before walking out.

At work, Dennis checked on her, but he kept a respectable distance. Ella had too much on her mind to analyze it or to reveal her newly single status. It seemed disrespectful to Owen and whatever they shared to jump right into Dennis's arms.

But when it was time to leave, Dennis was waiting for her in the hallway. "I want to go with you."

There was no arguing. His eyes were focused, his tone even and firm. With a short nod, she agreed. "Then let's go."

As they waited outside of Lila's school, Dennis started to apologize. "Maybe I should have told you sooner."

"You did what you felt was best, Dennis. I understand." She gave a small cry of frustration. "She isn't here." She dug her phone out of her purse. "Dammit. Missed call. I don't recognize the number." She called it and shot Dennis a semblance of a smile when he brushed the hair out of her eyes. "Hi, yes, I had a call from this number?"

"Yeah, it's me. Connie. There was an incident last night, and Lila is okay. She's fine. But Alex went outside to find Lila's boyfriend or ex - he was shoving her. Alex punched him and got taken into custody."

"What?" She turned to Dennis who stared back, waiting for an update.

"I bailed him out, and it looks like the boy's parents will drop the charges. They don't want their boy in any trouble for pushing around a girl. I guess he admitted to getting physical with another girl and having authorities question him. But anyway... I ...I wanted you to know."

"Thanks, Connie, I appreciate it. Really. I'm at her school right now. I'm not seeing her."

"Well, she should be there. If you can't find her, let us know."

As soon as she relayed the phone call to Dennis, her phone rang again. "Dad? She is? Okay, we're on our way." She sighed and explained, "She's at dad's."

Ted had the front door open before they even got out of the car. "Just fair warning, your mom's here too."

Ella nodded, brushing past her dad. "That's fine. Fair warning, Dennis is here too." She did not bother to stop and see if the men greeted each other or stared each other down. She only had one goal, and that was reaching her daughter.

As soon as she saw her mother, Lila started to cry. She jumped up from the couch, where Diana was also sitting, and ran straight into Ella's embrace. "Mom, I'm so sorry. I kept a lot from you. There are things ... I'm sorry."

Ella smoothed her daughter's hair back and managed a smile. "It's okay. But are you okay? I need to know you're safe."

Lila glanced over Ella's shoulder and saw Dennis standing a

few feet back. "I'm not with Brad if that's what you think. I'm not."

Dennis stepped forward. "I ran into Finn."

"Right. But Finn doesn't understand what he saw. And then Brad showed up at dad's place last night and dad... it was horrible."

They managed to move the trembling girl to the kitchen, a hot cup of tea set in front of her. Diana moved around like a ghost, silent and graceful, out of sight before anyone could acknowledge her presence.

After talking about all that Lila had experienced with Brad, all she felt being with Finn, the girl stared at Ella with huge eyes and trembling lips. Ella was reminded of the time Lila had fallen off her bike. But this was different. She was older, getting bounced around by life and emotions.

"There's something else," Lila warned, fresh sobs breaking through the words.

"Go ahead," Ella urged. "You can tell me anything."

"Mom, this has been eating away at me for over a year. But I caught dad.... with Connie. You were at work. I left school early. And I never told you. They were at the house, in your bedroom."

Ella braced herself, waiting for the rage and embarrassment of her husband's infidelities, but she was surprised to find those emotions absent. She only felt sympathy for all her daughter had to endure. "Lila. I'm so so sorry you witnessed that. I know what that's like. I do. And please do not feel guilty for not telling me. That was not your responsibility. You're a kid. You're my baby girl. Okay?"

And it made sense to her. Lila's distant attitude, the outbursts... it was all stemming from the secret she was forced to keep. She had felt in the middle, and if anyone could relate, it was Ella. She glanced up and caught her own mother standing there with an expression of shame and horror, and she felt a tinge of sympathy for her. Even for her.

Because life was not fair. There were setbacks, there were

mistakes. There were crossroads, and sometimes, the wrong path was chosen. But Ella was starting to believe that eventually, the person would find the way back if the desire were strong enough. Catching Diana's stare, she gave a slight shake of her head, as if to tell her to let go. To not hurt over those past mistakes any longer.

"Let's go home. You have to call Connie. I think I worried them when I said you weren't at school."

"Okay, but please, can I go somewhere first? I'll meet you at home. Please."

Ella nodded, already knowing.

**

Finn was stacking dishes in the back, the restaurant almost empty before the dinner rush. He half-turned as if he sensed Lila, and then he turned away. "Not now. I'm working."

"I know," she said calmly. "I just wanted to tell you that I love you. I am going to remind you of that until you know it." She paused and added, "Brad showed up at my dad's house. I … I thought it was you knocking on my window. And when I told him I wanted nothing to do with him, he got pushy. And then dad ran out, and things got crazy. Dad punched him."

Finn faced her, his lips turning up slightly. "Nuh-uh."

"Uh-huh. He did."

They grinned at each other before Finn remembered himself. "I'm still… I'm hurt, Lila."

"I know."

"It's going to take some time."

"I know that too. That's why I said I'm going to remind you. I love you. And I'll see you. Have a good night, Finn."

She walked away, sure that his gaze was following her.

Six Months Later

Dennis rocked back on his heels, staring out the window. "Is there anything to do in this town?"

"Yeah, unpack." Ella motioned to the box in front of him. "Seriously, I don't want to live in a sea of boxes, searching through them every time I need a pan or a brush."

"Boxes are labeled, El. Take a break. You've been a mad-woman all day." He reached up and tugged at her dress, laughing as she squealed. "C'mon. New house, new start. This deserves a break. I saw we had some glasses unpacked. Some champagne…" He hopped to his feet and pulled her to him.

"Kid still here." Lila sauntered through the living room. "Hey, Finn's picking me up any minute. Can I stay out a little past curfew?"

"No. Thought you were having dinner at your dad's?"

"Yeah. Then we're watching the baby. Dad and Connie have therapy tonight. But when they get back, Finn wants to take me to this one spot to watch the meteor shower."

"Oldest trick in the book!" Dennis cried out.

Ella stared at him. "You asked me to watch the meteor shower tonight." She burst out laughing when he winked at her. "Lila, call if you're going to be really late. Got it?"

Once they were alone, Dennis nodded toward a box in the corner. "I think you should unpack that next."

She eyed the box and then turned to him. "Where'd that one come from? It's not even labeled."

"Housewarming gift. Go on. If we're moving in together, I get to spoil you a little, right?"

She opened it slowly, her hands trembling. And inside the large box was a small ring box. Her future shined up at her through tear-filled vision.

ABOUT THE AUTHOR

Trisha Ridinger Mckee

Trisha Ridinger McKee resides in a small town in Pennsylvania where she works as an Instructional Production Specialist at Penn State University. When she is not writing, she is fishing, planting sunflowers, playing with bulldogs, and loving life. Since April 2019, her short stories and articles have appeared in over 60 publications. Beyond the Surface is her first published novel.

BOOKS IN THIS SERIES

Beyond The Surface

Ella is a middle-aged woman with a stagnant career, an exasperated teenage daughter, and a husband that has left to make a new life with another woman. Her first attempt at dating is a disaster, and in an attempt to refocus her life and rediscover her joy, Ella goes fishing. It is here that she meets Dennis, the older, captivating man that ends up saving her life and stealing her heart. But Dennis has a history, and Ella might just be in for the biggest heartbreak of her life if she can not get her emotions under control and face the demons from her own past.

Beyond The Dreams

Ella seems to have her life together, but Dennis is pushing for a wedding date, and for some reason, she is unable to commit to what kind of wedding she really wants. Lila is about to start her next phase of life in college, and that means letting go of her past, and that might include Finn.

Made in the USA
Columbia, SC
15 March 2021